Books *by HEIMITO VON DODERER*

EVERY MAN A MURDERER) 1964 (

THE DEMONS) 1961 (

These are BORZOI BOOKS, published in New York

by Alfred A. Knopf

Every Man a Murderer

Every

1964

Man a Murderer

by HEIMITO VON DODERER

Translated from the German
by Richard and Clara Winston

NEW YORK

ALFRED · A · KNOPF

L. C. Catalog card number: 64–11569

Contents

~~~~~~~~~~~~~~~~~~~~~~~~~~~~~~~

EVERY MAN

A MURDERER

―――〰〰〰〰〰〰〰〰〰〰〰―――

Part One

~~~~~~

✌❦ 1 ❧✎

EVERYONE'S CHILDHOOD is plumped down over his head like a bucket. The contents of this bucket are at first unknown. But throughout life, the stuff drips down on him slowly—and there's no sense changing clothes or costume, for the dripping will continue.

The man whose life is to be related here—his case aroused some curiosity within and even beyond the German borders, when in due course the facts became known—might almost serve as a proof that no one can ever wash away that bucket's contents.

When he was small, people called him Kokosch, in imitation of his own first babyish pronunciation of the name Conrad. What even as a child he had called his "realm"—and later, in choice and highfalutin language, "my boyhood realm" or "the land of my childhood"—was the jutting outcrop of a great city. The outcrop lay on the other side of a wide ship canal, its massed houses extending beneath a misty sky to the rim of the horizon. In fact, these houses were not everywhere massed in solid lines and streets. In many places they were divided, interrupted by vacant lots and grassy expanses in which stood ancient trees, spindly second-growth coppice, and shrubbery. Many a street had houses in a continuous row only on one side; the other side was empty. Here one looked out over heaps of crushed rock and piles of lumber. The view stretched from the rounded embankment of the canal, across it to the slashed and divided conglomerate of the city, and up and down along the water, which sparklingly turned in a slow curve to the left between its sloping banks. There loomed the gray-green foam of the treetops, and there the meadows ran down to the water. In the distance were factory smokestacks, ranged like arrows in a quiver; besides these, the squat cylinders of the gas tanks, glittering metal surmounted by structural steel, on which the fog sat in winter, in summer the tousled clouds of a vaporous horizon.

In the last house of that one-sided row near the canal lived Conrad's parents. They had a roomy apartment on the fourth floor. His father, Lorenz Castiletz, was not exactly a rich man, but what is generally called well-to-do. His business was selling textiles, and in addition he had long been the representative of two Dutch firms. He was rather envied for that, since that was what gave him a strong position. There was also an aunt who owned an estate—house, land, and farm—in the country, fairly close to the city. The result was that Kokosch—who was, more-over, an only child—never suffered from the want, often so dam-aging to health, to which other children were exposed during the war and the hard postwar years. By and large, such events by-passed the Castiletz household. In his long-ago youth his father had developed a heart condition by excessive indulgence in fencing. Moreover, at the outbreak of the war Herr Castiletz was no longer of age for the early call-ups, even if his weak heart had not made him unfit for military service. There was a difference of forty-seven years between Lorenz Castiletz and his son.

The father was a tall, good-looking man with black curly hair, which he wore rather long, and a strong mustache, both grace-fully, almost coquettishly, streaked with silver. Good-natured, kindly, and outside of business affairs extremely distracted and disorganized, he would sometimes be suddenly seized by a brutal, seemingly inward-turned rage, would turn black as ebony with fury and pour out awesome imprecations. In such cases the apartment was converted into a vacuum of terror, until suddenly the father would reappear with a friendly smile, ready to apologize to everyone, whether to the mother, whom he kissed, or to Kokosch, whom he took on his knees. But the experience of his father's sudden black rages made a more lasting impression on the boy than the subsequent reconciliations.

Once his raging progenitor encountered him in the white-painted vestibule, at an ill-fated moment, although Kokosch for his part was wholly innocent of any harm. He was about to set off for school, properly on time, after the noon recess. He was holding his schoolbag under him arm. His father had been talking to his mother in another room: all of a sudden his voice had grown loud, had quickly taken on that shouting, roaring tone. He came charging through the French doors of the drawing room and saw Kokosch standing in the vestibule when he had thought the boy already out of the house. "It seems you no longer obey orders as you should either, you brat!" he snarled at the boy— in a relatively low voice, which made the deepest impression upon Kokosch. "Get going, get going!" his father exclaimed, gripping the boy—who had begun to cry with fright—by the back of the neck and pushing him out the door. That afternoon Herr Castiletz was waiting after school—which alarmed the boy when he came out of the school, for it was not his father's practice to be there. But Lorenz Castiletz showered affection upon his small son, took the boy to a pastry shop and stuffed him with cake and whipped cream, and spent the evening helping him with his homework—which, as a result, was finished in a trice—and playing with him. He stretched out full length on his stomach to adjust the switches of the clockwork train set. When Kokosch's mother entered the room, she clapped her hands at the sight. Kokosch, too, was delighted. But the experience in the vestibule nevertheless entered his dreams. They were always frightening dreams, in which, oddly enough, he saw the brown jute matting which ran from the front door to the glass door of the reception room. He saw it with extraordinary distinctness, as if he were scrutinizing each fiber from close up, as though he himself were barely a few inches above the floor. That effect was always present in his dream of his angry father.

Lorenz Castiletz's sudden plunges into blackness always had the silliest causes. It never happened that he lost his head over any important or even mildly substantial matter. On the contrary, dropped collar buttons and rumpled ties, mislaid scribbles of things to be attended to—such trivia lured him into the abyss. Nor was it always only a metaphorical abyss, for it was connected with the darkness under desk and sofa where something had to be looked for, in a stooped posture oppressive to a man with a weak heart who inclined to apoplexy. In the end, usually having accomplished nothing, he was forced to rise out of the depths, his face brightly flushed.

Like many careless people—whose secret generally is that they take a thing and use it but never return it to its place—he insisted that something had been taken from him or mislaid whenever he did not find it in its place, which in view of the perpetual upheaval of the study would have been supernatural. Things were in some sort of order for the first two hours or so of the morning, during which time Frau Castiletz, in her husband's absence, would have tidied the room. But there, perhaps, lay the greatest danger; for such rationalistic intervention stamped out all those footpaths and cart tracks of habit along which objects may be lying at random, but where a swift and skillful memory, operating in the chiaroscuro of consciousness, can swoop down upon the object sought. This ability must be held among the most important and amazing psychic powers of disorderly persons. But precisely such powers are paralyzed by interference, so that the search has then to be undertaken by the clear light of intellect. The intellect, however, is a singularly delicate organ which demands, with painstaking strictness, a definite order in the arrangement of things. And woe betide if it does not find that order. Then plunges into the abyss may follow, indeed must follow, unavoidably.

No one could ever feel quite secure, therefore, in Conrad's parental home, since the onset of external disasters or bad news was not needed to make the situation intolerable. Rather, trouble was begotten within the household itself. Even without knowing Frau Castiletz, we understand that she was powerless to check such outbursts. There was nothing for her to do but to make herself as comfortable as possible under the circumstances, and not to provoke her husband Lorenz by contradiction when such eruptions occurred. She held sturdily to this course; indeed, there is no saying what would have happened otherwise. Yet her gentle acceptance in a way intensified the gathering storm—to the extent that Lorenz Castiletz sensed behind it a know-it-all tolerance, an established habit of no longer taking him quite seriously. And that was how he wanted above all to be taken—once he had reached the stage of ebony blackness.

Anyone who knew Frau Leontine Castiletz personally would also know that there was a phrase which precisely described her nature. It was a foreign phrase commonly applied to a particular type of color, the pale blue the French call *bleu mourant*. She was a *bleu mourant* person, and ever since the phrase was first spoken by someone, it rapidly gained favor behind Frau Leontine's back, first among her acquaintances and finally among her relatives. These last did not mind it in the least; they promptly made a noun of it: *"La bleue mourante."* Thereafter, the name Leontine vanished completely, unless its bearer happened to be present.

She was a pretty woman. Some said she looked exactly like her aunt as a girl—this was the aunt who owned the country estate. But Leontine was much more delicate, and the landowner, an attractive and distinctly buxom lady, looked somewhat overpowering alongside her. Perhaps that was due to age. Frau Castiletz was a full twenty-three years younger than her husband.

She was dark blonde, and her eyes floated in a rare violet blueness. These somewhat slanting eyes—the outer corners seemed higher than the inner—gave the impression of floating rather than of looking straight out at the world. In spite of their slant, they were large. But everyone who gazes straight ahead sends forth a ray of sight like a flying arrow, stronger or weaker as the case may be. In the case of Frau Castiletz, there was no such ray. Her vision seemed to spread out sideways like the rings around a stone thrown into water.

There was in fact something around her eyes like the ring around a clouded moon, a constant veil of inattention, sight spreading outward in rings rather than seeking and holding in focus what she was looking at.

Kokosch loved his mother intensely. He could play on the floor happily and noiselessly for hours when she sat in the room with her embroidery frame, which she always had with her, though she seemed never to look quite at it as she worked. Sometimes she gave the impression that she was slightly cross-eyed, but that was not the case.

On such solitary afternoons of early childhood, whose silence was broken only now and then by the ringing of a streetcar bell or the tooting of a steamer on the canal, Kokosch was undoubtedly happy and self-absorbed (and much later he would sometimes remember those times, and the distant noises also). From time to time he would leave his toys—a fort with soldiers, ships, the big train set, and other fine things—and would come to his mother. He kneeled on the rug in front of her and rubbed his head and face against her leg in its smooth silk stocking. Then he silently returned to his play, in which he was highly inventive. He could obsessively pursue single inspirations for days, and was extremely put out by interruptions. The disposition of his army outside the fortress seemed at first glance always the same, but his father, who was quite keen-eyed, once noticed that it changed from day to day. By cautious questioning he learned that his son's games involved arrangements that extended over an entire week and fully deserved to be called logical. Kokosch on that occasion explained confidingly and in great detail the important part played by the railroad, and showed his father the resulting alterations in the layout of the track.

Frau Castiletz was not the kind of mother who tells stories about her children. Otherwise she might have reported that the boy, without having a clock in the room (he could probably read time by then) and without hearing any striking from a church tower, would interrupt his game every half hour with amazing regularity—as she had quietly noted by checking her wrist watch —and would come to her.

It would in any case have been unbecoming to her to tell such maternal anecdotes. She did not claim the attention of her fellow men; she did not put herself forward. She merely sat by. No more. Her hair was curled and very loose; there was something tousled, dissolving, or disarrayed about her; and when she wore bright dresses she preferred, with quiet obstinacy, very large flowered patterns which made her look plumper than she was and moreover struck others as not always in especially good taste. Sometimes the patterns consisted of stylized flowers, a single one of which would extend down her whole back and even lower. It must be assumed that she deliberately chose and bought such fabrics. But no one ever heard her maintaining a view of her own in so many words or expressing any tangible opinion. She frequently had an air of amiable astonishment. When she spoke, her sentences disintegrated almost as soon as they were put together, just as her looks dissolved into rings as soon as they left her eyes. She always seemed to be drifting like a distant sail far out on the margin of life. There were people who in spite of all this considered her silly; but that was as incorrect as the assertion that she was cross-eyed. She was not silly. She was *bleu mourant*.

By descent she too came from the "branch," as people said

instead of "trade." Her father had in his time been a textile manufacturer; her dowry had been respectable, though not staggering. Nevertheless, quite aside from the inheritance which might be expected, Lorenz Castiletz had "married well," as the saying is in middle-class circles, when at the age of forty-five he acquired this girl of twenty-two.

2 &

CONRAD'S parental home constituted, along with the entire row of houses at the temporary end of which it stood, one of the last and most recent outgrowths of the large urban quarter on the other side of the canal. At its core, however, that quarter surrounded a dreary, not to say gloomy, tangle of old and in some cases ancient little streets. These formed the background to the later segments and incidents of Kokosch's boyhood history. For the time being, his life was bounded by an area defined by three points. The first point was his home, most notably Conrad's large, bright room, which had a wide, impressive view, as fourth-floor rooms are wont to have. The second point was on the other side of the canal: the school. It was no great distance away; he had only to walk back along the street to a big bridge, and there it was on the left, at the end of a long street with an upward incline. If a boy ran downhill after school, great speed could be attained along the sidewalk; naturally this was done in packs, not altogether to the joy of grownups. Lorenz Castiletz had wanted Conrad to attend this particular school, and had seen to it that the boy was registered early. For its five classes were auxiliary to a large institution in which young teachers were trained. The pupils served as educational guinea pigs, and, therefore, the school stood in the odor of particular modernity and progressiveness. The building, which was so large as to be almost gigantic, also contained an intermediate school, so that the children, as they scaled the ladder of education, could do so in the same place and go to school along accustomed paths.

The third point in the triangle that more or less enclosed Conrad's boyhood, and thus also his "realm" ("land of my childhood," "boyhood realm"), was located at what was at once its center of gravity and its outermost frontier: directly opposite those factory smokestacks which loomed like ranged arrows on the other side of the canal. Conrad was in the habit of working his way through the meadows, shrubbery, and woodlands thus far and as a rule no farther. For farther on were more houses and factories, then railroad tracks, and finally the infinitely high fence of a race track blocking the way.

Conrad was not one of those boys who are blessed with a governess until well past their elementary-school days. He was soon allowed to run about freely like a regular street urchin, so long as he came home on time. In this respect his parents were not strict; on principle, Lorenz Castiletz granted his son considerable freedom. Kokosch possessed that great talent—it is almost an art—which simplifies the life of every schoolboy just as it does an army recruit's: the art of not attracting attention. He did not attract attention either by knowledge or by ignorance; his performance remained a plain gray, as did his conduct; and so he passed from one class to the other as a fellow traveler whom the teachers took for granted. His parents did not require much of him on this score. Lorenz Castiletz was satisfied with his average performance; had it been otherwise, he would probably have beaten the boy.

Conrad's boyhood was the direct opposite of what in those days was called a "school tragedy." Its bitterness came from quite other quarters.

Directly outside the front door of his house began his "realm" proper—starting with the piles of lumber across the street, the patches of landscape visible between them, and across the canal the mass of buildings on the other bank. Alongside the house there were several future building lots, but these were not fenced in; they were open and still unleveled, with many small mounds and tiny mountains on which playing children had worn innumerable paths and passages, and riddled with trenches for tunnels and streets—in places the lots looked like the structures produced by certain rodents. A large signboard on two posts announced the owner's name and the fact that the lots were for sale. The sign had been standing for a long time; its boards were grayed by wind and rain.

This somewhat desolate area was separated from the real "steppe," or "pampa," by a wide footpath which ran at a diagonal toward the canal and the road which bordered it.

From there on the meadows spread out. Groups and lanes of young deciduous trees stood at their edges, dividing them. But here and there, solitary in the middle of a meadow, stood a giant tree, whose highest branches reached high, high, close to the blue sky, and merged with the rays of sunlight. Below, the huge trunk would generally be scraped smooth of its bark, for many generations of children had played hide-and-seek around it. If the tree happened to be hollow, deep excavations would have been undertaken in the surrounding earth to enlarge the hiding place. In time these had become regular pit traps. Perhaps they were dug for no other purpose than to dig. Someone could always be found digging deeper—two or three small boys and a girl, all with earnest faces, dirty noses and hands.

Wide stretches were covered with dense and, at first glance, impenetrable shrubbery. But there were narrow paths through the tangle, an endless number of them. No wider than a very thin man. To either side of these paths the bushes rose higher than a grownup's head. A child could discover with joy and surprise hollow spaces, even whole rooms, in these thickets, with walls and ceilings woven tightly of the long, tough vines of creeping plants. But before crawling into the green shelter of such a natural tent, you usually stepped into filth, and then saw that it lay about everywhere. The nocturnal tramps had had no inhibitions.

Of all the many boys from the neighborhood who knocked about this natural playground, there was a certain species who soon commanded Conrad's fascinated attention: those who would return from the water meadows at twilight on summer evenings, carrying large canning jars on handles of string which they had skillfully wound around the upper lip of the glass. These jars were filled with water in which swam tailed, four-legged creatures, some in brilliant colors, others pale and transparent. They were all sorts of newts, tadpoles, and similar creatures caught in stagnant eddies of the big river which flowed somewhere far off in a part of the city Conrad seldom saw. But there were two such stagnant pools in Conrad's own hunting grounds, and the boys came to prefer these because they were so rich in amphibians.

A pet shop paid the boys ten groschen for every good-sized amphibian in good condition. Apparently there was a demand for the creatures; they were sold to aquarium fanciers or to laboratories. It seems worth noting that Conrad learned of the financial motive for the laborious climbing, fishing, and probing about the ponds only long afterward, quite by chance, when he was almost grown up. A close corporation had excluded all undesirable competition.

Conrad soon made the acquaintance of the boys, and his conduct toward them was such that it should have made him popular with them. On the first afternoon that he accompanied them he used certain of their rather strange expressions, including the curious names they gave to the amphibians; from his lessons in natural history, little Castiletz was familiar with quite different names. But with a rather hasty adaptability and keenness of ear, he used theirs. In fact, he several times mispronounced one such name. The boys looked at each other and laughed, but did not correct him. Conrad proved to be skillful at catching the creatures. His catch, too, went into the big canning jars. When darkness began to fall, he drifted homeward with the boys across the meadows and undergrowth and into the first streets. Above the trees a long, reddish streak slashed the sky. In the gathering darkness the cars roared, the illuminated trains of streetcars tinkled their bells. The noise of civilization semed strange after the time spent slipping through the thickets, wading barefoot through some sandy ford, after standing for hours staring into the water, gazing intently at the movements of some tiny or possibly fair-sized and highly attractive creature until it came within reach and could be swooped up with a calm, extremely economical movement. Wriggling in the hand, a tangible triumph in the literal sense of the word, it lay in the handful of mud that always came with it, each time looking smaller than Conrad had expected.

On the way home some of the boys would drop off into side streets. They hardly bade the others good-bye when they left, and Kokosch did not notice them at all. In the end he walked with the last of them, who was headed in the same direction as he. Conrad began to speak; he asked what school the other boy went to, and where there were bigger salamanders in the water than the ones they had caught today. The other boy's replies were monosyllabic. At his front door he said good night with a curious formality, abandoning dialect for the occasion, and disappeared inside.

Back in his room, as soon as he had turned on the light Conrad looked for and found a small red pail that he still owned from earlier days, when he had dug in sand piles. He went to the kitchen, where supper was already in preparation, and filled the pail with water to test it for leaks.

After he had eaten, Conrad surveyed the homework situation,

and plunged violently into Latin and geography. At half past eleven that night, his father, on the way to bed, paused at Conrad's room, surprised that the light was burning so late.

"Well, my poor boy," he said. "Still so much studying to do for tomorrow?"

"No, Father," Conrad said truthfully, "I was finished by five this afternoon. But I want to have a little more time in the meadows tomorrow, and so I'm doing my homework in advance for day after tomorrow."

"Well, well, arranging our business affairs," Lorenz Castiletz remarked, laughingly. He stretched his arms above his head and yawned. "Well, go to sleep soon, my boy."

His mother, too, dropped by. Conrad pressed his head against her shoulder with an almost imperceptible intensity.

When Conrad arrived at the meadow the following afternoon with his red pail, he found the place still empty, the bushes by the bank not yet stirred by boys slipping through them, the water not yet rustling and splashing from wading feet. He set the empty pail down on the grass, near an old tree so crooked that for a while it ran along almost horizontally above the ground, and swung himself up on the trunk of the tree. It looked like a bench. Conrad sat down. On the other bank of the canal, where the water was deep, the tips of trees and bushes hung over it, here and there dipping beneath the surface. The sky was a pale but ardent blue, with distant high treetops poised in it like clouds.

The prevailing stillness oppressed Kokosch slightly, not so much with a sensation of silent pressure, which is the usual feeling, but with its spaciousness. He felt as if he were scattered through it, without being really able to yield to this feeling. On the other side of the water, the distant treetops floated on the heights. Behind him, the stagnant arm of the canal ran between trees and shrubs, now and then bounded by slightly sloping areas of flat meadow. It ended against a high embankment which belonged to the race track on the frontier of the "realm." To the left of the natural bench on which Conrad sat, the open "steppe" receded for a great distance. He would have preferred to have run out there now, if only it had not been impossible to run in all directions simultaneously. However, he remained sitting, almost motionless, gazing down at the red pail which lay in the grass at his feet. Suddenly he pictured his mother vividly as she had stood in his room last night. He felt a delicate but sharp twinge in the vicinity of his heart, jumped to the ground, and picked up the pail.

He soon succeed in catching two black salamanders of respectable size; not yet scared off by any of the other boys, the creatures had lain in a very shallow spot close to the grassy bank. As he dropped the second into the now half-filled pail, the bushes crackled, the water splashed up here and there, and the other boys appeared all along the bank. They must have seen Conrad first, but they had not called out. The boy who had walked with Conrad the night before asked him whether he had caught anything yet. Conrad showed him the two creatures and placed his red pail beside the group of canning jars which had been set down in the tall grass near the tree.

All along the strip of water there now sounded excited shouts from boys who had also made catches.

Conrad attempted to catch a third large salamander. He did not bother with two or three smaller fry, and attained his goal only after quite a while, and by moving to the other, deep side of the pool, away from the noisy boys. A large salamander, more than a hand's span long, sat on the edge of the water there, its big head almost raised above the surface. The slightest incautious movement might send him scurrying back into the depths. Besides, the bank was steep and accessible only by holding to the trunk of a tree. An overhanging branch would have been better suited to Conrad's purpose, but its swinging and rustling would have quickly spoiled his chances. Conrad considered beforehand each movement he had to make, all the while keeping his eye on the salamander. And his strategy succeeded. Then, with his prey held carefully in his cupped hands, he had to walk around the pool again to the point where his red pail, with the other two salamanders, stood. One of the boys was sitting by the tree. When Conrad picked up his pail, he found it empty, without water and without salamanders. "We thought we'd put them together right away," the other boy found it necessary to explain, pointing to the big jars, in which Conrad's catch were already swimming around with the other salamanders.

"All right," Conrad said promptly. "Then I'll catch some more, because I want to take some home myself today."

"They eat flies," the boy said, with a cunning wink.

"No, they don't eat flies; they eat earthworms and things like that, but sometimes they live for a long time without nourishment," Kokosch replied, and to his own surprise he made no attempt to accommodate to the other boy's speech. He sounded to himself as if he had been reading aloud from a schoolbook, and he laughed. The pail was half filled with water again, the new salamander put into it. But this time Conrad kept his vessel with him, which was more convenient in any case, since for his next catches he again went around the pond to the other, the deep side.

It was quite a time before he found replacements for the stolen creatures, but among these was the largest specimen Conrad had yet seen. Even after he once more had three salamanders propelling themselves around the pail by flicks of the tail, Conrad went on hunting, but he took his excess catch to the boys and added it to the stock in their jars. For the first time they showed some friendliness toward him—particularly the boy to whom he had, as it were, read a lesson from the textbook. They thanked him for the specimens he brought them, and all stood around the red pail admiring the "giant."

But when Kokosch grew loquacious and skillfully employed the manner of speech of his new friends, especially on the way home, they dropped back to their former terseness.

As soon as he reached home, Conrad initiated the maid into the secret of his new treasure. She was an extremely young, still quite childlike girl who was always well disposed toward the boy. In his room the two earnestly contemplated the amphibians and then decided to place the pail on the wardrobe, which seemed the safest place, and to obtain a larger and sturdier vessel.

There was a glazier near the school who also carried a large selection of glassware: mirrors, pitchers, bottles, all sorts of vessels for special purposes, and in addition aquariums of various sizes. They were entirely of glass and came in several shapes, shallow and tall. Conrad had often seen them in the small window of the shop without paying any particular attention to them. Now he recalled them. Next day he took stock of his homework and then ran through it in two hours—arrangement of business affairs, to use Lorenz Castiletz's phrase, which quite expressed his son's attitude. Then, taking his entire supply of cash, Conrad set out for the glazier's shop. There he learned to his pleasure that the prices were much lower than he had estimated, and so he was able to obtain a fairly large glass container as a palace for his salamanders. It was oblong and wider than it was high. Half filled with water—brought specially from the pond in a large old pitcher, along with floating duckweed and other plants—it served its purpose perfectly, and the black salamanders whipped about in it, with movements sometimes rather reminiscent of those of trout.

It was a strange time in Conrad's life. It was the salamander time. He woke during the night; his bed was placed so that he could see straight out through the second window without raising his head from the pillow. The silhouettes of several roofs in the hilly section of the city across the canal stood out against the dark sky. They were irradiated by some indefinite glow of light. The beam of a headlight traveled across the ceiling of the room. A distant locomotive whistle sounded from the railroad embankment near the race track. Not far from that, the salamander pond lay in darkness. Were his salamanders homesick, Conrad suddenly wondered. A soft gurgling was heard; the creatures often produced such small, nocturnal noises, which aroused in him a feeling akin to tenderness. He slid out of bed, took his flashlight, and standing on a chair cast its light upon the aquarium on top of the wardrobe. One of the salamanders was swimming up and down behind the glass wall, raising itself by gentle oar strokes of its flat tail, and in diving spreading the forelegs, which looked like short arms with tiny hands. The broad head was turned toward Kokosch, and the tiny dark pearls of the eyes looked tranquilly at him.

3

ABOUT this time Kokosch made a friend in school. It was his first, for hitherto his association with schoolmates had been only occasional and superficial, in school itself and at various playgrounds and athletic fields.

The boy's name was Günther Ligharts; he came from the north and was the child of distinguished people. When Lorenz Castiletz first heard his son mention the name, he recognized the family at once. They lived in a large house in the villa quarter of the city. Günther had made the first approaches, talking to Kokosch on the way home from school, and in the course of the chat walking part of the way with him, although his streetcar was in a different direction. Boys attending intermediate school no longer tore downhill on the long, straight street to the bridge over the canal. They strolled slowly now, and so had time for talks. In fact, they walked with deliberate slowness for the sake of these talks, and paused at the corners. Kokosch told Günther what luck he had been having in feeding the salamanders. He had dug up earthworms, but had scarcely hoped that the salamanders would eat in captivity and had therefore decided to exchange them from time to time, that is, to catch others and restore the erstwhile occupants of his aquarium to freedom in their native pond. But the first time he let a worm dangle down into the container, a salamander darted up to it, bit into the worm, and gulped piece upon piece with strange, rocking movements until the worm had completely vanished. Kokosch found out that he did not even have to release the other end of the worm, but had only to let it down a little: the salamander virtually ate from his hand. If Conrad did release it, another of the three black brothers would attack the loose end. A kind of tug-of-war at the bottom of the aquarium would ensue—the warriors prettily bracing their little legs against the floor. Or else the two would continue devouring the ends of the worm until their heads met, and then each would bite off his portion.

"Say, I'd like to see that," Günther said. "Can I come over some time?"

"Of course!" Kokosch replied, delighted. Günther walked him across the bridge. A steamer came down the canal and tilted its tall smokestack. The boys, leaning over the railing, observed the men and apparatus on its decks. As the steamer glided by beneath them, Conrad had the feeling, for a few minutes, that the whole bridge was sailing upstream.

For three days Kokosch kept his salamanders on short rations, but continued to gather worms of suitable size in his tin box. Toward five o'clock on the third day, Ligharts came, as they had arranged. When the doorbell rang, Conrad ran to the hall. In the brightly lighted stairwell the blond boy stood at the door, and Conrad again felt strangely moved by Günther's face. Although it was rather broad, and with the eyes set wide apart, its features were sharply defined, as though a draftsman had gone over each of his lines twice; and there was a delicacy of expression which suggested some luminous secret hidden at a remote distance back of the face.

They watched the entrancing salamanders darting, snapping, and swelling as they swallowed their prey. Günther could not get enough of it, and they fed out the whole supply in the tin box. After a while the maid came in; Frau Leontine had told her to bring the boys afternoon coffee and cake. They washed the worm slime from their hands in the bathroom, and then Conrad and Ligharts sat down at the small table by the wide window. Günther, who evidently felt at ease here, promptly helped himself. "You've got a nice view," he said, cake in his mouth. He swallowed and added: "This is a good room altogether—I mean, it must be good being here, and that's very important."

"Yes," Conrad replied. He paused pensively. "Yes, it is important."

Ligharts spoke an extraordinarily pure German, and never slipped into grammatical or dialectical irregularities. Yet his speech was of indeterminate origin; you could not have told that this boy came from the north. Intonation and phraseology seemed to draw secret nourishment, as it were, from all the German dialects, so that, for all its purity, Günther's speech never lacked warmth. Conrad could not grasp all the implications of this, but he felt it keenly after his own fashion.

"You're learning fencing?" Günther asked when he noticed Conrad's foil, mask, and gloves in the corner. "But you don't ever take part in the fencing lessons in school."

"My father thinks that for fencing you need more private teaching than you can get in school. He's still the president of the Hellas Fencing Club, and I take lessons there with what they call the young blood."

"I've often thought the same," Günther said. "I mean, that this practicing in long rows, thirty or forty of us at a time, can never be as good as private lessons. My old man thinks so too."

"Would you like to fence at the Hellas? I'll tell my father and he'll see that you're enrolled in the young blood."

"Oh yes! If you could arrange that, it would be fine."

Günther then began speaking about the salamanders, and midway asked whether Conrad knew a picture called *The Fight with the Dragon*, by a painter named Böcklin.

It seemed that Conrad did not.

"The dragon in that picture is shaped like a salamander, just like that one of yours at the top, only big and armored," Günther expatiated. And now an amazing breadth of knowledge was revealed. He knew all about this part of the animal kingdom—that, for example, the amphibians constitute an older branch than the reptiles, and that there are many survivals among them, so that to this day a very large type of salamander, more than three feet long, exists in Japan. Günther also spoke of the real dragons of earlier ages, of the serpent dragons and the flying dragons with thirty-foot wingspreads, of the gigantic wingless type that resembled moving mountains. And he described vivaciously and precisely the landscape of those earlier ages. The face of the earth under the hot blue sky of those times must have had the look of infinite emptiness and openness, he said, with herds of silent, magical beasts straying over the low, gradual hills, the plains from which the waters had just receded, with the rigid shapes of the forests of giant horsetails, and marshes swarming with life.

Conrad looked out into the twilight, which was already descending upon the quarter of the city across the canal, preceded by broad red streaks of light. A row of windows began shining in the reflected light. The things he had just heard seemed wonderful and new to him. But what really struck him with its novelty was that Ligharts must have looked into all these matters on his own. So you could turn your attention to something of your own free will and by your own decision. So you could go in any direction you pleased. He suddenly saw himself sitting by the water on the horizontal trunk of the tree, sitting perfectly still. But he did not yet know what that might mean.

"So you've studied all these things?" Kokosch said. "How did you happen to? What made you interested?"

"I really can't say," Ligharts replied. "Do you know how you happened to get interested in your salamanders? Did you ask yourself one day: what do I want to have? And was the answer: I want salamanders?"

"No, it wasn't like that," Conrad said.

"Of course not, and it wasn't like that for me either. But I suppose it ought to be. Then you would be—free, and doing what you want."

"Free . . ." Conrad repeated. A tiny gurgling sounded in the silence that followed. Almost surreptitiously, he looked up at the aquarium. Ligharts caught the look.

"Come," he said, "let me have a last look at your cute little fellows. They're jolly."

They stood on the chairs again and looked into the basin, illuminating the water with two flashlights, for Ligharts had his own in his bookbag. The delicate, deep black skin of the salamanders gleamed where the cones of light struck them, and their flat, oar-like tails seemed transparent.

4 ॐ

IT seems significant that Kokosch, in spite of much more frequent meetings with Günther Ligharts, still found time now and again for his friends who hunted salamanders, water snails, and aquatic beetles. He devoted himself to them; in fact, it might almost be said that he wooed their friendship. He even began to do so with sweets; he formed the habit of buying a bagful on the way to join them. Conrad had no special preference for sweets—in contrast to Günther, who pounced on them whenever they were available—but he offered them to the naturalists at the pond. Quite often they displayed an odd coyness, only to say at last: "If you don't mind," with a tight-lipped, sourish expression, before taking the proffered chocolates. Then they would fall back into their flat-nosed sulkiness.

Conrad behaved as though he had left unsettled some matter of importance with these boys and could not manage to get it done with. That in fact was how he felt about it. His efforts increased—and one day led him to a turning point.

Once again they were all busy by the shallow meadow side of the stagnant pond—Conrad beside the boy who had once advised him to feed flies to the salamanders. Suddenly a cry arose. A snake came gliding over the water, a harmless little creature of the kind called ring snake. The head, with its yellow cheeks, was raised above the surface, and the grayish silvery body moved gracefully under the water. These reptiles had become extremely rare in the vicinity, because of the presence of the boys. And the snakes were not sought as prey, since the pet-shop owner with whom these young entrepreneurs were connected did not buy snakes from them. All the same, the appearance of one, after so long a time had passed in which none had been seen, was something of an event.

In spite of the hullaballoo raised by the boys, the swimming snake kept to its direction and reached the flat bank. It was instantly picked up and hurled in an arc out over the water, into which it fell with a splash while two of the boys ran around to the other bank to keep it from reaching dry land and escaping from the pond there.

But the precaution was needless. As soon as the snake touched the water again, it began swimming back toward the same bank. What prompted the creature to return straight into the hands of its tormentors would have been difficult to explain—and the boys did not care to reflect on it.

Perhaps the steep bank on the other side discouraged it.

It swam, and then flew through the air again. Each of the boys tried to make the farthest throw. A rotten, fallen tree lay half submerged near the other side of the pond. The wreckage of its branches stood up, bare and broken. No one had yet succeeded in throwing the snake that far.

Something now stirred in Kokosch, something that may be called the awareness of a decisive moment. Here at last was his chance to release the thing that had lain compressed within him whenever he associated with these boys, like a spring held down. Now was the moment to release it, at any cost. He could tear the cords that bound him, could step aside, even if it meant that he would be left standing alone, with the others angry or even hostile toward him.

He contemplated this possibility and its prolongation, as it were, for several moments. But then the snake reached the shore. With an oddly heavy, violent, and awkward step, Conrad reached it first; he seized the exhausted reptile, now only twisting feebly, and swinging his arm in a circle once and then again, hurled it. And sure enough, his was the farthest throw. The ring snake struck, lifeless as a string, around one of the sharp-edged, broken branches of the half-sunken tree, and remained hanging there, no longer making the slightest movement.

For a while the boys stood looking at it. Then they eyed Conrad obliquely and without a word scattered along the bank to resume their fishing.

Kokosch, too, crouched down at a shallow spot. But he moved like a person whose hands do something utterly beside the point after a terrible accident, such as doing and undoing a button on his coat. Oddly enough, he thus caught a salamander after only a few minutes. The creature wriggled in his fist. He unclenched his hand and it slipped off. Kokosch rose and went away, across the short grass of the meadow, without being noticed by any of the boys.

His legs were very stiff; every step shook him right up to his head, as though he were moving on wooden stilts. He would have been quite incapable, just then, of running even ten steps.

His right hand felt cool and clammy from the water that still clung between his crooked fingers.

He walked heavily on and on, and came to a broad parkway lined on either side by tanbark-strewn riding paths. And suddenly, with a rush of motion, something charged toward him and dark horses' legs passed by, only two steps away; bits of the reddish-brown tanbark sprayed against him. But the riders were somewhere up above Kokosch; they were beyond notice, for he was staring at the ground before his feet. Again something came bearing down as he was about to cross the path, and he stood still. But this time the movement was checked in front of him; the big, heavy hooves pranced about a little; the tall, dark shadow of the horse did not pass by, but came to a halt in front of Conrad.

"Kokosch!" someone called in a clear, high voice from above. And Ligharts leaped from the saddle and gripped Conrad's shoulders. "Hey, I'm so glad to see you," he said, laughing. "What are you doing here? Shall I come with you? Oh, Herr Brokmann, please—" he called up to the riding instructor, an elderly man who was holding Günther's horse and smiling down at the boys—"please, this is my friend here, would you be so good as to take Daisy home?" He turned again to Conrad. "We were just riding home, you see. It isn't far now—I'll walk with you." "Daisy is her name," he added, patting his horse on the neck. "She's a darling. See, Daisy, this is my friend Kokosch. Take a look at him." He fondled the head of the brown mare and laughed again.

With his still damp hand, Kokosch patted Daisy's mane.

His head felt like wood; his teeth lay in his mouth as if they were dentures of stone; his body sank into the tanbark on which he stood, and he felt as if he were buried to the waist. But his lips moved and the words flowed out: "No, ride on ahead, Günther, don't let me hold you up. I was just down in the meadows for a while and have to go up to the café on the boulevard, where my parents and a flock of aunts are waiting for me." He produced a friendly smile and a wave of his hand in the direction of the well-known outdoor café. As he spoke, he felt that Günther, in his yellow boots and riding breeches, was a being composed of an inconceivably light, pure, and happy substance.

"All right then, see you tomorrow in school," Ligharts said, smiling. He shook hands vigorously with Conrad, stepped into the stirrup, and mounted. Kokosch exchanged a word with Herr Brokmann, and as they rode off Günther turned in the saddle and waved.

Conrad crossed the parkway, which was at a somewhat higher level than the two riding paths. In climbing and descending he felt a mild stab of fatigue in his knees. He was hot. And he was conscious of every part of his body, right to the roots of his hair.

His right hand was quite dry by now. He went along a narrow path between the shrubbery, passed through a group of second-growth deciduous trees at the edge of the broad meadows, and then stepped into the meadows. They seemed to him, in his weariness, a vast expanse extending forever under the setting sun. Yes, he'd had to fend Günther off; there'd been no question about that. "In such a state"—these were the very words he thought—it had come off pretty well. For the first time it occurred to him that he had never offered Ligharts a bag of chocolates, such as he so often bought for the fishermen at the pond, although Günther was mad about sweets and would even steal them if he had the chance. Conrad was now walking through the largest meadow. From the canal came the whistle of a steamer. No, it had not occurred to him to give Günther pleasure in that way.

At home the fever erupted.

He stood in the middle of the room and felt himself separated by a soft, invisible, intangible layer of something from the objects around him, as though they had moved away from where he was. The room seemed bigger. He did not look at the salamanders.

Frau Leontine came in and saw that Kokosch was sick. He had
to go to bed; a thermometer was thrust under his armpit; he was
given tea with milk and sopped bread for supper. He lay on his
back, his nostrils haunted by a smell like that of a marsh. The
mud at the pond had smelled the same. But as soon as he concentrated on this odor and tried to breathe it in, it vanished.
For a few moments Kokosch considered whether the smell might
not come from the aquarium and the salamanders. His father entered with the doctor, who had been sent for immediately. The
blanket was thrown back, his chest listened to, his pulse taken.
The doctor's head, with its very clean, white hair, to which some
austere and bitter scent clung, remained close to Kokosch for
several minutes. "You spend tomorrow in bed," the doctor said
with a laugh, "and the day after you'll be able to scoot off back
to school." He turned to Conrad's parents. "It's nothing serious.
If his fever is gone by tomorrow night, let him get up and go out
next day. Some people incline to sudden fevers that pass as
quickly as they come. It doesn't amount to anything."

Next day Ligharts came. He was plainly anxious, asked Kokosch
what was wrong, whether he was tired, whether he hadn't been
feeling ill yesterday when they met. Günther sat on the bed,
holding something wrapped in tissue paper between his knees.
Frau Leontine entered. Günther stood up and clicked his heels.
Kokosch lay on his back, suddenly terrified that yesterday's lie
about the café where he was to meet his parents with "a flock
of aunts" might come out.

"Is he allowed to eat ice cream?" Ligharts asked.

"I don't think it will do him any harm," Frau Leontine said.

A large white carton was produced from the tissue paper.
"Look, Kokosch, your friend has brought you ice cream," his
mother said. "I'll get you bowls and spoons."

It was a lovely afternoon, though drenched in a strange and
novel kind of sadness that seeped like ground water around all
things and events. Kokosch spooned his ice cream thoughtfully.

He felt perfectly well and recalled his depression of the day before with astonishment. The thermometer showed him to be free
of fever. The marshy odor had disappeared. Nevertheless, he
asked Günther to sniff the aquarium. But it had no smell at all,
aside from a faint redolence of water and plants. The salamanders
darted about cheerfully. Ligharts sat on Conrad's bed and told
him what had gone on at school. At Kokosch's suggestion, they
ran through the homework for next day, but there was not much
of that, and it was soon finished.

Right after dinner the following noon Conrad hurried to the
meadows. The sun brooded heavy and hot over everything. In the
vicinity of the pond it was still; none of the boys seemed to be
there so early in the afternoon.

Resolutely, Conrad stepped around a bush and looked across
the water. On the branch which jutted from the half-sunken tree
the dead snake still hung.

He stooped, found a stone; he was determined to, he had to
hit it. Sure enough, his missile pulled the dead snake from the
branch. While the stone clattered to rest in the bushes on the
bank, the corpse slid into the deep water and sank.

A boy had appeared at Conrad's side.

"What did you kill it for?" he said.

For the first time Kokosch experienced the limits of his own
capacity for expression, and of words. And so he did not answer.
As if under compulsion, he turned away and went home.

Next day, when he told Günther that he was going to set his
three salamanders free, his friend begged to go along.

"Have you observed them enough?" Ligharts asked. Kokosch
could not really decide what was involved in the word "observed."

"I want to go right after eating, in the early afternoon," he said.

"Good. Then I'll hurry, so that I can pick you up."

Nevertheless, it grew rather late, since Günther had to come
by streetcar from quite a distance. Conrad was restive; he paced
up and down the hallway while waiting for his friend. The two

boys then carefully lifted the salamanders out of the tank and placed them in the little red pail in which they had come. Wriggling around in the confined space, the three black creatures struck Kokosch as unusually large and fat; as he remembered it, they had been much thinner when first caught. Ligharts found a simple explanation for that. In the pond they had no doubt been unable to catch as much food as they had been given in captivity, so their rapid growth was only logical.

When Günther and Conrad reached the pond, the boys were already running about everywhere, and the canning jars stood in the tall grass by the tree. A few of the boys came over and glanced into the red pail, which Conrad was carrying by its handle—and then there were shouts and exclamations. The unusual size of these amphibians was plain enough to the boys.

"Why don't you put them right into the jars!" one of them called out.

"Sure—you want all three of them for yourself. None of that!" another snarled, planting himself in front of Kokosch.

"Get out of the way," Ligharts said quietly, in his precise enunciation. "We want to go down to the water."

By now the boys were standing in a compact mass, facing Günther and Conrad.

"What do you want to do at the water?" asked the boy who stood in front of Günther.

"We are going to set the salamanders free," Ligharts replied.

"Why?"

"Because it suits us," Günther said.

"Because it suits us"—the boy imitated him, with exaggerated pronunciation. Conrad, who had stepped to one side with his pail, saw something light and swift moving through the air. With a frightening brutality, Günther had slammed his fist squarely into the boy's face. The process was repeated as another boy attacked Ligharts. Their noses streaming blood, the two ran away, shouting savage curses over their shoulders and, as is typical of young roughnecks, threatening to call the police. Kokosch was stunned. He had barely had time to set down the pail, the whole thing had happened so fast. But Ligharts needed no assistance. The other boys had stepped back and seemed not in the least inclined to make an issue of it for the sake of their comrades—who had meanwhile vanished.

"Where are you going to set them loose?" a boy asked Günther, politely and with a rather affectedly precise enunciation.

"Over there where it's deep," Ligharts said, turning to Kokosch. They went around the pond, followed at a short distance by the others.

"Go alone," Günther said to Conrad, and he remained standing at the top while Kokosch negotiated the steep bank. Günther handed him the pail and turned to face the approaching boys. Kokosch, too, sensed how exposed his position was on the steep embankment, where he was forced to cling to a tree with one hand. Carefully but quickly he tipped the pail just above the surface of the water, saw his salamanders vanish with vigorous flicks of their tails, and hastily climbed back to Günther's side.

"What did you feed them with?" one of the boys asked; the pack were once more facing the two friends.

"With fli-ies," Ligharts replied, drawling the word. He looked calmly at the boys for a moment, then turned away, and he and Kokosch walked off.

"Why did you tell them flies, of all things?" Conrad asked after a while.

"I don't know—it just occurred to me," Günther replied.

5 🦆

~~~~~~~~~~~~~~~~~~~~~~~~~~~~~

THUS the salamander time came to an end. And many other things changed in Conrad's life—in fact everything, before long.

First of all came summer vacation, and its beginning meant the end of his association with Günther Ligharts, and not just a two-month interruption. Günther's parents moved to Berlin, and when school started again in the fall Kokosch's friend was no longer there. Word came from him at the New Year: a picture post card which showed a white Pierrot or Harlequin, his face faintly smiling under a tall pointed cap. Kokosch put the card away carefully in the drawer with his writing materials. He intended to answer it, naturally. Günther had neatly written out the address: Uchatius Strasse 23. Conrad often looked at the post card; the picture seemed to him to have a direct bearing on Günther. The Pierrot looked a little like him. But the card was never answered.

That summer vacation following the salamander time—later on, when the dim searchlight of memory passed rapidly now and again over those fields—stirred Conrad to amazement. For he had absolutely no consciousness of the vacation, although there must surely have been one between the end and the resumption of school. All that remained of it was what it had in common with other vacations: the common background of them all. His aunt's home and farm in a shallow dip surrounded by high grass, which shot up luxuriantly behind all the fences, wherever it was not restrained by a path or tilled field or vegetable bed. Fairly close by were the old-fashioned, latticed, and curlicued wooden verandas belonging to the fine houses of a village summer resort, parched by the sun and smelling of wood when you walked past them. Here and there were a few fences, against which grew lilac bushes, their blossoms long since turned to seed by this season, their leaves either shining with an oily gleam or mottled by the dust of the road. Farther on still, came the spurs of the mountain forest, and the railroad embankment, and on the other side of that the checkerboard plain began, intersected by roads and industrial canals and extending to the smokestacks of the factories and the distant city.

Later on there was nothing whatsoever to remember of this particular summer after the salamander time. Yet things must have happened: carriage drives with his parents, games with other boys, catching stag beetles or coming upon a hedgehog. Kokosch actually had to borrow all these things from other summers, thus filling up the shallow, high-grassed dip in the meadows which stood alone and lifeless. For at this spot his memory was just as shallow.

In compensation, Kokosch entered into the autumn and the onset of school as into a time of great change. Everything seemed to have been accomplished in his room during his absence; the room felt as if it had undergone alterations, although outwardly nothing had even been moved. Soon the accomplished fact surrounded him; the summer disappeared into the thin air, the salamander time likewise, and with it the water meadows also ceased to be present in his consciousness. The fields acquired a new attractiveness after the war broke out and soldiers began marching over them, drilling. But that lasted a very short time. After he had drifted two or three times between the lines of skirmishers and the violent barking of rifles with fire spurting from their barrels, after he had stood in the way of maneuvering machine-gun detachments and been forced to flee from the numbing chatter that rose to a roar almost at his ears, after he had several times been genially but firmly sent away by one of the officers (who knew that even such blank ammunition could be dangerous to boys, who insisted on seeing everything from as close as possible)—after that he'd had enough of the whole area. Moreover, the soldiers were not at all fine looking and grew less and less so. They were strained, elderly men, their uniforms full of dust and mud because they constantly lay on their bellies.

So that wing of Conrad's "realm" broke away. The water meadows disappeared, and forever.

But the new thing, which ever since the beginning of school had seemed to him to be hovering in the air, did not delay for long. It discharged, at first in frightening fashion.

After the autumn there came a time of clear, bright weather, with a little snow on the ground now and again. Kokosch stood at the window one day, looking down at the street, the piles of lumber, the sloping terrain, the gray and coldly glittering canal. Behind his back he sensed the strangely expanded room. The distance from the window to the corner near the wardrobe, where his foil and fencing mask hung, had grown tangibly larger. It smelled different, too, and fresh.

Only now did Kokosch hit upon a very simple explanation for this circumstance: during the summer his parents had had the hallway painted.

More amazed than the cause warranted, he went out into the hallway. Yes, it came from there, that clean smell of dry paint which produced a sense of distance or of newness. He stood, without switching on the light, looking past the umbrella stand, at the dark coats hanging in the dimness. But what surprised him most was his belated and slow perception of that natural explanation.

The apartment was quiet and empty at the time, no one home but himself. The maid, too, seemed gone.

Kokosch put on his blue quilted jacket, switched out all the lights, closed the door circumspectly—on the stairs he was strangely affected by the notion that he lived entirely alone in this house. Ah yes, the smell of that fresh paint in the hallway pointed toward—something new. Now he distinctly felt it.

The streets put on the bluish wrappings of early dusk, and their din resounded with doubled intensity. Kokosch walked across the bridge. He was bound for the glazier's shop. The salamanders' former palace had already been deposited there, and his present plan was to exchange it for other objects of glass, for flasks and retorts that could be used in certain chemical and physical experiments. He had a regular program in mind. When Conrad had come with the aquarium, the glazier had not been there, only his wife, who could not decide whether the big glass vessel should be credited toward the purchase of smaller ones.

The glazier himself, of course, was glad to make the exchange, at a slight loss for Conrad. Conrad was content. Once again he carried his entire supply of cash with him. In addition he had a slip of paper on which he had carefully drawn up a list of what he would need. Arrangement of business affairs. He wanted to try only a few specific experiments. This enterprise was to have its limits, was not to lead him on and on indefinitely.

"It must not turn into salamanders"—these were the precise terms in which he put the thought.

Now the choosing began. The glass vessels emerged from excelsior and paper, somewhat dusty but nevertheless gleaming. The glazier circumstantially reckoned the price of each item by weight, which was marked on it in grams. He had a way of pronouncing the word "gram" with a curious emphasis. Considering, making sure he had a firm grip, Conrad held the flasks, glass tubing, and magnificent long-beaked retorts in his hand—such things as he had seen before only in the natural-science laboratory in school. The instruments were what made the subject enticing. Choosing was difficult. Conrad fell in love with all these vessels; when he came to the test tubes he would gladly have bought the whole rack at one fell swoop. It was provided with holes like the egg board at home in his mother's cupboard.

He grew rather agitated, but in the end equilibrium was restored and three contrary points of view reconciled. These were his original list, the available types, and the state of his pocket-book. The solution he finally reached was pleasing. For in this case, too, the prices were lower than Kokosch had anticipated, and he was able to buy the big retort with a ground glass stopper, instead of a smaller one without a stopper. In addition he acquired ten test tubes. He had planned on three. But there was something about them that attracted Conrad. Moreover, the glazier had remarked that it would be better to have more of them. The sum involved was only a little more than the amount he had once spent on his salamander palace, although of course the cost of that had to be reckoned in.

After all, the new enterprise seemed to be turning into a salamander project. On his way home Kokosch was burning to take his carefully packed treasures out of their wrappings and look at them again. He decided to place them up on the wardrobe, separated from everything else. He would have, as it were, a special section in his room: the laboratory.

He walked with great care. Because of his fragile burden, he selected quieter streets leading down to the canal. Full darkness had fallen; here and there the dim yellow glow from the modest lights of suburban indigence fell upon the sidewalk from ground-floor windows, from groceries, from a tavern whose smell of raw spirits crept across the pavement. Then someone staggered out of the tavern and left the opaque glass door open behind him; some moments passed before a vexed hand closed it from within. Conrad made a point of hurrying past. But someone called to him: "Young gentleman, young gentleman!"

The voice did not sound in the least malignant, threatening, or coarse. It was only plaintive, feeble, murmuring. Conrad paused, holding his delicate burden carefully, and looked back. That prompted the man who had called to come somewhat closer; but he remained at a distance, either in order not to frighten the boy away, or out of some inexplicable shyness. Light from a low window fell upon a thin and sharp but good-natured face. The man's hat was covered with the dirt of the street; he must have fallen several times. Around the bridge of his nose and under his eyes were deposits of sweat, weakness, and fatigue.

That was all Conrad grasped in the few seconds that he looked back over his shoulder. For the briefest moment, but with great distinctness, he considered the possibility of stopping and asking what the man wanted. But the impulse was blocked by the frail treasure under his arm. He began to walk faster and faster.

"Young gentleman—listen, please," the voice called behind him, somewhat louder, though still weakly.

Kokosch sped around the next corner and strode along the canal toward the bridge. Only when he reached it and was in a more frequented section, did he feel safe. Now, of course, he had to be careful that no one jogged his arm.

He brought all his treasures home safely, subjected the dusty vessels to the rubbing of a clean white cloth, and finally placed them on display as he had planned. For a long time Conrad stood on a chair in front of the wardrobe. He already had a wooden retort-holder—he had bought it a few days earlier, in a bold foray. And now the big retort, with its ground-glass stopper, was with due deliberation slipped between the cork-lined plates of the clamp, screwed tight with moderate pressure, and the glass alcohol lamp put into place beneath it. A rack for the test tubes was lacking, to be sure. But they were neatly laid out in a row on absorbent cotton and looked splendid. The good-natured maid, who had brought the cleaning rag, helped and handed things up and exclaimed about everything, especially about the shape of the retort. With its long tube coming to a point, it looked just like the grocer next door, she declared, like Herr Köttel, who had just such a nose.

An unusually clear, bright time followed. After Conrad had arranged his business affairs for the next three days, he set up a table at the window in the late afternoon and proceeded with the first experiment, following the instructions in the textbook exactly.

It was the making of oxygen, and Kokosch went about it, not with dangerous sodium chlorate, but with harmless manganese dioxide. At the beginning of the experiment it all seemed implausible, and Conrad had only the most tentative faith in the formulas, similar to the feeling he had about mathematical formulas: they were hard to believe, but once you learned them you could use them to calculate very rapidly.

But then, when the gas, heavier than air, gathered in the tall collecting flask and the strip of magnesium he had ignited blazed up mightily when held in the oxygen—then he felt a joyous clutching around his heart, the sense of a quiet miracle of a world opening out.

Kokosch stood motionless, the ember of magnesium in his hand. Dusk was just beginning to fall.

Into the spreading silence there suddenly broke the clatter of running footsteps from the street below, closer and closer, more and more of them, and reverberating cries.

Kokosch took two steps forward and looked down. A man was running at top speed along the canal. His hat flew—for the how manyth time?—into the dirt of the street. But the harried man paid no attention. His shouting pursuers, a policeman among them, had just reached the bridge; the man had a long head start. He could have escaped. Into the meadows. Instead, he stood still. Kokosch shifted his weight from one leg to the other and pressed his hands against the windowpane. The hatless man down there stood behind a pile of lumber, which hid him from the eyes of his pursuers. For a moment he peered out, just like an animal. Kokosch could distinctly see the whites of his eyes. There was still time to run! But now the man opened his jacket, thrust his hand into some pocket, head bowed. And then the thing appeared, gleaming and dark, was pressed to his brow, elbow sticking out horizontally, and there came an overpowering report like the crack of a whip. Conrad saw the smoke still hanging in the air while the man below was transformed into a heap of clothes lying motionless on the ground.

The shot checked the pursuers; perhaps they thought it was aimed at them. But then the whole crowd came running up, along with many others who thronged to the scene, and built a wall around the man on the ground, so that Conrad could no no longer see him.

The incident, only a moment before sharp and small like the first flash at the end of the ignited ribbon of magnesium, quickly and fluidly spread out. The maid came running, then Conrad's mother. Then Sophie, the maid, raced downstairs to find out more about what had happened. Outside, the helmets of the police increased in number. A dreary whistle; the ambulance arrived; now a path was made through the crowd for someone, probably the doctor. In a short while he emerged from the swarm of people, got into the ambulance, and it drove away without its cargo.

For this man who lay beside the pile of lumber was no longer sick. He was, in a manner of speaking, far healthier than anyone else, for he was dead.

A bier sufficed for him, and with it and a guard of police to fend off the curious, the whole scene melted away. In its train the maid appeared, and recounted everything with the velocity of a chattering machine gun.

It seemed that the man had stolen a can of fish and a few other edibles from a shop, and had been caught in the act. He had wrenched loose and fled. Sophie described precisely the shop in which the incident had taken place; she knew it, its proprietor, his wife, her two daughters. . . .

Kokosch sat on the edge of his bed.

A few days later a literally diabolic happenstance occurred.

His mother called him. She was standing on a chair in Father's study, taking down the curtains, which were to be washed. She had also assembled various coverlets and doilies. Kokosch was asked to note these things down, item by item, on a sheet of paper. He started to go for a pencil. "Take one from here," his mother said. And so he wrote the items as she called them out, all the while looking around the room, which he seldom entered. Crossed swords, rapiers, foils, fencing masks, and so on decorated the walls, as well as group photographs taken at meets or parties in the club. In one picture Kokosch recognized two of his father's friends from the club who came to the apartment once a month for a kind of board meeting or something of the sort. On those occasions there was always a big supper and a good deal of lively talk among the men around the table. Even next day the odor of cigars could be smelled as far as the hallway. . . .

"Three valances, six side panels . . ." Frau Leontine called down. Kokosch wrote.

She descended from the chair and handed him a bundle of linen. "Take these, please." To free his hands, he thrust the pencil into his jacket pocket. Then he followed his mother, whose arms were also full, into the next room.

It is, of course, already apparent that the pencil was the heart of the matter. Two days later, when Kokosch was quietly going through his business arrangements for the next day, carefully making the necessary entries in French and geography—two days later the door suddenly slammed into the wall and an ebony-black father burst into his quiet room. As yet this ebony blackness lacked the bitterly sought justification, the switch to steer it into its dark orbit, the spark to set off the gathered forces.

"Have you by any chance . . . I've been looking for a good hour for . . ."

A spark leaped a gap and Kokosch experienced a terrifying flash of understanding. He was frightened literally to the marrow of his bones. He seriously thought himself done for. For brief moments he considered the possibility of simply denying everything. But already his icy hand was fingering his breast pocket, betraying everything. His terror became bottomless when he did not find the pencil at once. But then he produced it, wordlessly.

With such violence as if he were snatching his child at the

last moment from under the hooves of runaway horses—just so
Lorenz Castiletz seized the little stub of a pencil. Immediately
afterwards the first two loudly resounding slaps landed.

"Idiot! Brat! What were you doing in my room?"

"I . . ." Conrad said.

"What were you doing in my room, I asked!"

The next pair of slaps struck.

"I . . ." Conrad whispered.

"Speak, you moron!" his father roared.

But Conrad said no more.

"Are you going to answer, you thief!" Lorenz Castiletz shrieked.
Then the dance began. Kokosch, seized by the nape of the neck,
flew with a crash head first into the wardrobe. A kick in the back-
side, a punch in the back, and the next two slaps followed—
detonated with the regularity of a battery of artillery firing in
salvos. Kokosch cried, of course. His head was hot, his face
burning with a deep fire. Horror followed horror. He was driven
before his father, reeled out through the hallway, against the
French doors of the drawing room. Roared into his ear came the
reiterated demand that he speak, but he was quite incapable of
saying a word, even if any attempt to do so had not been
smothered by new thumps and blows.

Outside, from the margins of life, where a few isolated sails
still drifted, Frau Leontine came, very casual and *bleu mourant*.
As he was being pummeled through the hallway, Conrad heard
the key turning in the lock. He thought the maid was coming,
but his shame at once subsided into dull, spineless despair.

It was his mother.

He wanted to flee to her. But she was the faster; she was instantly in front of him, defending her child.

Without a word, in complete silence, for long moments in that
dim hallway the forces struggled against one another, the forces
on which everything depended, on which hung ultimately the
continuance of this family.

Lorenz Castiletz wanted to storm past his wife to seize the boy. But he ran into an invisible wall which he no longer had the strength to break through, detonated as he was and already carrying within himself the germs of collapse.

"The pencil . . . sneakiness—he was in my room—this—good-for-nothing . . ." These words were accompanied by the last gasp of the eruption, the last attempt at a breakthrough past Frau Leontine in the direction of Kokosch.

But his wife did not stir or lift a hand. Although the gaze of her large slanting eyes rippled outward rather than focused purposefully forward, so that it would have been difficult to say at what point it was directed, Lorenz Castiletz nevertheless felt it to be resting on his left hand, which held the recaptured pencil stub. The casualness with which Frau Leontine looked in that direction, and elsewhere, charged her gaze with such bottomless contempt as no curling of the lip or narrowing of the eyes could possibly have expressed. It was sheer, terrible disdain. For Frau Castiletz's face remained perfectly smooth and calm; it had just come from the distracted horizons of life far outside, from the blue mists of the distance floating up, itself *bleu mourant*. Thus she looked at the pencil—as well as elsewhere—and nodded and said casually:

"I know. I took it from your room. Conrad was just going to bring it back, but I needed him at the moment to help me take down the curtains and told him to put it in his pocket for the time being. That's how he happened to have it."

Lorenz Castiletz was now roused to, or subsided into, his own despicableness, which began to trickle down his left arm, cold and viscous, and over the hand which held the little stub of pencil. That despicableness was not despairing, or was accompanied only by an entirely spineless despair from which God himself could not have struck so much as a spark of courage.

He tucked the stub into his vest pocket. While Conrad still stood behind his mother, ears half deafened, in a hot and dry

isolation from himself and the world, studying with fixed attention a particular spot on that brown jute runner which led from
the front door to the glazed doors of the drawing room—during
this stillness that rotated slowly and evenly around its own axis,
there came the first moaning tokens of what was to be the most
frightful aspect of that evening: the moans accompanying the
collapse of his father, who but a moment before had been totally
ebony black. Conrad crept into his room. His back was heavy
and bent with, we are tempted to say, the certainty of death, as
if boulders were being hurled after him. For out there in the
hallway Lorenz Castiletz lay on the floor, kissing his wife's feet.
Leontine was so profoundly shocked that she turned completely
colorless, and though she was there in the flesh could be said to
have sunk below the horizon. Lorenz, then, kissed his wife's feet
and whimpered. Thank God today was the maid's day off. For
the whole evening continued in that key. Toward ten o'clock
Kokosch's mother brought him a plate of cold meat, salad, and a
glass of milk. She embraced him. Her gaze had by now entirely
dissolved in all directions. Her dark blonde, disheveled hair
seemed to be trying to follow the example of her eyes; it stood
tousled around her head like cirrus clouds in the sky.

Not until two days later did these events coagulate within
Kokosch. It happened at night, when everyone was asleep. He
started up out of a dream and with a jerk reached a sitting position. There was a hollow roaring in his ears, a true chasm of
noise which devoured everything and anything. It was still coming toward him, past the cold, small, solitary railroad station,
high and swaying, with a thin, twisting streamer of smoke, fiery-
eyed and sinister: the locomotive. His father, lying on the floor,
had turned the switch the wrong way, but Conrad remained
paralyzed. The smoke was horrible; he twisted like a thin string,
as if in pain. The smoking lanterns were spewing out red liquid,
from the nostrils, for they were the faces of the two boys at the
salamander pond to whom Ligharts had given bloody noses.

Kokosch sat up in his bed while the persuasiveness of the dream rapidly diminished, the sloping walls in which he was caught widened out and at last faded away entirely in the surrounding darkness. The beam of a headlight passed across the ceiling of the room. Kokosch listened. But he could not hear a single one of those tiny, gurgling noises from the salamanders on top of the wardrobe. Then he wakened fully. There were no longer any salamanders. Kokosch became composed, cool. He looked through the dark window at a few scattered, feebly glimmering parts of houses across the canal.

From out of the center of his coolness the tears welled, in a great hot current, like a thawing stream. He felt the wide rivulets coursing down his cheeks. They came and came and would not stop, like a hemorrhage. He wept because of Ligharts, because of his father, because of the dead man who had lain by the lumber below, because of the salamanders, because of what had happened and what was now, because of yesterday, today, and tomorrow, and so perhaps for a whole life.

6 🐦

THERE are stubborn stains of the soul. A while back it was the fashion to call them "complexes." Nowadays that word has become old hat.

Henceforth, before Conrad set out for school in the morning—on time, as always—he would pause for two or three minutes in the middle of his room and look around him in all directions. The fact was that he so intensely needed this brief time for composing himself that even as he washed and dressed he made sure that those minutes would be left to him. After this brief check-up of his surroundings Kokosch could feel somewhat reassured that nothing had been left out of order or unnoticed anywhere which might then launch itself menacingly against him. This watchfulness of his—we may well call it that—amounted to an alertness within him toward things and affairs beyond the sphere of those which can be listed—class schedules, time for a soccer game, arranging of business affairs, pencils, time for the fencing lesson. He stretched his senses beyond this sphere in an effort to learn something about the further, less definable circle of life which lay like a ring around the moon surrounding this inner ring and containing no particular things or affairs. There, too, disorder might abide; there, too, something might be forgotten; from that quarter, too, a possible menace might approach.

The upshot of it was that Conrad no longer could feel secure. He formed the habit of telling himself aloud that everything was in order, he had all his homework done, he need fear no scolding or punishment, his pockets had all been looked through and his belongings were all in their place. Yet all this was inadequate to repress the basic feeling underlying everything: that somewhere something was not in order and that a terrible threat must therefore be approaching, coming dangerously closer.

It often happens that grownups looking for a particular street or in need of some directions will apply to a bright and good-looking boy like Conrad for help. If ever this happened, Conrad would start with fright. Once a policeman in uniform, who seemed to be a stranger in this part of the city, asked where there was a stationery shop in the neighborhood—as a schoolboy he would know that, wouldn't he? But Kokosch was barely able to stammer out the information. After the man in uniform had set out in the indicated direction, Conrad stood almost numbed; but already he was beginning to fight against this state of mind. He felt as if he had been given a beating. He went home; the houses and sidewalk shimmered before his eyes as if they were under water, or presented the aspect of utterly blank plane surfaces, so desperately was he struggling and choking over this thing that had assumed power over him, that seemed to drive him down and away from his ordinary life.

Although all that was closer and more self-evident than the shirt he wore—he nevertheless conceived a strange idea which, had it been carried out, would probably have been an effective countermeasure.

One evening the board members of the Hellas Fencing Club met and the Castiletz apartment once more resounded with the hawking and rumbling of many voices in the dining room, the smells of fancy cooking and expensive cigars. Conrad was about to slip out of his room into the hall when he saw through the crack of the barely opened door one of the gentlemen strolling down the hall with that dignity and self-containment that persists even when there are no witnesses—the bearing of a man who thinks something of himself and his own opinion, but also respects the opinions of others, and is leaving the pleasant and continuing male converse for a brief while in order to let things take their course without him. Soon afterwards the maid, Sophie, appeared in the hall, and the gentleman, now on his way back to the dining room, dallied for a momentary tactile appreciation of her charms. Conrad was afraid they might notice that the door was open a crack—though he did not really fear it for his own sake. Apparently they did not, and soon the hall was deserted again.

At that moment, a strange thought rose up in Kokosch.

He decided to write down such observations. It was as if he sensed the possibility that knowledge gained about others would serve as a counterpoise to all the things that threatened him, as a kind of insurance against the constantly lurking dangers, especially the dangers he was ignorant of. Those others were not aware that he had been a witness; they had no inkling of what he knew. He began to forge his weapon, had already cut up some paper for establishing a kind of dossier—when his mother came and called him in to the party. The men had disagreed over the correct translation of a Latin proverb—they were in the habit of weaving many such into their conversation—and so they needed the "little Latinist" to set them straight. Which he did, precisely and with not a word too much, under the doting eye of his father.

There in the dining room, where the man glimpsed in the hall had once more settled into the pleasant vapors of conversation, wine, and cigars, the episode Conrad had seen lost its vivid actuality. Alone once more in his room, facing the blank sheets of paper, he felt unexpectedly numbed by the mounting problems of this sort of record. And where was he going to keep it? The result was that the whole plan was suspended for the time being.

A similar fate overtook his chemical experiments.

They were not continued, even though the collection of cunningly shaped glass on the wardrobe had considerably increased. The initially acquired treasures formed only the nucleus of the whole group. Now there was even a handsome little rack for test tubes, completely filled. All this glassware dated from the days after the diabolic incident with the pencil. Lorenz Castiletz had gone to the glazier's shop with his son, and bought from the gratified shopkeeper all the "grams" that Kokosch's heart desired. But the truth of the matter was that his heart no longer desired any of these things. Conrad felt exceptionally embarrassed by the whole business. However, he had no opportunity to say so or to extricate himself from the situation. For Lorenz Castiletz was now moving along his generous and warmhearted track just as forcefully and busily as Kokosch's little railroad cars used to run on theirs when the clockwork motor was wound and his father would lie on the floor working the switches.

It is a curious fact that afterwards Kokosch would occasionally tell his father a little about chemical experiments which he had not undertaken. With dignified swollen middles and slight coatings of dust, the retorts and flasks stood there on the wardrobe, gleaming again once a week, when Sophie dusted them—with care, out of fondness for Conrad, but at the same time privately reviling all this "magical junk."

Later on, when an occasion offered, they were all given away.

Kokosch, after all, was beginning to be a bigger boy, a big boy in fact. He was reaching the end of the lower secondary school and the plan was that he should go on to a higher commercial school, to prepare for a vocation similar to his father's. Even now, while still in secondary school, he was receiving lessons at home from a private teacher in commercial correspondence, stenography, and the elements of bookkeeping, along with practice in English and French, which he had learned earlier. In addition, he was studying the basis of all technical subjects, descriptive geometry.

The name of his private teacher was Albert Lehnder. A law student whose career had been held up by military service during the war, the child of once well-to-do people, he was now compelled to support himself and his mother. He worked in a bank, supplemented his small income by giving lessons, and must also have got in some studies, for from time to time he took examinations at the university. The really remarkable thing about Lehnder was that in spite of all this honest toil he by no means radiated virtue. Quite the contrary seemed to be the case, so that Lorenz Castiletz, for instance, although he was forced to respect the young man and had never heard anything to his discredit, nevertheless kept a mistrustful eye half cocked in his direction. Yet he would have vigorously disclaimed any charge that he felt suspicious of the young man.

Lehnder was a good teacher for Kokosch. The boy learned in order to please him, and Albert's special and well-tested technique consisted precisely in eliciting this state of mind. Thanks to it, he managed to have a good many of even his most difficult cases receive passing grades, so that he acquired a reputation for successful tutoring among the parents and could present top-notch recommendations. Moreover, this student and bank teller was a good-looking boy, in fact distinctly handsome—though it was handsomeness of a moist and hairy sort, we might say. Women ran after him. Perhaps Lorenz Castiletz had occasionally noticed that.

During those years of accelerating departure from boyhood, with antennae already reaching out into the emptier, more tranquil reaches of adult life—where, to the mind of a boy, people do nothing at all but sit together in the most boring fashion, with ostentatiously polished shoes, and talk, not showing any signs of intending to do anything, and consequently never damaging their clothes—people very much like the books they read, in which virtually nothing happens: during those years Conrad, since he was no longer so constantly occupied as he had been earlier, hit upon a strange sort of game in the drawing room in lieu of loafing around in the empty apartment. There was a large mirror in this room whose glass showed a faintly greenish tinge and perhaps the slightest tendency toward opaqueness. If he looked into this mirror when twilight was beginning to fall and narrowed his eyelids to a crack and gradually moved backwards—at a certain point in the game he achieved a thrill of fright. For suddenly an image was looking at him out of dark, empty eye sockets. The nature of the light and the squinting erased everything, from that particular point on, except those hollows in the face. Kokosch played this game again and again for some time. In the past he had taken no notice at all of the drawing room, but now he enjoyed going into it, especially when no one else was there. The close air of the room, filled with the clean scent of fine wallpaper and upholstery, and the sense that all the objects in it were more or less untouched and unused, affected him very much as had the one-time smell of paint in the newly painted hall: with a premonition of distance or novelty. As he inhaled it while he stood in that room, the particular fragrance could not help seeming good and attractive to him.

The game in front of the mirror took an even stranger turn when he moved in the reverse direction, approaching the mirror. For then he saw at first only his own dusky outline, then the more brightly illuminated surfaces of his face growing ever more distinct. But at the very moment when, as it were, he first recognized himself in the mirror, he found himself confronted by the empty eye sockets. Each time this happened he could barely keep from making a faint, very deep start of fright. And although Conrad managed several times in succession to suppress that start, and practiced in order to be able to do so, his efforts were usually a partial failure.

Nowadays, when he was out on the streets, he tended to saunter. In the past, he had always been in a hurry: because of Ligharts, because of the salamanders, because of the experiments, because of five dozen other things. Now he noticed many a matter that strikes the eye of a man who walks erect: the form of the clouds drifting before the setting sun over the canal, the distant silhouette of a building, the stream of vehicles and pedestrians on the bridge pouring out toward the water meadows on a Sunday in the spring of the year.

The commercial school which Kokosch later entered—after thorough preparation—produced a certain consolidation of the erect gait, if we may put it that way. It had been built only two years before, and in the spacious entrance hall one was greeted by composed and tranquil shapes, a great deal of metal, glass, tile, and stocky radiators glowing a dull silver color. Thanks to Albert Lehnder's lessons, Conrad was familiar with the most difficult aspects of the various courses. Moreover, Lorenz Castiletz kept the private tutor on, so that Conrad was always a bit ahead of his class. Nowadays, on the rather longer walk home, when he had talks with schoolmates, they were the more sedate conversations of groups of young people walking or standing. They no longer wore boys' suits, but collars and ties; this new kind of apparel affected Conrad inwardly.

In the commercial school there were also girls. The remarks made about them, at first sheer borrowings, soon became second nature.

7 🦆

~~~~~~~~~~~~~~~~~~~~~~~~~~~~~~~~~~~~~~~

AS is well known, every family is a fountainhead of unique anecdotes. These pearls of family humor are sooner or later gathered up by young people and carried on—usually throughout a whole life. For, basically, everyone thinks that there cannot possibly be any better stories than these.

Conrad, too, picked up such pearls. They were not all equally suited for retelling, say, to a group of his schoolmates. The most likely were those concerning the old colonel, a recently deceased uncle of his father, possessed moreover of a kind of inherited castle, who had passed his last invalid years after the war drinking his life away with resolute conviction. A well-stocked cellar served this end; otherwise, he turned every penny over three times, as the saying goes. In the course of a business trip through that vicinity, Lorenz Castiletz had set aside a day to pay his respects to this uncle; other male relatives had recommended such a visit as time well spent, both because of the uncle's quaint eccentricities and because of his excellent wines. He found the small, old manor house quiet and seemingly lifeless among the wooded hills of the Sonneberg district of Thuringia, the entrance

gate open, not a dog around to bark. Lorenz Castiletz mounted
the stairs, flanked by an unassuming row of stag antlers, to the
low-ceilinged first floor. Here, as he was looking around and
wondering which way to go, or which door to knock at, there
suddenly rang out a resounding male chorus. The song was that
Protestant church hymn which begins: "One thing is needful, O
Lord, and that . . ." The singers themselves then appeared; they
emerged from a big double door. Evidently they were two servants, and between them they carried a large empty basket of the
type used for laundry. Castiletz turned to them, intending to ask a
polite question. They did not listen. Both signed to him with a
regretful shrug of their shoulders, but did not interrupt their
singing for a moment. Stanza upon stanza rolled forth as they
descended the stairs, shouting rather than singing the hymn.
The whole house reverberated with the hymn as the descent continued; presently the song seemed to be coming from the cellar,
rising through open doors.

Lorenz Castiletz now noticed a door ajar. Stepping through it,
he entered an anteroom and then what seemed to be his uncle's
study, for the uncle was sitting there in an armchair.

The old gentleman recognized his nephew at once, although it
had been a long time since he had seen him. His only greeting,
however, was a mute, though hearty, nod and handshake and a
gesture toward a chair. His entire attention seemed to be devoted to the song rising from the depths. Soon the singing approached again. "One thing is needful, O Lord, and that . . ."
boomed right outside the door—but then the singing stopped
abruptly and the basket, half filled with wine bottles, was set
down on the floor before the old colonel. The old man promptly
made a choice for his nephew and himself. The nephew was also
served a breakfast whose hunting-lodge simplicity scarcely
matched the bottle of Ruppertsberger Gaisböhl 1907—a vintage
before which one might well have genuflected several times.

"The singing is so—so they won't swill in the cellar," the colonel said. "I have barrels there too."

Afterwards Lorenz Castiletz learned that this custom was fairly recent. Time was when only a single servant had descended the stairs singing and returned with the wine basket. But one day the fellow fell on the stairs, still singing—whether out of clumsiness or cunning remained unexplained. At any rate, a good many precious bottles were broken, and henceforth his brother, the gardener, had to go along, likewise singing. It bothered the colonel a bit that the men were tone deaf and that neither of them could harmonize a second voice. "Why, any drayman can do it," he complained. But the two obstinately remained tone deaf. Soon the story went the rounds among the relatives that down in the cellar one of the servants invariably bellowed for two while the other drank for two.

Now that was a tiptop story for a board meeting and supper of the Hellas Fencing Club, or for the ten o'clock recess at the commercial school. Soon Conrad's fellow students knew it, as did his father's guests.

The same could not be said for the tale of another relative, also deceased, from Kulmbach, where the famous beer is brewed. Uncle Christian had brewed beer likewise, all his life, with skill and expertise. But that was not his only talent. He was also practitioner of a second art not necessarily connected with brewing: magic. Uncle Christian was a first-rate magician, was in fact famous for it. As other substantial folk have a library room in their apartment, so Uncle Christian had a magician's cabinet. In tall, narrow cases all along its walls he kept a variety of those tools of the trade necessary to a magician: the top hats with double and triple bottoms, the dice, the cardboard tubes, the small tables, the packs of cards, daggers, balls, and tail coats. In one corner stood a large container made of heavy wooden slats, which he had made only recently. He had promised to appear at a charity fair, and was going to use this chest to give the audience a special surprise: to make himself, his entire, by no means thin—in fact, rather substantial—person, vanish entirely: to conjure himself away.

The trick was performed in a hall holding some two hundred guests, and was a complete success. The audience was given an opportunity to examine the chest closely. Then, with a friendly smile, the magician stepped inside and closed the lid behind him. In a moment it was opened, and everyone was allowed to come up to the chest and examine it again. It was empty; incomprehensibly, the magician had vanished as if he had departed for the hereafter.

He remained vanished. After some time the audience grew uneasy and concerned. But it was a long time before Uncle Christian's whole and substantial person was found in the false bottom of the curious box, whose lines and displaced perspective had deceived everyone. Uncle Christian was dead. He had died of a heart attack, perhaps brought on by the heat, so the doctor said. But this explanation somehow failed to set peoples' minds at rest and dispose of the matter, as might have been expected of unsuperstitious people.

Conrad had far less success with this story. In fact, he scarcely tried it out. It was probably not one of the gems presented to the Hellas Fencing Club either. Nevertheless, this anecdote was especially dear to Conrad's heart. Had he told it, he would not have been merely acting the part of a son carrying on the traditions of his forefathers. The story had a more vital, personal, and autonomous aspect. For that very reason, perhaps, he kept it to himself.

But the young man soon felt the flicker of desire to experience something on his own. An incident that could be shaped to a point, or neatly rounded off—as you will. In short, he wanted to create an anecdote of his own.

The adolescent was lured by the spirit of adventure. And a big city offered a large enough arena for it. After the sudden departure from boyhood, everything had appeared as lean and clean as the entrance hall of the new school building which he passed through every morning. Now, out of the urge not only to hear but also to create stories there sprang up victorious a power to take steps against that bareness in the foothills of adult life.

For everywhere, in that street, on those stairs, "life" could surprisingly and incredibly come at one!

Conrad was not yet aware that life is only rarely inclined to do anything of the sort.

He could only think that he would know how to give it a good reception, and maintain an erect gait! Incidentally, collar and tie already belonged to his new, his urban romanticism; in fact, he could no longer conceive of it apart from them.

Here lay the root of much purposeless running around (purposeless when compared with the busy and action-filled world of the boy). But now these roamings no longer took place in the lonely realm of the water meadows, but a great distance across the canal, in the central parts of the city. Here even lay the root of the appointments and the walks with girl students, enterprises which as yet scarcely sprang from their proper and natural soil.

It was quite out of the question, in all these enterprises, to experience disappointments, or to recognize failures as such. So boundless were the expectations that no disappointment, and no fulfillment either, could in the slightest diminish them. The spirit of adventure bent the as yet unknown environment to its will with such violence that the environment could not possibly have sprung back into its proper shape.

It no doubt suited Conrad's amiable but mooncalfy purposes that one day, when he had already passed his fifteenth birthday, he was sent on a journey by himself. This was during the first half of the summer vacation. Various relations (that is, in the category of "a flock of aunts") had insisted on borrowing the boy for a while, because they had not seen Conrad for a long time and were interested to see how he was growing up. Lorenz Castiletz may have looked somewhat further into the future when he arranged that his son set out quite soon after this request was made, and well equipped. And so he was bound for two cities in central Germany, not too far from one another, from aunt to aunt.

He traveled by express, second class. With a small, shallow yellow suitcase. Collar and tie so much a matter of course they need scarcely be mentioned. Quite superfluously, he asked a railroad official about the train, which was already in the station, its last car sporting red lights.

The second compartment he came to in the next to the last car held no old ladies and gentlemen—a type of humanity Conrad avoided. Its inmates seemed in the merriest mood: they promptly toasted him when he entered, and he too was given a glass of liquor. Evidently they were not going to allow the newcomer to disturb their gaiety, but proposed to include him in the company. Two exceedingly well-dressed young men had put their feet up on the opposite bench. A third sat at the window next to a blonde girl, beside whom Conrad was seated, "so that she'll have some fun too," as it was put. As he responded to the toast, Conrad tried his best to imitate the northern intonation of the whole company, and especially of the two dapper young men; he felt that it was indubitably superior to his own. The girl asked him in a friendly way, with almost a touch of maternal concern, where he came from and where he was going. Conrad confined his replies to essentials. Gradually, however, he entered into the mood of the others, was no longer so bothered by the smell of the spilled liquor, which mingled with a strange and penetrating kind of perfume, both superimposed upon the odor of stale coal smoke which is the railroad smell.

They had spent no more than ten minutes laughing, chatting, and drinking when the young man sitting at the window, apparently in obedience to a sudden inspiration whispered something to the giggling girl beside him and then quickly brought out a large, whitish object from his baggage. He tossed it to the two other young men, who caught it and passed it on to Conrad.

It was a human skull, a "death's head," as it is call
owner, a medical student, as it now developed, was tak
specimen with him on his vacation, for studying, so he sa

All sorts of jokes inevitably followed. And it was su
that they put a hat on the "old boy" and tuck a cigar b
the jaws, which were held firmly at the joints by two
springs.

This was the sort of thing Conrad had been waiting f
create stories of his own. He studied the skull carefully,
all sorts of high-sounding notions spawned inside his ow
looked into the empty eye sockets, which, however, were
fully illuminated by the light from the ceiling fixture. Brief
was touched by the recollection of his strange game in the d
ing room, but only briefly; it did not fit here, and he banishe

"Man or woman?" he asked the owner tersely and matte
factly.

"Used to be a man," the medical student replied, laugh
"Undoubtedly a very fine fellow. Quite good-looking even n
though a little pale."

But suddenly, with howls of glee, the skull was snatched fr
Conrad. A tremendous idea had burst like a bombshell upon t
two young men.

In the next compartment, they said, there was a girl ridi
alone. We'll be coming to a tunnel in a few minutes: let's ho
the skull up to the window.

General screaming and laughter at this proposal.

"On my cane!" one of the well-dressed young men cried.

"Won't hold it," the student said.

"Oh, come now, you mean to say this fat club won't?" He
showed it. It was one of those walking sticks that had come into
fashion at the time, a kind of short baton of bamboo. With a
handkerchief wrapped around it, the metal tip fitted into the
hole at the base of the skull where the spinal cord had once
emerged.

"Let's give him a turban too!" the medical student exclaimed. He knotted his silk scarf firmly around the old boy's temples. The cigar was removed. It was really an extraordinary sight.

Conrad was suddenly aware again of the smells, the spilled liquor and the penetrating, slightly oily odor of a pomade, soap, or perfume with which he was not familiar. Dimly, he recognized the now bygone possibility that he might have taken a seat in another compartment, and as he pursued this idea, he perceived that this possibility was by no means past and gone. He suddenly laughed aloud with the others. But his head hurt as he did so. He was feeling the effects of the drink.

"Who's going to—hold him out?"

"I will!" Conrad cried.

"Bravo, young fellow," one of the smartly dressed young men said. "Quiet from now on!" he ordered. "A ghostly silence must prepare the act. We'll reach the tunnel in about ten minutes."

They lowered the window all the way. It was partially open anyhow, because of the sultry air.

And suddenly they slipped with a roar into the tunnel, whose walls seemed made of smoke. Even the ribbons of brick rushing by no longer gave the impression of being solid substance.

Conrad sprang to his feet and seized the walking stick. He noticed the medical student leaving the compartment behind him, followed by the girl. They disappeared into the corridor, sliding the door shut behind them.

The two young men had likewise stood up. "Careful now, young fellow. Keep it close to the wall of the car, or there might be an accident," one of them said quickly and emphatically at Conrad's ear. A tremendous, crashing noise roared out of the blackness as he went to the window. Conrad held the cane so that the handle pointed in; that way the old boy's charming, turbaned countenance was in the right position, turned toward the car. Since the cane was short and easily handled, he had no difficulty at all, hardly had to lean out. For greater security, the

two young men held Conrad's shoulders. For a few moments Conrad plainly saw the skull against the square of light from the window of the adjoining compartment, which was also open. He thought he heard a brief scream—it sounded something like the falling and breaking of dishes—and immediately pulled the skull back in through his window. Even as he did so, he realized that higher pitched and clearer noises were roaring in the air like a thousand devils, so that he had probably been mistaken. He put the cane down.

"Didn't she scream?" Conrad asked the other two.

"Not a bit. We would have heard it through the wall. The noise was terrific, but still . . . Well, I suppose she didn't even look and all our fine plans came to nothing. And now the tunnel's far behind."

The shattering roar had in fact ceased as if totally absorbed by the soft palate of a great mouth behind them. Now the train ran on, with its gentler rattling noises. The medical student and the girl entered from the aisle.

"Could you see in?" one of the young men asked.

"No. The curtains were drawn too closely, without a crack between them. It doesn't seem to have worked—at any rate, nothing stirred." He removed the skull from the cane and replaced it in his suitcase.

"Just as I thought, she didn't even look. Was probably lying on the bench with her head to the window and reading or sleeping. But our young fellow here did a fine job. Well then, cheers!"

They drank again. But the misfired practical joke seemed to mark the point at which the evening's exuberance had passed its peak, having been vented in the prank. At the corner by the window the student sat beside his girl, holding his hand over his mouth and yawning. He did this several times in succession, though he did not look really sleepy. He had a long face, soft and weak-looking, with a slight dampness, apparently of perspiration, on his temples and on the bones above his somewhat hollowed cheeks. He looked quite old for a student, a grown man in fact, with that indefinite aura that goes with adulthood. It was not just, as with Conrad, the novelty of collar and tie. The blonde girl beside him seemed a bit on the thin side, but she had an air of good nature. Her large dark eyes were wide open and glistening now.

At the next stop the pair said good-bye and got off. The two young men and Conrad also soon reached their destination—Conrad last of all, and long before daybreak. Alone in the compartment, he had almost fallen asleep at the end of his journey, and roused himself with a start when the train stopped at the station where he was to change to a local. . . .

This third "self-made" anecdote, which had fallen short of becoming a real one, stuck out of Conrad, so to speak, for a long time, like a nail driven only halfway into the wood. But no one was caught on it, that is, the moment never arrived when he could interlard it into a conversation. Moreover, it had not come to a neat conclusion. That, and perhaps a somehow embarrassing memory of the smell always associated with it, resulted in its suffering a fate even more wretched than the story of the Kulmbach brewer: it was never told at all.

Except for a single time, on a cold and dreary autumn day. Conrad was brooding in his room, had nothing to do and did not want to do anything, could stick to nothing; in short, was in that state of mind in which people can keep nothing to themselves. His father, in his study, was the only other person in the house. Conrad went to him—which was unusual. He found his father at his desk, but not working; he was reading a thin paperback volume. The room was very cool, scarcely heated; inclined to apoplexy as he was, Lorenz Castiletz loved coolness. Conrad slumped into an armchair near the desk, and, with a kind of semi-blindness and perverseness, lacked the sensitivity to gather from his father's friendly question, "Finished with your homework so soon?" that he was intruding. Instead, he produced his story for

the benefit of a listener—distinctly the wrong one. Lorenz Castiletz, who had sat leaning forward over the desk top, taking in
the anecdote with increasing vexation—which Conrad sensed but
obstinately refused to feel—Lorenz Castiletz suddenly became
very angry, though not quite ebony black. He told his son in a
sufficiently loud voice that he ought to be slapped for such a
silly prank, which could have had some terrible effects; moreover, the father said, he had half a mind to slap him now for it.
With which he ordered his offspring out of the room.

With that, the protruding nail was driven at a single blow up
to its head into the wood; in fact head and all, so that you would
have had to examine the wood very carefully to find the spot
where it had been hammered in. Or, to phrase this more bluntly,
Conrad forgot this first attempt of his to assign more definite
shape to his youthful romanticism. He forgot quickly and readily,
because too painful a memory was now associated with it.

8

HE underwent other relapses from the erect gait during the first
two summer holidays after his entrance into the commercial
school. But rarely were the actualities and compelling necessities
of the boyhood world again illuminated from within. Yet it was
still possible to spend a whole day, barefoot, dirty-handed,
crouching on all fours at the brook in order to dam it up with
boards, stone, moss, and mud. If such an artificial lake was still
there the next day, deep and long and already clear to the bottom, it was like a newly discovered country, conquered territory.

Conrad felt the urgent need for a ship; he ran into the house and actually found one still left from his one-time so carefully guarded fleet. It was even in fairly good condition, standing on one of Aunt Berta's big chests; she had dry-docked the steamer behind canning jars. Now she fetched it out, to Conrad's unbounded joy.

But there was a certain faint poignance in these games, a certain awareness of an idyl to which he had only temporarily returned. For a moment Conrad felt that keenly, as the ship, its clockwork clicking, glided sturdily upstream, delicate furrows streaming away to the right and left of its red keel. Younger boys are tougher; they are immune to such side-glances and side-feelings.

But once even these emotions were blown away by a sudden and great surprise.

At the bottom of the clear water sat a crab.

The creature, so rare as to be almost extinct in the vicinity, must have come from the shallow little brook into the novel deep water. Conrad had often looked for crabs here, having heard from the old gardener that there had once been some. Yet all his groping under the stones and roots of the bank had only resulted in his withdrawing his own hand wet and muddy, but never that strange shelled and clawed form of life. In this respect, the brook had seemed lifeless and vacant.

Right now, the thing he saw at the bottom of the water was visible only because his ship was casting its shadow upon the spot in question, cutting off the reflection of the sky and making the sand and gravel and the thing on it visible. Yet, because of his previous disappointments, Conrad at first thought the shape must be an illusory lump of gravel. And so he was not really excited. But then, lying on his belly, his face just above the surface of the water, cautiously feeling about with a short stick, he made certain. Suddenly there was no doubt about it, for with a movement of its tail the crab made a jump backwards, almost

to the shallow upper end of the pool. The sturdy *Minnesota*—
that was the ship's name—its clockwork long ago run down, had
meanwhile drifted gently with the feeble current and had come
to rest athwart the dam.

Conrad, his heart pounding, rose to his feet swiftly, poised on
the bank, and then with a single step straddled the spot where
the vexed and disturbed crustacean crabbishly crouched. Then
he leaned forward and, placing two fingers at the armor of head
and thorax, lifted the crab out of the water. A vain switch of the
tail, so that drops of water were sent flying, and then a slow
kicking motion with the little legs and a waving of the outstretched, open claws in the air. But these weapons found no
enemy to grasp.

Conrad set him down in the shadow of a bush. It was a rather
large specimen and therefore, as Kokosch well knew, some
twenty-five or thirty years old. For a moment this notion struck
the boy as very strange. The crab remained motionless for a
while; but shortly it raised itself oddly high on its legs and
stalked toward the margin of the pool. Conrad did not molest it.
The crab made much to-do about clambering into the water; it
slid its head and thorax in; for a while he could see it crawling
along the bottom, and then the reflection of the sky removed it
from sight.

Conrad remained motionless, sitting in the grass beside the
bush. Then, in the silence, he suddenly heard the murmuring of
the water; it had its say, delivered itself of its various messages.
For a moment he had almost been carried away by the experience and the triumph, had almost yielded to the impulse to run
to the house, to report his find. But the big cooking pots in the
kitchen rose before his anxious inner eye. And Conrad vowed to
keep silent. The vow made him more composed. He sat in stillness made visible as the white reflection of a cloud deep beneath
the surface of the pond. His glance fell upon the *Minnesota*, waiting so modestly, as if at a pier. And Conrad thanked the ship.

"*Minnesota,* I thank you, you are a good, a sturdy ship," he said under his breath. He remained sitting in the sun without stirring. He was happy.

But no crab time ensued, and the paradoxical anxiety that the experience might turn into "salamanders" did not come to pass. His plans to create more pools above the existing one, closer to the woods, were never carried out. At first these plans had seemed essential, since new basins had to be established for the *Minnesota* (the existing one was no longer usable; navigation in the pool would disturb the tranquil inhabitant—although, on the other hand, there was a certain charm in the idea of the steamer's sailing above a monster of the deep!). And then, such plans were hatched (at night in bed) in the hope that a new basin might lure another mysterious guest out of the brook. Who could say —it might mysteriously be a much-inhabited stream.

However, the plans were postponed, though only till the end of the vacation, he told himself; and then one day the *Minnesota* went into dry dock behind the canning jars.

Return to city and school. The room, with its impressive view over the canal, smelled strangely empty, dusty, and at the same time promising. Within a few days, everything was transformed, the gait once more erect, while in the region above Conrad's diaphragm all sorts of expectations quivered. Even before the end of the holidays, Conrad had met, actually for the first time, the mute, deeply veiled companion of almost all adult life: boredom. He had lounged around a great deal, sat on benches gazing down the old-fashioned, latticed, and curlicued wooden verandas of the villas, along the fences with their faded lilac bushes which separated the gardens from the street and whose leaves either gleamed with an oily sheen or were covered by a thin layer of dust.

That winter he turned a leaf in a new direction whose beginnings are always regarded as exceedingly important and are always described anew—although one may take another view of the matter. In the case of Conrad Castiletz, at any rate—painfully and breath-takingly though this arrow penetrated his diaphragm—only one aspect need detain us here. Finding his way for the first time into the real heart of his part of the city, that drab and even sinister tangle of old and ancient streets, he neglected not a single one of those precautions which the joyless informativeness of his schoolmates had communicated: knowledge to which he had given more precise outlines by reading up on the matter. Those briefings, incidentally, had taken place some time in the past, and at first Conrad had felt the information only as a troubling and oppressive burden, and had forgotten it again as quickly as possible. Now, however, he turned back to it, and to books also: arrangement of business affairs. After everything was clear and the needful obtained, he set out, toward evening, on a mission whose strangest experience remained the entirely new interpretation which he gave to all life in the streets about him as he walked with such designs in mind. Everything outside these designs seemed utterly odd and inexplicable—thus, for example, that a truck loaded with wine casks had stopped at a tavern and was discharging the contents of its mighty vats through hoses into a cellar hatchway.

Conrad stepped over these wine-filled hoses and went his way. Twilight fell; he crossed the large, wide, traffic-thronged avenue, which here led slightly downhill, and turned to the left into the maze of ancient alleys.

From that evening on—it came off well and properly, and was afterwards so evaluated by Conrad—he had acquired a more comprehensive and more detailed conception of that old quarter of the city. Previously, this district had existed for him merely as a known fact. The occasionally glimpsed houses made of older and darker stone had held no meaning; he had thought of them as all standing huddled together around a tiny square. But now there stretched out a world in itself, a complex network of alleys, doorways, half-curtained windows, narrow staircases, old archways, and dimly illuminated rooms. All that could communicate a certain kind of contentment, and certain paths within the network came to be preferred to others—because habitual, in fact. But not through frequency, not at all. It is significant that Conrad was never placed in the position of having to forgo such gratification because of lack of money. Not that his allowance was so large; but he was not the kind of boy who sent every banknote which came his way flying in that direction.

Thus the young man led an orderly existence, and at Easter his last school year began.

As for his tutor Albert Lehnder, Conrad forthwith informed him of his new activities. Whereupon Lehnder asked him about precautions, and when it was clear that Conrad knew what to do and that the matter had been taken care of, he thenceforth passed over the whole matter with a certain disdain and a note of mockery.

9 🦢

FOR Conrad's next and last school holidays Lehnder was invited by Aunt Berta (who had met the young man at the Castiletz home on a visit to town) to spend the summer in the country. Lorenz Castiletz concurrently hired Lehnder to accompany Conrad as his tutor and general supervisor. "So the boy will have someone to talk to and some guidance." As a matter of fact, bridge was an important consideration. Lorenz Castiletz loved the game, as did the aunt, and Conrad already played quite well; only Frau Leontine proved utterly incapable of learning it. Consequently they sought and found a fourth for the summer months in Lehnder.

Aunt Berta, for her part, found the young man an agreeable guest on other scores. Lehnder read many books and could, if required, talk about them in a manner calculated to please a lady of intellectual pretensions. And since she painted, he also took up art, and the two were to be seen seated—presenting remarkably different shapes from behind—on camp stools, their little easels before them, thoughtfully besieging a group of trees, an old hut, a brook lined by bushes, or some other picturesque scene. Lehnder, who kept at this new hobby with a certain dogged obstinacy, displayed some skill despite his unpracticed hand. But the jokes which Lorenz Castiletz cracked when he was alone with his wife referred chiefly to the contrast between the burdens on the two camp stools. Painting itself was sacred in this house and hung, mocking its very nature, in naïve horror on all the walls.

Conrad had ample time to stand, sit, and lie around, looking distinctly handsome the while. His long, slender legs in knee-length socks, his shorts of light-gray duck, which like an antique tunic fell halfway down his thighs, a negligently open shirt and bare arms—this costume, combined with the relaxed, catlike movements of a boy who had always engaged in vigorous physical exercise, gave his appearance a touch of casualness, of having been lightly dashed off, as if a master's pencil had sketched it, say, as Conrad appeared over the crest of a hill, the blue sky behind him. For the rest, his face also had a feline quality; at least there was something catlike in its delicate lines, in the very large eyes, which resembled his mother's, and in its sometimes mildly astonished but always amiable and friendly expression.

Albert Lehnder fell into the habit of saying the following things to his pupil daily.

"You're looking good today."

"You looked marvelous playing handball."

"Don't brush your hair too far back from the forehead."

"You look best in a blue shirt."

He gave him Plato's *Symposium* to read, in a masterly German translation—and as is well known, our mother tongue can do greater justice to the Greek text than any other language. Conrad read through the text out of doors, lying on a grassy slope, never suspecting that he was venturing onto one of the most exposed and windiest peaks in all the history of thought. What affected him pleasantly was essentially the washed and ventilated quality of this whole world and of these men who talked together and drank diluted wine. The simplicity of certain comparisons, like that between the bow and the lyre; the matter-of-factness with which warfare, so much discussed in the past several years, appeared in these conversations as a natural component of men's lives, which in truth were otherwise directed toward other goals —all that appealed to him, wafted around him like the fresh breeze which from time to time played about the hill where he lay. And so he glided, drifting in the blessed smoothness of the reading, over all the difficulties, as the *Minnesota* in former days had glided over the monster lurking in the depths.

Lorenz Castiletz saw this book in his son's hand, and Conrad often left it lying on a sideboard in the hall. But the father in this case lacked the knowledge to consider what the boy was reading. Plato—he was an old Greek or Roman, an inhabitant of schoolbags and therefore in some way useful.

Otherwise, it is quite possible that Lorenz Castiletz would have been precipitated into a paradoxical pondering, guessing, and weighing in the balance—in which case his own stone would have rested in one pan of the scales, the massive figure of Aunt Berta would have burdened the other, and Albert Lehnder would have been in the middle as the tongue of the balance.

Albert Lehnder, incidentally, questioned Conrad rather insistently about his reading but the boy's attitude remained cool and remote. The tutor was on the point of feeling contempt for such meager responsiveness, contempt or outrage—emotions justifiable enough when pertaining to the realm of education. But Conrad innocently rebutted all charges in advance; his concise report of his impressions of what he read proved the direct opposite, and he mentioned many a detail which showed he was by no means unaware of the quality of the text.

Consequently, Lorenz Castiletz could cling to his original theory. The jokes he'd made at the beginning seemed more than ever apt. Any number of small things seemed to bear out his insinuations. His basic attitude toward what he thought was going on was one of condescending approbation, to which he gave a comic cast by his exaggerated discretion in knocking at doors, retreating, keeping out of the way. If after dinner the black coffee was taken out on the lawn, with everyone lying on big blankets—which was one of the customs of the household when the sun happened to be shining brightly—the smaller blanket was always reserved for the lady of the house and Lehnder, the larger occupied by the Castiletz family. Each time Lorenz thought it well to arrange this specially, as though it had become his particular office.

There were also half and whole days when Lehnder tramped about the country with his pupil, or dropped in at the neighboring summer resort. Here the tutor made no effort to conceal from the pupil his interest in "this dame" or that. They found it particularly amusing after supper, if there did not happen to be a bridge game, to go across to the inn for a "nightcap" in the form of a gigantic stoneware mug of beer. Ceremoniously raising their mugs, they would address each other as "Hildebrand" and "Hadubrand" (the Sohrab and Rustum of Old High German poetry). Each time they would laugh so idiotically that the beer would come foaming out of their noses.

Years later, Lehnder asserted that he had been very happy all those weeks.

Once a great buzzing sounded from the inn. The terrace in

back was illuminated, and from the open windows there rang out into the warm summer night the thumping and tootling of a brass band. Waiters and waitresses, their fingers crooked around the handles of beer mugs, scurried across the terrace as a short cut from the bar to the hall. It was eleven o'clock. Conrad and Lehnder quietly slipped out after the bridge game.

The annual summer dance of the local fire department was taking place; the firemen were also providing the tremendous blare of music. Conrad, without bothering to cross through the other room, climbed straight through the window, and Lehnder behind him. The well-known young man was greeted from many sides, and Lehnder likewise. Country people and vacationers were dancing freely with one another. Albert soon floated away with a young woman he had noticed several times, the dance offering a respectable, as it were rustically innocent, opportunity to meet her. The music, too, was innocently rustic—modern dances performed rather broadly, with reinforced bass, but amazingly firm rhythm.

Conrad did not care for dancing. The indolence of his years was the chief obstacle. And to plunge into this crush! In the corner stood a grand piano, which was not in use. He leaned against it. When the music stopped, a blonde and slender young person in a white dress came toward his place and, climbing on an empty chair which stood beside Conrad, lightly and demurely sat upon the piano, evidently returning to her accustomed seat. Her bag lay there beside his elbow.

When she was perched there, she and Conrad smiled. He moved the chair a little nearer, under her feet. Her slender legs in their silk stockings rested beside him now, against the dark, receding curve of the piano.

They began talking to each other, volubly and about all sorts of things. There was a mutual supporting, a mutual bracing of their voices, and a reaching out conducted by the eye. He brought her something to drink. Then the music resumed. Smiling, excusing herself on the grounds of tiredness and thirst, she declined one invitation to dance, then a second and a third. Conrad stood in front of the piano, facing her, chin propped in his hand, looking up at her as he talked. He observed that her large, dark blue eyes were glistening intensely.

She was tired, had long been wanting to go home, she said.

Might he accompany her?

A glance at Lehnder, a signal that they would meet here again, and he helped her into a white coat. They stepped out into the night, already turning rather cool.

"Who is the gentleman?" she asked.

"My friend," he replied.

"Visiting you at the estate?"

"Yes. Do you know where I come from?"

"Yes. People said when you climbed in the window."

They walked along the highway for a stretch. Then they turned off. From gardens and meadows, dense and strong, came the ambrosial fragrance of vegetation, intensified by the nocturnal exhalations of the trees. Part of the rowen hay still lay on the mowings. Conrad saw the moon poised like a sickle above the village, and here, on the fence-lined, unpaved road between the fields, the chirping of the crickets sounded uninterruptedly.

Since he had earlier taken her arm, now on the sheltered road Conrad considered that the moment had come; he slowed down, stooped, and laid his cheek against hers. He also pressed her hand, and she responded. Then they stood still. Turning fully toward her, he drew her close at last and kissed her mouth very slowly, his arm resting, quietly, gently, and easily around her shoulders. Her lips were very hot. Only now did he realize fully how much shorter she was than he. After the first kiss her head remained unmoving where it was; she continued to hold her mouth toward him, like someone being given a drink. Conrad went on kissing her; he kissed her eyes, cheeks, neck, and hair, which lay close and thick upon her head, and breathed the slightly oily fragrance of a hair tonic unfamiliar to him, or something of the sort.

"Aren't you cold?" she asked softly, without changing the position of her face. Her hand lay on his arm, bare in the short-sleeved shirt. Her face was directed straight toward the moon, which mirrored itself in her shining eyes. Conrad only shook his head and kissed her again. He did so without exaggerated tenderness.

"I'd so like to go to sleep now—I'm dead tired," she said, without making the slightest effort to free herself. She spoke with great gentleness and in an apologetic tone, without the least suggestion of resistance, prudishness, or coyness. "Will we see each other tomorrow?" she added softly.

"Yes, of course," Conrad said quickly. "Where?"

"I'm staying with the washerwoman, Frau Rumpler, by the brook," she answered—they were standing in the same position—"do you know the little house?" Conrad nodded. "There is a footpath on the other side of the brook. You know it?"

"Yes, certainly," Conrad said.

"Then would you be on this path near the bridge about four o'clock tomorrow? All right?"

"Tomorrow at four then. I'll come up the path from below, from the sawmill, and head for the bridge near Frau Rumpler's house," Conrad repeated.

"Yes—you'll be sure to come?" she said.

"Sure to," Conrad said eagerly. Only then did they change position and turn, to walk arm in arm down the road to the railing which fenced in the washerwoman's little property. The white cottage lay back from the road under the weak moonlight. At the gate they kissed again.

"What's your name?" he asked, smiling affectionately.

"Ida. And yours?"

"Conrad." He pressed her close. After the garden gate shut behind her, he saw her turn once more on the path to the house, which ran between dwarf fruit trees. Then she disappeared.

He walked back to the highroad, thinking that it had worked out well. Now that he was alone, he was much more conscious of the scents rising from the meadows. On the highroad a couple came along, singing, arm in arm. When Conrad re-entered the dance hall, the music had just stopped momentarily. He saw Albert Lehnder at a table with a largish group, including the young woman with whom he had danced earlier. Albert beckoned. Conrad went over to the table and was introduced. "Well . . .?" Albert said, and once again he had his slightly mocking tone. At the same time he was quite obviously delighted because he could see that the others were taken with Conrad. They all looked at the boy.

"Weren't you cold, with your arms bare?" the young woman said, smiling.

"No, I wasn't at all cold," Conrad replied innocently. At that they all laughed. Someone offered him a glass of wine. Shortly afterwards the party broke up. There was a good deal of tramping back and forth in the streets among the old-fashioned villas with their wooden verandas, and at the end they brought Albert's girl home to her garden gate.

"How do you like her?" Albert asked when they were on their way home.

"All right," Conrad said. "She's really pretty, with that raven-black hair."

"Like a Roman woman!" Lehnder said emphatically. "But what about you—I suppose you've already reached the goal of your desires?"

"No, tomorrow," Conrad answered simply.

"What's that—you've already fixed it up?"

"Yes, in a way."

They reached home and stopped talking. Taking their shoes off, they sprinted across the lawn and climbed into the house through the open kitchen window.

Next day Conrad crossed the dusty village street and at the sawmill started up the footpath bordering the brook.

It was five minutes to four.

He walked upstream. Behind him the noise of the saw sounded like a rapid, gasping, but perfectly regular breathing. The flow of the brook was thin; in many places the stony bed was almost dry, for all the water was diverted to the sawmill and poured into a wide wooden race. The drop was considerable here: these were spurs of the wooded mountains. There was a small weir to divert the brook. From this point on the path was accompanied by water tumbling over rocks and rushing swiftly. There were benches along the path. The rich foliage of the trees hung low over it, and the bushes on the steep slope to the right spread half across it, so that the sunlight that pierced the leafage to dance upon the water was broken up into innumerable curlicues, circles, and bars.

By and by, Conrad saw the small bridge near the washer-woman's house. There was a white gleam in the sunlight between the shrubs on the other side of the brook, and the girl crossed the narrow bridge. She looked toward Conrad and waved. He quickened his stride. She approached with a soft, springy gait, smiling in a rather deprecating manner, as though she felt she should apologize for what she was doing, for this rendezvous—apologize to a society imagined as being present—but with a sense also of being unable to help herself.

She was dressed all in white again, but in something lighter, airier. Now, by day, Conrad saw clearly that she was very pretty. A sudden hotness came over him.

"What were you called as a child—as a small boy?" she asked after she had shaken hands with him and kept his hand.

"Why," he answered, "I don't really remember—yes I do: Kokosch." And so he swallowed the already spoken lie.

"Kokosch!" she exclaimed. "May I call you Kokosch too?"

"Yes," he said, looking into her eyes. And then his glance glided down over her shoulders.

"When it turns cooler in the afternoon, so many ugly people

come walking here," she said. "I always see them from the window."

"Then let's turn off to the right, into that little side valley, for our walk," Conrad proposed.

Arm in arm, they left the path after some hundred paces and walked down a slight incline between two wooded slopes that widened out. They followed a small rivulet that was a tributary of the larger brook.

Deep in the woods, when he drew her close, she hid her face against his shoulder.

He lifted her like a real man, in both arms, and laid her gently down on the moss.

"Why, Herr Castiletz . . ." she said twice. Later he would often remember that. Her head, with its thick blonde hair, lay to one side.

He scratched himself slightly on the pin while opening the brooch that held her dress at the neck.

Otherwise all went well. She hid her face against his shoulder again.

"I'm twenty-four years old," she said softly.

"And I am eighteen," Conrad answered without embarrassment, since these figures meant nothing at all concrete to him. She stayed as she was, saying little. He noticed that her eyes gleamed moistly. From the village road the horn of an automobile sounded.

On the way home, later, it occurred to him that his seventeenth birthday had been at the beginning of the summer vacation, which seemed to have gone on for a very long time. But he thought that he had not consciously lied, not in the manner of that first lie, which he had so quickly taken back. For a moment he grew thoughtful in the face of the difference in their ages. Then he envisioned Ida as she had crossed the bridge and approached him.

It was very warm. At one point, to the left of the road, the

sinking sun created a wide lane filled with a golden glow in the
sparse woods. When Conrad reached home, Lehnder winked at
him, then shrugged his shoulders and said: "Well, well."

All went well. Almost every day now, Conrad walked upstream
from the sawmill along the path, beside a brook at first silent and
then, farther up, rushing over its stony bed.

Almost daily, then; but he was not so very smitten with Ida.
Perhaps one reason was that deep-seated and inexpugnable disdain in the blood of the middle class for everything that can be
had for nothing, that need not be paid for. Whenever he thought
of the return to the city and school, of autumn and winter, there
arose in him as a particular form of pleasure the image of that
ancient quarter of the city which, stepping over the wine hoses
and passing beyond them, he had come to know for the first time
this year. Ah yes, it had its place and had kept it.

But this factor changed on a particular day which imprinted
itself deeply on Conrad's mind, so that the scene of the experience, too, was carried into the heartwood of memory. The scene
was modest indeed, bare, smelling of boards heated by the sun,
and of wet clothes: the inside of a dressing cabin at the local
beach. Outside the water plashed, boys shouted, and from on high
the sun fell through the louvered transom.

The entire Castiletz family had gone there to swim, together
with Albert Lehnder and Aunt Berta. Conrad had already removed his scanty clothing when he heard his aunt's voice at the
right, in front of the door of the adjoining cabin. As this door
was opened, the sunlight entered and shot a swift arrow or flash
of light through a small knothole in the board wall, about eighteen
inches from the floor. Conrad knelt down and looked through it—
why, it would have been hard to say; he became aware of what
he was doing after he had assumed this cramped position.
Through the knothole he could see the entire adjoining cabin.
Conrad observed his aunt slide the bolt and then draw her light
summer dress over her head. Sitting on the bench, she removed

her shoes and stockings, then stood up—and, inexorably, it went on. At last she stepped into her bathing suit and drew it up. Conrad fell away from the knothole like a ripe plum falling from the tree. His whole body was trembling in wild oscillations. But he succeeded in sitting down on the bench, without making any noise.

As if there were a fire and he must rush to the rescue, he sped, clattered, tore in thought down the whole isolated, variegated pattern of alleys, gates, half-draped windows, archways, and dimly lit rooms in that old quarter of the city which only a short while ago, in foretaste, had filled the post-vacation time with a particular kind of contentment. But now it had all been rendered lifeless at a single stroke. He felt curiously confined and deprived of his freedom, cast from a lofty eminence where he could survey a whole landscape into a narrow, rapidly moving channel which carried him away from his fastidious sensual innocence. But not at all in the direction of the fat woman whom he had just seen, but in the direction of Ida. In those moments, strangely enough, the young bourgeois learned to respect the things that life customarily gives gratis; and while he fought the senseless notion that he was drifting with the water in the wide sawmill race—drifting upstream, no less, toward the little bridge near Frau Rumpler's laundry—he implored all the spirits of past pleasures to accept, or rather to evoke in him, at least a fraction of that mysterious intensity that Aunt Berta had unsuspectingly stirred in his trembling limbs. Stirred, and a moment afterwards generously transmitted to Fräulein Ida Prangl.

Conrad sat, cramped and askew, on the little bench in the dressing cabin, with a body that would have given any instructor in an Athenian school of wrestling—the philosopher Plato, say— the hope that he could ultimately guide this youth to victory in the Olympic Games.

The next time Conrad climbed up to the wooded dale beside modest Ida, he felt himself being swept into that remarkable millrace; and the waters now poured toward a blonde head which smelled a little of a hair oil or pomade that Conrad rather disliked. Yet, when this smell came to him, say, in bed at night, it aroused memories of the girl with particular force. Now, however, as he lay beside her on the moss, the faint perfume was almost disturbing.

But there were other smells, of pine needles and of the soil of the forest, smells so pungent that it seemed as if there must be mushrooms nearby. The long trunks of the trees rose like the newels of old winding staircases among their radiating branches. Conrad was aware, more than he was able to see, the dark, narrow tops high up against the blue of the sky.

The couple rose and walked through the woods to the ridge which formed the watershed. Here the conifers gave way to scattered deciduous trees; down along the slope the trees stood among grassy meadows. There were pretty paths, little brooks, and benches. The dip into which they descended afforded no view of the plain with its hint of the great city far back; instead it curved up in hills again. They discovered a farmhouse and drank milk in a small pavilion. Conrad felt transported into another valley which he had seldom entered. It was as good as new, rather in the way that the drawing room at home had struck him as new when he was just beginning to leave childhood behind. The sun shone on the table, on the girl's shoulders and white dress, and in the stillness the murmur of the brook could be heard; it had its say, delivered itself of its various messages. Conrad now noticed that the smell of paint, of which he had all along been rather pleasantly aware, came from the freshly painted scrollwork that ornamented the posts and the façade of the pavilion. Between two of these posts the outline of the hills stood like a framed picture, the wooded slopes here and there streaked with the colors of autumn.

10 &

BACK in the city, he continued his relationship with Ida Prangl, and thus the affair was placed firmly against its proper background. She was a seamstress or milliner, and that vacation in the country air had been painfully sewed and saved as essential to her health. She lived in a sprawling factory district of the city and they formed the habit of meeting in this neighborhood, which was new to Conrad.

There existed in the city a kind of educational club for commercial students where movies were shown and lectures given on practical or intellectual subjects. In the evening, of course. And the club had the advantage of being located in a quarter of the city very distant from Conrad's home.

As soon as school began, Conrad found it advantageous to join this institution. His parents raised no objection. And so, on such evenings, he boarded the streetcar and rode on a line he otherwise scarcely ever used to the suburb where he met his new girl friend.

The brightly lit car howled up and down its scales through busy streets, rolled resonantly through the underpasses near a railroad station, and at last whizzed along the wide and noisy main artery of Ida Prangl's neighborhood for a long stretch without stopping. Here there were innumerable shrieking lights making every imaginable announcement of every imaginable need, dominating the whole width of buildings with gigantic red and blue ribbons. The avenue cut a glittering gorge of desirable and desired vivacity into an otherwise quiet and somber quarter whose houses squatted evenly in their dirty gray. The fences and great gates of the factories, interspersed among the rows of houses, were also of this color. The name of the plant would stand over the entrance in smoke-blackened wrought-iron letters.

Conrad rode to the last stop on this big avenue, got out, and waited on the same side of the street.

Evening discharged all sorts of persons into the avenue. Children carrying beer mugs passed the white, glaringly illuminated windows of a laundry. Young workmen, strolling arm in arm, their hairy chests all but forcing open their shirts, needed almost the whole width of the sidewalk for themselves. From the tavern came the sound of a phonograph and a tempting smell of food, while a big, heavy automobile glided almost noiselessly and indifferently past. There was a burst of laughter from some girls.

Now she came, emerging from the turmoil and the flashing lights: Ida, with her springy walk, her blonde hair, hatless, slender in the coat she wore in spite of the mildness of the evening—the autumn generously exhaling its last resources of warmth. Once again her heart-shaped face held a slightly apologetic smile as she greeted the boy Kokosch by placing her small, very warm hand in his.

Around the next corner the couple left the main avenue. In the quieter streets they put their arms around each other and walked slowly down to a park which lay spread out between the factories and the last stop of the streetcar.

Darkness had long since settled over the streets. Here and there the dim, yellowish glow of modest lights from modest houses fell upon the sidewalk, from ground-floor windows and arched doorways in which stood elderly women who eyed the pair as they passed. When Conrad had first walked here with Ida, no recollection of one-time romantic inclinations had risen in him, no sense of adventure at all. This was a world of a different sort which now enclosed him on all sides. This was a world which contained within itself a wholly strange kind of pattern. He had felt that at once on his first slow walk with Ida "through her streets here." Now and then, in moments of singular alertness, he pricked his ears, as it were, to listen to something beyond the immediate neighborhood, as though he were seeking to learn something about an outer ring surrounding the life here. Yet that life held no particular affairs or relationships which he could have singled out. At such moments he would turn to her face, "heart face," as he called it, and it seemed to him mild and dear.

In the park, with one accord, and exchanging jokes, they would seek out an unoccupied bench as far as possible from the gas lanterns—which was not always easy. Here they would kiss; that was how they initiated such sessions in the open air, under the bushes, which were already beginning to lose their leaves: here and there between the branches the lights of houses could be seen. Her hair no longer had that unpleasant perfume; she did not use it now because he had once made a remark about it. In fact, she seemed to have washed her hair very carefully, for it was free of any oily scent. Now her hair exhaled its blonde color only as a dry fragrance. Strangely enough, at night, before Conrad fell asleep, the former perfume of her hair always returned to him, together with images of their first times together.

They talked, too. That is, he did, and she looked at him and seemed to be very happy during this talk, which was of the kind Conrad would have heard at the "Educational Club for Commercial Students" if he had actually gone there.

Toward ten o'clock Conrad would board the streetcar at the stop by the car sheds. He stood on the platform of the last car, and she stood below and said she would go to the post office on Monday to get his letter, she was looking forward to it, and she would answer right away, using the code word, as always— yes? Perhaps they could manage another outing next Sunday, all right? He leaned forward and squeezed her hand once more as the streetcar started.

During the ride home from that remote part of the city, Conrad was always at peace, inwardly satisfied, as if he had taken care of a matter whose value was beyond a doubt, something which unquestionably had to be attended to, which under no circumstances might be neglected.

"So you are going on with it?" Albert Lehnder said when Conrad told him a little about it. "Hm. Out in the suburbs. A bit bothersome. I must say, that would not be to my taste."

The Sunday after that remark was made, Conrad did not meet Ida "out there in her streets," but at the edge of town, almost where the country began. Which meant, at this season of the year, plunging into colors of autumn deeply embedded in sunlight and carved out of the blue of the sky. Wide swaths of gold marched through the woods. Conrad would leave home directly after Sunday dinner; during the meal he would surreptitiously glance at the clock. Not so much because his heart ticked with the seconds in eagerness for the rendezvous. Rather, he was concerned that nothing be disarranged, that he should arrive on time, be first out there, so that he could wait for modest Ida in the way that had already become habitual.

And she came, walking softly, springily, with a slight hesitation and with her smile; both enveloped her in a kind of aureole, in a faint ring like that around the moon on misty nights. They walked together toward the woods and then uphill and over rises along whose sides were scattered a few old and a few modern villas, spots of brown and white among the green of trees. Once it rained, and they sat in a café near the streetcar line, in a white-painted room with round tables.

Conrad stopped talking and ran his mind over his affairs. He thought it well to use the opportunity of this rain-spoiled outing to make sure that everything was in order: school (tomorrow); fencing (day after tomorrow). Yes, all was well, as far as he could see. Suddenly Ida, who was sitting beside him, entered his mind; he had scarcely been aware of her up to this point. Good, he thought; he could enter her in the list. But was she also in order? And for a moment he listened alertly, probed his surroundings, as though some menace might be approaching.

"What are you thinking about, Kokosch?" she said softly and somewhat shyly, placing her small hot hand on his.

He looked squarely into her face.

"Whether—whether you are a white raven," he replied. His eyes betrayed a certain anxiety now; they figuratively gnawed at her features.

"What's that?" she said. Her "heart face" was wholly unfolded.

"Or—a salamander after all," he added.

"A salamander?" She laughed. But beneath the laugh flowed an undercurrent of comprehension; its dark bottom showed through her eyes and dulled their gleam. In reply she only pressed his hand hard, while a brief pain, a plaintive twitch, flitted across the corners of her mouth.

"No, you don't understand what I mean," Conrad said. He too smiled painfully, in his own way.

Their outings generally ended at nightfall in a small weekend inn at the edge of town which a schoolmate had recommended to Conrad. That was one reason why they chose this particular vicinity for their Sundays, quite aside from the hilly charms of the landscape here on the very outskirts of the city. The inn stood by itself, close to a large suburban railroad station. It had a pleasant restaurant and bar through whose back door you could unobstrusively reach the stairs that led to the rooms. These were quite comfortable, although furnished in a curiously old-fashioned style. There was electric light, of course; nevertheless, every room had gigantic candleholders of turned wood, and jolly, hugely curved, and curlicued easy chairs. The washbowls, on the other hand, were as small as if made for dolls. The inn smelled somewhat of sun-parched wood and wallpaper. It felt rather like being on the inside of old book bindings.

Conrad and Ida walked along the wall of a park. Here and there in the glow of street lamps the stones of the wall gleamed a soft green, for they were coated with moss. They entered the inn by the side entrance this time, without bothering about the little restaurant. They mounted the stairs, followed by the chambermaid. The steps and the corridors were covered by a hemp runner the same color as the one in the Castiletz hall.

Ida switched out the light. They stood close to the window, through which fell the weak, distant, nebulous glow of the arc lamps above the tracks of the railroad station, like artificial moonlight even colder than the light of the moon itself. He slid down the shoulder straps of her slip. For a second her eyes gleamed up at him in the darkness; then she hid her face against his bare shoulder, whose classical shape was bathed by the pallid light.

Under his generally selfish but prudent caresses she remained still, and from time to time kissed him. Once he found her face hot and wet. He asked why she was crying. "Because I love you," she replied. He said nothing, and for a while lay quiet in the darkness. Then he went on as before.

Lehnder's criticisms multiplied, and increased in vigor. He seemed to fear that this affair was becoming rooted in Conrad, and he seemed to disapprove of that. "Such things have to be temporary. Or else sooner or later you'll be placed in an impossible position and made responsible for a baby which of course won't be yours. I know the way it is. She's perfectly well aware of who you are; you told me the first evening that she knew. Naturally. In that little village."

He also said: "Getting involved in this sort of mess so early is the worst thing anyone can do. It sticks to a person and remains a permanent disability."

And on another occasion, later: "That sort of thing must be temporary. Write her a couple of pleasant lines. Say your parents have found out the whole story—that you carelessly left a letter lying around and now aren't allowed out any more."

Conrad awoke in bed one night. The window stood high, clear, and sharply rectangular, for the curtains had been removed for washing during the day. A few of the roofs in the hilly section of the city across the canal gleamed in the moonlight. He lay wide awake, as though he had slept soundly all night. Lying on his back, it was as if he were floating in the center of that outward, indefinable circle of life which lay like the moon's ring around the inner circle, but which no longer contained any single, specifiable things. Things were in order, insofar as any firm ground of resassurance in regard to them could ever be attained. But now, as vividly as if someone were suddenly striking him in the side, came a cry from outside: Ida.

From the vicinity of the race track a long, wailing whistle of a locomotive sounded and faded away.

Conrad's heart gave a little jump. That must be put in order. Yes. He whispered it to himself in the darkness.

The next Sunday was approaching. There was a difficulty. He no longer had money, at least not enough. (Strangely, it did not enter Conrad's mind to arrange to spend their time together in any but the accustomed way—in which case he could have cut the cost considerably.) There had already been four outings this month. To appeal to his father before the first of the month, when he received his allowance, would be altogether unusual. And it would be difficult to borrow from his mother—for this particular purpose. Conrad put it off from day to day. He put it off from minute to minute. At one point he even thought of borrowing from Sophie, the maid.

But that possibility, too, was postponed and neglected. He became curiously stiff in his joints when it came to carrying out any plan for obtaining money—although other sources were open to him. There hovered over him, or dwelt within him, an inexorable leaden weight; it was as if he were constantly dragging it along behind him wherever he went or wherever he ought to have gone. There were persons from whom he could easily have borrowed, were it not for this perplexing, embarrassing weight he had to drag around. But by Sunday he had done nothing. Sunday dinner was a torment.

He did not take the streetcar. He walked across the bridge in the face of a cloud of dust whipped up by the wind. And he rang Lehnder's doorbell. With that, it was done, although it was still theoretically possible for him to reach the meeting site on time. But he would have had to ask Lehnder for a loan. In itself this would have been the easiest course from the beginning, except that its purpose would have been transparent—and especially today, on a Sunday. He recognized that it was impossible and out of the question at the very moment that Albert's approaching footsteps informed him that his ring had not been in vain, that his tutor and friend was at home.

So was Lehnder's mother. As Conrad bowed before the pleasant and intelligent old lady—she was a Prussian from Silesia, her mind clear and her courage unbroken in spite of all the changes in her circumstances—as he bowed, the last possibility of keeping his rendezvous dropped away. With dull pain coupled with relief, he found himself sheltered by inevitability, guarded by a wall of overwhelming circumstances from any further doubts or considerations. He felt that he wanted to stay with Lehnder, at all costs not be alone now. Lehnder was content, and so after a while they walked across the bridge (the windiness was over and the bridge bathed in warm autumnal sunlight) into the water meadows and strolled about there. To Conrad a strangely thin light seemed cast over everything, over the Sunday promenaders, the music that poured from various booths. Everything had a kind of borrowed reality.

The following morning Conrad dropped the letter into the mailbox—which for a few moments he vividly pictured as a great white vacant space. The spirits of order did not speak up. They did not give the expected sign of lively assent, and his self-confidence did not rise like a balloon when sandbags have been jettisoned. Conrad lingered a little in the sunlight in front of the mailbox, feeling the movement of the street around him more distinctly than his own quietude. Then he walked back to his house.

"What did you write her?" Lehnder asked that evening.

"What you suggested," Conrad said.

11 ॐ

~~~~~~~~~~~~~~~~~~~~~~~~~

"WHY, you already know how to handle it splendidly," Frau Anny Hedeleg said, leaning over the arm of Conrad's chair. He sat in front of a newly acquired calculating machine—the "champion of calculators," as the advertisements said—practicing on it. Since the beginning of the winter there had been nothing more for him to do or to learn in school, and so his father had taken him into his office as an assistant for the evening hours, so that he might gain some practical experience. And it turned out that he knew a good many things that perplexed even Frau Hedeleg, old hand though she was. Doctor Albert Lehnder (Doctor of Laws by now), with his special approach and his dynamic methods, had scored one of his triumphs. Though of course this student had been a special case. Old Castiletz had invited Lehnder to his study (with the sabers and foils on the walls) and expressed his high appreciation, in token of which he handed the tutor the sum of 200 marks, quite apart from his regular fees. Albert was a decent fellow, as he proved by candidly informing Conrad of this windfall and presenting him with 20 marks as his share in the spoils.

Frau Hedeleg continued to lean over the chair, comparing her own totals of the invoices, which Conrad had added up on the machine simply for practice, with the results obtained on the machine. All five totals agreed.

"Then you already know how to work the thing and what to watch out for," she said.

"Yes," Conrad replied.

The tip of her firm right breast pressed so distinctly against his shoulder that it was as if someone were jabbing him with an elbow to call his attention to something. Since there was no longer any good pretext for her to be leaning forward, the fact of it rapidly outgrew the previous sound business reasons and swelled into an empty space, filling the vacuum with an entirely different content.

Something swished through Conrad's head which might be expressed in the words: "This is something I've got to experience," and which, moreover, instinctively taught him—and he followed the promptings of this instinct in a wholly relaxed way—not to move, to leave his hands resting on his knees and so, instead of a withdrawal, to provoke a closer approach.

That took place. Her cheek came closer and closer to his; still without contact, he could feel the warmth of her skin like a delicate down upon his face. Only then did Conrad close the gap of a fraction of an inch by a very slight movement of his head, hardly a movement at all, but enough to bring cheek against cheek.

They were alone in the office. The clock read fifteen minutes after seven.

Her hands must have slid from the arm of the chair to his shoulders, but Conrad did not notice when. He only felt the result.

The two remained motionless for a little while. Then they turned their heads slowly, just a little, until the corners of their mouths touched, and kissed in a curious way, from the side, with only part of their lips. It was Frau Hedeleg who first used the tip of her tongue.

Conrad's hands still rested on his knees.

At last he raised his right arm, composedly, without any tension. He placed his hand lightly against her head, kissed her squarely on the mouth, turned to her and put his left arm around her shoulders. She leaned down still more, and he drew her to him.

"But Herr Conrad!" she murmured, giggling. "I must not seduce you."

"Why not?" he said quietly.

"Why, listen to that!" she replied, and kissed him on the mouth. "Would you believe it!"

They fell silent.

"When will I be seduced?" Conrad said.

"Suppose I say—tomorrow," she answered, looking into his eyes.

"Then I shall be very happy," he replied at once.

"I must go, it's so late," she said.

Standing, they kissed a good many more times.

"Seduction tomorrow?" he said.

"Seduction tomorrow," she replied, in his arms, whispering close to his ear.

"Please leave by yourself now," she said then, somewhat more loudly. "I'll stay here, turn off the lights, and lock up."

"And what about tomorrow?" he asked.

"Do you know the Café Belstler? Yes? Will you wait for me there after the office closes?"

"Yes," he said. He pressed her hand, kissed it, and left.

Next day they did not sit long at the Café Belstler. But they sat hand in hand, and at brief intervals the hands pressed one another hard. A pair of lovers. At seven o'clock she went on ahead, to her home. Her husband had to start work at the power plant at eight, as he did every night. And at eight fifteen, with exemplary punctuality, Conrad entered the apartment. In all other respects he had adhered to Frau Hedeleg's instructions. He had hurried past a particular door, where, she told him, the worst gossip in the apartment building lived; he had made sure in advance that this door was closed and had assured himself that no one was peering out at him from the stairs. And if he had met anyone on the third floor, which was Frau Hedeleg's floor, he would have deliberately continued on to the fourth and fifth floors, as though he were looking for someone who lived up there —anything but the prearranged refuge of Frau Anny Hedeleg. However, all went well.

When Conrad entered the street, he saw, looking down a side lane, that he was not far from the point at which he had once stepped over the wine hoses. Oddly enough, this circumstance gave him a distinct feeling of composure and security. He passed through the wide, arched entrance of a rambling apartment building with several courtyards and a number of different staircases and found the third on the left. As he climbed at a moderately rapid pace and almost without a sound—feeling as though he were climbing into something, a railroad train, say, which would then ride away on the readied tracks—as he climbed the stairs, he was overcome by the kind of goose flesh that you get when the water in the bathtub is too hot. It was utterly still in the stairwell. From somewhere came the weak noise of a pail filling under a faucet, a sound at first sharp and drumming, then soft and plashingly, purringly content. As he passed the second floor, the noise disappeared.

Here was the door marked Number 18. And as if yielding and opening before the pressure of his gaze alone, the door turned inward slightly, a crack appeared, a bright face smiled out of the darkness. He could hear the bolt softly and ringingly slip shut behind him while from in front an extraordinary softness and warmth enveloped him. Trumpets and drums of excitement sounded, and his own body immediately responded. He felt thin fabric slithering over her skin. Now they stepped out of the dark hall into a lighted room, and he saw that she was wearing a kind of kimono or dressing gown.

The god who presided here shook him powerfully, as though the heavenly archer's rosy little fist had seized Conrad Castiletz by the back of the neck and was stripping the clothes from his body almost as quickly as Apollo robbed Patroclus of his armor in the battle by a single buffet of his palm between the shoulder blades. Conrad reeled, glimpsed something like a red couch, lost his balance, and fell upon it. Perhaps he "looked good," as Albert Lehnder used to put it. At any rate, Frau Hedeleg, her eyes a frozen spark, was with him; there were arms, shoulders, a great deal of white skin and very little taut chemise, from which, under Conrad's unruly grasp, breasts sprang forth like an explosion.

All went well. The new drawer fitted into the bureau of Conrad Castiletz's life. It closed smoothly and opened when it was needed. But never undesired. Frau Anny had appointments and relatives (a flock of aunts?), and Conrad too could not absent himself from home too frequently in the evenings. But she was most amenable to waiting placidly until he wished to come again and would tell her so (after work). The Café Belstler dropped out of the picture; he came directly: eight fifteen.

Lehnder had no objections. He was acquainted with Frau Hedeleg; she had been a trusty employee of old Castiletz for ten years. "All very well," he said. "Though at bottom absolutely uninteresting."

At bottom Conrad thought differently, though he did not dispute Lehnder's opinion. Ever since the affair with Ida, Kokosch was always privately prepared for a wet blanket from Albert. Albert himself—likewise privately—had put Frau Anny behind him a good while before.

12 🦢

ONE evening she said:

"Can you guess, Conrad, whom I'm going to meet tomorrow."

"How should I know?" he said, continuing to fondle her bare arm.

His indifference was too genuine not to be upsetting, in fact insulting. However lacking in jealousy a lover may be, tact calls for him to simulate a little. Hence the second barrel that Anny was withholding was fired somewhat sooner than she had intended, speeded by vexation.

"Your papa," she said.

"Terrific!" he replied, and kissed her in the armpit.

She felt a strange chill, like a cold draft from an open cellar door. She drew her arm against her side, thus shutting off her armpit. Conrad sat up. A change had passed over his face after all, but it was not what Frau Hedeleg had wanted to evoke. He felt that at once. No, this change had another source entirely.

For some minutes he sat looking off into space, as into some deep hollow, utterly absent. Then he spoke with great animation:

"You know, that's great—look, you have to describe it to me exactly—will that be amusing." Then he laughed; his face composed itself rapidly. The draft from the cellar door made Frau Anny Hedeleg's flesh creep. She wrapped herself in her moral scruples, which pleased and warmed her.

"Oh," she said, "I would never have done it, never have arranged to meet him, but he simply would not let me alone. He insists on going for a walk with me or meeting me in a coffeehouse. After all, there's no harm in that. Still, it is embarrassing to me. When I think of your mother! She would have a fine opinion of me. And yet nothing is going to happen that in any way ..."

"Why not?" Conrad said.

"Now look here—" she exclaimed.

"Meet in the Belstler," he suggested. "That will really top it off."

Next day Conrad bought a blue quarto notebook. This time the difficulties about where to store a record such as he intended to keep were solved with surprising ease, the moment he entered his room at home. For behind the wardrobe protruded a flat yellow suitcase. The locks were handsome and strong and could each be opened only with its proper key. It was an expensive piece of luggage. Lorenz Castiletz had bought it for his son at the time of that first trip.

Conrad listened. It was quiet; there seemed to be no one at home. He opened the lid; close, virginally sterile, clean air wafted out of the suitcase, reminding him for a brief moment of the family drawing room, where the furniture was always under linen slip covers.

A picture post card lay in the suitcase.

It was the one that Ligharts had sent him long ago. He thought he had not seen it for years, and could not recall when he had placed it here. The white Pierrot, or Harlequin, was still smiling under his high pointed cap, and slightly resembled Günther.

Conrad looked out the window at the gray houses across the canal. Then he deposited the new notebook in the suitcase along with the post card, closed both locks, and put the keys into a side compartment of his wallet which could be closed by a snap, and which he had never before made use of. . . .

Frau Hedeleg chattered away. Conrad listened with strained attention, summarized a number of points in his mind, and when she paused repeated them to himself, running rapidly over certain phrases so they would stick in his memory. At first his behavior did not strike her as peculiar. Since the whole story seemed to tickle her vanity enormously, she was too self-absorbed to notice him.

"Actually the whole thing was so awfully funny. And now I'm so happy that I can be with you again," she concluded.

"Café Belstler, yesterday's date, 6:30. She: I thought all I was for you was a good secretary—he: on the contrary, I've been in love with you for years—she: Herr Castiletz, you make me terribly happy when you say that, but after all I'm married—he: so much the better, so am I—she: I would never have expected anything of this kind from you—he: do I look so old?—she: no, certainly not—he: will you believe I never dye my hair and my teeth are better than many a young man's (shows her). Then tells the anecdote about the uncle in Thuringia with the two servants who had to sing when they went down to the cellar . . ."

"What are you mumbling?" Anny asked in astonishment.

He had not been conscious of mumbling.

"You know, I heard a perfectly marvelous tango recently," he said casually, "but my trouble is I can never remember the tune without the words. I seem to have forgotten a whole line of the words."

"Could it be this one?" she said, whistling the melody.

"Right!" Conrad exclaimed gratefully.

At home that night, Conrad mentally reviewed the whole account, dashed down cue phrases, and then set it down in writing. He worked at fever heat, though he took care that his handwriting should be neat and precise. At intervals he would say under his breath: "Hm—salamanders?" By two o'clock it was all done, the notebook locked away in the suitcase, and he was dead tired.

Barely a week afterward another rendezvous took place between Frau Hedeleg and her boss. Again Conrad was informed in advance. "He simply insisted on it," Anny had complained. Conrad remained home on the evening in question, and dined alone with his mother. "My husband will not be home until half past nine, Sophie; have his supper ready for him then," Frau Leontine said to the girl.

The dining room lamp brooded above the table and its crockery. The white tablecloth reflected its light as a block-like plane upon the ceiling. "Well, Kokosch, you'll be all done with school at Easter," his mother said merrily. "You're already a young man."

"There's still the Reutling Textile School," Conrad replied.

"Oh yes, of course . . ." she answered, cheerful and distracted. The sail jibbed, the vessel swerved toward an unknown horizon. Her eyes, slanting and amiable, looked past the food; she forgot to eat and nibbled at a radish.

At this moment, Conrad's knowledge by no means inhabited the middle of his head, and those "romantic" elements which he had expected from such a piquant situation did not materialize. He had expected his knowledge to be a continually exploding shell (if there were such a thing, to the joy of war-makers) around which everything else would radiate: mother, the dinner table, the lamp, the dark corners. Instead, that knowledge remained thin, had slipped off somewhere to one side and did not even fill out the wrappings of secrecy under which it lay. In fact the casual, harmonious conversation with his mother sufficed to make it disappear altogether. Moreover, the conversation itself took shape, instead of remaining what it was supposed to be, merely a painted wall mysteriously blocking off the view of the real landscape of life. Ah yes, that was what it was supposed to be, and that was what this whole evening should have been. But it was turning out differently. Conrad felt that the affair had been a total failure.

"You aren't eating at all, Mama," he said, interrupting his thoughts.

"I am so!" she replied, and with serious gaiety she held up her radish.

"But that won't do at all," Conrad said, laughing.

"I'd only forgotten," she admitted candidly, helped herself to the food, and ate quite substantially.

Lorenz Castiletz came home somewhat before half past nine. Conrad, as he heard his father's heavy but elastic footstep in the hall, had the distinct feeling that something uncanny was happening. For the first time he knew, though only for these few moments, that his father was—alive. As a rule, sons are aware of this only in the form of a pallid, featureless, self-evident fact.

But as he entered the room his father changed into the form appropriate to himself, that is, into an authority, although a beloved one. Conrad subjected him to a sharp scrutiny, feeling honor-bound to make a few observations. But their sum total was quite thin. The old boy's curly hair, shot through with a good deal of silver, seemed to be pasted slightly to his temples, and in general it could be said that he looked overtired. But he peeped jovially under the nickel covers which Sophie, the maid, now lifted from the bowls, and began eating and chatting and laughing with Conrad's mother. Perhaps it was due to the excessively completed impression that every grown or even older person makes upon the young—who, though they themselves may already be involved in elaborate hypocrisies, tend to assume that all appearances are genuine. At any rate, in the given situation Conrad could no longer conjure up with anything resembling vividness, a picture of what he knew had taken place. The knowledge, which had earlier slipped from the center of consciousness to some obscure corner, seemed well on the way to drop out entirely.

Once in bed, with the light off, he was struck by the thought— as though by an arrow shot from the ceiling—that Anny might have invented the whole story. He pictured her face, and saw in it that possibility. It was a dark face, dark in spite of her light complexion; there was the same darkness in its corners as in the dirty gray of the big factory gates which he used to pass with Ida. Her face was clearly before him; he could see it plainly.

But if Hedeleg (for so he called her in his thoughts) had lied, how could she know that his father would be late for supper on this particular evening?

But of course she could easily know that; she had been working for his father for ten years, would know, for example, when some important Dutch or English agent was in town and would be expecting his father to call at the hotel. Hedeleg had often had to be present at such conferences, as stenographer. She might well know all about it in advance.

Conrad tried to reason the matter out more closely, and fell asleep.

13 &

ABOUT ten days after these "events," toward evening, within a few hours and with utter reticence, Frau Lorenz Castiletz died. The sail finally vanished below the horizon and did not reappear. A few white, rippled clouds dissolved in the void at the edge of the sky.

The cause of this sudden decease was said to be a thrombosis.

In every kinship group there are deep thinkers, and one such remarked that in her *bleu mourant* way Leontine Castiletz had simply forgotten to go on living, and had therefore died, out of absent-mindedness.

For the husband and the son this misfortune, which had come crashing suddenly and unforeseen into their lives, lingered in the mouth like the taste of a sour fruit. The sourness mingled with the secret belief that they might still avert disaster if only they refused with sufficient forcefulness to accept it. Such is the clarity and brashness with which men at times see through the relativity of all so-called facts. Facts, you might say, are the common folk among the phenomena of life—though a tough-fisted lot.

In the Castiletz apartment the event lingered for two weeks like an invisible fireman's net, spread everywhere, causing everything to rebound, making it impossible to stay in any one place, to keep at any one activity.

Father and son visited the grave with flowers—our mute gesture-language toward the dead, which we hope will be understood.

The sky on that first day of spring displayed those hazy and disconnected cloud formations which correspond to the vacillations of the earth at that season, the hovering between death and life. In contrast to the sky, the walls of the funeral chapel located amidst the fields of graves now gleamed white in the sunlight, now lapsed into a gentle gray.

Conrad had not wept since a certain night in his boyhood. Even the loss of his mother did not produce in him that alternating feeble and strong, warm and ultimately hot ring around the eyes which tears can rinse and cool. He experienced the essential quality of the event like something hidden behind many walls, as a pressure which seemed to be forcing him in a certain direction. For the first time, he sensed, something had really happened in his life, stood upon his road like a firmly set post, dividing the way into a before and an after. All that had been before, he felt, could in some way have been undone. But this was final. This finality was new, and it irritated like a foreign body.

He noticed that his father, who stood at the foot of the grave, was unconsciously biting the brim of his hat, with a face that was small and wet like that of a crying infant.

A few weeks later, on the red couch, Frau Hedeleg wrapped herself in a warming fur of self-laceration, for the draft from Conrad's direction was alarmingly chill. Her last report, weeks back, had been more than usually detailed, so that Conrad had scarcely been able to keep up with all the material. He had finally had to interrupt Anny when the points began to pile up beyond his ability to register them in his memory. But the numerous details, some of them distinctly raw, had, in sum, dispelled Conrad's suspicions and steeped the whole story in truthfulness.

"I can no longer look your father in the eye," she said.

Conrad had observed that for the past quarter hour Anny had been gearing herself for a sob. When she at last succeeded in producing it, he said: "You don't have to look him in the eye."

"What's that?" Frau Anny asked, floundering in a vacuum.

"Keep looking at your account books."

Ah well, this affair with Hedeleg was no longer good for much. Moreover, the time for his final examination at the commercial school was fast approaching; and although Conrad was fairly well prepared, he did need a while to collect himself. He made a point of having ample time for that purpose, so that he could make sure that nothing had been left unordered or neglected which might turn up to plague him in the course of the oral examination or the written work. But nothing turned up, his affairs were well arranged; in short, he passed the examination brilliantly. Lehnder had expected nothing less. "What a pity your poor mother could not live to see this!" Lorenz Castiletz said. He embraced Conrad and wept. His face seemed to have shrunk of late, to have finally and really become smaller. Frau Hedeleg had vanished from Conrad's view, since he had not gone to the office for some weeks before the examination. Now, at the Easter holidays, a graduate, he left behind him forever that modern building with the large, bright entrance hall in which compact, low radiators stood, gleaming a pale silver.

Conrad went out to the country, and was alone there. Aunt Berta now lived in town and was taking excellent care of his father, who had broken down at the mere thought of the country, replete as it was with the peaceful and happy memories of the past summer. As a young man who had recently lost his mother, Conrad received the natural sympathy of the maids, gardeners, and farm hands. These people had in their own way been very fond of Frau Leontine, their feelings for her having been evi-

denced by the manner in which they had greeted her each time
the family came for the summer, by the way the news of her
arrival had been bruited about, and by the great bunches of
flowers that had adorned her room throughout her stay.

The woods were still gray, but not lifeless; their dampness was
full of presage. Every space between tree and tree could be intensely felt as an opening in whose vibrant silence the waters
rushed. A vase of pussywillows stood in Conrad's room. Sunlight
filled the empty house.

The common people let the new dead rest, do not start them
up by repeated mention. Whenever the folk about the house
spoke of the summer past, they paid silent tribute to Frau Leontine. Once the old gardener smiled and remarked that, by the
way, that girl from the city, the one the young gentleman had
seen so much of last fall—he remembered her, didn't he—had died
a few weeks before. In Salzburg. He'd heard about it from Frau
Rumpler, in whose house the girl had lived; they were distant
relatives.

"Everyone dies," Conrad thought. Literally that. And then he
felt shocked, for he had included his mother in the phrase. Died
in Salzburg. He knew something about the location and character
of that city, from school, and knew it was mountainous there. But
now, deep within himself, he saw Salzburg on a perfectly level
plain, a towering castle of a white, dry color set in an endless,
salty steppe.

"Must have been sick in the chest," the gardener commented.

It did not occur to Conrad to go to see Frau Rumpler, the
washerwoman, to find out more about it. But on a walk he found
himself nearing the small bridge over the rushing brook, and he
turned into the little dale and walked through the deserted, cool
coniferous woods along the slightly uphill path. The silence of
the dark, arching branches remained unaffected by the now loud
gurgling and plashing of the little tributary. The tiny waterfalls
and basins had their say, as if thrust back upon themselves by the
pressure of the surrounding stillness.

Conrad reached the summit. Here the conifers receded. He looked down the incline over the denuded pastures which stretched among the hardwood trees. Trees and bushes were bare, like tousled hair, scarcely differing in color from the gray boards of a bench set in front of them, and yet tense with an inner glow that the dead wood lacked. Down there, in the light that trickled deep into the ground, lay the narrow road and the scattered farms. Conrad raised his eyes and looked at the opposite hillside. Along the curve of the hill were etched the first sharp bright greens of spring.

EVERY MAN
A MURDERER

Part Two

PART TWO

∿∿∿∿∿∿∿∿∿∿∿∿∿∿∿∿

❧ 14 ❧

FATHER CASTILETZ lived long enough to set his little son—
who in reality had become a grown man and taller than his father
—upon a well-prepared track. Conrad had enrolled for the two-
year course at the training school for the textile industry in Reutlingen, Swabia, and emerged an accredited "textiles engineer." A
well-prepared track: just as once Father had set the tiny cars of
the toy train upon their tracks, and off they rolled. In the case of
some people there is simply no deciding whether they are weak
or competent in confronting life. Proceeding on a strictly scientific
basis, we find ourselves unable to make a judgment. These people
never go crashing into anything and never knock off any of their
corners. We know what we know about them, but the facts take
on no coloration of strength or weakness. These are the pupils
who travel along and never give their parents anything to worry
about. The teachers have grown accustomed to them without
really knowing whether or not they are good for anything. These
are also the recruits who are least bellowed at. They are the
people whom one does not sound out. Conrad Castiletz was a
perfect example of this kind of person. As a boy he was miles
apart from the boys who are always being discussed by their near
and dear with heavy sighs, who go flying out of one secondary

school into another, only to flunk out again, and who later change their occupations and their goals much more often than a Kirghiz changes his shirt. This kind of young man will, for example, regard the study of medicine as a fine tonic note from which to run the gamut of all possibilities. The temple of his learning includes so many separate apartments, rooms, and chambers, and has such a multitude of important gates opening into such a variety of fields, that in practice the young man is permitted to revolve in an extraordinary manner around himself. But suddenly it is he who is standing still, and in the revolution of the years, as on a rotating disc, the same examination dates flit by again and again, while the subject matter to be mastered grows out of all bounds. Each one of us is vulnerable to various mischances occurring on the plane on which we move; and any medium-sized disaster, a little less money or the death of an uncle who has been paying the bills, suffices to drive our disciple forever out of the temple of Asclepius. Nothing so dreadful about that. People of that type have at bottom a very firm and secure relationship to existence, and they can look into life through extremely various windows, yet see it always exactly the same and quite attractive. The switch is thrown, the former track is abandoned, a new one flashes far ahead in the brilliant light, up to the dark mouth of the tunnel, which obviously will provide a smooth passage. A student has become an engine driver on the "underground," as they say in London, the "subway," as they say in New York—while in Vienna it is known as the "Stadtbahn." Now the train leaves the rumbling tube whose walls as it thunders past seem to consist of smoke, though smoke there is none. The hurtling vehicle leans into the curve; at any angle the swaying luminous scene of the city appears with the receding lines of streets like a gridiron, crossing and recrossing, and with innumerable harsh and dim, sick and twinkling earthly stars. So the city looked once, seen from the hills, where our student sat with a group of his fellows, singing student songs, and—it remains the same.

But no, such corners were not for Castiletz. Conrad proceeded steadily along the prescribed track. It would never even have entered his head to shift from the track his father had built so long ago, on his trips and in his prudent relations with old business friends. He had seen to it that Conrad traveled also, and well equipped. A flock of aunts, too, could always prove useful. The son left the school at Reutling after two years—his time there had been strangely empty—and at once was able to enter a large plant, as a volunteer for the time being, in a smallish city in the South of Germany. Another young man would not have found it so easy to reach the mouth of this particular channel, whose further course seemed to old Castiletz to offer a good many pleasant prospects, not only in an occupational sense. But Herr Lorenz, who had aged greatly and whose hair was completely gray, did not speak of that.

Conrad arrived in the town in the midst of a pouring rain— which is said to bring luck. He left the railroad station, whose low, sprawling brick building reminded him slightly of the railroad terminal in Munich. He walked across a paved square bright with bouncing raindrops, and, as he did so, had the feeling that the town proper must stretch out to a considerable distance on his left. Later it turned out that that was so. The small hotel was on the right, across the square; the railroad station diagonally opposite.

Not until he was inside the bright lobby did he recollect—as if making up for something which had utterly slipped his mind while he was leaving the railroad and going to the hotel—that this was not the first time he had been in this city. His relatives. Ah yes, and he also had a letter to deliver. It was in the suitcase, with other letters. The most important of all was the one addressed to Councilor Veik—although the "Councilor" was a purely honorary title, of course. Tomorrow he would have to call at the factory at the proper time.

Conrad supped alone in the dining room; there was not another soul there. Outside, the square was dark; the rain was coming down harder, with a soft rustling. The waiter who served Conrad, bespectacled, had a rather sourish haughtiness. Since under the circumstances it was not very enjoyable to linger at the table, Conrad ordered a cup of coffee sent to his room, and went up.

He opened the suitcase and laid the letter out, where it would be ready for the morning.

Then he stood still in the middle of the room, looked around briefly, and remained in that position for some time, staring down and to one side. Precisely, as one runs up a scale in practicing the piano, he thumped mentally through all his affairs. Yes, to be sure, everything was in order.

There was a knock. Conrad started. For a moment, while thinking over his letters, visits, errands, baggage, money (which was ample!), he had been completely lost to the world.

He drank his coffee standing by the table. Then he went to the window. It was wet; he could see nothing outside. He opened it. The rainy night, with its watery, dripping, splashing, and drumming noises, rushed up to the edge of the brightly lighted room. The building stood at an angle to the street. He could see two or three dim windows. Below was a courtyard with piles of boxes and a tin roof; light from the hotel windows, perhaps from the kitchen, showed other litter toward the back of the yard. Conrad looked across at the windows. As he did so, there came to him—despite the totally different atmosphere—the distinct memory of his Aunt Berta in the dressing cabin next to his. Then Reutlingen. He wondered. Throughout his stay there his life had felt like a flat stone being skillfully skimmed over the water by a boy—everything on the surface. Yet Conrad had gone through three love affairs in Reutlingen, had happily graduated from them, one might say, in the sense that nothing disorderly or inconclusive had been left behind. Several times he had taken one of these girls up to the famous Achalm, which loomed above the city, crowned with the ruins of its medieval castle. The girl had meant nothing to him, nothing at all; he had been as indifferent to her as to the tables in the garden of a restaurant where he had often sat—which, as a matter of fact, was the last memory that came to him of his time in Reutlingen. He closed the window. The thin white curtain whispered. Suddenly warmth flowed through him. The room was very bright. He prepared his suit for the morning, hanging it carefully on a hanger. Then he washed his face, brushed his teeth. Lying between the crisp sheets, listening to the silence, he suddenly felt the life that would now be coming to him, felt that he loved this city, which he scarcely knew, because in it he could live alone for the first time, here, with his suitcases, with, with—with collar and tie, so to speak. At that moment Conrad became a romantic person. He put out the light and for a moment pressed his cheek into the pillow. "Yes, that's it, of course—life," he whispered. And slept.

15 ଌ

THE conference room of the Carl Theodor Veik Textile Plant was reached by a somewhat narrow and steep staircase. Around a small mahogany table were grouped four lean leather-covered armchairs. In the middle of the table stood one of those devices which contain everything necessary for smoking, but which have never really met the personal requirements of any smoker. Such devices are usually given as presents; if the recipient is head of a firm, they find themselves sooner or later placed in the conference room. If he is a dentist, they end up in the waiting room. Such things are symbols of humanity in an environment which otherwise represents the maximum in impersonality. The same might be said of the potted plant which stood on a small stand in one corner of the conference room.

After the attendant had ushered Conrad Castiletz into the room and shut the door, the young man continued on a few steps, following the law of inertia, and stopped in front of the single window. From here he could look, past a protruding part of the administration building, down upon the roofs of the shed, which extended jaggedly for some distance, like a line of slanting, extremely proper handwriting. Beyond were the slopes of hills, with trees still partially green.

The prospect surprisingly resembled the one from the stairwell of the Reutlinger Textile School, about from the fourth floor, where glass cases held many old and new models of various looms and spinning machines. Here, too, the view to the right was blocked by the building; the same type of roofs was spread out below, and beyond, though considerably higher, had risen the Achalm, with its vineyards and woods.

In back of Conrad a pleasant-spoken girl opened the door and requested him to follow her.

A long row of small, bright-yellow desks, and on each of them a typewriter: the office opened before him like a straight street when one has just come around the corner and is looking down it. But the noise was by no means overwhelming. Most of the typewriters were covered; dictation was being taken at only two or three desks. Conrad crossed the office behind the girl, and was conducted to the quarters of the president. A quantity of green leafy plants lined the window, in front of which the landscape of two facing desks presented itself.

"Well now, Herr Castiletz, I've been expecting you daily," old Veik said pointlessly, but laughing affably. "Ah yes, looks just like his father, but blond instead of gray, hahaha. . . . Arrived yesterday?" The manner in which he scrutinized the young man could not be embarrassing to Conrad because the Councilor seemed much taken by the young man's appearance. "Well, well, congratulations, Lorenz!" he called out loudly, addressing the absent father, "such a giant of a boy!" A shadow flew over his face, and his large, floating blue eyes suddenly became still. The eyes well suited the thin, straggly blond beard. His whole face looked diluted, thin, like a clear soup.

Now they were in conversation.

"You probably know," old Veik said, puffing at his cigar— Conrad, a non-smoker, had politely declined the proferred cigarette—"you probably know that we have two outfits here. The textile plant, the firm of Carl Theodor Veik, where we are now, and on the other side of the city, the webbing mill, Johann Veik and Sons. Two very different industries, as you will admit, which by now have virtually nothing to do with each other. Nothing at all, in fact. Here we are concerned with keeping up quality, with mixtures and patterns, with the movements of fashion; there with quantity, mass production, productivity. And also, of course, with the prices of jute, hemp, and flax. You have been in Reutlingen. Hm, well, the technical school in Kottbus would have given you a better background for wool, but it doesn't matter; with your good Reutling background you'll quickly get the hang of the work here. But now tell me this: are you interested in the manufacture of webbing? Sincerely?"

"Yes," Conrad said quietly, obediently, for his father had particularly impressed this point upon him, "in fact I think I rather prefer that branch."

"Well now, listen to that!" old Veik said with animation. "Of course you'll start here, with me—your father wants it that way, and after all there is more for you to see and learn here. Yes, certainly. I suppose you'll ask me how the two happened to come together, a webbing mill and a textile plant. Actually, it's only that I own both. Originally they were two separate firms founded by two widely separated branches of our family. But various circumstances, in the end the death of my elder brother and the fact that my younger brother Robert chose a different career, permitted them to be brought together. Now I have Director Eisenmann, splendid old fellow, in charge over there—well, you'll meet him soon enough. . . . Here, why don't you take this with you."

He reached behind him to a bookshelf and handed Conrad a thin volume in album format.

"This is the history of our firm, and also of my family for the past half century," he said. "We brought the thing out last year, to commemorate our fiftieth anniversary. Take a look at it at home; you'll find a good many things that may interest you. Incidentally, I said 'at home,' but I suppose you're stopping at the hotel. Where do you intend to live? With your relatives in town?"

"My father wants me to take a small apartment of my own."

"Excellent. I know something that will suit you."

He reached for the telephone and dialed a number. Smothered by the earphone, a voice replied, whereupon Veik asked: "Treasury, District Office?" and then: Extension 83, please," and finally: "May I speak to Herr von Hohenlocher?"

Now the voice from the telephone sounded full and more human, and old Veik suddenly began to laugh; evidently the person on the other end of the wire had said something amusing.

"Well, then, my dear Herr von Hohenlocher, the young man I mentioned recently, our engineer-in-training, has arrived. But he's not to be staying with his aunt; he's looking for a little apartment . . ."

More words on the other end; old Veik laughed again. "What's that?" he cried into the telephone. "How did that go? 'Whoever enters the family dies in it'? Marvelous! Be careful it doesn't happen to you, Herr von Hohenlocher. Ah yes. Well, I'd like Herr Conrad Castiletz to see that place of yours . . ." At this point, Herr von Hohenlocher of Extension 83 in the District Office of the Treasury appeared to speak somewhat more lengthily.

Old Veik replied: "Fine. I'll send him at four. Many thanks . . ." He hung up, but promptly dialed another number.

Obviously it was a lady whose choked voice emerged from the earphone.

"Manon!" Herr Veik said energetically. "You yourself—how nice—how are you, darling? Yes? Look, I'll be bringing a guest for luncheon today. Young Castiletz. He arrived yesterday. . . . Yes, a giant of a boy. So long, see you soon, darling."

He turned to Conrad again. "I'm sorry I couldn't ask you to come until half past eleven. We've operated some newly installed machines—Jacquard machines—for the first time today, and I wanted to be on the spot. That put me behind on the mail, and I had an appointment with Director Eisenmann at half past ten. I hope you spent the morning pleasantly, seeing our town . . .?"

He mentioned a number of sights. And Conrad had in fact looked at them. Some, incidentally, he had seen that time years ago—way back in the remoteness of time, on that first exciting foray into a virtually adult life.

"As for the plant here," old Veik said gaily, "just plunge right in. Plunge in and lend a hand wherever you please—for the beginning, I leave that up to you. Get on a loom and weave if that strikes your fancy, or relieve a man at the pattern looms, or try your hand at knotting, or sit down here in the office at a typewriter or a billing machine. I'll want you here in any case for the foreign correspondence—that will bring us together a lot. Here, you see, this desk is orphaned. Six months ago my dear friend Secretary Schröder sat here—now heaven has him."

For a few moments he looked thoughtfully down at the closed roll-top of the second desk, and was silent. But then his gaiety returned.

"Your father told me you're excellent with English and French and even know some Dutch. . . . That so? Splendid; keep your knowledge polished; it's invaluable in this work. I'll certainly have to call upon you for languages. We start tomorrow morning, then, at seven."

He impulsively extended his hand to Conrad, who shook it.

"Here in our plant you have the whole production process right before your eyes, from the spools to the finished fabric, except for the dyeing. We have that done outside as piecework. . . ."

Conrad was glad to hear that. He had never liked the large, low-ceilinged hall in Reutlingen which you reached when you turned to the right on emerging from the school building, and walked past the boiler room. The warm and sweetish, yet dull and somewhat muted odor that spread over all the machines and apparatus in the dyeing plant, the absence of that vigorous beat of shuttles flying back and forth, or of the humming of spindles —the relative silence soaked in insipid odors—he was glad to be spared that here.

"Well, now, it's already twelve," old Veik said, glancing at the clock. Almost at the same instant the siren rang. The noise in the adjacent buildings—the tall spinning mill, the long, shallow weaving shed—ceased abruptly and it was then that this molten, indistinct mass of noise made its presence felt, when it was gone. It was strangely like a process deep within one's body, a displacement in the body's quiet, unknown functions. Even next door, in the office, noiselessness had ensued, and when shortly afterwards Conrad and the old gentleman passed through the room, they found it empty.

16 ಶ್

DELIGHTED and ill at ease, Conrad sat opposite his hostess at the table and afterwards, while his experiences of the morning continued to reverberate within him in curious freshness and colorfulness, like a tapestry full of living figures unreeling behind

the lovely head of Frau Manon Veik. There was the walk across
the mill yard to the left of Councilor Veik, the now silent plant,
a window through which he caught a glimpse of many small
discs, parts of machines. Then the ride in the heavy, swiftly moving car, the unexpected view, as it turned a corner, of the busy
main street of the town down which Conrad had strolled slowly
that morning. . . . All that vibrated within him and at the same
time moved in a series of scenes past that erect head with the
high coiffure of thick, snow-white curls which perched above a
rosy face like a rococo wig. A face in which the dark eyes were
slightly slanted. Her gaze veered off in a vague sidewise direction, with slight hauteur, in an ultimate, reticent disregard of
things, and even of the conversation in which she nevertheless
took part with extraordinary affability and keenness. Someone had
once shown Conrad portraits of women by the Parisian painter
Marie Laurencin. Here sat a living Laurencin, a charming young
woman disguised as an old lady. Leaning forward slightly into
the world, indefinite and inscrutable, painted in pastel. Henceforth, to himself Conrad called Frau Manon Veik, Madame Laurencin.

It did not escape Conrad that the one among his flock of aunts
who lived in this town was mentioned in the conversation in a
manner which was not only intended to display good will toward
the nephew but to indicate clearly that the lady in question belonged to the top circle of the city, socially speaking. Conrad for
his part talked with great warmth and intimacy about his Aunt
Erika—Frau von Spresse was her name—and mentioned his boyhood visit with her and how he had at that time seen something
of the city, which today, however, struck him as completely different.

"Once again a proof that life's center of gravity is subjective,"
the Councilor said laughingly, and somewhat circumstantially
laid down his napkin. "I have an acquaintance who spent four
years in Outer Siberia—he was a Russian prisoner of war. The

trip there—in the cattle cars of a transport train—lasted for several weeks, during which he understandably enough observed the country and the people and the whole stretch of the railroad with great interest. Four years later, he told me, when he was being repatriated, he seemed to be passing through a different country and using a totally different railroad line which he had never ridden on before. That is how the world changes with our condition. In youth, I suppose a few years are enough to change it completely. Later on things grow more monotonous."

In the foreground of his consciousness Conrad superficially followed old Veik's talk; he ran his mind along the surface of it, the way a hand runs along a banister. Meanwhile, he was thinking distinctly, in the following words:

This afternoon, look at the apartment. Then check the alarm clock, get work clothes out of the small suitcase and have them ready. Find out shortest streetcar route to the factory, riding time and walking time. Leave fifteen minutes earlier than necessary, to be on the safe side. Tonight, look at the album. Tomorrow, see Aunt Erika—she's obviously important.

"Another example of things being up to oneself," Frau Manon said. "I have long been convinced of that."

"We might also say," old Veik commented, "that the more a person is, the greater the number of things which are up to him."

"Yet, as a matter of principle, wouldn't that have to apply to everyone, if we assume it for anyone?" Conrad asked modestly, but speaking clearly and slowly.

"Right and logical!" the old Councilor replied. Again he laughed. Apparently he often laughed without reason. This laughter was an expression of his personality, as in other men a particular gesture might be; that is, it was a trait rather than a sign of any special merriment. The Veiks came from the Rhineland, and the old man's manner was in many respects characteristic of that region—as were his deep kindliness and the amount of wine which was served at table.

"And now I must give you a little information about that fine fellow Herr von Hohenlocher, and your apartment," Veik said, turning to Conrad. "This Herr von Hohenlocher, Herr Castiletz, is Government Councilor in our District Office of the Treasury, and a delightful person—incidentally, from a very old and prominent family. He lives in a building which has only small apartments, three on each floor, and he has rented a whole floor for himself, although he's a bachelor. But, then, Herr von Hohenlocher likes a secluded life and can afford the luxury of having no neighbors. At the moment, however, he is subletting two rooms with bath. You would be undisturbed there, you'd have your own entrance; it so happens that that suite of rooms is separated from the rest of his apartment. It isn't at all expensive. Moreover, the streetcar connection to the mill, in fact to both our mills, is extremely convenient, no transfers necessary."

"How long it is from there to the textile mill?" Conrad asked.

"I can't say exactly, but I should think at most twenty minutes. From here, of course, it will take you almost half an hour to reach Herr von Hohenlocher's, but this is an entirely different district and we've come by car. I'd gladly have my chauffeur run you over there, except that I need the car now because I must return to the mill. Here is Herr von Hohenlocher's address—he's expecting you at four o'clock, and my wife will explain the route to you—won't you, Manon? You'll find your way easily enough."

"No trouble at all," Conrad said. "I simply take Line 3 from here and . . ." And he proceeded to describe the route exactly.

"*Donnerwetter!*" the Councilor said, laughing. "I call that fast orientation."

"I studied the map of the city during my journey, and this morning I supplemented my theoretical knowledge with some practical experiments," Castiletz said without so much as a smile. This approach somewhat stunned the old gentleman, but apparently in a favorable sense.

Shortly afterwards the car could be heard softly purring down the driveway, and the gate clanged shut. Conrad was sitting opposite Madame Laurencin in the adjoining room, at a small Turkish table on which tiny demi-tasses steamed. Abruptly and without any visible reason he felt weirdly affected by the situation in which he found himself. The feeling was distinct, though utterly irrational. He shifted a little on the heavy tapestry upholstery of the couch. It was his inward uneasiness manifesting itself in a small, hapless external movement.

"And how do you like it here among us?" she said.

"I am happy," he answered abruptly, lifting his gaze from the design of the small tray, with its inlay of mother-of-pearl. Now, looking at Frau Manon Veik, he observed her features much more distinctly than he had before, when he had only noted that her eyes were far apart and slanting. Now her features seemed to him more vigorous than he had realized, more impressive in a way, yet still those of an old woman. There was a Persian hanging on the wall directly behind her whose center was a bright blue; with the result that for several minutes he visualized Madame Laurencin against a new background—not that of the factory or of busy streets, but against a pale sky in which a few wind-driven clouds scurried. The blue aureole hovered for a moment in the big room, with its heavy, dark-upholstered furniture, its many rugs, and the wide, arched opening into the dining room where they had eaten. Framed in one of the windows at the rear of the room was the sunny top of a tree, in vivid autumnal yellows.

"And what, aside from your youth, makes you especially happy?" Frau Veik asked.

"Why, that isn't easy to explain," he answered. "It's just—just life," he said exuberantly.

"I hope it fulfills all your expectations, Herr Castiletz—and I mean all of them," she said smilingly. She raised a liqueur glass. "Let us say, then: long live life."

Conrad bowed slightly and drank to the old lady. It must not

go unmentioned that at this moment he was close to telling her
the anecdote about Uncle Christian and his magic box—a sign
of a Castiletz in a particularly genial mood. But he did not get
that far. The conversation took another turn, in the course of
which his mood of open-heartedness toward this motherly listener prompted him to tell her something strange: that if he ever
married, it would have to be a woman older than himself.

"Well, Herr Castiletz, when the time comes, that should not
be a difficult requirement," she said, laughing. "As a rule, men
look for younger women, you know."

He had expressed his attitude on this question with masculine
dogmatism, and perhaps for that very reason Madame Laurencin
did not take his odd dictum seriously. But the beautiful old
woman was mistaken about that. For Conrad, even as he spoke,
had been thinking of Reutlingen and the three girls from whom
he had graduated (on the Achalm), with vivid dissatisfaction
(afterwards). The three had all been younger than he. Madame
Laurencin, meanwhile, had come to rest on another subject which
seemed to be more interesting to her. Namely, the social life of
the town.

"There are some really delightful houses here—you'll get to
know them, of course. But first of all there is your aunt, Frau von
Spresse. I regard it as an extraordinary sign of spirit and personality for an elderly, childless woman who is alone in the
world and has some means to maintain a fine house—and a really
charming one besides—and receive guests often. She has practically succeeded in establishing a 'salon,' as people used to call
it—to the extent that anything of the sort can exist in an
industrial city like ours. And her hospitality is really sheer al-
truism. She makes everything as pleasant as possible; her house
exists entirely for the guests, and serves as a meeting ground
for the most diverse persons. To me, it seems an abominable custom to do a great deal of entertaining only for the sake of the
daughters and to stop as soon as they are married off. Yet that

is the custom in Vienna, or at any rate used to be, as bald as you please."

"You lived there for a while?" Conrad asked casually; all this scarcely interested him.

"Yes, as a girl, for about two years. Have you never been there?"

"No," Conrad replied. Unexpectedly, a dark, listless shadow passed over his features, and he added: "I have not even been in Salzburg."

His obvious change and the troubled look could not escape her. She asked: "Does that city have any particular significance for you?"

"No," Conrad said slowly, "not at all. It's quite all right. But—isn't Salzburg, I don't want to call it very gloomy, solitary, I mean, or let's say—austere?"

He knew at once that what he had just said was nonsense, and yet it seemed to him less foolish than his telling the story of Uncle Christian would have been.

"Why, what makes you think so!" she exclaimed, no longer concealing her astonishment. "On the contrary. Salzburg is one of the gayest and most beautiful spots in Europe. Haven't you ever seen it on a picture post card?"

"Yes, of course, it's only that I have this prejudice . . ." And in a kind of bold desperation he took the lead and drew their talk back to its former track, only to get it off this toboggan slide on which he had come close to making a fool of himself.

She yielded to his efforts and continued her description of local society and its present doings, not failing to mention that she and her husband—"unfortunately we are childless"—could not imagine life without conducting cheerful open house. And at the end she added: "By the way, we're about to have a very promising addition to our social life. My brother-in-law Robert, my husband's younger brother, has been appointed chief magistrate of the District Court and will be moving here with his family.

The Veiks are all Rhinelanders to the core, and Robert Veik especially—their household is often like a beehive. He had two daughters—though now there is only one of them left—a very dear
girl."

"Didn't your husband also have an older brother who died?"
Conrad asked.

"Yes, Max Veik. He died four years ago. For more than twenty
years he ran the webbing mill, where old Eisenmann is now in
charge. You will meet Eisenmann, of course, and it is certainly
worth the trouble to get to know him."

17 ཙ

~~~~~~~~~~~~~~~~~~~~~~~~~~~~~

TEN minutes before four o'clock Conrad got off at the right stop
on Tramline Number 3, checked his position once more on the
map of the city, and walked slowly up slightly sloping Hans
Hayde Strasse to Number 5.

He walked past the house, since it was still too early (eight
minutes to four) and unobtrusively studied the brown-tinted
four-story building, which stood rather far back from the street,
with a sizable garden in front, divided by a wide driveway and
arched entrance, through which a courtyard could be seen.
Farther up the street, the bright autumnal foliage of a public
park gave a sense of spaciousness and openness. The leaves were
now glowing brightly, for the sun had broken through a blue
portal in the clouded sky. He looked at the map again, was about
to cross the street toward a golden birch tree at the edge of the
park—and suddenly jumped back. From the narrow side street

along the park a gigantic, bright yellow truck, a tank truck as he realized in a moment, was rolling almost noiselessly but very fast toward him. The driver blew his horn. Conrad folded the map to compose himself after his momentary fright. He walked into the park, which was clean and completely deserted. He could look down paths lined with white trash baskets, to fine, spreading lawns whose edges were everywhere spotted yellow and white from fallen birch leaves. In the distance the jagged gables of some fine private houses could be seen. He noticed that Line 3 went around a bend here, close to the park, and that there were stops in both directions at this point. He could have got out sooner and gone the few steps downhill instead of up. He made up his mind to wait for the street car here in the morning, instead of below. By the time he had considered this, it was time to turn back (two minutes to four).

Inside Hans Hayde Strasse Number 5, whose exterior was a warm brown tint, everything was painted white, at least as far as the first story, where Herr von Hohenlocher lived. Three white doors opened on the hall, where absolute silence seemed to prevail. But then Castiletz heard a noise from inside, like the crack of a whip, but muted by the doors. The door at the left end of the hall had an empty metal frame for the name card; the middle door, where the hall took a turn, seemed to be sealed off—it had no knob. Here, on the right-hand door, a smooth brass plate read: Hohenlocher. Conrad rang. Inside the whip cracked again.

The door opened wide. Conrad confronted a creature whose extremely large bright eyes were the first thing that entered his consciousness. They had a kindly, inviting look and were set in a small face with a sharply pointed nose. It was a face whose age and color seemed at first glance as indeterminate as those of a faithful, much-used tobacco pouch.

Conrad was about to explain his purpose, but this seemed unnecessary. The servant—so the tiny woman seemed to be—helped him out of his coat and indicated a door just as tall and white as the one he had entered from the hall. He knocked. From inside, a man's voice called out, loudly and genially: "Come in!" As Conrad opened the door, another shot cracked; inside the room the report sounded very loud.

Everything in the big room seemed slender and tall—wardrobe, windows, curtains. A man in a silk lounging robe, belted with a sash, rose from a wide divan. At his chest hung a large Zeiss artillery glass. He now shifted the long-barreled practice pistol which he had held in his right hand to his left. This was Herr von Hohenlocher, and Castiletz at once thought of a large pointer. The man's step was that of a dog, short and loose, and his beardless face was creased in short loose folds.

"Hohenlocher," the pointer said in response to Conrad's polite introduction of himself. "Please sit down, Herr Castiletz. And excuse the bang-bang business. But I had to get one more shot in; I was lying just in the right position."

"You shoot lying down?" Conrad asked, quickly and courteously adjusting to the situation.

"Yes, I'm that lazy. Look at the target over there."

At the other end of the long room a large, strong target of light-colored wood hung over the fireplace. In its center was the paper bull's-eye.

"And what is the glass for?" Conrad asked.

"So I can see my hits clearly while lying on the divan. After each twenty shots I change the target sheet."

"Marvelous!" Conrad exclaimed. "First you shoot and then you look through the glass."

"Of course. I can see the target as though it were in front of my nose, and need hardly change my position. . . . But you want to see the apartment, Herr Castiletz. Frau Schubert will take you right over. If you care to take it, make the arrangements with her."

He pressed a button.

Frau Schubert led the way across the hall (while a shot

cracked behind them) and unlocked the door with the empty name-plate frame.

The small apartment had the restrained freshness and coolness of long-unused rooms that have been kept immaculately clean. The two rooms—across the hall, Herr von Hohenlocher had made a single large room of two such rooms—were furnished in the modern style, the pieces clean and smooth. In the dim light of late afternoon, glass and metal shone quietly in the stillness. A window of the bedroom at the rear of the apartment opened on a semicircular courtyard. Conrad was struck by the fact that the rear of the building was not of the same color as the façade that gave on the street. It was painted white instead. He was also surprised that the view looked gently downhill over many roofs, toward the heart of the town. The sky with its shifting clouds momentarily showed small and distant things bright in rays of sunlight, only to have them fade again in mist. Reflecting the changes in the sky, the white stucco of the rear of the building now shone with a vivid white, now melted into a subdued gray.

Conrad knew that he would stay here. He looked down at the cobblestones which paved the yard, and discussed the details of his tenancy with the little old lady. Among them, that she would have to wake him at fifteen minutes to six in the morning ("I'll set the alarm for half past five, and she'll come also, to make certain," he thought). Then he produced his wallet. And recollecting paternal instructions, Conrad gave Frau Schubert five marks beyond the wage they had agreed on for her services, as a kind of initiation fee. If a mouse could smile, it would seem that Frau Schubert did so on this occasion.

"It will be best," Herr von Hohenlocher said when Conrad returned across the hall, "if you send Frau Schubert to the hotel right off. Have her pay your bill there and fetch your baggage."

He was carrying bottles and siphons, and placed them on a small table beside the divan, whose pillows lay scattered in disorder.

"What will you have?" he asked. And when Conrad, who scarcely ever drank, faltered, he remarked: "Take gin—the most sensible drink anyhow." He filled a small, bluish glass for Castiletz.

"Well then," Herr von Hohenlocher said, "that's the most important thing: having a home."

18 ह&

~~~~~~~~~~~~~~~~~~~~~~~~~~~

FRAU Schubert was dispatched, and Herr von Hohenlocher reached from the divan to the telephone to connect Conrad with the hotel.

"Councilor Veik," Conrad said, after making his call, "said something to you about me a while back, if I am not mistaken, Herr von Hohenlocher."

"Yes, but nothing of importance, nothing that could interest you," Hohenlocher replied with negligent candor. And at that moment a prudent, unself-centered, solid middle-class instinct in Castiletz for the first time took note of the man's superiority, which existed quite independently of the great difference in their ages. "He only mentioned that he would be having a new volunteer for his sweatshop, the son of a business friend. What time do you have to start at the mill in the morning, by the way?"

"Seven o'clock."

"Shortly after midnight, in other words. I'm curious whether you'll make it to general manager."

"Hardly," Conrad said, laughing. "I'd be happy if my training would eventually qualify me for a decent job anywhere."

"Hm—I see the situation rather differently," von Hohenlocher said after a silence. He tossed away his cigarette. "In the first place, not anywhere, but here. Secondly, you're not out merely to qualify, you've got to succeed with trumpets and drums. For the rest, you aren't going into industry in order to retire after twenty-five or thirty years of doing your duty as an Oberregierungsrat. That sort of thing is best left to people like me. In your case, something altogether different is at stake."

He looked at Conrad through half-closed eyelids He had couched his remarks in a casual tone, as though he were speaking of remote, inconsequential matters. And yet there was a precision and definiteness about his words, a kind of unsparing definiteness underlying it all.

"And what would that be?" Conrad asked modestly. In times past (for a reason that may be remembered) he had fairly often cut meetings of the Cultural Club for Commercial Students; he was still keenly eager to learn.

"Power," Herr von Hohenlocher said, yawning slightly. "I don't care about it and it could never tempt me. I merely state the fact."

"I am simply obeying my father's wishes," Conrad replied, on the retreat, "and I am sure that's best."

"Undoubtedly," Herr von Hohenlocher said.

He was a difficult person to disagree with. He presented his own opinion frankly and without embarrassment, but always in a casual manner; and, if need be, he withdrew it, just as one might close a proffered cigarette case after someone has stated that he is a non-smoker. In general, Hohenlocher did not seem to feel a need to have his say. When he talked, it was like a form of doodling; he could stop talking at any moment, because he did not care (because of indolence). When he listened to someone, he would very rarely interrupt him. Now he fell silent, reached for the switch, and turned on a small lamp with a colored shade fastened to the wall above the bed. It was beginning to grow dark.

"The Veik family consists chiefly of women and old men," Herr von Hohenlocher remarked, after he had drunk down a glass of gin with Angostura bitters.

"But no old ladies, it would seem," Conrad said quickly, pleased at this chance to give his impression of Madame Laurencin.

"You mean the Councilor's wife? Yes . . . the other one is cut out of the same cloth—that is, she's also youthful and lovely, and also far younger in years."

"You are referring to the magistrate's wife, the—the one who is to be transferred here, as I hear?" Conrad said, with obliging courtesy.

"Yes, Robert Veik's wife. Her name is Gusta. The other Frau Veik is childless, as you probably already know. Gusta Veik had two daughters—now just one."

"The other died?"

A cry sounded from the street, the penetrating cry of a small girl who has been caught in a game of hide-and-seek. Herr von Hohenlocher turned his head, and Conrad did likewise, partly out of politeness, partly because he was startled and the movement helped appease his fright.

"Hmn, died . . . she was killed," Hohenlocher remarked, yawning again.

"What!" Castiletz said, leaning forward.

"Her own fault, completely. She was the victim of a murder and robbery."

"Murder—but what do you mean, that it was her own fault?"

"A dear girl . . ." Hohenlocher said, in a kind of monologue, speaking under his breath. "Also—rather impressive, insofar as you can say anything of the sort about a nineteen-year-old. But crazy. The Veiks are very rich people—well, I suppose you know that. Naturally, the brother, too—our future chief magistrate— he is also part heir to the mills, you understand, and in addition they have a huge fortune. Well, she was mad, foolish about jewelry to such a degree—I've never seen or heard the like. The old fellow doted on his younger daughter—the girl was named

Louison—and in the course of a few years bought her a veritable Nibelung hoard. Simply fantastic, I tell you—not the sort of jewelry collection you'd expect a young thing of barely twenty to own. All choice pieces. In the end they cost her her life. She traveled a great deal, visiting relatives here in Germany and abroad, and every time she took the whole of the Rhinegold along. Her father should never have allowed it—in fact, I'm not sure he knew. From what I've heard, she was always extraordinarily reckless, used to toy with the rings, if possible in the presence of strangers in hotels or in trains. It was inevitable. Incidentally, not a single piece of the jewelry ever turned up again."

"Was the crime solved?"

"Not to this day."

"I see—when did this happen?"

"I no longer remember exactly. It must have been somewhere between four and six years ago, perhaps even longer."

Faced with such a dramatic story in this new and attractive environment, Conrad swelled once more into a romantic person. He took a large swallow of the gin. Before leaving the gentlemen to their talk, Frau Schubert had shaken up the coke in the stove, and now a faint reddish glow showed through its mica plates at the dim, far end of the long room. The cooler and whiter light above the divan, the unaccustomed drink in the tiny glasses, and the conversation—Conrad saw it all as if from outside, with deep appreciation.

It struck him as a rather jarring note when Herr von Hohenlocher remarked: "Such are the illnesses of the excessively rich. And some die of them."

And after a while: "She somehow took after her Aunt Manon, although there was no blood relationship at all."

"Really?" Conrad said. He had risen to his feet and (perhaps to give the scene an even greater romantic tone) moved over to the stove. From there, he aired his thoughts on the way Frau Manon Veik called to mind the pictures of Marie Laurencin.

"True," Herr von Hohenlocher said. "You're quite right. The other girl, Marianne, looks like her father, whereas Louison had her mother's dark hair. But there was no trouble recognizing the girls as sisters."

"What a terrible shock such a thing must have been for the family," Conrad said. "And—there's something that surprises me."

"What is that?"

"Well, forgive me—but, after all, it's understandable that I'd like to know a bit about my future employer—it's useful and necessary to me, if only so I won't say anything tactless—forgive me, it just occurs to me that Frau Veik spoke of the active social life of her brother-in-law and his family—which, under the circumstances, strikes me as somewhat odd . . ."

"Not so odd when you are more familiar with the total picture —aside from the fact that more than half a decade has passed since the calamity. Incidentally, hadn't you heard anything about it? Your father has known Herr Veik for a great many years, I believe."

"As far as I can recall, my father never mentioned the subject to me. Perhaps he himself didn't know, or had heard only vaguely; after all, they are only business friends, as the phrase goes. And then—since my mother's death my father has—changed amazingly. He's aged a good deal and is very withdrawn. As a matter of fact, I think I heard the name Veik for the first time when arrangements were made for me to come here, which was only about three weeks ago. Perhaps, too, my father didn't want me to have any preconceptions. I don't know. I'll ask him some time."

"Preconceptions . . ." Herr von Hohenlocher repeated. "Ah yes, very wise. As far as the social life in the Veik household goes, it centers around Marianne. As long as her younger sister was there—the two girls were barely a year and a half apart—Louison was the undisputed leader, although Marianne is an extremely pretty girl, tall, blonde. . . . But Louison was the more distinguished of the two, and distinctly more interesting in every respect. Her father's official favorite, as was perfectly evident to everyone. She had something southern about her, like her mother —a curious type. . . . Rumor has it that her sister was pretty unhappy because of her. Someone told me that an engagement of Marianne's was broken up because of Louison, although apparently Louison did not attempt to take advantage of the situation. . . . Well, in any case, the situation was fairly obvious at the time. The father has now turned all his affection toward his one remaining daughter, as though to make up for past neglect, shall we say. . . . It's understandable. The result is that the Veik household perked up after a suitable interval."

"Ah yes, of course, now I understand it," Conrad remarked, still standing by the stove.

"I've just remembered something else," Hohenlocher said slowly and reflectively. "Marianne once said her sister Louison was a kind of 'Manikin Zack.' That's a kind of little man who means bad luck—'a certain kind of little old man—when I run across them in the street, everything goes wrong.' That was the way she put it. The idea might be from E. T. A. Hoffmann. And Louison was her 'Manikin Zack.' A sort of hobgoblin specializing in breaking up engagements, I suppose."

The casual way in which Hohenlocher brought forth his indiscretions as if talking to himself probably had its source in such boundless indifference that Castiletz could not possibly fathom it. At moments this indifference could rise to an attitude of amusement toward the subject on hand, but it could equally well take the form of complete forgetfulness of these matters within a few moments.

Thus, in the next breath and in the same tone Hohenlocher continued: "About Frau Schubert—I wanted to tell you something you ought to know. She's a bit cracked on one subject— imagines that she is going to get married. I believe she even has some cad whom she—takes seriously. The hopelessness of it is self-evident—I mean, you only have to look at the little creature.

Naturally, the cad misbehaves from time to time, or perhaps regularly, chases after other women, and so . . . Well, all that is uninteresting; but, at any rate, that's when the weakest spot in Frau Schubert's character emerges—let's say, the Schubertian *punctum minimae resistentiae.* A matter that's somewhat difficult to describe. . . . I suppose the Creator has given every character a built-in, deliberate defect in its mechanism which is at once that character's greatest danger and its greatest blessing. The latter in the sense that you only need to discover that spot and you can use it to lift the rest of the character off its hinges, to liberate it completely. . . . Well, probably such phenomena have their divine purport, or, at least for good believers, the slogan would be: every character defect a mission in life! Well, cheers! Of course the dangers inherent in the defect probably win out most of the time, and the particular point which should rightly serve as the starting point from which a person can lay hold of his entire life becomes; in most cases, the point where life lays hold of him. As I say, I suppose everyone has such a point. Frau Schubert stands and falls with her self-deception, with her idea of marrying this man some time in the future. When this self-deception is pressed to the wall too brutally by facts, she doesn't free herself by yielding to the facts; she breaks step the way a horse that doesn't want to jump breaks step in front of the hurdle, and even tries to shy away completely, which of course it can't do. Life isn't a race course with high hedges on either side, or at any rate the hedges aren't so visible; they're discreetly arranged and you don't see them. . . .

"In any case, our dear Frau Schubert always breaks away. Goes around with a tear-stained face, but furious, small, and contracted like a wet fist. It's an odd kind of dull rage that seizes her —altogether hopeless fury; it's as though she's gone off the rails completely. Well, it's nothing new that all types of escapism are basically pathological; that's all it is with her. She runs away from her weakness and insignificance as a woman and escapes into tantrums, so that she won't have to recognize the facts. Once I found that she'd eaten nothing for three days, out of fury. Toppled over like a dry twig. Another time she cut herself, almost deliberately in my opinion, while cleaning vegetables, and then did nothing about the rather sizable cut for a whole day. That was deliberate beyond a doubt, or, let's say, purposeful—and the kitchen was as gory as a slaughterhouse. I suppose you'll ask why I don't throw her out. But, in the first place, she's the best of souls, reliable, and in the course of years she's been beautifully trained in running a bachelor's household. She doesn't bring me pumps when I want black oxfords, and she knows that you don't wear a woolen tie with evening dress. In the second place, these fits of hers come rarely, just once every year or two. And, in the third place, she amuses me. I'm curious to see how the thing is going to turn out. If things look bad, I make a practice of turning off the main gas valve at night and locking the little door that covers it. . . .

"But to get to you, that is, to my advice on how to handle her. You have to be on guard and not let her tell you her troubles with that contracted little face like a wet fist. For, once she starts, you're driven to cheer her up with reasonable arguments, and those are precisely what she doesn't want to hear, as you can realize from what I've said. Because in that case you're tugging in the wrong direction; namely, toward life. But pathological mechanisms aren't so simple that you can just pull them out like a crooked nail from a board. Such treatment doesn't even work on normal emotions. So—don't let her tell you her griefs. As soon as she begins, put on a show of glassy-eyed coldness that will send her out of the room. That's something a man has to learn, alas. False fraternizing is a total waste of time—only the right kind of fraternizing makes sense, and then it's a different thing entirely. A tremendous mistake, to adjust to every fool who comes along, to be obliging, understanding, kind, and good. Of course, you may thereby be putting on an excellent imitation of universal love and charity, but you stumble over your own feet and in the end fall on your nose right into your own bitterness, rancor, sentimentality, in short into your worst potentialities, as into a bog. And you end up malicious. Nobody can sustain such indiscriminate great-heartedness. It is equivalent to making out checks on a bank where we have no account, as an English writer once put it. No, Herr Castiletz, I beg you, cultivate those glassy eyes, as glassy as possible. There's no other way, and no other way to handle Frau Schubert either. Besides, no one is entitled to provoke another person at his weakest spot. The glassy eyes may not look so nice, but morally they're unquestionably on a higher plane than kindly calf's eyes."

Herr von Hohenlocher had evidently felt it incumbent on him to explain all this at length, but the subject so bored him, not to say exhausted him, that he dropped into silence and settled down among the pillows in his corner of the divan. Conrad, who had long since abandoned his romantic post by the stove and returned to his former position in the armchair near the small table with its assortment of bottles—Conrad, on the other hand, seemed to have reacted to his host's lecture with an increase of tension. His eyes flickered over the glasses as though seeking to draw from these fragile, transparent vessels a firmness of outline which he could not quite attain because words were not so readily at his command as the glass was at the drinker's.

He leaned forward and said, his gaze still fixed upon the table: "You mean, then, that it is more advantageous, in fact both useful and necessary, not to adapt readily to every person or group one falls in with, not to be too yielding and amiable . . . but, rather, that it's better to stand alone and take what I suppose must be the other alternative: present a cool and reticent personality. And that, by extending that alternative, one will give far less offense, in fact be more sought after. . . . You mean that such an approach promises far greater advantages?"

Castiletz had spoken rather stumblingly, not looking directly at Herr von Hohenlocher. Had he been looking, he would have spied behind Hohenlocher's half-closed lids a variety of glassy eyes, with which he was regarding his guest like some strange plant in an herbarium. Both remained silent for a while.

At last Hohenlocher said: "All right. You say: advantages, advantageous. My feeling is that something else altogether is involved, the sort of thing generally called bearing. And whatever profit or loss bearing brings with it is only of secondary importance. Its justification springs from another source entirely."

Conrad looked up. He knew he had made a mistake. Perhaps more than that: a mistake which he was making not for the first time in his life; one that was important, significant. He struggled in vain to detect what it was, to pinpoint it clearly. In short, to make order. Simultaneously, there arose for him, for the second time in his life and in an entirely new form, the thing that until now had been represented only by his father: authority.

But without the blackness of ebony.

19 ࣙ

~~~~~~~~~~~~~~~~~~~~~~~~~~~~~

FRAU Schubert appeared in short order, announced by the purring of a cab in front of the house and by a highly audible, humorous interchange in the hallway with the driver, who helped carry up the bags.

"We would like some coffee," Herr von Hohenlocher said. "And make the fire in Herr Castiletz's apartment." He turned to Conrad. "You may as well put off unpacking until it's warm. Should you prefer to eat at home, let Frau Schubert know, and she'll give you your supper. She generally reckons a supper at seventy pfennig."

In giving this information, Herr von Hohenlocher managed to convey the fact that he preferred to eat alone.

A silence ensued, and lasted a long time. The coke cast a quiet red glow through the mica plates of the stove.

Once Herr von Hohenlocher broke the silence to say: "Ah yes, new things and new surroundings often come upon us very rapidly from outside, and very thinly, just the concept, like the name of a city. But then these empty frames fill, more and more; their contents impose obligations by extending far beyond the mere facts. And then what you have is—life, as people so neatly put it. But it all begins with picking some train from a railroad schedule and traveling somewhere."

"How fine it is—life," Conrad said with a passion that seemed disproportionate in view of Hohenlocher's casual way of speaking.

"At the age of forty-five I can only second that statement vigorously," Hohenlocher replied. And then they spoke no more.

Across the hall, Conrad found the small apartment bright and warm. He was happy. Had not Herr von Hohenlocher's counsel shut his mouth like a heavy lid, he would inevitably have "fallen into conversation" with Frau Schubert. But now, as things were, conversation was stillborn, and their exchange of remarks was restricted to practical matters—where Conrad's suits, shoes, and linen were to be put. There were also a few trifles, including fencing equipment, but none of the troublesome and elaborate paraphernalia of the smoker, the pouches, bags, pipes, ash trays.

There were only a few books, all in a small, flat, yellow suitcase. Conrad opened it. The first book to meet his eye was *Ribbon Manufacturing*, by Otto Both. Beside it lay Dr. W. Zänker's *Dyeing*, Volume 211 of the Library of Technology. In addition, by the same author, *Chemical Treatment of Wool*. An unpleasant subject! Insipid smell! Conrad, only now realized that he was somewhat tipsy ("take gin—the most sensible drink anyhow").

On the inside of the suitcase lid was a pocket of rippled satin, secured with an elastic. Conrad peeped in and checked on the blue notebook. He lifted *Dyeing*; Plato's *Symposium* lay underneath. But he left the books in the suitcase and said to Frau Schubert: "Please put this suitcase of books up on the wardrobe and push it to the back."

The mouse with the bright, inviting eyes promptly climbed on a chair and, pushing comically, for she was very tiny, carried out this instruction.

"You have very nice linen and so much of it, young gentleman," she said, as she busied herself putting things away.

Conrad answered—nothing at all.

Everything was arranged with the greatest precision. The toilet articles too, so that everything would go smoothly next morning. With a remarkable certainty of instinct, Castiletz packed his brief case with blue work clothes, not the white smock the textile apprentices at Reutlingen wore at their machines.

It was rather like days of long ago, when school was opening in the fall, when he had nosed a little in the new books which opened somewhat stiffly and still smelled of the bookshop, not yet of school. He would stand in the middle of his room, which seemed strangely big compared with the rooms in the country, and had a promising fragrance, hinting of newness and distance. Yes, everything was new (and yet in order), and he had managed to put a certain interval, a coolness and freshness, between himself and everything else: the room, the walk to school next morning, the books.

Here, too, everything seemed to be new, or renovated, down to the smallest item. The bright, blond furniture, whose fine, smooth lacquer still gave off a faint odor, and whose rounded corners were accented with narrow bands of red, so that the compact modern shapes dominated the room all the more emphatically.

Yes, now everything was ready, really ready. He washed up in the neat little bathroom, which particularly delighted him. Frau Schubert reappeared with his supper.

An hour later, Conrad went to bed in the room at the rear, whose windows looked out upon the now dark courtyard with its cobbled paving. On the night table lay the map of the city and the album Herr Veik had given him, the anniversary volume of the firm of Carl Theodor Veik (the "sweatshop," in the parlance of Herr von Hohenlocher). Conrad lay on his back. Everything was sounding within him at once, like vibrating strings of a musical instrument; but it was all harmonious and somehow happily ordered. Suddenly he felt—although his supper had been ample—an intense hunger, which lasted for several minutes. He vividly pictured a "Kimmicher," a type of puffed and pointed pastry peculiar to Reutlingen. But the hunger passed, and he realized he would scarcely have been able to eat a "Kimmicher"; he would have left it lying on the night table. Something else emerged from behind thoughts of pastry and dropped down upon him: the vision of a blonde girl, not too young—and so it turned out that his hunger had been of a completely different kind. Castiletz tossed in bed, then sat up, unfolded the map, and pursued his conquest of the city where he was to live in this delightful apartment.

He wanted to habituate himself quickly to the city; he wanted to know everything. He had reason to be grateful to Herr von Hohenlocher for telling him a few things about the boss's family. . . .

And then it suddenly seemed to him that Herr von Hohenlocher loomed among all his crisscrossing and intertwining notions like a battlemented tower, rang and sang in all the vibrating strings, drew all the cables toward himself like those short, barred posts atop roofs to which a whole constellation of conductors run. Ah yes, his neighbor loomed in the background like the measure of all things, his every word binding. Conrad wondered; he felt pressure coming from that side.

And so the young researcher at the foothills of life reached for the album.

A golden cord with tassels laced the binding, and the heavy

pages were of handmade paper. Cool, clean, large leaves, obviously de luxe, with fine printing, and with rather good lithographs tipped in, pictures of the mill, with every imaginable machine and the people who ran them—in essence, the volume was the apotheosis of several thousand lives. The heaven, as it were, into which they had entered after a life spent under those spreading, staggered roofs, those low roofs with half gables and skylights which everyone has seen, though perhaps only in a passing glimpse from an express train: a neat row of boxes entering the field of vision and then out again, while the smokestacks leap like red rockets high into the blue; and then all has vanished, receded to vagueness behind the swaying horizons of memory. But these lithographs showed the life that flits by us in its permanent form, with its permanent odor. And the candid accuracy of the artist's crayon (a photographer might have done better at meeting the requirements for this festal volume) had put everything down: not only the huge and complicated machinery in the long sheds, but also the homeliness of young women who spent their lives over spindles, and the old-fashioned look of an age entangled in necessities, redolent with the oily odor of progress.

But Conrad Castiletz did not see all this in the book. That touch of horror and anxious constriction which attacks the layman when he enters industrial plants and sees them in operation, that distaste for unpleasant mineral odors which evoke the forests in which we once dwelt—all that was alien to Conrad. From school and the practical work he had done on holidays, noise, smells (so long as they were not of dyeing), and the quality of light in halls full of machines, whether looms or spinning machines, were familiar, cheerful, habitual to him. He did not regard such things from outside, like a passenger, but was filled and stimulated by their innumerable artful, inspired, and witty interconnections.

At the technical school in Reutlingen there had been some schoolmates who were not blessed with such inner equilibrium.

Students of Conrad's kind maintained a certain friendly reticence toward these others. It was clear from the first who would leave the school after six months or a year, not having accomplished his purpose, to turn elsewhere, in some unknown direction. There were those—rare exceptions—who were unhappy at Reutlingen, who were beyond the aid of teachers or fellow students. Association with them would scarcely have been profitable, would only have been upsetting. You sensed their unreliability and their capacity to change schools as well as aims in life quickly and frequently, And while you might be tempted to feel pity for them, that feeling was checked by a secret knowledge that at bottom they felt quite all right in their given state and that they commanded a certain freedom which you yourself lacked. Part of that was the ability to shift to another track—which, when Conrad seriously considered it, was a difficult concept to grasp. Actually, he could not imagine doing it. But these other students could; they felt unhappy, said so to whomever would listen, and one day vanished from the school—and were thus in some way superior, and therefore not to be pitied. Conrad had, for example, run through these emotions toward a boy at the Reutlingen Textile School who was there at the insistence of his father, a prominent textile manufacturer from Swabia.

Conrad now saw this young man before him, in the semi-shade of imagination, a little to the right of the book whose pages he was turning, to examine the picture of a winding frame and then of a warping machine (he thought both drawings "first rate"). He saw the narrow head with large, somewhat moist eyes, and the hair at the temples, allowed to grow long and form sideburns. The two were standing in the hall leading to the director's office, with some other schoolmates, and the boy said: "I wish I were anywhere else in the world but here!"

The others let this remark pass—what could they have done with it, or with the gesture of distaste with which the boy had jerked his chin in the direction of the weaving room. But, curiously, Conrad, after returning home from the school in Reutlingen, had met this schoolmate in his native city. The young man had been working there for some time; he had a good position in a bank. . . .

And here was the portrait gallery of the Veik family, up at the front of the book. All of them in the trade. A man with big, very kind eyes, standing beside his wife; he had a ponderous double chin, an imperious face. Remote men with the high-buttoned suits of the eighties.

Conrad managed to read: "He set a fine example to all his employees, not only by his unswerving industry, but also by his kindness and helpfulness . . ."

At this point Conrad realized that he could no longer concentrate on the album. Ah well, he was still far better prepared than he used to be on the night before the first day of school in the fall. . . . The last sentence he had read floated with strange and detached distinctness over his head and rose toward the ceiling, where the muted glow of the lamp on the night table hazily rested. An odor suddenly brushed him, descended upon him for a moment—a fragrance that he knew he did not really like, that was unpleasant, something like hair tonic. And yet it was refreshing, pleasing—ah yes, like a tumbling brook. But now a man's face pressed forward, for moments floated close to him out of the soft, cottony background of reverie: tall and long, soft and weak, seeming a little damp on the cheekbones that showed through its thinness.

"Ida!" Conrad said distinctly, as though he were calling her because the little stream, or whatever it was, had been checked and was drying up. He was awakened by the word he had spoken aloud, which hung over the silent pieces of furniture.

Conrad utilized his last conscious moment to switch off the light. The dream situation into which he immediately sank could easily have been explained by Hohenlocher's words, which now seemed to him strangely high-pitched and soaring. They were certainly illuminating. But he could no longer arrange these words in syntax or form them into sentences. All he could recover of them was: "New things come thinly, very thinly. The empty frames fill. First you've picked out a train."

20 ॐ

~~~~~~~~~~~~~~~~~~~~~~~~~~~~

THE empty frames filled. With their appropriate contents, of course. And while they filled, the weeks and months passed like a few days. Once Conrad took a short vacation, to visit his father, for whom Aunt Berta now kept house. Except for the summer months, she was there in their old apartment, and she had taken over Conrad's old room. As a result, the room dropped out of sight, as had the water meadows at the end of the salamander time. Those meadows, incidentally—as Conrad observed on a disgruntled wintry walk, which he soon cut short—were no longer what they used to be. They had been carved up into recreation grounds for various clubs. Large areas were closed to anyone who was not a member of one or another of these organizations. There no longer was any place for the solitary stroller.

Conrad found his father in reasonably good health. The board of the Hellas Fencing Club still met at their house, and as the only lady present at these gatherings, Aunt Berta had soon adapted to the teasing tone. Now Albert Lehnder was also included in those evenings, although he had never had anything to do with fencing. But he was welcome for his good qualities, and for his social talents. Lehnder, incidentally, had made a valuable connection in Berlin. That is to say, he had a kind of patron there, and now that Lehnder had passed his examinations and was beginning his clerkship, this man had promised him a place in his law firm. Lehnder was preparing eagerly for the profession; in external as well as inner qualities he seemed very well suited for it. Albert's excellent Prussian mother was still alive, and he still lived with her.

Once a week father and son exchanged letters: they reported on their health and their business affairs; Lorenz Castiletz was placing his in what businessmen call "liquidation." He wanted to retire. An agency, even one with the finest connections, is always to a large extent linked with the times. Under some circumstances it can bring in a brilliant income, but it is a dubious thing to hand on. Recognizing this, Lorenz had never regarded his son as his business successor. From the first, he had steered him toward the other, better career in industry. Now he proposed to arrange his financial affairs to the boy's best advantage. And when the father thought these matters over, he could see that Conrad's situation was even better than was apparent. Moreover, his advancement seemed assured; by and by, the tone of old Veik's letters became one of highest praise.

And so Lorenz Castiletz's old age, in spite of the loss he had suffered—he paid weekly visits to the grave—began in a tolerably happy fashion. To a son who had turned out as well as Conrad he could afford to write jesting letters such as this:

"You ask about the calamity of Louison Veik. That question, I might say, indicates that I have been a poor educator; for it proves that I had no success in impressing you with the importance of reading newspapers, although I remember telling you, when you were starting commercial school, to take a newspaper every day and make a habit of reading it carefully. I grant you, I did not mean the crime news. But obviously you did not read that either, although in those days it would probably have interested you more than the financial page. Well, joking aside, I remember very well that terrible and still unsolved

murder. The jewelry was valued at an enormous figure. As for
when it happened, as near as I can date it, it must have coincided
more or less with your visit to Aunt Erika. Probably it happened
while you were away, or else you would have heard us talk
about it. I don't know any of the details. When I read about
it in the newspapers, I wrote to my friend Veik, expressing my
sympathy. I did not myself know the poor girl."

After this letter, Conrad observed a change in his personal
habits. When he came back from the plant in the evening and
Frau Schubert served him his coffee, she would also bring him
the newspaper to which he had been subscribing for several
weeks. Reaching for the paper became as much a ritual as the
donning of house coat and slippers which preceded it. Herr von
Hohenlocher—whom Conrad seldom saw—once came across the
hall and witnessed this idyll. "Jolly house slippers you have
there," he said, contemplating the checked symbols of comfort
(but also of worse things) on Conrad's feet; they were trimmed
with a sort of pompon.

"Yours are handsomer," Castiletz said sincerely.

"Old evening shoes—the best things to wear around the house.
No need to buy them special," Herr von Hohenlocher replied. He
stretched, and took his departure.

There were changes, though Conrad did not observe them.
Now, when he came home from work in the evening and got out
at the streetcar stop by the wintry, bare park, and when he
walked down Hans Hayde Strasse—the street was entirely transformed. This was not only because it was winter and a different
light slanted upon the row of houses opposite. Rather, a number
of details which had previously loomed large for him had now
leveled out. For example, the big red sign of a teashop which
used to warn him that his streetcar was approaching the turn
leading to the park, and that he would soon be at his stop. Now
he no longer noticed that sign. There were dozens of other land-
marks; yet he did not make use of them. Dully and surely, it

was the whole fabric which showed him the way. And it was the same throughout the city. A good many things looked absolutely different, especially the factory, which had now opened out into innumerable details. Likewise the home of Councilor Veik. Never again would Conrad see those two large rooms, the dining room and the adjoining drawing room, as he had on the first day, when he sat with beautiful Frau Manon Veik by the Turkish coffee table, and looked through the arch-shaped opening. The window at the back no longer showed an autumnally golden treetop, but that was the most minor difference.

Vaguely, he sensed the habituation that had taken place—sensed it even at home in his small apartment. And it pleased him, because from the very first moment he had sought it. Still and all, each fragment of home that flashed by now and then in swiftly passing and elusive recollections surpassed in luminousness everything and anything here. Those older memories floated in a strange and alien light, like that of a brand-new morning which had not yet shone upon anything. The images of the past were bathed in a light that had not been before in the world: images of the way to school, the bridge, the street at night, or the bend in the canal with the factory smokestacks on the other side of it, ranged like arrows in a quiver.

In his vocational life, a second stratum had already been laid over Conrad's initial impressions. After a few months, old Veik had laughingly (always laughingly) declared that he must now pluck Conrad from his beloved looms and spindles and banish him to the second desk in his office, where all sorts of work awaited him. Around this time, a conversation also took place between Veik and an elderly master weaver from Mill III, who remarked that Herr Castiletz was a man with a great deal of varied experience whom they would miss. They had seen what he could do as early as his third day in the mill, when there had been a "reed break" and the new volunteer had leaped in to help retie the broken threads.

Nevertheless, Conrad now had to stay in the office and help Councilor Veik, who, it seemed, was not too sure of himself in matters linguistic. There was a great deal of foreign correspondence; the personnel in charge of these matters had to be relieved somewhat; and the most important letters were composed by the chief himself, assisted by Castiletz. However, Conrad had to draw up the drafts for a good many letters on his own. These were then shown to old Eisenmann, who was versed in a number of languages. And he said Conrad was doing splendidly. But the upshot of this was that Councilor Veik lost his secretary. Director Eisenmann waxed so eloquent about the young man's gifts that Councilor Veik had to give him up to Eisenmann and the webbing mill. And thus there came about that second stratum which was laid over Conrad's initial impressions.

The director made his remonstrances wearing a short fur jacket, which he had not taken off. He had arrived at the mill in the firm's automobile, climbed the rather steep steps, passed through the conference room (with its smoking paraphernalia and its potted plant) and the office, and come to a steaming stop in Councilor Veik's office. There he now sat, elbows propped on his thighs, holding his shrewd Swabian head somewhat tilted, and with a small group of furrows between his eyebrows which seemed to rule out all possibility of contradiction.

"My dear Veik, I must say—you have made arrangements with Peter Duracher; he has given up his job and will be here in another month, sitting at that other desk where Herr Schröder, bless his memory, used to sit. Herr Duracher is a first-class textile chemist besides; and, after all, you are thinking of building your own dye works. And, besides, you need someone who can have power of attorney. For my part, I'm asking nothing of the kind. But I must have the volunteer. I find myself forced to insist upon that, especially after all I've been hearing about him over here at the mill. As things stand, I simply can't handle all the work. Besides, I'm only asking for a man who costs—nothing."

"As far as that's concerned, we can't let that go on much longer," old Veik said. "But, in this case, that's beside the point. However, you'll have him, Eisenmann. You'll have him, if you don't eat me for lunch. That's all I ask in return." And he laughed. As usual.

A few days later Conrad entered what seemed another world (as he promptly wrote to his father). And oddly enough, afterwards, from the vantage point of the webbing mill, he discovered in himself a kind of distaste for the textile plant, for its flabby and close atmosphere, which contained a whole gamut of odors, beginning with the smell of sweat and fat from the fleeces, which were partially cleaned there, and going on to the point at which the fabric once more acquired a kind of artificially produced animal character in the "scour." In the progressive steps of manufacture of the cloth, the fatty, animal odor was gradually replaced by that dead smell typical of tailor shops.

At the willow and the mixer—the latter like an upside-down Vesuvius, for the exhauster sent an incessant whirl of feather fibers into the conical crater of a mountain of wool—you were still inconceivably far from the slowly moving cloth that grew as the shuttles shot back and forth. Spatially as well. For in between lay shed upon shed. The combing. The carding. In wide, ethereal cascades, the gauze descended. Of the boys at the winding machines, old Veik said: "They come in when they're done with school, at fourteen or fifteen, and in time, according to their abilities, they'll go on to all the other jobs." In the fulling mill the machines rumbled violently in tall, closed, upright boxes, and when you opened the door and looked into the works it seemed as if someone in long trousers was hastily and incessantly clambering up a chimney. In the drying room, on the other hand —the hot one—it seemed simply like a tailor shop, but one on a gigantic scale.

It was a totally different world in which old Eisenmann now had Conrad Castiletz scurrying about—to all the places that he himself could not get to at the moment, for lack of time—but where nevertheless he somehow followed, or, astonishingly, was already there when Conrad arrived. The brightness was intense; but this was not due solely to the fact that the major part of this mill consisted of recent, very recent structural additions. The material they worked with in the webbing mill was different, the smell pure and bitter, akin to a saddler's or a ropemaker's workshop. From the end of the ribbon looms the finished product dropped into clean, light-colored wooden boxes, dropped in dry, reptilian windings: venetian-blind cords, straps, belting, yard upon yard, blue or red threads mixed with the sandy color of jute, hemp, or flax. No shuttles flew. The noise was less than that of the textile mill; between the looms, each of which was handled by two girls standing on the running board, you could easily talk. An even rattling and rustling was the sound that filled these sheds. In long rows the nappers swung eccentrically, and the drums of wood or aluminum rested like round shields on the looms.

Within a few months, the men in the webbing mill grew used to regarding Conrad Castiletz as a kind of director's adjutant, who had to pitch in everywhere, in the works and in the office, and to whom everyone turned, whether for a particular English phrase in a letter, or a stuck winch, or simply a bell in the office that was on the blink. His obliging temperament, and the fact that he always knew just what to do, encumbered him with the worries of a jack-of-all-trades, but at the same time forestalled the usual jealousies of older persons in the mill against a newcomer. Later it turned out that a large number of the workers had initially taken Conrad Castiletz for a young relation of Director Eisenmann.

Eisenmann treated his adjutant with frequent outbursts of typically Swabian rudeness, and always addressed him by his first name—which was perhaps another reason that the mill workers assumed ties of blood between the two. But as his curses would take on a milder cast, old Eisenmann would pat Conrad on the back and offer him a cigar. The first time this happened, Conrad had, with considerable presence of mind, accepted it without trotting out his non-smoking; the gift found its way to the nearest workman. And old Eisenmann went on for years offering his assistant cigars without ever having seen him smoke.

Among other changes, certain initial streambeds of the life here dried up. Among these was Tramline 3, along with the stop at the once more green-clad park, along with the big red sign of the teashop. It is true that Line 3 was just as convenient for reaching the Johann Veik and Sons webbing mill as it was for the textile mill. But Castiletz no longer took the streetcar to work. One day old Eisenmann had curtly and in his usual rough tone declared that Conrad need not come to work quite so early in the morning, but could report at the same time as himself, since he intended henceforth to claim his services exclusively. And now each morning at half past seven Conrad took up his post in front of Number 5 Hans Hayde Strasse. A few minutes later the mill's auto turned the corner, with old Eisenmann sitting in back (minus his short fur coat). Hans Hayde Strasse was conveniently on his regular morning route to the mill. The car stopped for a moment, the adjutant was taken on board, and the vehicle set sail again. In the mornings it was best not to talk to old Eisenmann; if you did, you might hear some perfectly horrifying expressions, as well as some more classic, milder ones.

On the occasion of one of the last streetcar rides that Castiletz took to and from the factory, he met an old acquaintance of his first day—and was nearly run over by him, as was Frau Schubert, who really provoked the incident. It was at the birch tree by the corner of the park. The birch was now, in the spring, quite green—not a glaring yellow like the tank truck which came rolling almost silently but rapidly out of the narrow side street along the park. Castiletz was just about to cross the street, which he could have done without difficulty if Frau Schubert had not

been, on this particular fine spring evening in one of those states
that Herr von Hohenlocher had described with such precision.
She came running straight toward Conrad, and Conrad knew
the moment he saw her exactly what was the matter with her. She
looked down at the ground. With a small, compacted face like
a wet fist. She ran ruthlessly straight ahead, and in the middle of
the street, toward Conrad, who avoided her, whereupon she
jerked toward the same side, and then the game was repeated,
this time toward the left. By then the tank truck had come up,
all four wheels braking hard, with a tremendous screech. Castiletz
simply pulled Frau Schubert back toward his side. She looked
up at him like a person at the bottom of a deep well. But he had
made Hohenlocher's glassy eyes a rule of conduct, and he simply
let her stand.

21 ♘

~~~~~~~~~~~~~~~~~~~~~~~~

THE frames filled, with their appropriate contents, of course. In
time the frames themselves became invisible; the contents no
longer required them, were held together of their own accord,
enclosed Conrad Castiletz on all sides. The idea that he had once
simply picked out a train and ridden into the blue—this idea no
longer inhabited his mind with any vividness. Details of his
changed situation and disposition did emerge now and then from
his own interior, in the brief and hazy light of a casual side glance,
which, however, would stay on long enough to show Conrad
some astonishing features. Like the fact that here absolutely
nothing had as yet been "graduated" from—to use the phraseology

he had once indulged in at Reutlingen. Now and then the sudden intense hunger before going to sleep bothered him, and the vision of a "Kimmicher" would arise—but never so close to the surface of consciousness that he was prompted to keep some trifle to eat on his night table. A keen and suspenseful attention toward the female half of the population of the city had become virtually habitual with him. But although certain narrow streets in the old part of town had by no means escaped his notice, he treated the matter—as the result of certain chance obstacles and post-ponements enforced by circumstances—in the same way as he had the "Kimmicher."

He played tennis. Chiefly on Saturdays and Sundays in a court laid out in the spacious garden of Councilor Veik's villa. Castiletz played a great deal, and after a while with notable skill ("You looked very good at tennis today," Albert Lehnder used to say). Old Veik loved to sit for hours on the raised platform which is usually reserved for the umpires at tennis tournaments. There, on the dark-stained wooden stand he enjoyed the sunlight, whether up front on the bench, from which he attentively followed the game, or stretched out in a deck chair shielded by a huge, multi-colored parasol—there was plenty of room for the chair on the wide platform.

Manon Veik in singles against Director Eisenmann (in the Councilor's private language this combination was known as "the old boys"; he used the phrase in English). They played quite a respectable game, however, and Eisenmann was far from having an easy task. Since she placed her shots well, he went puffing about the court, and quite often was beaten. Old Veik would not miss such games; he would leave his chair for the bench up front when the pair entered the court, and from up above they would be urged on, laughed at, and often cheered for some particularly good shot.

As a rule, however, the young people swept over the reddish gravel. Their games were intensely serious, often extremely fast and hard. There were several fine competitors among the girls as well as among the young men. In time it became customary to give a handicap in doubles to the side on which Conrad Castiletz was not playing.

The sun poured down upon all these activities, upon the tennis court and the Councilor's huge, multicolored mushroom of a sunshade. One day the parasol was furled; in autumn such protection was no longer needed. The furling was done by Herr von Hohenlocher, quickly anticipating old Veik. Herr von Hohenlocher was filled with a rare vigor on this day. He was, moreover, to umpire the singles match between Castiletz and Peter Duracher, the new confidential secretary at the textile mill, whose playing strength had not yet been ascertained, for this was his first appearance on the court.

Hohenlocher crossed the wide platform to the bench where the Councilor sat, while down at the net Castiletz and Duracher tossed a coin to decide who would play facing the sun. Above the white shirt collar the South Tyrolean's strong nape glowed in the sun as he gazed down at the falling coin. Duracher was shorter than Castiletz; he was about forty and looked rather as we imagine the ancient Romans to have been, with broad shoulders and thick, curly black hair. Some might have called him extraordinarily handsome, with a straight nose and a medium-sized but sturdy frame. Now both men looked up. Herr von Hohenlocher, instead of taking his seat, raised his arm above his head and waved with a curiously slow motion toward the path that led from the house to the tennis court. Several young people, girls and boys who had already played that day, were coming along the path, accompanied by two ladies with whom Conrad was not acquainted. Hohenlocher and Veik clambered down from the stand.

In succession, Castiletz experienced two altogether different feelings, each of which was produced by his encounter with a new face. He was introduced to Frau Gusta Veik and then to her

daughter Marianne. Frau Veik's appearance was mild and re-
tiring. She had intensely black hair, with the merest sprinkling
of gray, and was lovely. Her daughter, on the other hand, had
the air of a person who means to assert herself. This was forth-
rightly expressed in a rich cloud of blonde hair and a milk-white
skin, as well as in a conspicuous fullness of the hips. In the nar-
rowness of the face around the mouth and eyes were those first
lines which make self-assertion necessary in a girl of twenty-nine
—or perhaps come from habitual self-assertion. Conrad looked
at her calmly and for quite a long time while he held her hand
and bowed slightly. He noticed as he did so that beneath Marianne's very clear, white forehead the base of her nose was rather
deeply hollowed out. She wore her clothes somewhat longer than
was the fashion. Conrad observed that; he observed also—when
the party settled down on the bench to watch the game—that
Fräulein Veik had somewhat thicker calves than fashion decreed.

And now he had to play; the new arrivals had no intention
of holding up the game between himself and Herr Peter
Duracher. He stood in front of Marianne after she had taken
her seat, and reluctantly left the particular spot on which his feet
rested. There took shape within him a strangely clear sense of
the contrast between the girl's thin, almost gaunt face and her
otherwise womanly appearance.

The pair began to play—and during the very first set were
amazed. For neither could make progress; each encountered a
wall; neither could take the lead, and the game went on for an
excessively long time. Their playing strength seemed almost equal,
and the conditions were quickly balanced because the sun
dropped down behind the tops of the trees. There was applause
for single plays on one side and on the other. But results were
almost insignificant. The game proved strenuous for both players.

Conrad was still breathing heavily when he threw his brightly
colored jacket over his shoulders. They walked across the garden,
he and Fräulein Veik somewhat ahead of the others. He pressed

his handkerchief against his chest, which was damp where his
shirt was open, and felt her looking at him. "You'll catch cold;
put your jacket on," Marianne said, and he did so. She had smiled
as she spoke, the lines of self-assertion deepening in her face.
Inwardly, Conrad moved toward Marianne, and with awakening
consciousness. Both of them failed to notice that the rest of the
company had chosen another path branching off at an angle
through the park-like garden. They heard voices and laughter
from the side, among the trees and shrubbery, but did not notice;
together they continued strolling toward the entrance to the
orchard, where beside a trellis stood an old pear tree with a bench
running around its trunk, the wood grayed by sun and rain. In
streaks here and there among the tops of the fruit trees the golden
banners of autumn had already been raised. Marianne pointed
to the pears hanging in the crown of the tree, and with five agile
movements Conrad reached them, with no concern for his fine,
porcelain-white trousers. He shook a branch lightly; three or four
fruits thudded onto the grass. Marianne stooped; Conrad was at
her side again and picked the pears up for her. The girl's rounded
hip, the moss-green cloth of her dress taut over it, touched him as
he did so. When he straightened up, pears in hand, he saw that
she was sitting on the bench.

He held out the pears and she took one. They did not talk.
Once she breathed deeply and sighed slightly. As she did so, she
looked quietly at him, just as he had imagined she would. In her
eyes there were standards and comparisons unknown to him. He
sensed this, and it made him uneasy.

"Why, where have the others gone?" she said at last with equanimity, and stood up. The two of them walked back to the fork
in the path.

22 ࠗ

AT the beginning of the winter a sizable reception was held in Magistrate Veik's new home, which Conrad had already visited shortly after his game with Peter Duracher.

This time he set out together with Herr von Hohenlocher. As they emerged from the cab and entered the brown-paneled hall of the house, they encountered the architect Georg Lissenbrech, an acquaintance of Hohenlocher—or, to put it more precisely, an item in Hohenlocher's "collection," which contained some remarkable specimens. When you looked closely at them. Outwardly, however, Lissenbrech was only a very good-natured-looking and somewhat portly gentleman who now made a highly dignified appearance in his dinner jacket. The three ascended together a sweeping staircase. Beyond the first wide glass door they found Frau Gusta Veik receiving her guests, her body plunged entirely into the blackness of a full-length evening dress from which her powdered shoulders emerged like white pinions. But the greatest radiance came from the central sun of the house, namely, the host himself. Tall, broad, firm, with the irrestistible force of lavish good humor he drew everyone into his circle. He had a faculty for making young people his confidants with three words jestingly tossed toward them like a beach ball or a pillow. Conrad felt a light nudge in his ribs; old Eisenmann pumped his hand and said: "Delighted you're here too, my boy." The throng grew larger; Conrad barely managed to greet the Councilor, who seemed small and frail by comparison with his brother. Then Conrad kissed Frau Manon's hand, and the current washed him into the next room and the next. At last he found Marianne, blonde and resplendent, in a dress of shimmering cloth. The neckline was fairly high; the satin glittered over her firm breasts. The bodice was cut like a short jacket, in old Spanish style; but it was set into the flowing folds of the skirt, which terminated in a flounce of ostrich feathers. Marianne did not have hands enough to shake all those held out to her; guest upon guest came up. Herr von Hohenlocher, Lissenbrech, and Castiletz made their way out of the turmoil. Room after room. It grew quieter. "Cigarette after the first assault?" Hohenlocher said to the architect. They stopped, alone; they were in a small salon at the end of the long suite of rooms.

The two smoked. Conrad, who did not know this distant room, looked around. The light of a host of electric candles under topaz-colored shades flooded the room, but concentrated upon a large portrait which hung above a dainty writing desk.

It was the portrait of a woman. But he stood in front of it and gazed into it as if it were a landscape. Done rather in imitation of the eighteenth-century manner, the portrait showed the face and dazzling shoulders of a girl in the first bloom of youth. Seated in a massive armchair, she held three or four flowers out in front of her with her left hand. But her gaze was directed elsewhere, straight at the viewer. The somewhat oblique eyes, beneath which the full cheeks seemed just slightly puffed, were a deep blue; but her hair was black and thick around her white brow. The background of the painting was light, nothing but a few dissolving clouds brushed in casually.

Confronting this portrait, and in a fraction of a second, Conrad became vividly aware of something he had never before conceived: the possibility of a life altogether different from his own. Even switching into another track became imaginable—became, in a strange way, a reality. The noise of the guests rang more strongly from the adjoining rooms, thundering and rumbling like a long string of cars. Conrad heard it sounding up against the margin of the monstrous silence within himself, the margin of an abstractedness such as he had scarcely experienced since his boyhood. True enough, he was following his track. But alongside it, within arm's reach, an entirely different track ran. He looked into the mute face of the girl who looked at him out of the picture, and it was like seeing into some distant horizon, into the last green streak of an echeloned evening sky. But in the midst of this sudden breakthrough to a wider comprehension, which remained nevertheless incomplete, a second face intervened: not beautiful, yet belonging against this particular horizon and no other; soft and weak, a narrow head with big, moist eyes, the hair coming rather far down on the temples. It was that schoolmate of Reutlingen who had left, Conrad decided. But no, it was not he. Then the vision of the moment vanished.

"Who is she?" he asked Herr von Hohenlocher, who was standing behind him. He indicated the portrait.

"The bogy man," Hohenlocher replied quietly. "Louison Veik, the dead girl."

The architect seemed rather alarmed by this expression; he looked down at the floor, regretfully, placatingly. Conrad, as if sensing a mysterious echo of the past few seconds, suddenly remembered distinctly the smell of fresh paint, somewhere back in time; at any rate, it came from himself, he was certain of that. Silently, the three men lingered before the portrait; no one moved, even when the swelling noise from outside came rushing toward them, and then crossed the threshold. Crossed the threshold, and there stood Marianne Veik in the doorway, her blonde whiteness framed by the intensely black ebony.

She looked up at the picture only briefly, and then into Conrad's eyes. He let his gaze rest on hers, and distinctly felt once again that a measure was being applied to him which, in the existing situation, could no longer be so entirely unknown or incomprehensible to him.

23 ᛒ᷾

WE may, with a touch of malice, state that Conrad Castiletz stumbled into his entanglement in an orderly fashion. In fact, Herr von Hohenlocher is supposed to have remarked something of the sort. Of course, orderliness has many aspects. Every regular activity, bar none, even if at first it occupies a person greatly, strains him and completely absorbs him, is in time built into the structure of life. And habit requires a constantly lessening output of energy—in fact, in the end a scarcely noticeable effort. Castiletz had long since reached that state of equilibrium. In mute understanding with old Eisenmann (saying as little as possible, especially in the mornings), he did his daily work, which soon brought nothing new, only repetitions of previous contingencies. Monthly, he received a good salary, which, together with the ample allowance from Lorenz Castiletz, constituted an unusually high income for so young a person as Conrad.

In this secure position, with the scales balanced, Conrad sat at Frau Gusta Veik's tea table and studied the childhood pictures of Louison. He looked at them in veritable absorption and listened to stories about her. Again and again a distant horizon with an incomprehensible view opened out, a faint glow which emanated also from the dead girl's portrait, which he now for the first time saw by daylight.

Frau Veik dropped the photographs back into the box and pushed it aside with a mild, horizontal movement of her hand, spreading silence over the subject she and Conrad has been discussing. For now Marianne's footstep could be heard outside in the hall and on the staircase.

As always, as soon as she entered she covered up for Conrad

the softer horizon that had just been thrown open. There was no note of infinity about her, no touch of the distant margins of the sky. She did not need them; she was a limited vessel of known and nevertheless overpowering contents.

Usually the three of them had tea together. Sometimes the magistrate himself joined them, and then they drank Wachenheimer Luginsland. Herr von Hohenlocher came sometimes too, escorting Frau Manon Veik. He was perfectly indifferent to everything, but nothing escaped his notice. Now and again Frau Manon invited Marianne and Conrad to her house; there, too, there were only the three of them, for no one else was expected. All this familial life was presented to him like a pretty, decorated bowl; and, in spite of his modest disposition, Conrad was obliged to realize that he and Marianne were inside the bowl, while the others looked benevolently over the brim.

In early spring, after the last dances of the season, the tacit engagement was announced. Everyone had expected it, Herr Peter Duracher first of all; in fact, he had made his prediction at the onset of winter, and it had long since gone round the circle. For Duracher was seen everywhere, to the pleasure of the ladies and, in spite of his mature years, of the girls also. Their mothers seemed less enthusiastic at seeing a divorced man their daughters' dancing partner—a man, moreover, who had been forced to make heavy reparations to his former wife, which seemed to indicate that the blame had been his. . . . That, too, had long been common gossip. But the tanned athlete danced like a dream, and it was also said that he was a terrific skier, a match in that sport even for the skilled Tyrolese.

Duracher, then, had been one of those who had entered the small salon with the topaz-colored lampshades behind Marianne Veik—at that first reception in her father's house—the time Marianne had stood between the ebony doorjambs, looking at the three men in front of the portrait of her dead sister.

The parents had not imposed too long an engagement upon

Marianne and Conrad. However, it was protracted beyond the intended time by circumstances.

24 ॐ

IN town society, opinion on the match was divided. Either it was said that Conrad had made a coup; or else it was emphasized that Marianne, a girl so much older than her fiancé and with no special talents, ought to be more than content with such a handsome young husband (whom she never would have caught if it had not been for all her money; scarcely anyone forebore to say or at least to think that). It occurred to no one to imagine that the two might be in love and happy. The difference in their ages aroused concern here and there—old Eisenmann being one of those who commented that Conrad would not have an easy time of it.

For the rest, he congratulated the "boy" heartily, and simply, with nudges and pokes. This took place around four o'clock on a drizzly spring afternoon in Eisenmann's office, where Conrad was getting ready to leave, for he was to take the car and drive over to see the Councilor at the textile mill. Eisenmann wanted Veik to have a look at his figures for the latest tax return for the webbing mill. Conrad put the rather bulky document in his pigskin portfolio and set out.

The car swept in a wide curve up to the mill, rumbled, bumping softly, over the mill's railroad track, and stopped in front of the administration building. On the narrow, rather steep staircase to the office, Conrad recalled his first ascent of them, more than a year before; but all that was now small and remote inside him, as if seen through an inverted pair of opera glasses.

"Something new has come up, the Councilor said. "That is, a new plan. And I'd like to ask you to take a close look at the project when you have the chance—later on, that is, if we decide to go through with it. We no longer want to send our stuff out for dyeing, but instead build our own dye works."

Herr Peter Duracher came in and greeted Conrad. "Ah yes, Herr Duracher," Veik said, "when the plans for the dye works are drawn up, will you let Herr Castiletz have a look at them—he's interested in such matters."

"Yes, of course," Duracher said.

"The new proposal comes from Herr Duracher," Veik added. "And the first rough estimates appear highly encouraging."

Conrad drove home in the car and sent it back to the webbing mill. A fine drizzle of rain was drifting with the wind into Hans Hayde Strasse. The stairwell was unlighted, in dense dusk. As Conrad turned the key in his lock, the door at the other end of the hall opened.

"Herr Castiletz," Herr von Hohenlocher said, "may I ask you for a small favor. You're a technician, and I'm rather worried about something I've just noticed."

Conrad withdrew his key and crossed the hall.

"Please, would you be so kind as to ring my doorbell while I'm inside. I'll explain what it is all about in a moment; I only want to check once more." Whereupon Hohenlocher vanished into the dark vestibule and partly closed the hall door. Conrad pressed the button. "Aha, yes, I was not mistaken!" Hohenlocher exclaimed. He opened the door for Conrad and switched on the light in the vestibule. "You see," he said with some excitement, "when someone presses the button, up above the door here, where the bell is, I see a bright spark. I noticed it a little while ago when the mailman came and I had to open the door myself because Frau Schubert is away at the moment. I crossed the dark vestibule and then I saw the spark. Is something wrong—is it likely to produce what they call a short circuit?"

Conrad looked up above the lintel of the door. A curious wariness assailed him, and that alone restrained him from making himself important in the slightest degree.

"No," he said tersely. "It's all right, there's no danger. If you like, you can ring once and I'll look at it in the dark."

"Well?" Herr von Hohenlocher called from outside. "Do you see the bright spark?"

"Yes, of course," Conrad said.

"What is wrong up there?" Hohenlocher asked.

"Nothing," Conrad replied with a touch of firmness. "Every electric bell produces a spark as long as it rings and as long as the interrupter is functioning. The reason we are seeing the spark is because the little wooden lid which ordinarily closes the housing has come open, from being shaken I imagine—perhaps by the heavy tank truck that passes here sometimes. We ought to have Frau Schubert climb up on a ladder and close the thing. Otherwise the box will fill with dust."

"Well, I am immensely relieved," Herr von Hohenlocher said. "Ever so many thanks, Herr Castiletz."

Conrad shook hands with him, bowed slightly, and said: "Good evening." He went to his apartment. After he had closed the door behind him, he stood in the small, bright vestibule with the distinct feeling that he had behaved correctly, had in fact acted very well.

There in the stillness a sudden thoughtfulness overcame him. Were there any faults of his which were on the point of—slumbering? This last word, which he suddenly felt to be just the right one, affected him like a tincture which clears a murky solution. As he entered his quarters, turned on the light and found the room warm and the stove going well, it struck him that Hohenlocher had once more wanted to amuse himself, this time over the "pomposity of the technicians" (a phrase he had recently used). Perhaps, too, he had been having his little laugh at Conrad's readiness to take an interest in this "case." Even granting the touching ignorance of technical matters that some persons seemed to enjoy displaying, this affair with the bell was a little unbelievable. Hohenlocher had a way of cosseting his whims and crotchets. But most of all he liked to cultivate odd people, whom he would then encourage in their peculiarities. . . . There was Lissenbrech, for instance. Hohenlocher praised him. Only because he was amused by him. . . .

"Well, I don't care to have a place in his cactus collection," Conrad thought distinctly, in those very words. He stood at the table in the middle of the room, enjoying the brightness and incisiveness of his interior monologue the way someone engaged in physical exercise might enjoy the movements of his body. And as he stood there, and before he had put on his slippers— which he was about to do—this inner brightness expanded some-what, pressed outward into the spaces of his present life, lightly touched some of the notions with which that illuminated cavern was filled—all around the hollow space there was a kind of ring, like the ring around the moon, beyond the space occupied with specific things or affairs. . . . And, much closer to him, concealed behind this or that wall, lay a certainty which extended into the future: that he would possess Marianne. For seconds he was left alone with this notion. All other thoughts were put to flight by it. But he had to curb it at once—proving that his sense of self-preservation was still wide-awake. Hastily seeking some other matter to occupy his mind, he hit on the vital point which he had forgotten and which had been disturbing him all along.

The dye works. Of course—he'd known something was amiss.

He heard Frau Schubert inserting her key into the lock in order to bring him his coffee, as she usually did at this time. In fact, it was a good deal earlier today. She must have noticed that he was home.

"Frau Schubert, please get that yellow suitcase down from the top of the wardrobe."

And just as the little mouse had once thrust it up, so she now climbed on a chair and with some difficulty dragged it down.

When she left, Conrad wanted to settle down with the newspaper. But he found it impossible to settle down behind the convenient barrier of this once recommended and now habitual occupation. Instead, he went to the suitcase and opened it. This he could do most conveniently, for Frau Schubert had placed the handsome piece of luggage across the arms of a chair. After removing the books, Conrad could have closed the suitcase at once, for Dr. Zänker's *Dyeing* lay right on top, as did *Chemical Treatment of Wool*. The books felt somewhat heavy in his hand. The chemistry of textiles—a science in itself—was his weakest side. There he would have to go easy in conversation, and not expose his ignorance. But at any rate he could refresh his knowledge. Oh, well—he placed *Dyeing* on the table with the other book, went over to the suitcase again, and looked in.

He really had nothing to look for there. He paused only for a few of those apparently empty moments in which a man's body and mind mingle completely while the self hovers with outspread wings over God knows what abandoned valleys and gorges of the past. With no special purpose, his hand merely seeking to avoid the books, which at the moment seemed too heavy for it, he lifted the elastic tab of the crinkled satin pocket on the inside of the lid, saw a blue notebook, and took it out.

Something was protruding from it at an angle. It was a picture post card. Long-buried splinters of one's remote past, even the most shapeless and stupid of them—notes passed in school; stick figures drawn long ago—one recognizes them with a profound feeling of naturalness, almost like parts of one's own body. This, however, was not shapeless. The white Pierrot, or Harlequin, smiled as of old under its tall pointed hat, and resembled the boy Günther Ligharts.

Conrad opened the notebook and read his own handwriting. He knew very well that its striking evenness was due to the fact that the whole thing had been written down at one sitting, on a single night:

"Café Belstler, yesterday's date, 6:30. She: I thought all I was for you was a good secretary—he: on the contrary, I've been in love with you for years—she: Herr Castiletz, you make me terribly happy when you say that, but after all I'm married—he: so much the better, so am I—she: I would never have expected anything of this kind from you—he: do I look so old? . . ."

Under the thumbscrew which tightened as he read, Conrad struggled desperately for a word that would restore clarity and order as had that phrase about his faults "slumbering." But nothing came, and his hand released the notebook. At last he hit on: "youthful follies." It was as dim a phrase as "boyhood realm" or "land of childhood," phrases which he had summoned up to express his feelings that time he had first come home on vacation and had walked disgruntled through the partially built-up, partially fenced-off water meadows that the various clubs had taken over.

He approached the stove, and was on the point of opening the hopper through which the coke was poured.

He stood by the stove, having placed the notebook on a chair beside him.

The bell rang in the hall. With a brief thought in the direction of Herr von Hohenlocher, Conrad went out, opened the door, and saw the visored cap of a telegraph messenger.

25 ३◆

~~~~~~~~~~~~~~~~~~~~~~~~~~~~~~~~~~~~

NEXT morning Conrad arrived in his native city by express train and rode through the broad, noisy streets in the dim light of a dreary day. A coating of dampness covered the pavements. The cab rolled across the bridge to the other shore of the canal—though Conrad scarcely noticed—turned to the right, slid along the side street, and stopped in front of the house, which was now no longer the last in the row, for in the meanwhile four new ones had been added. The piles of lumber opposite, by the embankment of the canal, had vanished.

His father's funeral did not take place until the second day after his arrival. The end had come gently and swiftly, he was told—a heart attack, medically to be expected sooner or later. Aunt Berta had taken the arrangements in hand, for which Conrad was grateful. He walked beside her at the funeral.

On the following day he paid another visit to the cemetery, this time by himself, and stood at the graves of both his parents, who now lay side by side and, as it were, merged, for they had almost vanished under a mound of flowers and wreaths. The restless springtime sun had broken through the clouds here and there, wantonly crosshatching distant buildings and the walls of the memorial chapel between the rows of graves, only to fade again. Strips of pavement had been dried by the wind; but the gravel cemetery paths remained damp, and the ground in front of the graves looked hard and wintry, the grass gray and not yet sprouting.

For a moment something caught Conrad fiercely by the throat. He thought: Mother. Then that was checked.

Like a dart of flame from the cold ground, it leaped up at him: Marianne.

That future yawned, within arm's reach. From the moment of his return, he spent almost every free hour with her, fitting himself into the frame of his future possession. And he felt with particular pleasure the slight resistance from that dividing line drawn by what was, in this regard, her excessively strict upbringing. If Conrad sometimes fleetingly brushed against the barrier, he enjoyed leaning against it with the knowledge that his bride stood behind it. He gave no thought to that; it seemed the necessary condition. Moreover, he sensed that once she was his wife, her conduct would be precisely the reverse. Marianne had grown slightly sterner in her expression since the engagement had been announced. We might say that she had firmed—if that were not such a repugnant stock-market phrase.

She had entered into certain rights, at least to the same degree as Conrad. Her rights were cherished beneath that pure white brow, below which her nose sprang from a deeply sunken base. From there they radiated outward in the form of an expectation, or a demand, which could be felt by everyone who addressed her. She was a bride-to-be.

26 &

ONLY by being constantly around Marianne, seeing her continually, her throat, hand, and forearm, the tautness of her dress, the rich curve of her calf—only thus did Conrad imagine that he could somehow fill out and survive the waiting time, which had been prolonged by the period of mourning. And it was long after the honeymoon had begun—at Bologna, in fact—that he for the first time became fully aware of the relationship and the resemblance between the faces of Marianne and Louison. Hohenlocher, he recalled, had mentioned that it was not hard to see that resemblance.

His wife slept beside him, and the light was on. She lay turned toward him, about an arm's length away from him, one cheek pressed into the pillow as she slept. She had slid down the pillow a bit, so that her cheek was pressed upward a little toward her eye. He realized this by comparison with the unchanged cheek, which pointed up the excessive curvature the other had taken on. And at that moment it struck him like an arrow—that this sleeping woman was Louison's sister. In the silence a long-drawn-out whistle sounded from the railroad station, which was close to the hotel—sounded and faded away. Conrad pictured his boyhood room, as it had once been, not as he had found it on his recent visit. He was tempted to awaken Marianne.

It was a real honeymoon. Under the high blue sky a second, invisible and clear as glass, enclosed the couple. As they sat in the train that carried them from Bologna across the Apennines to Florence, the heat flowed toward them through the awning that flapped in the wind—heat mingled with streaks and streamers of cool mountain air. And then the plain below turned into a sublime landscape painting in which Pistoia lay, tight, compressed, a city set in the big picture window of the open expanse.

In the evening, when they raised their glasses at dinner and looked into each other's eyes, Marianne's sparkled. She preceded him up the stairs, quickly and eagerly. Even before their first night she had walked like that. In Florence they looked at the merry "Journey of the Magi to Bethlehem" of Benozzo Gozzoli in the square, isolated, small, and almost lightless room, the attendant holding up a powerful lamp on a long cable so that they could see all the major and minor figures. Afterwards Conrad said: "This room looks as if it had once been a bridal chamber." Her fingertips, which had lain softly and lightly against his as they left the palazzo, pressed his hand; her back hollowed, and for a second she shook herself as if shivering.

When they returned they moved into a large apartment complete down to the last detail. It was not far from Conrad's previous apartment, was in fact located on the street which ran along the park and into Hans Hayde Strasse. The newlyweds occupied the entire second story, whose windows faced partly on Hans Hayde Strasse and partly on Weissenborn Strasse and the park. The entrance of the building, Number 17, was on Weissenborn Strasse. Below, there was a garage, and in it Marianne's car. But she did not drive it herself; she maintained a chauffeur.

Herr von Hohenlocher was there for a farewell nip of gin (the most sensible drink, anyhow) when Conrad cleared out the last of his possessions from the flat. Frau Schubert was in charge of the packing; she did not presume to chatter, but her every wrinkle and pore breathed out happy approval of a marriage. Herr von Hohenlocher stood around during the cleaning up, largely in the way, wearing his silk house coat, sash and all, with a bottle under his arm and glass in hand, since there was nowhere in the room where he could safely set anything down. "You should hold an auto-da-fé before she packs up the rest," he commented. "There are things one doesn't take into marriage— I mean, letters and such stuff." He indicated the shelves on which notebooks, newspapers, and books were heaped.

But no, Conrad had nothing of that sort, nothing at all.

He suddenly reached into his trousers pocket, took a key from the side compartment of his wallet, and unlocked the flat yellow leather suitcase. The blue notebook which had once before almost succeeded in escaping was removed from the satin pocket. Herr von Hohenlocher produced his lighter, after Conrad, still a non-smoker, had vainly searched for matches. With a clumsy, hasty movement, missing his aim, Conrad pushed the uprush of flame toward the maw of the stove; he bumped his hand against the grates and dirtied it, but at last the ignited notebook fell into the stove's black innards. The draft caught it; it spread apart in charring pages, and rushed up, flaming brightly. Then Conrad realized that he had burned Günther's Pierrot post card. It had been tucked into the notebook, and he started in real alarm. For the span of a thought it seemed to him that nothing so clearly marked the beginning of a new segment of his life as this circumstance.

27 ?~

~~~~~~~~~~~~~~~~~~~~~

THE vestibule was very large, almost square, and its floor was
covered with gray-green carpeting. On the right, at a considerable distance, a number of modern metal chairs stood lost in the
expanse. To the rear, the daylight cast its milky whiteness on the
squarish glass doors which led to the living quarters. Of these,
the bedroom was on the left, facing the park. Next to it was a
large, strikingly barren room which so far held nothing but
wardrobes. This was called the "dressing room" and could some
day be transformed into a nursery. Adjoining it was a small salon
in strict Empire style, with Marianne's desk and the other
appurtenances of a lady. At the angle of the house was the large
living room, with windows on both sides, facing Weissenborn
Strasse and Hans Hayde Strasse. It was airily furnished, that is
to say, not in an excessively opulent manner. There was no
carpet, but, rather, a large area of gleaming parquet and two
groups of small golden armchairs, at present wearing chintz
slipcovers. There followed the dining room: dark and sober, as
befits punctual dinners announced by a clock as sonorous as a
church bell. Adjoining this was the master's study. Rising from
the vast diplomat's desk, he could appear in the doorway the
moment the cathedral bell sounded. For when the soup strikes
twelve, the clock must be on the table—oh no, excuse it please,
the other way round, of course, for to place that clock on the
table would have been wholly unsuitable, since it was six feet
tall or more.

Besides, the Castiletzes dined at half past twelve; the car
brought Conrad from the mill for that purpose. In fact, it was
only on Sundays that Conrad came to the dining room from the

diplomat's desk—at which, for the present, he never wrote. The glass top was placated by a number of ponderous objects and a leather writing case beside which lay a huge ivory letter opener with a heavy silver handle. This, the wedding gift of Director Eisenmann, would no doubt have been a fine weapon for a neolithic man.

These stretches of furniturial landscape, which at evening darkly surrounded the young couple's illuminated bedchamber, did not immediately fill with life. At first they only raised demands, especially with regard to constant care by housewife and servants. The ever-present, tart odor of new varnish and the sterner smell of leather spoke inaudibly and incessantly. That is to say, these rooms, which (in Conrad's mind) had not long before been filled with the tumultuous images of his expectations, like a crowd incited to the point of riot—these rooms now stood pacified. Although furnished, they were in a sense empty. And the process of filling them was hampered by a hitherto unencountered difficulty: his regular working day. For his work now required a considerable output of energy, in fact often reduced him to complete exhaustion; and the fact that this condition disturbed Conrad by no means reduced the drain on his strength. He now rose heavily in the mornings and was always concerned about and anticipated difficulties with the maid, the alarm clock, the time.

In the study, or "library," as they had taken to calling it, a monstrously large American bookcase had established itself. Its demands were not easy to satisfy, but satisfied they must be, for the shamelessly gaping emptiness of the shelves was unendurable. Conrad possessed no books. The contents of the yellow suitcase were only a bad joke and a drop in the bucket (in any case, *Dyeing* and *Chemical Treatment of Wool* were usually to be found on the vast desk, though in the evening Conrad needed only to feel the chair beneath him and fatigue made reading altogether impossible). Marianne, too, had never bothered with books. Now, however, she went prowling about her parents' household and confiscated, in addition to an encyclopedia and some four or five feet of classics, a part of her deceased sister's library. This consisted of a great many books, but Marianne took only those that seemed to promise interesting reading—novels whose titles sounded attractive or whose settings, when she leafed rapidly through them, appealed to her.

The outcome of these literary measures was that the couple henceforth took to reading in bed at night. Marianne, incidentally, went in for nothing less than André Gide's *Counterfeiters*, which she enjoyed.

Conrad, for his part, opened an adventure novel translated from English, and for the first time saw Louison Veik's signature. The sight of the name struck him like a direct contact with a nerve, or like the arrival of a surprising message. He instantly closed the book again, and glanced at his wife, who lay with her back to him. Conrad turned to the title page again. There it was: Louison Veik. The handwriting was not fashionable; nor was it nervous. It looked like one of those handsome, careful hands of the old days: each letter had flowed from the pen rounded and distinct. Castiletz did not read much that night. Two or three times he interrupted his reading to look at the signature again. Soon sleep overcame him.

Next day, which was Sunday, they dined with Marianne's parents; this had become the established practice, as had a tea hour given by the young couple at five o'clock in the small Empire salon adjoining the "dressing room." There the maid, before taking her Sunday off, would have prepared everything so carefully that nothing remained to do but to plug the cord into the outlet. The room and the time of day, late afternoon, with twilight falling, offered complete and rounded comfort into which it was easy to slip and easy to remain. Moreover, there was an element of piety involved: the custom dated back to the very first days of Marianne's and Conrad's joint household.

It was on this Sunday and at this tea hour, some time around the beginning of the month of March, that Conrad for the first time had a fairly elaborate and detailed talk about Louison with his wife. He had stretched out on the floor, on a polar-bear rug, as was his habit. The small gas fireplace had been turned on; its curved copper shield threw a low, straight path of light and heat against Conrad and, over his body, at the legs of Marianne, who still sat at the tea table. The sharp path of light made the twilight in the small salon appear much deeper than it was. The room seemed almost dark.

"I have nothing of hers, just trifles," Marianne said. "Everything was given away. Incidentally, we used each other's things now and then. We were confirmed on the same day, although I was older, and Aunt Manon gave each of us a similar pair of beryl earrings, set in gold. After a few years we switched them, so that I really have Louison's now."

"But I've never seen you wearing them," Conrad remarked.

"No," Marianne replied, "I never wear them. One thing I'm sorry about today. Among the things that were stolen was a small and not particularly valuable gift of mine that Louison was very fond of and always had with her. It was a cigarette case, or rather, actually a delicate little snuff case of old silver that someone insisted on giving me, although I never smoked. Louison started smoking quite young, so I gave her the thing, although the person who had given it to me even had my initials engraved on it—M and V."

They fell silent.

Conrad stared into the white glow of the gas flame and after a while said, speaking somewhat more loudly than the silence called for, as though he had to break through a certain blockage of the words in his mouth: "Just how did that awful thing happen? How was Louison killed, and where?"

After he had spoken, there was a short pause, but his wife's reply came firmly and fluently: "Her skull was completely shattered with some blunt object. It happened on a train, at night. . ."

As she spoke, a scream was heard from the street; it mounted to the piercing pitch of despair, filling the room in spite of the closed window. A moment before, they had heard the horn of a car violently blowing three or four times.

Conrad jerked around and stared up at his wife, who was now sitting bolt upright, her eyes aghast, but her head not turned to the window. Then they both rushed to the window, colliding, and wrenched it open.

What had happened was clear from the scene below. A child in a white coat had run from a young woman walking on the sidewalk, had pulled free of her hand and gone tripping across the street, just as a large, handsome car turned the corner from Hans Hayde Strasse into Weissenborn Strasse, its horn blowing. The driver must have realized with horror that the child was paying no attention to his repeated signals; instead, she ran straight toward the car. Seeing the little girl almost at his left front wheel, he had at the last moment desperately swerved. The car jumped up on the sidewalk by the park, almost over-turning, smashed through the low railing close by the birch on the corner, and came to a stop with its front wheels in the soft ground. At the crisis the mother had screamed, giving her child up for lost; and the fact that she had lost hope had been ex-pressed perfectly in her scream. That was what had made it so dreadful. The hastily gathering crowd now begun commending the driver, while some tried to soothe the child—who in those few seconds that decided her life or death had simply crouched, in sheer terror of the huge vehicle swerving wildly in front of her.

Conrad closed the window and drew the yellow curtains. His wife stood motionless for a few moments longer. A harsh furrow had appeared over the base of her nose, giving her face a dark, obstinate, almost violent expression. Castiletz looked at her with amazement—and anxiety. He suddenly and clairvoyantly sensed that, as frequently happens with strong-minded persons, an intense fright was threatening to veer straightway into anger. She turned abruptly and left the room, but without closing the door to the hall. He saw her cross the wide, carpeted expanse of floor, open the bathroom, and switch on the light. Then the door slammed loudly behind her.

There was a rumbling in Conrad's chest, as though the hollow within were revolving around itself like a mill wheel. The thing he had realized—as he watched Marianne crossing the hall—was as unconnected with the events of the past few moments as it was irrefutable in its certainty: he no longer desired his wife.

Conrad leaned against the panel of the door and looked out into the hall, which was partly illuminated by the light from the salon. This new home suddenly seemed like a magic circle whose spells and keys had been lost, so that he was trapped inside it.

He listened. Not a sound came from the bathroom.

With slow footsteps—his legs seemed reluctant to obey him— he started into the hall, and reached the island of table and chairs. The metal of the furniture gleamed in the light that fell through the door. Conrad sat down carefully, like a man with a wooden leg, not moving the chair.

There was continued silence. Then he pricked up his ears: he heard water splashing. That was almost reassuring.

And then loud, stertorous sobbing, swelling evenly. She wept like someone drinking long and deep.

Conrad started up. His legs felt cold to above the knee. But they bore him in five steps to the door of the bathroom. The sobbing was loud, close. "Marianne," he called, knocking. When she did not answer, he tried the door. It yielded; it was unlocked. His wife stood right behind it.

"Good Lord . . ." he said, in an interrogative tone.

"Yes, good Lord!" she retorted, the tears welling from her eyes. "You say that now—but you started it! All that's needed is to mention her name—and it means misery for me. You sat for hours with Mother, looking at her pictures—will I never be free of her? Never! She ruined my life; when I was a girl she tormented me half to death. . . . And now you come along—and again it's Louison, Louison. How horrible it was, that scream! That was her, she did it. She doesn't want us to enjoy our tea hour. We'll never have another, never again. But I don't want Louison, not here. . .

"No!" she screamed, her voice suddenly piercing. "No! Enough! She spoiled everything for me, always, even as a child—oh, you have no idea—I never want to hear her name again. . . ."

He was almost glad that she was raging. Had he been able to examine his own feelings more closely in those strange moments, he would have realized that he was glad that it was impossible to take his wife into his arms to console her. With an absoluteness that forced him to accept the emotional foreground and gave him the calm to do so, the dead girl lay in the background like a landscape, no matter how wildly the living sister gesticulated. And if there were a way out of the encirclement of the present situation, the way out was remote, but in some manner attainable, like the last green streak of twilight sky above the horizon. Conrad was perfectly calm; and so, in a curious fashion, he remained faithful to Louison Veik in the midst of the roaring tempest.

There was a tinkle; something bright shattered and rained down into the bathtub. Marianne had seized the nearest glass and hurled it against the tile wall. Then she sagged into Conrad's arms, her face resting on his shoulder. He smelled her hair, which had a dry and doll-like, innocuous fragrance, like flax or cotton.

28 ߑ

IF anyone says, "Nonsense!" in regard to something, it generally shows that he was not inwardly dealt with the matter.

It must be admitted that Conrad became increasingly aware of one distinct disadvantage in no longer having a bedroom to himself. Those brief moments of composure which he needed to survey the nearer and farther realms of his life and to see whether all was in order—those moments had more and more become associated, during the past several years, with the moments before dropping off to sleep and after awakening. And now, when he spread out these rings, beginning with the innermost one, he promptly encountered his wife on his right hand. Across the way, at Number 5 Hans Hayde Strasse, it had sometimes happened that he would feel the impulse, at night, to conduct some such rapid survey of his living space. At such times he had actually got up, continuing erect what he had begun in a recumbent position. Here, married, that was not possible, for it would have raised questions.

Conrad was rarely home alone. And in the beginning it did not help much even when he was. These rooms were singularly noiseless, for the building was relatively new; all the doors and locks closed and snapped to without a sound. Footsteps in the wide hall were completely muted. The result of all this silence was that he felt like a ghost, uncanny even to himself, when he wandered through these expanses of space totally at his disposal. Moreover, he often thought himself alone when he had for some time ceased to be so, when Marianne had meanwhile returned. Even the sharpest ear could fail to hear her arrival—if, say, he sat in the "library." For the front door made not the faintest audible sound when it was opened; the modern lock obeyed the lightest pressure.

In time, to be sure, the broad divan in the study developed around itself the enclosing ring that shut off the rest of the apartment, and the room became a kind of secondary bedroom. Its firmness held even when the apartment was moderately animated by Marianne or one of the servants. All such animation remained moderate. Coming from a large household, which in the last few years preceding her marriage she had run practically alone, Marianne encountered no domestic difficulties or complications— especially since she never lacked for excellently trained household help.

Thus Conrad Castiletz was able to spread around him the necessary ring after all, with the divan as its center. And now that he could again practice his old vigilance, he was able to come to an accounting with a good many aspects of his life that required reflection. The first which came under consideration was this marriage of his. What struck him about this, when he gave thought to it—and what struck him as the decisive point—was that the venture was not at all in vain. After all was said and done, he had renounced his freedom in full consciousness of what he was doing. (Being no thinker by profession, Conrad did not examine this vague concept any more closely. Otherwise he would have come to the conclusion that the notion of freedom had taken shape in Reutlingen.) In this sense, then, everything seemed to him to be in order. Moreover, that order was reinforced by another reassuring fact: as his father's heir, he had become well-to-do in his own right and could almost have lived on this scale out of his own means. There was no way of proving that the money he was due to come into had made any impression upon the Veik family. And yet Conrad knew for a certainty that this factor had been considered within the counsels of the family, and was held to his advantage. He had also learned— from Eisenmann—that the plan was afoot to invest the son-in-law with the power to sign for the firm at the webbing mill; the directors were hesitating only because of his extreme youth. Eisenmann wanted this recognition of Conrad's position; in any case, although he looked so young, his lack of years was never present in anyone's consciousness. It was impossible to think of him as "not mature enough." He gave the impression of being thirty—the most indefinite of ages.

But from his post on the divan such musings were still inner rings and, as it were, preludes. They would begin when he had coffee brought in to him in the study at six o'clock, as in his bachelor days—only not by Frau Schubert, but by a middle-aged chambermaid, who also placed his slippers in front of the divan and carried away his street shoes.

For several days there had been flowers in the room—a little attention on Marianne's part. Among them were two pots of flowering hyacinths. Their novel, invigorating fragrance struck Conrad's nostrils along with the smell of the newspaper he was reading, and won out. He lowered the newspaper and leaned back. As expected, in fact as if on signal, memories vivid and shining pressed forward, recollections of former areas of his life. This sort of thronging or wafting up of memories had occurred frequently during the past few days. All those images pertained to his early home; all floated in a strangely disturbing light, like the light of a brand-new morning. The taste and smells that belonged to them, and even the appropriate physical feelings, entered his whole body. And as he absented himself from the life he was actually leading at the present time, Conrad very gradually began—to have a past. And strangely enough, that past loosened the embrace of the here and now, caused it to appear no longer only as progress by comparison with the earlier state, but on the contrary as an arbitrarily added supplement of foreign material, like a wooden leg attached to a living stump.

It always struck him, when he had come thus far—come, that is, to the point of wondering at this massive desk in the room, for example, or at his having a wife who would be coming home —it always struck him that Louison's face was the truly vital, kindred continuation of his past life, not a supplement of foreign and arbitrary material. She, too, stood in a disquieting light, but it was the same as that in which his earlier years presented themselves. That light reached to the crooked canal with its distant factory smokestacks, and the streets down to the water and the bridge—everything that Conrad had not seen and not noticed the last time he was in his native city. This light reached to a certain point, and if he looked closer, Ida Plangl stood at this point, by the last streetcar stop, stood and waited. From there on, as he moved toward his present here and now, everything became coarser and darker, opaque as the wood of this heavy furniture; became a kind of gigantic lid, of those nature as a lid he now had a certain knowledge. For that was the true and most secret effect of Louison upon him. She had appeared at this present end of his life, on the side of the lid under which he now lay; and yet she was made of the same material as the first part of his life, which extended back from that last stop of the streetcar where Ida waited.

Not a thinker by profession and utterly unaccustomed to meditation, Conrad would start up with a shock after a few seconds of such finespun reflections. The coffee would be splashed out of the cup because he had knocked against the small table by the divan. But the images that had thronged his mind had attained such denseness, proved so real and resistant, that they left behind in him the feeling that something, something had to be done.

He did not know how to use that feeling, how to do anything with it. Nevertheless, the singularity of it guided his footsteps in a singular direction as he now, passing by the desk, crossed the room and opened the door to the dining room and then to the large corner drawing room.

It was perhaps the first time that he had taken this route. He was accustomed to enter his study from the hall and to leave it the same way.

The room was empty, highly polished; the small armchairs were hidden under chintz slipcovers and lined up along the walls. It was still daylight; today, on a Saturday, Conrad had taken his hour of rest somewhat earlier than usual; he had not returned to the mill after the midday meal. As he walked over the echoing and slightly creaking parquet flooring, he had the feeling that he was approaching some decision, or some weighty and important matter. It was like feeling his own breadth and solidity; he was conscious of his shoulders. At the window facing on Weissenborn Strasse, he pulled the drapery cord. The curtain swished back. He opened wide both sides of the casement window and looked out at the park.

The weather had turned mild. The park showed no green; it lay exposed, fading into its own expanse and into the innumerable fine lines of its bare branches. It was still; there was no noise from the streets. Conrad became acutely conscious of his own former apartment, off to the right and behind him, down on Hans Hayde Strasse; he felt it as small and compressed, pushed out to the furthest rim of his being by this new environment which surrounded him.

He was supposed to see his father-in-law this afternoon; such visits were quite frequent nowadays. He had really come to a friendly footing with Magistrate Veik only quite recently. Herr von Hohenlocher, to be sure, maintained that it was impossible to know the "two Veiks" because they "smothered everything and anything and everybody with their invariable cheerfulness." But he was wrong about that, at least in regard to Conrad's father-in-law. Yet Hohenlocher went so far as to suggest that Conrad someday bring one of the two brothers a really disagreeable bit of news (their tax situation offered no such opportunity), or ask them a favor which would be distinctly inconvenient for them, "in order at last to see the true faces of these professional smilers."

That was not true. Robert Veik, in fact, was even disposed to a certain melancholia. Conrad thought of the good many hours in the course of the past winter which he had spent with his father-in-law in Veik's study, chatting about this and that, about a good many things, in fact in the end about almost everything. . . . It had been an entirely new atmosphere for Conrad: the deep easy chairs into which one sank; a sip of Rhine wine from the glass now and then; each time astonished anew at the subtly varied and brilliant fullness of the taste. They sat in a mist of cigar smoke. And there, for the first time, Conrad had made the acquaintance of those small, light, imported cigars. They were a part of the picture. He liked them, although he did not smoke elsewhere, only at these chats.

Now, standing at the open window, he looked forward to another chat, and this afternoon became animated at the prospect. Marianne had gone shopping in town with her mother; in the evening he and Marianne were going to the opera, and therefore he must be back in time to fetch her and to change his clothes. As he considered this, and as he closed the windows and pulled the curtain, he once again felt the enrichment accorded him by those few minutes on the divan, despite the uneasiness they had brought in their wake.

Since he had a good deal of time, he decided to walk. The door closed noiselessly behind him; you never heard so much as a click from this lock, and Conrad had formed the habit of pressing his palm against the outside of the door to make certain that it was securely shut.

The air was filled with dampness. The gravel in the park was still soft, and the view over the lawns and clumps of trees veiled. Everything smelled of earth. Conrad regained the asphalt near the teashop with the large red sign. Here began a long but narrow street down which the streetcar—Line 3—ran. This was Wackenroder Strasse, whose other end terminated in one of the main avenues at the center of town. Shop was ranged beside shop here—small shops that dealt in everyday things. The sidewalk hardly had room for two pedestrians. The streetcar bells tinkled, and where the cars stopped, the waiting automobiles growled at the passengers boarding and leaving, to hurry up about it. Over this bustle, in which each person's destination seemed fundamentally different from his neighbor's, twilight began to fall; but it remained hanging like a tent above the middle of the street, caught on the procession of street lights which long before its coming had already begun to glow. Conrad entered the enormouly wide König Strasse. Here night had already been proclaimed, prematurely, so to speak; but the still open, still dusky sky had to retreat and escape to the darkness above from the ladders, rows, zigzags, and bends of marching lights on the avenue, rows of letters in red and blue, gigantic slates covered with brilliantly green writing, and a few distant but powerful glowing points on the eaves of the roofs. On the roadway the cars pulled ribbon upon ribbon of light along with them.

29

"NO, my dear Koko" (this was the magistrate's name for his son-in-law, a simplification of the childhood Kokosch), "that is hopeless. There is nothing more to be done about it. There are cases in which reason has to abandon the field. Here fate clearly wants to teach us a lesson. In my long practice I have naturally seen one or two crimes that were never atoned for, perhaps for lack of evidence. But, in Louison's case, the prosecuting attorney could not even draw up an indictment; there was not even evidence enough for that. The man Henry Peitz was never formally charged, and the police were forced to release him after a short time."

A streamer of smoke floating horizontally over the table gradually dropped away to the right; its edge touched Conrad's wineglass. At that moment he felt that it was impossible to let Louison's case alone, altogether impossible for him, that is.

The magistrate fell silent. His big, shaved face looked troubled, but by no means crushed by grief and the burden of life. Even now it preserved the vigorous expression of a composed intelligence. It was not a bold intellect; it probably never stirred up those depths which might have cast doubt on its own proficiency. But it was surely adequate for the tasks of this life, and humanly ennobled by the vibrations of experience, including the experience of sorrow. Robert Veik's face had something northern about it. With his stubby nose, broad cheeks, and not very deeply embedded eyes, he might have been taken for a Swede. His blond hair was short and curly, and still thick at the back of his head.

"Quite aside from that, I myself, after carefully considering the matter, had to conclude that Peitz was entirely innocent. And I had to think of how one would feel oneself, an innocent man arrested on suspicion of robbery and murder, and held in custody for weeks The man must have suffered a considerable business loss, besides, for which he had no legal redress—to say nothing at all of the moral damage."

Such was the wall Conrad Castiletz had come up against—and irrationally, in spite of everything, he was looking for a door in it. All the while they had been sitting there, he had been studying a large photograph, framed and under glass, which hung on the wall above the leather sofa. It was really a portrait, though not of a person, but of a cat. An Angora cat, whose beautiful head filled the whole of the picture. The profundities in those wide open, convex, and oblique eyes exerted, even from the photograph, an effect that was almost overwhelming. The head of the cat had the majesty of a kind of animal deity.

"That was Louison's cat," the magistrate said, noticing that

Conrad had been staring at the picture. "His name was Chichi Peter, and he died not long after she did. She loved him dearly and often said that he looked like her, out of empathy."

"She was not so far wrong," Conrad said eagerly, "as far as I can tell from pictures of her. . . . Those oblique eyes, somewhat pressed upward by the cheeks, for example . . ."

"You often look like a cat yourself, Koko," the magistrate said.

Albert Lehnder used to say the same thing, Conrad recalled.

"Then Louison and I may have remotely resembled each other, by way of cats," he countered.

"Quite so," the magistrate exclaimed, laughing. "But, in all seriousness, there is some facial similarity between you and Louison; I realized that the moment I saw you, the first time you came here. It's a fact, and it certainly is remarkable."

They fell silent. Robert Veik refilled the glasses. His face disappeared behind clouds of smoke, and out of the midst of the clouds Conrad heard him saying: "Yes, she is sensitive about that—Marianne—as you no doubt have had occasion to notice by now. It's the sort of thing you understand better when you know the past. The man involved was an important person—no longer living, incidentally. What brought him to Leipzig was an exhibition of contemporary French painters; he was supervising the hanging of the pictures. As a matter of fact, of the whole group, he himself was the best known abroad. The most famous of them, you might say. Derainaux was his name—you've probably heard it. He was thirty-five at the time, much older than my girls, at the height of his career, and a fine figure of a man. After the show opened, he gave a talk in German on contemporary French painting. My wife and I attended, and Marianne went with us, more by chance than out of interest in the subject. A few days later Derainaux came to our house. Everyone used to come in those days; we knew practically everyone in Leipzig, our circle of acquaintants was like a large net which caught all the big and little fish. The person who had arranged the show happened

to be one of our friends. I liked Derainaux immediately. He was
the most natural man I've ever seen, a Breton by birth and so
really of Germanic-Norman descent, but blessed with all the
charm of a true Parisian. As far as Marianne was concerned, I
saw the whole thing right from the start. It was like the bursting
of a bud, one of those quiet but inhumanly powerful explosions
which have always made me feel that spring is an uncanny and
cruel season. I regard a flowering orchard as a place of violence.
It was love—I don't say a great or passionate love—but love as an
indivisible magnitude, a prime number of life. It was a force,
like the inertia of a planet or the precisely measurable pressure
in the capillaries of the stem of a plant. Derainaux, as far as I
could see, was not thrown into any such unequivocal emotional
state, though he himself may have thought he was. He suc-
cumbed to a kind of enchantment. I rather think that he was
enchanted by the sudden appearance in the flesh of a fixed conception which he as a Frenchman had of the German girl, the
German Gretchen. Seen from the French point of view, so to
speak. . . . We're always happy when we see a type perfectly
typified. We want the Englishman to be as English, the Viennese
as Viennese as possible. It's a kind of testimonial to order in the
world, order in spite of everything. . . . At any rate, Marianne,
as she was in those days, amazingly and delightfully confirmed
that order for him. And so Derainaux stayed in Leipzig. He
stayed month after month, rented a studio and set to work. At
the time I distinctly felt that for Derainaux, the artist, all this
was his 'German experience.' Just that, no less and no more.
Have I said 'more'? Well, actually there cannot be anything
'more,' more than an experience, that is. . . ."

But Robert Veik broke off, preferring not to luxuriate in his
own words. For a space he forgot to go on with the topic; he
dropped the thread he was spinning. His heavy, strong, benevo-
lent face, whose features told at least this much, that he had
fought bravely to attain a balanced view of life (and what bet-

ter praise can we give a mature man, I ask?)—his face clouded over with pensiveness. It was the look the gods confer upon those who suddenly see something long familiar in an entirely new light, the inward turning of expression that comes with insight.

"There are situations in life," he said, continuing at last, "in which we foresee what is coming without taking measures to fend it off. Yet we neglect to do so, not out of carelessness, or because we are postponing taking action, with a bad conscience. In fact, we feel no twinges of conscience at all, which shows that the paralysis from which we suffer has a deeper, or perhaps a higher, origin. But then when the foreseen event at last takes place under the foreseen circumstances, we feel we are entitled, in some strange way, to regard it as invalid because, after all, we anticipated it long ago. We see that sort of thing most clearly in connection with trifles. The glass at the edge of the table, for example—we know it is going to fall, and know it long enough to do something to prevent the fall. But we don't take the glass and set it farther back. When soon afterwards it lies in splinters on the floor, we are reluctant to recognize that anything has happened, precisely because of our foreknowledge. This phenomenon might be explained rationally as due to a remote memory in every man of a condition in which he was not yet born and isolated from the rest of the universe, but actually existed only as a tiny fraction or atom of God. And God's conceptual power or imagination is so overpowering that each stirring of it promptly carries matter along with it, moves and shapes, obstructs or smashes matter. As a general rule, all man has kept of his sublime source are the pretensions, not the powers. And those pretensions promptly assert themselves when something happens which is already over and done with in his imagination. Nevertheless, it goes ahead and happens, and the happening offends man and shows him the impotence of his feeble spirit.

"I've gone into all this in order to describe the state, the state of equilibrium I might say, in which I found myself when confronted with the situation between Derainaux and Marianne. I foresaw the whole thing. I suppose my wife did too; she understood it in her own fashion, and took action. Quite quickly, in fact. She contrived to prevent Louison's appearance on the stage, which proves that she had the same view of the case as I, only she did not feel the inevitability of the outcome, of which I had not the slightest doubt. Louison was in Paris at the time and wrote that she would like to spend the rest of the summer in Deauville; she was staying in Paris with some friend of ours, who used to go there every year. Originally, my wife was by no means pleased to have the child gone so long. But now she encouraged Louison, saw to it that she had plenty of money, and even wrote that she might also come to Deauville. . . . Well, those are details which I watched as if they were a glass of water on the point of falling off the edge of the table. I felt that all my wife's arrangements were at bottom pointless, and I was right. Two weeks later, Louison turned up in Leipzig."

Conrad, remembering hints that Herr von Hohenlocher had once dropped, listened with greedy eagerness. Every scrap of information concerning Louison was precious to him. She, not Marianne, was to him the central figure in the magistrate's story. He avidly absorbed these facts whenever opportunity offered. Tact and consideration generally forbade him to ask anything of his own accord.

"The essential thing about the next incident," the magistrate continued quietly, "seems to me that it was far from being the first time such a thing had happened. It was the first time only in this particular context, given such insistent pressure in the capillaries of life. But basically a mechanism was operating which I'd watched since the childhood and adolescence of the two girls. I'd noticed it quite casually, I say. As a glass perched at the edge of the table, but one which had not yet fallen and made a real smash which would have forced—at least in hindsight—a clear recognition of the danger. . . . One significant aspect of the whole thing, to which we'd gradually grown accustomed, was the fact that when the girls were small everyone would be much taken with Marianne, charmed by her rosy cheeks, her straw-blonde braids, her firm, plump legs, and sensible way of talking. People paid less attention to Louison initially. There was something all dark and thin and soft and modest about her, so that she receded into the background. But, sooner or later, those who at first adored and spoiled blonde, sturdy little Marianne would succumb to Louison.

"I might add that parents are none too ready to see their children, nor children their parents, as real living human beings. Rather, they conceive notions of how the others should be. There seems to be no room in children's minds, for example, for the idea that a father, say, may have a life of his own, a life story of his own. . . . Well, to my mind the parents, since they have more awareness of the problem, should shatter such delusions. But when you have been observing something out of the corners of your eyes, it takes more strength than you will believe to fix your full gaze upon it, give it the sharp outlines of a fact with a frank look, or by the magic of a word clearly formulated in the mind. . . . No, you go on looking out of the corners of your eyes— and so the glass remains standing on the edge of the table. You'll soon see what I am getting at, in the case of Derainaux. You see, earlier, from the very start, I'd had a dim knowledge of the peculiar relationship between these two children, the love and the hatred. And, as a father, you simply repudiate hatred when it appears between children, instead of looking straight at and into it—trying to get at the reasons for the hatred, I mean. Later on I did think it over closely, and had many talks about it with my wife. In her own way she understood it much as I did, and, like me, too late. At least the real clarity of vision came too late.

"There are bridge people. That is the formula I found. There are people who serve as bridges leading to others, and their true relationship to those others consists solely in this function. In the end they are passed over, walked on. Such was the compulsive mechanism between Marianne and Louison. It always had been. But later on the mechanism started grinding the heavier, more nourishing grain of life, instead of the partiality of aunts, the friendliness of children, and all sorts of pampering presents, which in the past had regularly shifted from little Marianne to Louison. . . . You see, people talked a lot of nonsense about the matter. They said, for example, that when Louison came back to Leipzig her 'spirited nature and her understanding of the problems of an artist such as Derainaux immediately put humdrum Marianne in the shade.' But these were clichés. That was merely the form that the eternal relationship took in this particular case —although of course it is understandable that people mistook the given content at the time for the eternal form, or mistook the grain for the mill, to be true to the earlier figure of speech. To this day I am deeply convinced that even if Louison had been there from the start Derainaux would have begun with Marianne; he would never have missed out on his 'German experience,' but would have put her behind him in the same fashion, without ever having had her—I trust you will forgive my putting this so bluntly. Perhaps in an artist the presentiment which I spoke of earlier is really more intense and his imaginative life is to some extent closer to the mind of his Creator and sole Sovereign. So that this imagination can at least change him, if not the life of the outside world. . . ."

In Conrad's mind one vague thought crossed with another. He recalled the evening when his father, upon entering the dining room, had promptly been converted once more into a father and hence into a figure of authority, whereas during his absence Conrad had succeeded (knowing or believing him to be with the Hedeleg woman) in seeing him as "alive." Then, again, Conrad felt, and not for the first time, a strange guilty conscience because of the scene with Marianne after the awful scream from the street . . . although everything was in order there, that is to say, strictly speaking he was completely innocent of having brought about that shock to his wife's nervous system. And yet, when he was with his parents-in-law, the incident came to mind quite often. He had even wondered whether Marianne might have told her mother something about it.

"Well," Robert Veik said after a pause, "I've really told you everything worth telling. Louison was now forced into playing a part—her essential part. But no one would believe she was forced, least of all her older sister. Not Derainaux either, who tried to win Louison without the slightest prospect of success. Perhaps she appeared like a greeting from his native land, not so much in a local sense, but in a much more profound sense. . . ."

As his father-in-law spoke, Conrad felt as if something stronger than himself were carring him along, as if it were lifting him from his secure footing. And his hands, which sought to seize the reins of order, caught hold of nothing. They were empty. For some minutes he floated along that way, as if over thin ice; then the ground underfoot became solid and opaque once more.

"Of course it's true that she showed 'understanding of all the problems of an artist.' Given her nature, she couldn't help doing that. She had an extraordinary respect for Derainaux—much more than that, as a matter of fact: with a precise and sure instinct she sensed his true stature. And ultimately that is all that counts in dealing with a man of the spirit. Given such a recognition of stature, any specific criticism is automatically eliminated because every frailty on the part of such a person takes its place in the organic whole. As a man, the Frenchman meant nothing at all to her. To this day, though, my wife and I are the only ones who really know that. We knew it at the time, long before Derainaux's flight from Leipzig. But, imagine, we could never dare even to hint such a thing to Marianne. Her suffering was so terrible, so much like the suffering of a wounded animal, that she had to attribute to Louison every bad intention imaginable, all along.

As if to stupefy her grief by hatred, a hatred which like a live spark leaped back along her whole life to her childhood and enlarged the situation I've described, magnified it in retrospect and made it seem Louison's doing."

Conrad remembered the casual and, as it now seemed to him, frivolous manner in which Herr von Hohenlocher had sketched in this story. He felt sudden vexation—but at the same time something akin to envy for such a detached conception of these matters. In fact, he actually longed for Herr von Hohenlocher's indifference.

"The following year that terrible thing happened to Louison," Veik said.

"When exactly was that?" Conrad asked, though it was unnecessary to do so; his father had given him all the particulars, that time he had inquired.

"It will have been eight years ago this coming summer," Robert Veik replied.

Conrad could have burst out with the fact that at the time of the misfortune, or shortly before, he had been in this very city, a boy of sixteen, visiting his aunt, Erika von Spresse. But at this moment, after the avidity with which he had absorbed Veik's story, he felt a tangible and almost oppressive fatigue. This made him shrink even from the small effort of saying what he had to say, and from the possibility that he might then have to answer questions. He remained silent.

"Derainaux did some ten paintings of Louison," the magistrate continued after a while. "Those paintings were magnificent and in his best manner—except for one, which arose out of a passing conviction—I might also say obsession—that Louison's personality could best be expressed in the style of another age. And so he did her as if he had been a contemporary of Watteau. Of course the thing failed; that is to say, he did a 'perfect likeness,' which was really almost an atrocity in terms of painting. Derainaux left that portrait to us. That is, it remained in his studio, and after we ceased to hear from him, we took charge of it for safekeeping. Two years later, we read his obituary notice in the newspapers. My wife went to Paris, hoping she might find the great portraits of Louison among his works. At the time Derainaux painted those pictures, it had been impossible to persuade him to part with a single one, although we were prepared to pay any price he asked. But he wouldn't give up a single one; he carried them all off with him. In Paris, immediately after his death, the dealers fell upon everything. Nevertheless, my wife did manage to see all the remaining paintings, and not one of those portraits of Louison was among them. They had disappeared without a trace. Probably he destroyed them all. The result is we have only the one which hangs in the little salon. You know it, of course."

With that, Conrad's father-in-law concluded his story. After a brief pause he resumed the conversation on another plane, touching upon one subject and then another, including his professional career. He made the rather curious remark that his position and work as a high official in the judiciary seemed to him somehow not quite compatible with the lavish tone of his household and the luxurious style of life of his wife and daughters. To his wife, who came from a Rhineland industrial family, that sort of thing was natural. But he felt a magistrate should live like the elder Cato. Then he fell silent for some time, and at last remarked that after Louison's terrible fate his practice on the bench had become a torment to him; he dreaded every criminal trial. His scholarly studies in the history of law, he added, gave him some ground for hope that within the foreseeable future he would be exchanging the judge's bench for the chair of a university lecturer. In all honesty, he would be extremely happy to do so.

For Conrad it was time to go. As he walked through the wide French doors and down the staircase into the warm hall, he felt something beneath him like a new room. It was nothing he could enter yet, or even peer into; but its presence exerted an upward pressure, was somehow sustaining, so that Conrad felt as if he were walking with lighter step, bearing a smaller weight. The residential street on which Robert Veik's house was situated—Benningsen Strasse—led straight to the end of König Strasse. Conrad felt a sudden resistance to the idea of plunging into its turmoil of traffic and jagged ribbons of light. It was as if all that would act like salt on some open sore. Since there were cabs on the corner, he took one. As the cab turned into Wackenroder Strasse, it veered so sharply that Conrad was jostled to one side. He saw that the narrow street which earlier had been bustling was almost deserted now.

Marianne was dressing. Conrad made haste, and when he re-entered the bedroom, in his evening dress, she was sitting in front of the mirror, choosing her jewelry. She wore white and silver, this time with a deep décolleté; her bosom seemed broad, full, and almost overpowering, her shoulders jutted back firmly like swan's wings as he stood behind her chair. Conrad leaned forward slightly and reached over his wife's bare shoulder into one of the small open dressing-table drawers which held a number of jewel cases. He picked up one; it was of leather, marbleized a greenish brown. He snapped open the lid, and a pair of earrings lay before him on ochre-colored velvet: green beryls in heavy gold settings.

"Are these the ones?" he asked.

"Yes," she said, half turning to him.

"Won't you wear them some time?" Conrad said.

"Not tonight," she replied in a conciliatory tone. "This dress only looks well with pearls, though I don't like pearls. Besides, the gold setting is too heavy to wear. After a while they hurt.

He bent over the low neck of her dress; his lips moved softly, close to her right ear.

"Wear them some time—at night," he said.

In Marianne's eye a little star splintered; it splintered into a kaleidoscope of possibilities. Among these may well have been the impulse to clench her fist and hit her husband in the face.

But she was turned toward him, and as he raised his head slightly their glances met. In his was grief, not intense, but intelligible. In her words and tone there now recurred an attitude and a movement that dated back to the earlier days of their marriage. Perhaps it was a movement akin to that with which she had once mounted the stairs in front of him, on their honeymoon in Italy. And so, out of the kaleidoscope in her eyes, a mild central pattern came into focus. And she said: "Yes, if you like." For not only he hoped. So did she.

EVERY MAN

A MURDERER

Part Three

∾⑃ 30 ⑂∾

RARELY INDEED does a vessel of connubial bliss set out from port without, sooner or later, a bogy man's creeping out of its hold and appearing on deck. And to tell the truth, that means little, especially when we consider that marriage is itself a succession of complicated balancing acts and oscillations between its constantly threatening, almost institutionalized end, with periodic relapses into continuability. Among the crew of our ship, incidentally, Frau Schubert was to be observed right from the start (Herr von Hohenlocher permitted her to augment her earnings by such outside jobs, now and then). While the young couple was still in Rome, she had swarmed up the ladders with new curtains.

Otherwise, for entertainment and society, whoever happened to be around had signed articles on the good ship *Castiletz*. For instance, Peter Duracher, with all the "young people from the tennis courts," a group containing several whited sepulchers tanned by the sun. Herr von Hohenlocher called these male and female disciples of Duracher the "Caterva"—as the Roman historian Sallust had once called Catilina's band of friends. Not that he thought Duracher, whom he could not abide, a Catilina. From his own collection, Herr von Hohenlocher contributed the architect Lissenbrech. He had once taken Conrad, long before the engagement, to call on Lissenbrech, so that he might see an exact model of the battle of Redfontein in the Boer War. This was one of the attractions at Herr Lissenbrech's. In fact, at intervals there would be a new battle, from Hohenfriedberg to Saint-Privat, from Colombo to Königgrätz, all represented with many thousands of tin soldiers, miniature works of art, meticulously correct in uniform and arms. They ran, fired, fell, knelt, or lay wounded on huge tables several square yards in area; they poured in assault waves up the slopes of artificial hills, sprang from burning houses (Lissenbrech was always on the lookout for handsome models), or rode to the attack on horseback, in bright uniforms with hussar cloaks streaming out behind them. Not a detail was missing. Back at the Boer camp at Redfontein, the cows were being milked, water pails were carried, and the meal cooked. Underlying these spectacles were precise historical, geographical, and strategic studies, and when Lissenbrech put together one of his battles, it represented a particular hour on the memorable day, and the exact stage of the battle at that time. According to the inventory Lissenbrech kept, he owned sixty-two thousand five hundred tin soldiers.

He was not bellicose. He had honorably served his country, but was hardly one of those people who have not lived through anything more important than the war years, so that in their own sense of personal value these years form a kind of tumor which can never again be absorbed into the rest of real life; which remain hard and intact, occasionally breaking open and pouring out the same stories in the same excessive manner. An oppressive manner too, for these stories are used to keep down the up-and-coming youth, who must respectfully bend before these anecdotes, although they are in no way to blame for not having participated in those grand events. The good architect Lissenbrech was not that kind of storyteller; his role as director of battles could not be explained in any such simple fashion. In fact,

as you got to know him you ceased to understand the hobby at all.
It seemed difficult or impossible to establish any connection between his personality and this game of his.

Occasionally, however, the connection flashed upon you as you
watched him standing at the enormous table surveying his regiments. It flashed with a bright, a white glow in his blue eyes,
which suddenly became transparent bullets and, like a foreign
body, like a dangerous explosive, cast a flicker over his face, his
person, and his comfortable home. Then you realized that this
good-natured, if somewhat irritable, man was capable not of
vexation, but of wrath, of a profound, incurable, inward-turned,
inward-consuming rage.

Perhaps that is why the regiments marched—who could say?
Herr von Hohenlocher, for his part, owed to the architect an
experience which, he often said later, was among the most un-
forgettable in his life: he could not think of his life apart from it;
without it, he would not have been able "to regard this life as
lived."

For two weeks before that sunny autumnal afternoon when
Conrad Castiletz had been introduced to Fräulein Marianne Veik
and had played such strenuous games of tennis with Peter
Duracher, Frau Erika von Spresse had held another of her intellectual evenings, the kind she so favored. (Herr von Hohenlocher was probably exaggerating when he compared Conrad's
aunt with that infernal goat from whose udder the devil's grandmother took the milk for her morning coffee. But Frau von
Spresse was gaunt enough, in all conscience.) The evening passed
in a thoroughly genteel and copious manner; genteel since everyone deemed it necessary, along with the black fabric of evening
dress, to display some artistic or intellectual pursuit like a white
tie; copious because everything was provided which a guest's
heart could desire, including the services of a string quartet.

Hohenlocher and Castiletz skulked outside during the music,
and in the intermission stepped into that room decently finished

with tiles and marble which adjoined the spacious cloakroom. Herr von Hohenlocher opened one of the white-painted cell doors, and immediately stepped back, startled, and stood still, shaken by so overpowering an impression that his eyes filled with tears. Castiletz rushed to his side. Almost simultaneously with the opening of the door, a cataract roared in the cubicle.

Erect in the clean bowl stood the architect. Barefoot, moreover, with trousers rolled up to his knees, at regular intervals activating the flush—as he began to explain, while his good-natured face, in the grip of this embarrassing situation, reflected a shock that might have dated back to the fourth or fifth year of his life.

His new and much too tight patent-leather shoes, together with his socks, stood quietly in a corner of the cubicle, while his tormented feet received intermittent gushes of cooling water. The architect thought it necessary to explain that the lavatory was not so handy for a foot bath; moreover, he had feared that one of the servants might come in from the cloakroom and find him in the unusual and ridiculous attitude of bathing his feet. Yet in his urgency he had failed to bolt the door properly.

But what use was it to come forth with such reasonable explanations of the situation. A curtain of tears veiled Herr von Hohenlocher's face, while his laughter became almost inaudible, so rapid was its rate of vibration.

However, Lissenbrech was rescued from his predicament. As soon as Hohenlocher had caught his breath, he rushed to the telephone and could be heard rapping out: "Schubert? Wrap up those old patent-leather shoes of mine, take a cab, and bring them over here to Frau von Spresse. And hurry!"

She came, and brought release from torture. Even before she arrived, the rescuer had pulled off one of his own comfortable shoes and the architect had tried it on—with one eye laughing and one weeping.

Conrad sometimes saw Herr Lissenbrech at Hohenlocher's, on

evenings when Hohenlocher had a few friends in for drinks; Conrad was fairly often invited on these occasions. There he met, for example, Doctor Velten, a neurologist who had enjoyed Hohenlocher's special esteem ever since, bored and wearied by his patients' endless accounts of their sufferings, he had curtly remarked to one such hypochondriac: "Please, while you talk put this mask over your face," and handed him a carnival mask that happened to be hanging on the wall. Whereupon the patient sat, with a huge red nose and a white walrus mustache, gravely confessing his inhibitions and obsessions. Thus the consultation provided some amusement for the doctor, who had all he could do to keep from laughing. Doctor Velten was a public health officer and found his modest salary quite sufficient; he devoted all his free time to research on the mental retardation of children. However, there were a number of mature ne'er-do-wells and semi-idiots who insisted on ventilating their dubious inner lives to him alone. They crowded his consulting room, and he often had to flee from their endless importunities. Doctor Velten was an unusually tall man, oddly careless in dress; he looked rather as though he had forgotten to undress the night before. He enjoyed considerable prestige in professional circles. In his manner of talking he outdid Herr von Hohenlocher in his game. Listening to the doctor, you had the impression that he was simply dropping his sentences the way you might lose matches from your trousers pocket.

This time, when Castiletz arrived at Hans Hayde Strasse 5 around nine o'clock in the evening, a fourth man whom he had not seen before was leaning against the stove in the big room. He introduced himself as Chief Inspector Inkrat of the city police. Herr von Hohenlocher had included Inkrat in his collection under the zoological classification of *Varanus aridus Inkrat.* And the fact was that there was something dry and reptilian about the man. You were struck, when you looked closer, by the way his head was sheared clear of everything that was not absolutely indispensable. Hardly any eyebrows or eyelashes. Almost completely bald. His gaze seemed to come from lidless eyes, and it would have seemed quite natural for them to be occasionally veiled by a nictitating membrane. The pear-shaped head scarcely ever moved, and the tall, broad-shouldered body similarly avoided every needless change of position. Hard muscles seemed to be in a state of rest beneath his clothes. His speech was sparse and lean too, dryly reptilian. It seemed never to suffer disarrangement or rearrangement from onsets of emotion.

Varanus aridus shook hands with Conrad and resumed his position by the stove. Doctor Velten sprawled across part of the divan —beside which stood the table with the drinks—distributing his length negligently here and there, while the architect, more rounded and hamsterlike, sat all of one piece, leaning forward, arms hugging his knees, at the edge of the couch. Today there was a second table covered with bottles, at which Hohenlocher, toward the rear of the room, was busying himself.

"Have a drink," he said to Conrad. "You're going to be tested in a moment. After all, you should still know something; you escaped from the schools more recently than the rest of us."

"So long as it's not a question of dyeing or textile chemistry," Conrad said, tipping the bluish glass. The gin tasted remarkably good to him. Herr von Hohenlocher refilled his glass.

"No, you're being tested on history," he said.

"Into the schools, out of the schools, only the good Lord loves scholars and fools," Doctor Velten said.

"I beg your pardon—what is the bearing of that?" Herr von Hohenlocher asked.

"None at all," Velten said.

"Then it's all right," Hohenlocher replied. "Now, Herr Castiletz, what do you know about the Spanish Inquisition?"

"Hm," Conrad said. "They burned people at the stake . . ."

"They weren't the only ones," came the voice from the stove.

"Unsatisfactory," the architect opined.

"Take your seat," Herr von Hohenlocher said to Conrad.

"We were talking . . ." the architect explained, turning to Conrad. "But what interests me most about the whole story," he went on, "is this: how do we happen to have such accurate, well-founded information about the internal organization and practices of the sinister institution?"

This inquiry was greeted with general silence. Quite a while passed before a dry voice from the stove said: "The last secretary general of the Inquisition—in the nineteenth century, no less—was a man named Llorente. He was hostile to the institution. All the archives were accessible to him, and after the dissolution of the Inquisition in Spain, he published a documentary history of it in several volumes. Our knowledge derives principally from them."

Having delivered himself of this statement, his mouth snapped shut like a letter box. It was wide, but almost without lips.

"Knowledge as catastrophe," Doctor Velten said. Actually, he was thinking aloud and happened to omit a few words.

"But how is it you know all that?" the architect said with frank astonishment.

"I once wanted to write a study of the secret police throughout history. The Inquisition might be considered a kind of police empowered to enforce dogma. In connection with these researches, I read Llorente's book."

"What a fascinating project!" the architect exclaimed. "And by a specialist in police work, into the bargain. Won't you finish it?"

"I never began. Never got beyond the planning stage."

Conrad snapped at the subject. A breath of that romanticism he had felt in this very room not too long ago touched him. Today too, as on a cool spring evening a while back, the coke (shaken up by Frau Schubert) glowed behind the mica plate of the stove, and the big room was illuminated by the warm, muted light from the lamp over the divan.

"I've always thought how dreadful it must have been to live in such a time, in Spain, I mean, when the Inquisition was active there," Conrad said. "The slightest suspicion, or a denunciation, was enough to put a man in line for horrible tortures. How could anyone have enjoyed his life or taken up any interests . . ."

At these last words Conrad suddenly thought of Günther Ligharts, of his childhood room and the glass tank with the black salamanders up on top of the wardrobe. But this memory glided into and out of his mind so rapidly that he did not even have time to wonder about it.

"In the long perspective, we see the terrors or grandeurs of an age all crowded together. At the time, they were distributed and floated along in the current of a whole general mood, the temper of the age. Many things must almost have been taken for granted. If I were to exaggerate a trifle, for the sake of clarity, I would say that most people noticed the Inquisition no more than the contemporaries of the great age of art in Italy noticed the 'Renaissance'."

The letter box closed after this speech.

"Besides, the Inquisition in Spain was directed chiefly against the wealthy and the aristocrats," the architect remarked. "In other words, against a restricted class of people."

"Because of the confiscation of property. Besides, good firewood is expensive in Mediterranean countries. Perhaps the question of profit or loss played a part in the matter," Herr von Hohenlocher said.

"I can think of a few persons who might well be burned at the stake," Doctor Velten commented. "Among my patients, too. Very dry schizoids. They could even be used for fuel, if chopped small."

"A good doctor must be a good man," the architect quoted. Rotund and hamsterlike, on the edge of the couch, he rocked slightly, laughing to himself.

Conrad pressed on toward more romantic notions, which these interjections were disturbing. "Such bodies have existed even in modern times," he said. "Think of the famous 'Third Department'

of the Russian Imperial police, the Ochrana. I once read a novel
about it, set in Petersburg."

"All very well," Herr Inkrat said. "The Ochrana may have become notorious because of extraordinary circumstances. But don't
overlook the fact that every country in the world maintains, and
must maintain, a secret police."

"It really is a curious notion—that by some casual, foolish little
detail one might arouse suspicion and as a perfectly harmless
person be constantly under observation." Conrad took pleasure in
kindling his own interest as one blows on a tiny flame.

"Well, no one needs to worry about that," the professional
policeman said lightly, with reptilian immobility. "We don't
know and fortunately we never find out all the things that are
often set in motion against us and then come to a halt at one
point or another without our ever being aware of them. Otherwise no one would be able to sleep peacefully; we would spend
our time splitting split hairs—in the end to be used for firewood
as one of Doctor Velten's patients. No, I take a different view
of it. You might say that there is a dossier on each of us filed
away somewhere, and from time to time items are entered in it,
additions and guidelines. Once it is complete, it probably turns
out that everything that was later written down was already
present in the watermark of the paper. And, to return to the
matter of the secret police—they are only a kind of symbol,
nothing more than a general fact of life rendered visible at a
particular place and in the form of a necessary institution."

"There is a dossier on you, Herr Inkrat, contained in this bottle,"
Herr von Hohenlocher said, handing him a glass of gin. At which
Varanus aridus stirred at last. He moved with astonishing speed
as he took the glass and drained it.

"It is amazing," Doctor Velten said.

"What is amazing?" the architect asked.

"Why . . . the authoritativeness with which you speak. Just
now, for example. That was excellent, in all seriousness, Herr

Inkrat. But every judgment, every opinion, remains amazing to me, in the final analysis, whether it is more or less incisive and accurate . . . The quickness of your mind, too. It would interest me to learn whether you . . . whether you've ever before thought all that you just said, put it into words, I mean, said something similar."

The uncertainty and pensiveness with which he spoke ruled out all implications of irony. Again Doctor Velten seemed only to be meditating aloud.

"Once upon a time I wrote it down in virtually those words, as notes for an introduction to the book I wanted to write," the reptile said. "But I think I know what you are getting at, Doctor, and I must admit that my feelings on that point are the same as yours."

"Pay attention, Castiletz," Hohenlocher interjected, as he filled the glasses. "Here you may learn something else besides how to get drunk."

"Yes—and what do you think of . . . I mean, what is your opinion on the—amazing—phenomenon of human judgment?"

"I am no psychiatrist," the letter box replied slowly. "And so I cannot analyze this thing as you might be able to do. I can only treat it logically. Our amazement at the rapid decisions and judgments that are being formed around us all the time, and delivered in respect to everything imaginable, comes, I should think, from the nature of these judgments, which are really only expressions of the life spirit. They appear as judgments only in form, and wear a logical garb that language imposes on them, whereas in truth they are made of the same substance as any other of the blind manifestations of life. They are only other forms of aggression or defense, of the organism's attempt to maintain its own value or diminish that of others, of the effort to proclaim what one would like to believe because it bolsters one's own vital forces . . . In short: what we regard as 'judgments,' fascinated as we always are by the logical form in which wholly illogical life appears, are essentially no different from the swift gesture with which we fend off a mosquito, or from those changes in facial expression which occur as we talk to different and differentiated persons in a group. On such occasions we don't wonder at the swiftness of our automatic reaction. 'Judgments' are similar adjustments, only draped in the costume of logic which language puts on every reaction as it emerges from our mouths. Arbitrarily filled test tubes containing the cloudy liquid of life—that is what judgments are. Only they happen to stand in the rack of logic. They are produced at least as rapidly as a smile, a clearing of the throat, a spasm of vexation. Essentially they are nothing but the complexion we happen to be wearing at the moment, or our temporary preference for falling asleep on our right side and then shifting to the left. In fact, the way most people make judgments consists in their simply generalizing their own secretions or excretions."

"Cheers!" Herr von Hohenlocher said.

"Critique of judgment," the architect remarked.

"No, only of sham judgments," Inkrat said impassively.

"I beg your pardon," Herr von Hohenlocher protested. "If I am required to pass judgment on a tax question tomorrow, will my decision be just a secretion?"

"Yes," Herr Inkrat said. "If you are in the habit of reacting spontaneously to the tax declaration of someone who is a complete stranger to you, it will be."

"One can't possibly ask for a spontaneous reaction," Doctor Velten remarked.

"Oh, but it is possible to consider a temperamental response the more meritorious one, humanly speaking," the architect said, and they all turned toward him, since this was the first time he had stated an opinion of his own. "For example, one might feel infuriated simply by the look of a person's handwriting and react by fiscally annihilating the individual as far as possible." As he spoke, his eyes protruded slightly, like transparent spheres.

"Listen to our general, who should be a tower of calm deliberation!" Hohenlocher exclaimed. "But I think it's even worse that a
criminologist does not believe in logic, when he should be riding
high horse on it."

"In practical life, purely logical judgments don't exist," Herr
Inkrat said, still posed motionless by the stove. "And certainly
not in criminology. No case has ever been cleared up by logic.
In medicine, too, there is no such thing as purely formal, scientific
diagnosis, as Doctor Velten will tell you, if he is not too lazy."

"Too lazy," Velten said softly, in a doleful tone.

"He treats madmen by putting masks on them," Hohenlocher
said. "Where is the logic!"

"Logic remains only a duty and a standard that we must try to
approach," Inkrat said. "But a policeman has a far deeper relationship to the criminal, as a doctor has to the patient; and these
deeper relationships are the means by which whatever is done is
accomplished. Incidentally, I might remind you that for the past
seven years I have not been a member of the criminal police—I
imagine you know since when. I'm in the much more innocuous
personnel section."

"Since you *secreted* wrongly in the Louison Veik case," Herr
von Hohenlocher said with a certain spiteful satisfaction. He
wrinkled his nose.

"Quite right," Inkrat replied. "I reached the limits of crimino-
logical science there, and had myself transferred to another
department."

"This young man is married to the victim's sister," Hohenlocher
said, indicating Conrad.

Inkrat scarcely moved; he only turned his head slightly in
Conrad's direction. "Well then," he said, "you no doubt know all
there is to know about that mysterious affair. As much as the
police, anyhow—which is to say, nothing."

For the first time Conrad felt that he was beginning to be
pursued by something which he had hitherto always followed of

his own accord. The conversation had surprisingly and without any intervention on his part turned to Louison. He had a strange feeling of embarrassment. Nevertheless, he promptly took up the subject; he could not have let this opportunity slip away.

"Actually, I know even less," he said. "That is, I'm not even acquainted with the outward details of the murder. You must understand that it isn't easy for me to ask the family questions about it. A short while before my father died, he wrote me about it, but he passed over those very details of fact which would have interested me, since they are what make a thing of that sort vivid. And I was just fifteen at the time of the crime, and did not yet read newspapers. I'd be grateful to you, Herr Inkrat, if you would tell me anything you know about the murder of my wife's poor sister."

Conrad felt, after he had spoken, a certain satisfaction in having made his request so courteously.

Hohenlocher waved a bottle. "Let's have the story!" he urged. "I myself would like to hear it told in order, one thing after the other, for a change. The newspapers printed only the usual nonsense dashed down in haste. Come, oblige our young fellow, since he's asked so nicely. Castiletz, incidentally, you're a very polite person; I'm glad to give you a testimonial to that effect. But before Sherlock Holmes' story, one drink all around!"

"Kiss your arse, Hohenlocher," Inkrat said. For the first time that evening he laughed. His long bones began to move; he freed himself from the stove and sank, extending his limbs, into a leather-covered chair.

Frau Schubert appeared with black coffee and champagne glasses. Lissenbrech, too, had by now settled into a comfortable armchair and no longer seemed so folded, hamster fashion, around his own stomach. He was leaning back, though a considerable volume of his person protruded. Doctor Velten alone remained as before, sprawled over the divan, while the others formed a semicircle around the table with the drinks.

The table held, in addition to other smoking supplies, an open box of small, pale, imported cigars. Castiletz, who was beginning once more to be carried away by the "romanticism of the situation," like a swimmer in a strong current (simultaneously he was floating on some sustaining wave which seemed to be associated with the phrase "young fellow")—Castiletz leaned forward, took one of the little cigars, used the cutter, and tucked the cigar into his mouth. This was a first performance, and he was conscious of all the attractions of novelty. It was the first time he had lit a cigar anywhere but at his father-in-law's, and thus in a sense independently, on his own. In fact, it was no less a first time, no less marked an era, than—than burning that Pierrot post card from Günther Ligharts. That was what he thought of at the moment.

"Since when do you smoke?" Herr von Hohenlocher asked. And since Conrad, instead of giving a straight answer—which would not have been easy—merely smiled significantly, Herr von Hohenlocher added: "Like a bank director."

"The facts are as follows, and can be told in a few words," Inkrat said, after he had established himself, as immobile as before, in his new position. "On July 25, 1921, the night express which ran between Stuttgart and Berlin arrived at Erfurt about half past four in the morning. In the course of the routine check of tickets, a second-class compartment in the next-to-the-last car of the train was found locked. The conductor opened it with his key and found the body of a young girl, whose head was horribly broken open. Everything was spattered with blood. A suitcase lay on the floor; its contents had fallen out and were scattered over the compartment. Clenched in the dead woman's hand was an empty jewel case. The window had been opened. The body lay across the rear bench—rear from the point of view of the train's motion. Apparently the murdered girl had struggled and twisted about violently. The conductor behaved in an exemplary fashion; he locked the compartment again, reported the crime

to his supervisor, and fifteen minutes later we were on the spot
with the squad."

"You were there—I mean, with the homicide squad?" Herr von
Hohenlocher said. "I had no idea."

"Yes, I was stationed at Erfurt at the time. A year after this
episode I was transferred here, at my own request. Naturally, the
investigation led me into frequent contact with the victim's
parents—in the course of the affair I often went to Leipzig to see
your present in-laws, Herr Castiletz, for that was their home at
the time."

"What did your men discover?" Doctor Velten asked.

"Their first task, of course, was to take exact note of the facts
and make the necessary arrangements. Just before this was done,
however, there was a remarkable incident which led to the only
clue we were able to find and follow up—though, as it turned out,
it led us nowhere. The train, of course, had been held up and
all the passengers had to be checked. The last two cars were
uncoupled and switched to a siding. And no one in them was
allowed to leave. We herded all the passengers into one car—
that had been arranged with the police at the station the moment
the report reached us. As you can imagine, the passengers were
not exactly overjoyed. But the layman hasn't the remotest idea
of how subtle a business such an investigation can be. In view
of all that is involved, the police can't possibly act in an ac-
commodating manner. They must concentrate on doing what has
to be done. I hurried ahead to the railroad station, with an experienced detective, to make sure the measures we'd ordered
were carried out. We'd drawn up a plan in a few minutes, and
my strategy depended on there being no railroad official in
either of the detached cars. A few minutes before the rest arrived
—I mean the investigating commission, which consisted of chief
inspector, doctor, photographer, and so on—we entered the
second-class car and stood in front of the locked door of the
compartment, where the detained passengers had assembled,

some of them angry, some inquisitive. And now I made my
experiment, which was based largely on the suspicion that had
leaped into my mind the instant I heard about that obtrusively
open window. That detail seems to have especially impressed the
conductor who discovered the corpse, and it had been passed on
to us in the very first report. I'd heard it on the telephone, since
I was on night duty. I didn't like that open window—I'd almost
say that I felt a kind of resentment against it. The statement it
made was all too plain, all too apparent; it pressed forward insistently, so to speak, demanded to be heard. . . . For that reason
I thought I'd make a stab at seeing about the door—I could always
come back to the window later on, if I needed a missing brick
for my structure. We'd ordered all trainmen to be kept out of
the car for the simple reason that each of them carries a compartment key. As you know, even when a compartment is bolted
on the inside, it can be opened from outside with the proper key.
Travelers sometimes carry them, although, strictly speaking, their
use is supposed to be reserved to railroad personnel. Well then,
we stood in the aisle in front of the locked door, and that gave
me the pretext to inquire politely whether anyone had a compartment key, since I needed one at the moment. No, sorry, no
one had such a key. I then ordered a search. There were some
thirty-five passengers, among them several ladies—we had to send
for policewomen. In short, there was quite a bit of excitement
and the procedure took some time. We used a compartment in
the second car. Meanwhile, the rest of the commission had arrived
and was at work in the murder compartment, which I'd eventually
opened with my own key. I too was in there when a report was
brought to me that a compartment key had been found on one of
the passengers. I took a look at the man, remembered at once
that he had been standing near me in the aisle when I asked my
question and that he had replied no, with alacrity. The key was
attached to a ring with the rest of his keys. I had this man
arrested. His name was Henry Peitz, and he was highly indignant."

"None of these details were in the newspapers," Herr von Hohenlocher said.

"No," Inkrat replied. "There is no reason to give the papers information on our methods. If Peitz had been tried in court, of course, all these points would have been dealt with during the trial."

"Were no fingerprints discovered in the murder compartment?" Conrad asked in high excitement.

"The ones we could find were her own," Inkrat said. "However, you must not overestimate the importance of that. The criminal world has long ago caught up with the science of fingerprinting. At least the major criminals have; they wear gloves whenever they pull a job."

"What happened to Peitz?" the architect asked. His eyes were extremely animated once more, and seemed to have become bright and transparent.

"He was detained, of course. The others were released after we took down their names and addresses, searched their baggage, and checked their identification papers. There was no trouble about identifying the dead girl, incidentally, since she had her passport with her. She had come from Zurich, which meant that she had been in the train since four o'clock the previous afternoon, and had a ticket to Leipzig, where her parents expected her to arrive in the morning. Now, of course, we were obliged to inform them of the tragedy. Also, it was essential to determine a number of important matters. Thus we learned about the jewelry which had been in the jewel case. We had assumed something of the sort right away; the whole picture obviously added up to a murder in conjunction with robbery."

Approximately at this point in Inkrat's story Conrad reached an understanding of his present condition. He was drunk, that was all; he had no tolerance for alcohol. Very simple. That was what produced this feeling of numbness which had overcome him, surrounded him, so that everything he was hearing condensed thicker and thicker around him, seemed to be besieging him. At the moment it was all too complicated for him to make any order out of it. But that somehow it must be put in order was beyond question. A thoroughgoing ordering was in order. The way to that ordering led to and through a notebook in the suitcase. Yes, that was it. This vague notion brought him a certain relief. He had only to fetch that notebook. But—like a man awakening from a dream—he suddenly saw these nebulous images with greater clarity and fixity, and, even as he did so, they seemed irrational to him, utterly lacking in reality, not at all hopeful.

"Among Henry Peitz's baggage was a bag of golf clubs. The doctors stated that an instrument of that type could possibly have been employed to commit the murder; but they were inclined to think that some shorter and cruder blunt tool had been used. The position of the dead woman on the back bench of the compartment, even assuming that it had been changed by her death agony or by the rocking of the train, together with the nature of the head wound, suggested that the attack had come either from straight in front of her or, even more likely, from the left side, that is, from someone seated on the opposite bench, close to the window. Experiments showed that with an object the length of a golf club it would have been nearly impossible to strike with sufficient force, among other things because of the protruding baggage nets. The golf clubs showed no trace of blood—although any bloodstain could have been removed without great difficulty. Moreover, the bag seemed to contain the full complement of clubs—you know, a complete set is needed for golf. All, without exception, were coated thickly with coal dust or soot. But that was also true of the murdered girl's head wound."

"On that detail, I should have hanged him," the architect said amiably. "For the sake of simplicity."

"A fat man is supposed to be a kind man," Doctor Velten countered.

"Easy there, easy there, gentlemen!" Inkrat exclaimed. "A few

more facts and you certainly would not have hanged Henry
Peitz. You would have had to let him go just as the police finally
did."

"On account of false *secretions*," Herr von Hohenlocher said.
"Or in this case: the generalization of them."

"Call it that if you like," Inkrat replied. "Now listen to the rest.
The doctors could not say definitely whether the soot on the
wound had come from the instrument that dealt the blow, or had
been deposited afterwards, because of the open window. The
railroad line, I may remind you, passes through a mountainous
area, the Thuringian Forest, between Grimmenthal and Erfurt,
and there are a number of tunnels. Given an open window,
smoke and soot would have poured into the compartment—
there is no question about that. Peitz testified that he belonged
to a golf association in the Westphalian industrial region. This
statement proved true. The traps on the golf courses of that
association contain rubble and slag from the mines of the vicinity,
which would account for the dirt on the golf clubs. Moreover, a chemical examination showed that the dirt on the golf
clubs differed in type from the soot particles which clung to the
open wound. I am not a chemist and so was not able to check
this particular item personally. The distinction seems to be that
railroad soot is a pure product of combustion, precipitation from
smoke, whereas the other would contain particles of coal. Well,
be that as it may, at any rate our difficulties and uncertainties
began there. The coroner's finding was that "death had ensued
a few hours previously, though possibly before midnight." Theoretically, that left the possibility of the entire stretch between
Stuttgart and Erfurt. Louison Veik was seen alive at the Stuttgart
station—by someone who knew her, I mean, a friend named
Maria Rosanka, who came to meet her at the station, since she
was passing through the city. This woman stayed with her until
the train left at half past nine that night."

"Rosanka!" Hohenlocher exclaimed. "Why, that must be the
painter."

"Quite right," Inkrat said.

"A charming person and crazy as a loon," Hohenlocher re-marked. "She enjoys staging her own comedy, and I like that about her. Tall, thin, brown, a woman made of leather, but with a broad, oddly foolish face. I did not know Louison Veik had been her friend."

"All the same, an important witness," Inkrat said.

"Is this Fräulein Rosanka still living in Stuttgart?" Conrad asked, politely.

"And how!" Hohenlocher said loudly. "Oh yes, she's still there. She's having another show: I saw a notice of it in the papers. But now go on with your story, Mr. Holmes. What about Peitz?"

"I shall be getting to him in a moment. I was saying, then, that we had to consider almost the entire stretch. That meant searching for any loot that might have been thrown out of the train. The same thing could have been done with the murder weapon, as well as with towels, handkerchiefs, or other items used for removing bloodstains. But these details are not impor-tant here; there are many more which must always be taken into account in such cases. With all that, we kept a particularly sharp eye on the stretch through the Thuringian Forest. The train had passed through there toward dawn—that is, at a time when even the most sleepless traveler usually nods off for a while. Besides, experience tells us that railroad robbers frequently prefer stretches of tunnel, because of the din, which drowns out indi-vidual noises or possible screams. So we went over that area with the greatest care, but without success. Naturally, the police also considered whether anyone had left the train during the night, getting off at a station before his destination. But nothing of the sort could be traced."

"But is it conceivable," von Hohenlocher asked, "that such a quantity of precious jewelry could disappear completely and not a single piece of it turn up in all these years?"

"That particular aspect of it does not strike me as such a mystery," Inkrat replied. "Naturally, we issued an exact description of the jewelry, and sent the report around. But we did not really hope for much. That kind of loot, with a high value in gold and gems but without unusual or unique artistic value, is extraordinarily difficult to trace, since as a rule such things never reappear in their original form. A criminal who is capable of robbery aboard a train does not go to a pawnshop. Stolen jewelry is often broken up into its smallest fragments, actually melted down in many cases, and disposed of through so-called fences, or sold abroad, pearl by pearl and stone by stone. In this case, incidentally, the booty consisted of gems, chiefly emeralds, which have risen enormously in value in recent years. There were no pearls. [As these words were spoken, Conrad thought that here, perhaps, was one of the few traits Louison had shared with Marianne, who also did not like pearls.] The very fact that not a single item ever turned up suggests a professional criminal, a man with good connections and a capacity for judicious restraint. No such qualities, unfortunately, applied to our Peitz—not a bit. In addition, if any of the loot had been thrown out of the train at some definitely marked point along the track—which is quite often done—the criminal would be running the risk of losing all or part of it to some chance finder. I say 'part' because the package might break open from the impact and scatter its con- tents widely. . . . Just consider the likelihood of single pieces, or the whole batch vanishing in the natural irregularities of the ground, especially on wooded and mountainous terrain. A single rainstorm and every trace would be lost. As a matter of course, we alerted all the villages along that stretch, and the railroad officials did their best. But our hunt was in vain—was perhaps too late. We must recall the times, the year 1921, that bad period after the war when everywhere honesty had been shaken to its foundations. A reward was offered, but it did not come to the value of the jewelry. All in all, the disappearance of the loot remains the least astonishing aspect of the affair, especially when I consider its other mysteries."

"But now to Peitz, to Peitz!" Herr von Hohenlocher demanded.

"Yes, we are coming to Peitz," Herr Inkrat continued. "I only wanted to cast a few sidelights on the details and the difficulties of such an investigation, and I haven't by any means mentioned everything. . . . I said before that we had to consider the whole stretch the train had traveled from Stuttgart to Erfurt. In this connection the conductor's report was of some value, but led to little. Louison Veik's compartment was reserved as a so-called 'ladies' compartment' and was not supposed to be used by male passengers. Immediately after the train left the Stuttgart station, Fräulein Veik retired to it. Fifteen minutes later, the conductor entered the ladies' section, in which she sat alone, and checked her ticket. He was, in fact, the last person who saw her alive. Thereafter she did not appear in the aisle. The curtains were drawn and during the night no woman, who might have entered the compartment reserved for ladies, boarded the train. So Louison Veik had it to herself. The conductor could not say whether she had bolted the compartment from inside. Once the ticket had been checked, there was no reason to disturb the passenger's sleep. However, she had not dimmed the light. Her compartment was the first one in the car, which meant that it adjoined a compartment only on one side; on the other side the aisle widened out into a platform. Neither a passenger nor any member of the train crew heard a scream or any suspicious noise. Fräulein Veik's neighbors in the next compartment were a group of young people who were having a merry time drinking and laughing. They did not travel far; by midnight all of them had got off, and from then on this compartment remained empty. In the next, Henry Peitz sat with a businessman and a government official from Berlin. They were strangers to one another and did not fall into conversation. It was important to find out whether Peitz had left the compartment and when; but since his companions had gone to sleep, it was impossible to obtain accurate information. Once, about two o'clock in the morning or thereabouts, Peitz is supposed to have left the compartment, evidently bound for the washroom. Neither of the other two men could say whether he'd had anything in his hand, or hidden under his coat, or had taken anything from his baggage. Peitz had occupied the window seat, the government official had stretched out on the opposite bench, and the third man was on the same side as Peitz, sleeping in a slumped position in the far corner. It was he who stated that Peitz had been out once, since Peitz had had to clamber over his legs. As for Peitz himself, the most striking circumstance in his favor was that he was still on the train at Erfurt. But the merit of this was somewhat vitiated by his being drunk at the time of his arrest. A half-empty bottle of cognac was found in his baggage. So that he might have overslept. But as you can see, this assumption was not very probable."

"What kind of person was this Henry Peitz?" Doctor Velten asked from his sprawling position on the divan.

"Hm—physiognomically speaking, a rather common type in our times and in big cities. One of those persons who very quickly, via various shortcuts, fall into the pattern they are destined for. Perhaps they have found it by the time they are fourteen or fifteen. Along with that, they acquire a way of dressing, moving, and talking which suits them perfectly. Peitz was a dapper-looking fellow, and by ordinary standards a rounded personality; he retained those qualities even when he was beside himself with indignation—and we had plenty of opportunity to see him in that state. I don't imagine, for example, that people of his type go through that unhappy period of boyhood when everything seems stale and sad; I mean those curiously awkward states that descend on boys, when their nimble bodies seem belied by an inner heaviness. No, Peitz must always have had a harmonious character, never at odds with himself. As you may know, such people incline to be critical and self-righteous. They're inclined to make large demands on the world, as a matter of course. They're on the whole light, slender, blond types, without too much crude strength, although they do have spunk. But if they feel weak at

some point, they tend to take offense. That is, they gladly seize
the chance to, and go through all the motions of being outraged,
all the while quietly enjoying the magnification of their own self-
esteem resulting from the injustice being done to them. Throughout the interrogations Peitz would sit askew on the chair, his
body stiff, inclined to the back and to the side. He would not
lean back comfortably. His very posture made it clear that he
felt every question to be a personal affront; or else that he expected to be insulted and was leaning back in order to increase
the distance between himself and the impudent questioner. His
face went along with this whole personality. The outer corners
of his eyes were set deeper than the inner corners—just the
reverse of what you would see in a Japanese, say. He also had
that form of overhanging eyelid which is called 'epicanthus.'
I am firmly convinced that even if we did give him a hard time
for a while, we were helping him fulfill his idea of himself, at
least that 'insulted' aspect of his character. Peitz tended to
screech at us during the hearings. He would rant about the
damage this incident was doing to his reputation and to his
credit, but what angered him most was that he had to get to
Berlin, where he was supposed to appear in court that very day
in connection with an important lawsuit. We checked on this and
it turned out to be the truth. Peitz owned a business in Berlin,
a large specialty shop for electrical goods. He had no police
record and his reputation was good. In his fury he threatened to
take all sorts of measures against us, issue complaints and what
not—but of course these threats made little impression on the
police. In the end, however, all our incriminating evidence boiled
down to nothing. The only suspicious factor was his reaction
when I asked for the compartment key. . . ."

"*Secreted* compartment key," Herr von Hohenlocher threw in.
He had evidently decided to ride this word for the rest of the
evening.

"Very well then, the secreted compartment key. But we had

to admit that the reason Henry Peitz gave for holding back the key suited him excellently, just as did his gestures, his sitting askew, his epicanthus. He simply said that he'd done it out of annoyance: he had foreseen that this incident would cost him enormous inconvenience. Besides which his thoughts had been fixed entirely on the court case which was to be heard that morning. And also, he asserted savagely, I had been out to get him from the moment I saw him; he'd sensed that as I stood in front of the locked compartment door."

"There is something for you, Herr Lissenbrech," Hohenlocher said. "A fit of rage at the mere sight of a stranger who is subsequently to attempt one's annihilation by legal means."

"Hohenlocher—someone should get rid of you," Doctor Velten called out.

"I'm afraid it is impossible to talk seriously with him," the architect remarked, smiling benevolently.

"Yes, it is, and I do my best to keep it that way. Life is so much easier when no one can talk seriously to you. You enjoy a great deal more peace."

"That may be," Herr Inkrat said. "But to wind up the story: the prosecutor decided that there was not enough evidence to charge Henry Peitz with robbery and murder. I forgot to mention that a check of his financial situation proved him to be a very solid citizen. The file was sent back to us, pending discovery of further evidence. And no further evidence turned up. We had to release Peitz. Try as we might, we could find no other clue aside from that damned compartment key."

"The end of Sherlock Holmes," Herr von Hohenlocher said. Herr Inkrat nodded good-humoredly. For some little while there was silence.

"Do you think Peitz innocent?" Castiletz asked. He threw out this question rather abruptly; after all the drinking, his tongue would no longer entirely obey him.

"Although I am no longer a criminologist, Herr Castiletz,"

Inkrat said immobilely, "I am still a policeman. And that involves a specific attitude of mind. To a policeman, everyone is guilty who has not decisively proved his innocence. Henry Peitz was unable to do that. He had to be released for lack of proof."

"A nice set of people, these policemen," Herr von Hohenlocher said.

"But necessary," Inkrat replied. "Unfortunately there are no police regulations and therefore no legal recourse against cynics and parasites of your type."

"Bravo!" Doctor Velten cried from the divan.

"Down with him!" Lissenbrech said grimly, raising his glass.

Laughing, all touched glasses with Herr von Hohenlocher. "It's been another of your delightful evenings," Lissenbrech announced. "We thank you, dear host."

Hohenlocher, however, held out his hand toward Herr Inkrat—like a conductor directing the applause to the orchestra. Inkrat gave a silent bow.

As they were taking their leave, there was another amusing incident in the hallway outside.

Conrad, possessed by the notion that he must fetch something—it seemed an entirely reasonable idea at the moment—strode rapidly to the door of his former apartment, took his key ring from his trousers pocket, and tried to unlock the door.

A great hallo of laughter arose behind him. "Hoho!" Herr von Hohenlocher cried. "Not here, not here, steer back to the conjugal port!" And turning to the others, he added: "There you have it: a bachelor, even when he wasn't one for long, always yearns to return to his old stall."

31 ⑧

wwwwwwwwwwwwwwwwwwwwwwwwwwwwwwwwwwwwwwwwwww

FRAU Erika von Spresse's house was one of the most distinguished in town, and looked it even from outside. The walls were adorned with murals. In the vast garden, where the rose bushes were still carefully wrapped in straw, marble busts gleamed along the paths (Plato, Pascal, Giordano Bruno). In the arbors, scattered little refuges for quiet meditation, were statues (Aristotle, Sophocles, Leibniz). You could scarcely be a walker in this garden; you had to be a peripatetic.

At the moment, these features looked rather bald, since the true glory of any garden design emerges only under conditions of full growth. Until then, a garden makes a rather spindly impression, with stalks, stems, and lattices standing somewhat forlornly in the thin and pure light of early spring, when everything looks as if it has just been created. Everything looks temporary, that is. Yet it would seem that this house could the more easily send its civilizing emanations beyond the boundaries of the garden as long as the hedges were not yet a tangle of growth. If Czerny's *School of Velocity* sounded through the open window, or Frau von Spresse leaned pensively at the slanting window of her attic studio, brush in hand—it really should have sufficed to make a cultivated person out of anyone who walked by the house once or twice. At the very least, people passing on the slightly sloping street should have sensed, in a mysterious, fluid fashion, the aura of a higher form of existence.

Conrad came up the street with the hot sun full in his face, so that it literally interfered with his walking. For him the whole of this spring felt like a purely external matter, like a noisy process whose power he sensed, but only as if he himself were in a closed and draped room.

In the hall, with its oak-paneled cloakroom and magnificently tiled adjoining chambers, he blinked in the semidarkness as the maid took his coat, which had kept him too warm during his walk.

His visits to Aunt Erika had been quite rare in the early days of his stay in the city. But since his marriage to Marianne Veik— which is to say, since his final proving of himself in every respect—Frau von Spresse seemed to value his company more. She often asked how he and his wife were, and several times invited them to come to see her. Herr von Hohenlocher, with his shameless candor, had long ago remarked to Conrad: "Keep on good terms with the devil's grandmother, or rather with her milk goat; it would be simply stupid not to. After all, you may have children some day. Very well, you have enough and to spare; but one is duty-bound to do everything possible for one's progeny. The woman is richer than anybody knows and has performed the feat of bringing her whole fortune intact through all devaluations, with the help of various nameless infernal advisers. You are the first in line. So do the prudent thing." He followed this with: "Since you've taken to smoking cigars, you look like a general manager in the making. The paunch will come in due time."

Conrad accepted Herr von Hohenlocher's arguments in regard to Frau von Spresse without undue resistance. He followed the course recommended. But he was always bothered by the suspicion that Hohenlocher's aim was no more than to create, or to draw, out of him a certain type—the type of the "general manager," say—for his own amusement. The role called for a set of carefully cultivated connections and prospects of inheritance. Hohenlocher seemed uncannily sure of himself even in regard to the paunch that would carry out the picture.

As for the "progeny," of which there was so far no sign: perhaps only Frau Gusta Veik was privately a little sad at having no grandchildren.

This time Conrad was calling on his aunt alone. The maid led the way, and Frau von Spresse received him at the tea table. Today the table was set in the library, for the house naturally contained one, and in the word's most oppressive sense: not only yards but cubic yards of books. The backs of leather- and cloth-bound volumes came up nearly to the wood paneling of the ceiling. There were special ladders on little tracks for reaching the top shelves. The maids knew their way about the library perfectly, and could bring out any book asked for by catalogue number. In the middle of the hall—for the library was large enough to be termed a hall—stood a showcase in which the letters of some famous men were displayed under glass. (There was even a letter by Adalbert Stifter, a writer Frau von Spresse was particularly fond of.) In addition, as a curiosity, there was an astrolabe, an instrument useful in astrology. Some guests, especially those who prided themselves on their association with the Spresse household, would maintain that it was the astrolabe that had belonged to Senis, with the aid of which Wallenstein's horoscope had once been cast. "An old possession of the von Spresse family."

It was cool here—that was Conrad's first sensation. The door to the garden stood open, and the sun was beginning to go down. Frau von Spresse extended her hand for Conrad to kiss while the maid poured the tea. Conrad's aunt was truly gaunt. Now, with the light from the shaded lamp falling sideways upon her, she looked almost flat and two-dimensional, like a tin soldier. Conrad suddenly felt that his presence here was grotesque. No feelings of "romanticism" stirred, in spite of these elevated surroundings.

"Well, how are things at home?" she replied in answer to Conrad's polite inquiry about her health.

"Good, thank you," he said. As in falling asleep we sometimes feel a little jerk, as though we were dropping down—and in fact our limbs actually twitch—so Conrad, to his surprise, suddenly fell into a totally empty space of recollection, and he came very close to making an involuntary movement. As a boy he had been in this house, after all, although in all likelihood he had rarely entered the library. But the garden, the vestibule—his impressions of everything here were at variance with an older layer of sight and feeling. All the same, he had been rather grown up at that time ("I was already wearing collars and ties," he thought). . . .

She dispelled his abstraction with a question.

"Your wife is going in for sports a great deal, so I recently heard."

Conrad was sure that it would be utterly impossible to convey to Aunt Erika the thoughts that had just passed through his mind. Why was that impossible? She would not have understood a word. And why should that be, since she read books all day long and in addition painted? He felt cold here, in this room, with the stern-eyed tin soldier. Had Conrad been less "textilian" (the word was Hohenlocher's, of course—but for whom, we may as well state, this story would never have been written)—had Conrad been less "textilian," he would have been able to define what it was about Frau von Spresse that was so discomfiting. The trouble was that she lacked absolutely all capacity for visionary thinking, as a plant that has been in a press lacks sap. Consequently, she could busy herself day in and day out with the fine arts and the sciences without ever feeling burdened by her activities (she had even written a book entitled *Madame Reads*, and subtitled "Masterpieces of World Literature Reflected in the Souls of Women"). But how could anything burden her when the real proportions of all things were completely unknown to her and would always remain so? However, Conrad could not even think of the simple word "unimaginativeness."

"Yes," he replied to his aunt's question. "I think it's very good for her. I only hope she doesn't overstrain herself."

"Even women are going in for sports nowadays, not only girls,"

Aunt Erika said. "Marianne didn't use to play tennis, did she?"

"No, not so far as I know," Conrad replied.

"Well, no doubt you'll make her an excellent teacher and partner."

Conrad began to fall prey to a kind of paralysis. On the way here, while getting out of the streetcar and then walking slowly up the sloping street, he had been feeling a certain excitement, for he had had in mind to obtain certain information from his aunt. But these plans dropped away into vagueness; he forgot them entirely and was seized only by the desire to leave as soon as he decently could. At last the maid reappeared, closed the wide glass doors leading into the garden, and turned on a nearby radiator. Conrad accepted some more of the tea, which was no longer hot.

"I don't think I'll play much tennis this year," he said. And, because he felt it the best way to block any further questions, he added: "We're terribly pressed for time these days." In truth, the thought of playing tennis or engaging in any sport was at present just as alien to him as the advance of spring in the whole outside world. He felt altogether unprepared for the habitual activities of the oncoming season.

"Herr Peter Duracher, who is more or less the leader of all those young people—your wife sees a good deal of him nowadays —is supposed to be some kind of expert in sports," Frau von Spresse said.

"Not only in sports," Conrad replied. "He is an expert in textile chemistry. But, as a matter of fact, he is also an extraordinary athlete. The whole group is frequently at our house."

He felt he had to emphasize this last fact, and threw the sentence out as a kind of self-defense. (It occurred to him that the whole group was at the swimming pool, where Duracher was teaching them the crawl—that was the reason Marianne had not come along on this visit.) Perhaps Conrad's tone, as he spoke these last words, betrayed weariness or indifference—at any rate, his defense was not offered in time, or with sufficient animation. It did not stop Frau von Spresse from raising a heretofore invisible lorgnette and training this weapon on him. She looked at Conrad for several moments. Then, as if to save face, she trained the lorgnette on the table, rang for the maid, and had the tea things taken out.

32 ଙ୍ଗ

~~~~~~

THE project for a dye works at the Carl Theodor Veik mill was dropped. In that year of 1929 there was no need to have an especially keen nose to sense the economic depression; it was already obvious.

For Conrad, the immediate result of this was that the two books which had lain on his desk for some time vanished again: Dr. W. Zänker's *Dyeing,* and *Chemical Treatment of Wool,* by the same author. The two little volumes had not looked particularly elegant on the diplomat's desk; especially *Dyeing,* with its brick-red binding, detracted from the general effect. The chambermaid had long before come to regard the two books as a part of the desk furnishings, to be dusted off along with the fantastic paper knife which had been a wedding present from Director Eisenmann. Conrad no longer needed to seek shelter behind Director Eisenmann in case it should occur to Councilor Veik that Conrad should return to the textile mill in order to pick up additional knowledge of dyeing. Not that Eisenmann would not have pleaded his cause, had it been necessary. With or without the short fur coat.

As for Duracher, he was deprived of the chance to shine by virtue of his command of textile chemistry, but he made up for it by riding high in sports. Even Frau von Spresse was aware of his prowess, and now Duracher had more free time than ever. In general, everybody had more time; that was one queer feature of those days. In that respect Conrad had lied.

Marianne changed. Nowadays, when she lay reading in the twin bed beside Conrad's, her arms, emerging from the short sleeves of her nightgown, were deeply tanned. Unquestionably she was growing much slimmer—everyone said so. But the real change had its locus beneath that tanned brow, where her profile was deeply curved in above the nose. She was resolute. That was what her face expressed these days. A will and a way had taken root firmly beneath her brow—whether this way had to be trodden with tennis racket in hand, or in hard hours of ski gymnastics in preparation for the coming winter, or at the swimming pool, learning the proper breathing technique which transforms a woman's face into a fish's head with mouth rising to the surface at regular intervals. Conrad, however, avoided speaking with her about her efforts in any but a purely matter-of-fact fashion. And when the talk turned to sports, which happened fairly often, he would take his stand entirely within her own area of interest, at once and without premeditation. There was probably no firm ground on which he could take an outside, critical stand. She seemed scarcely to notice that he did not participate—although he used to be fairly adept at games. Certainly she did not take it amiss.

A tennis game was in progress. Marianne was being coached by Duracher, who had posted one of the young men—for some inscrutable reason he was called Peggy—on the other side of the net. Duracher himself, standing three steps from Marianne, supervised her every movement; now and then he would call out a correction. The platform was being used by some of the crowd for sun bathing; most of the spectators of this beginners' lesson were seated on the benches at the edge of the court. Among them was Conrad, but he wore street clothes. Today he was feeling better than he had for some time. What he particularly enjoyed was a certain inattentiveness to his surroundings which gained him space. Amid all the shouts, laughter, and conversation around the court he—and perhaps he alone—heard the cries and trills that came at intervals from the birds in the garden, especially those in the orchard. He listened to these with a pleasure which perhaps derived from the knowledge that he had a more extended sensation of space than those who were discussing Marianne's chances to develop a good stroke, or who confined their conversation to the objects and persons closest at hand. The sun poured down. To Conrad it was the first April sun of the year which he had really felt.

But after a while he bade his wife and the others good-bye. The temptation of the empty apartment, of solitude, became overpowering in this absorbing, spacious stillness of the spring season—a season that, no matter what noises were tossed into it, swallowed them up as pliantly as a swamp, a mute swamp filled with anticipation. Conrad, too, had changed. About the same time that those two books vanished from the desk, other objects made their appearance. These did not remain lying on the desk, but found a place in its drawers: several boxes of cigars and, recently, packages of cigarettes also. And a bottle or two of the "most sensible drink anyhow" found their way behind the untouched and immobile row of classics and the encyclopedia. Nowadays, in the late afternoon, when the maid brought Conrad his coffee and slippers, a bluish glass stood on the tray also, for use as required.

By now, in fact, Conrad was perfectly able to spread himself out in rings while lying peacefully on the couch.

He lay there; it was quiet; no traffic outside. Warmly, the alcohol he had drunk rose up toward his head, stretching itself out to act as a lining for all his thoughts, every outgoing and incoming notion. Of late, when he lay there and invited his "thoughts"—thoughts which even Herr von Hohenlocher could no longer have called purely "textilian"—the first thing that came was the sense of the presence and the opening up of a way. In this respect, and speaking in purely formal terms, there was undoubtedly a certain resemblance between the attitudes and situations of the two spouses. Each saw a way, but the ways diverged.

She on hers was looking energetically ahead, under that fore-head with its sharply indented nose. Her face nowadays often wore an obstinate, almost violent look. And she held on to her way with her hands, firmly and definitely, although at heart she was a little disappointed and therefore defiant. Whereas Conrad's way was not nearly so clear. He only sensed something. For the present that was all. When these intimations came to him before he had primed himself with tobacco or some of "the most sensible drink anyhow," they would be bright and clear, like the spring sunlight pouring into the ground so that you could almost believe it penetrated a foot deep into the earth and spread its light among the roots. Then there was a sensation of something lifting like a lid, something that covered a certain part of his life. And then it fairly often happened that as he rested on the couch he would once again recapture the declining light of that after-noon when he had suddenly started up and sped across the adjoining dining room and over the creaking and reverberating parquet floor of the wide living room, and there opened the window.

He fell into the habit of waiting for the onset of this state, as soon as he was alone. And, to be precise, he availed himself of the "most sensible drink anyhow" only if that state failed to come of its own accord. But it usually did come. The result was that Conrad had developed a highly curious relationship toward drinking, at this time of day, anyway. It consisted chiefly of his having the small, bluish glass standing beside him, filled. Most of the time it was later carried out, still full, by the maid; and she, for her part, might easily have become a tippler if the stuff had not burned her mouth and throat so dreadfully. Such Hohenlocherish aids were employed by Conrad largely as symbols of the new age that had dawned. Seldom were these symbols dishonored by actual employment.

But sometimes he would reach for the newspaper, which he frequently let lie unread nowadays. And when he looked up from his reading and out into the room, the room would suddenly bore him, would lie lifeless and opaque before him, refusing to offer enough space, to become a light and casual container for his thoughts. In such cases he would reach for the glass on the tray, drink, and lie back. Then the warming and reviving gin magnified his "thoughts" and daydreams, caused them to swell, and they would drift like flocks of clouds being driven by the wind toward, almost always, the same region of his soul. At least, that was how it had been of late. The "way" would become visible again. But some unknown had smashed the approach to the bridge—an unknown who hovered somewhere out there in that outermost, no longer specifiable ring of life which lies like the moon's ring around the closer area, distinctly filled with its own objects. Eight years ago that same unknown had contrived to slam the door of life in front of Conrad Castiletz's nose, and to wall up the doorway. At the bottom of his heart he considered the fate of Derainaux, the unfortunate painter, to have been the easier one. For himself, so it seemed, the broken bridge loomed over a chasm as mysterious as it was hopeless.

33 ह≫

wwwwwwwwwwwwwwwwwwwwwwwwwwwwwwwwwwwwww

INEVITABLY, such notions eventually led to feelings of vengeance. And if there were any object in the vacuum to which these could attach themselves, it would have to be the portrait of Henry Peitz which had taken shape in Conrad's imagination after he had heard Inkrat's story.

This development, no doubt, prompted Conrad to make an appointment with Herr Inkrat and on a very warm day in April to call on him at his home. It was situated behind a large, not especially beautiful, church. Perhaps the Romanesque portal of the apartment house, with its pillars and capitals, purported to be a kind of emanation of the neighboring structure. Conrad stepped off the steaming asphalt and out from under the blue sky, and wound his way up a whitewashed stairwell. Inkrat opened the door. They stepped into an excessively large room, resembling Herr von Hohenlocher's in its proportions, but lacking any personal flavor. The furnishings looked as if they might have been taken over along with the apartment (Inkrat lived with his mother); possibly that was also true of a number of unexpected, resplendent battle paintings in broad gold frames which adorned the walls: French dragoons with waving plumes advancing to attack. The piano, too, seemed not to pertain to the owner of the room and gave the impression of having stood uselessly about for unimaginable ages, with jaws clamped shut.

Here, too, there was a glass of "the most sensible drink anyhow"; and Conrad now availed himself of the offered cigarettes. (Incidentally, old Eisenmann would still offer Conrad a cigar now and then, but by long-established custom these were the foreman's rightful spoils.)

"I assume that something specific has brought you to see me," *Varanus aridus* said.

"Yes," Conrad replied. He suddenly felt very good. This scene had its romantic elements; it might have taken place in one of those mystery novels which in the past he had sometimes picked up for entertainment. Some of their titles flashed through his mind, along with the thought: "I really might seriously look into the whole affair." Immediately afterwards he thought of Günther Ligharts. All this went through his mind in a matter of seconds, while he gazed at the round-arched choir of the church visible through the window.

Inkrat waited in his immobile fashion.

"It concerns our conversation of the other day," Conrad went on. "That is, the case of my sister-in-law. I don't want to raise the question you've already answered—whether you consider Henry Peitz guilty. But your story set me wondering about something else."

"And what might that be?" the lizard asked without raising his voice at the end of the interrogative sentence, so that it took on an indifferent or superior sound.

"I wanted to ask—I know so little about this field—whether, in a case like Henry Peitz's, there would be surveillance after his release. In other words, whether the police keep an eye on such persons afterwards, and if so, for how long?"

"Herr Castiletz," the lizard replied with lidless gaze and total aridity, "they certainly do. As a matter of principle, anyone who has ever had anything to do with the police in any way remains thereafter more or less under surveillance. Of course I do not mean this literally. But the principle remains. If any police force in the world abandoned this basic principle, the assumption that crime is always threatening, just as the doctor feels about disease —it would be betraying its obligation to guard society. The physician, the policeman, and—I say this in order to delineate this type of mentality all the more clearly—the prose writer, the novelist

or narrator—have all made the greatest sacrifice that can be made
in the realm of the mind: they have committed themselves to
seeing the world as it is, never as it ought to be. That is to say,
they do so insofar as they are pure representatives of their type.
What is more, they repudiate all those claims to the world's
being different which reside in hidden corners of the heart or
sleep in some cradle of dreams. For such minds, there is only
one reality, there is no second reality they may escape to, perhaps with the pretext that it can some day be made real. But
this is where the realm of another type begins, a type which is
just as self-sufficient, but can live and act vigorously and finely
only by taking entirely different spiritual nourishment, and only
by assuming an entirely different mental posture—though without abandoning the value and the necessity of that first posture,
let alone refuting it—not even if they could shape the whole world
to their desires. Otherwise the world, no matter how fine it was,
would lose its balance and tumble into a void. Old as the human
race is, very little is known about the natural history, the biology,
of the mind. You see the indispensable figure rising out of the
pedestal which is its underlying, appropriate way of life and
basic attitude. If for one reason or another you attempt to put
the figure on another pedestal, you'll end up with two pedestals
and one shattered statue. Just consider the almost heroic modesty
that is involved in a man's applying his mental force to the at-
tainment of a single goal: to be able wholly to assent, without
excepting anything, without wanting to change anything. To
offer a counterpoise to all things within the self. To be able to
feel as a matter of deep and real experience that this world is
always in order, always hung correctly on its hinges. And thus
in the end we may attain, without whole personalities, a knowledge and a capacity already possessed by every loafer who stands
leaning against a fence and who from the start sees the world
just as it is, though it may be that he only sees it from below,
sees it squirming on its belly through the mud. . . . For that rea-

son, I say, in the final analysis to be on the police force is to be in one of the few places where you can attain a seasoned conviction that criminals are necessary. Hence you can always be ready, without anger, to deal with them."

Although we have remarked that Conrad's "textilian" rigidity had eased considerably—this was still too much for him. The thought flashed through his mind that Herr Inkrat might be an excellent theoretician, but that in practice he could hardly be the kind of criminologist needed for a case like Louison Veik's, where the ability to talk more or less cleverly mattered damned little. And because Herr Inkrat was something of a dud as a detective, Conrad himself had to wander around a solid wall without a gate in it. With a very faint superiority that trickled out of the innermost chambers of his being—the greatest power the amateur has over the professional in such a situation—he turned the conversation back to more concrete channels: "Do you know, Herr Inkrat, what this man Peitz is doing today, and where he lives?"

"No," Inkrat said. "As you know, I washed my hands of this case years ago. Probably he is still in Berlin, running his business. During the time we had him under official surveillance, by the way, we were unable to observe anything unusual about his conduct."

Conrad fastened his gaze once more upon the gray rounded shape of the church choir outside, as though this were the wall that he would break through just as soon as he selected the right spot. Dusk had settled deeply over the room, and Inkrat switched on a lamp. The light, leaping abrupting into all the corners, stirred Conrad to greater animation.

"The chief thing I came to ask you, sir, is really a purely legal point," he said with considerable sprightliness. "Namely, whether I would have the right, as a relation of the deceased, to attempt to solve the case on my own?"

If Inkrat was surprised, his immobility concealed it. He said quietly and in a tone of perhaps genuine indifference: "There could be no objection to that."

They fell silent. Conrad could feel upon his skin that Inkrat was subjecting him to study. The lamp on the desk behind Inkrat threw its light full into Conrad's face. A clear, sharp image rose to the surface of his mind: he saw himself sitting over wine in his father-in-law's study. Opposite him, above the sofa, hung the portrait of the cat with the eyes of an animal deity. And he felt, as though it were still present as a physical memory in his limbs, that fatigue and numbness that had overcome him when the magistrate finished his story about Louison and Derainaux. Now, here too, in the cone of light from the lamp, and under the scrutiny of Inkrat, a kind of circumstantiality numbed him. His tongue felt paralyzed and he was incapable of the effort of articulating what he wanted to or ought to say: that he himself, as a boy of fifteen, had been right here in this city at the time of the crime, visiting his aunt, Frau Erika von Spresse.

"May I ask you," Herr Inkrat said, "whether you have some definite theory which has led you to this idea of investigating on your own?" He immediately softened the force of this candid question by adding: "Incidentally, I can tell you that if you do have, and if in the course of your work on the case you should find it strengthened, you are under no obligation to inform the police of your discoveries if it seems better to you, in the interests of completely clarifying the case, to postpone direct intervention by the authorities."

Conrad instantly felt himself to be wholly master of the situation. Yes, he did mean to look into the matter. As things stood, he had plenty of free time he could devote to this. That was simple and clear. He would take this case in hand and put things in order. A sudden self-confidence filled him, rather similar to the feeling he had had the time Herr von Hohenlocher, simply to amuse himself, had asked him about that silly business of the spark in the electric bell. In this mood of resolution, he was able to pass over Inkrat's question. He thanked the inspector for his kindness, bade a polite good-bye, and descended the white-washed and now illuminated staircase.

34 🦆

〰〰〰〰〰〰〰〰〰〰〰〰〰〰〰〰〰〰〰〰〰〰

WHEN he stepped out on the sidewalk, it was half past six and the shops were still open. He had only a five-minute walk to his home; the street on which Herr Inkrat lived branched off Wack-enroder Strasse, which also faced the front of the church. After walking down the seemingly endless long side of the building, Conrad turned the corner. The traffic on Wackenroder Strasse was heavy at this time of evening. He found it oppressive. More-over, he now remembered that he had of course forgotten some-thing: he should have asked Inkrat for an exact description of the stolen jewelry, if possible with pictures. These must be in the police files. He would have to take care of that detail some other time. Noted. Conrad stopped in front of the window of a stationer's.

He looked at the many things displayed—portfolios, blotters, paperweights, and fountain pens in all sizes and colors. But some-thing deep within him kept him from going in and making a purchase which in view of his clear intentions was perfectly sensi-ble. He suddenly felt the desire to take a stand at a sufficient distance from all this, to place it apart from him once more, before he took on this affair of Louison, so that when he did become engaged in it, he would be doing so out of wholly free choice. As this impulse came to him, he thought of Günther

Ligharts; but the image of Günther was in a sense much too close for him to be able to observe it or define it to himself. Immediately after this succession of thoughts, he went in and bought a blue quarto notebook.

When he got home, Marianne had not yet returned. Conrad withdrew to the "library room."

Of course he had read detective stories. But this enterprise was different from the start; there was no doubt about that. He had the distinct feeling that he was not simply taking up and attacking this case—although that is the way it should have been. A freely chosen direction! That was it. The phrase gave him enormous satisfaction, as in the past that other phrase about "slumbering faults." As the words "freely chosen direction" came to him, he saw himself as a boy perched on that tree in the water meadows, by the edge of the pond, close to the ground, sitting on a horizontal branch as if on a bench. He saw himself looking out into the meadows. He also saw the little red pail. Just now he did not think of his mother.

Then Conrad undertook the necessary first entries. First, as an unsettled item: "Exact description of the jewelry." He paused for a moment to fill in the blank on the cover of the notebook with the words: "Louison Veik." Then his pen began to race as he conscientiously set down all the facts that Herr Inkrat had related at Herr von Hohenlocher's. Conrad was engaged in a hard struggle with them, that is, with putting them into words, when the maid tapped at the door leading to the dining room, then opened it to invite him to supper. Conrad caught a glimpse of Marianne already seated at table. He slipped the blue notebook under the desk blotter.

The following afternoon, when he returned from the mill, the notebook lay on top of the blotter.

Conrad realized, of course, that for a maid with a duster and rag, such a notebook on his desk would necessarily fall into the same class as *Dyeing* or *Chemical Treatment of Wool*. This insight disposed of any resentment he might feel toward the girl—but in no way improved the situation. That evening he did not continue his entries, but instead locked the blue notebook in a desk drawer.

At first there was no change, nothing noteworthy, in Marianne's conduct. Conrad could not tell whether she had entered the study during the day, or whether she had, by chance, not been in the room all day. Later, when they were in bed, occupied with literature, as they were every evening nowadays, he received a kind of answer to his inward questions, reflections, and fears.

As she read, Marianne lay facing the lamp, and hence had her back to him. The tanned nape of her neck emerged firm and sturdy from the white nightgown, crowned by her blonde hair, which had been growing steadily lighter of late. Her hair looked somewhat coarser than in the past. All at once Conrad noticed that the green beryl earrings were missing.

He started in alarm. The answer, though imparted by so trivial a fact, struck him harder than a harsh word. At the same time it was unassailable because of its possible ambiguity. His efforts in regard to Louison, his action—which consisted merely in having visited Inkrat and having bought a notebook—became fixed by Marianne's removal of the earrings. Something was definitely determined, and consequences seemed bound to follow. It was simply too hard for Conrad, too oppressive, to accept this mute speech without contradiction, and to reconcile himself to it.

After some hesitation, he said: "Marianne darling. . . ?"

She did not answer. Ah well, perhaps the book was engrossing.

"Marianne—what have you done with your beautiful earrings today?"

Several uncomfortable minutes passed before she answered, lightly and firmly, without changing her position: "I lost one of them and can't find it. There's no sense in wearing the other alone."

"Of course," he said, promptly accepting the statement. He was quite grateful to her for putting it this way.

Some time thereafter, incidentally, the couple changed their sleeping arrangements—in perfect accord. Conrad moved first to a wide sofa in the "dressing room," later to the divan in the "library." There were several good reasons for this. Conrad read longer and longer at night, whereas Marianne had to rise very early nowadays, since Duracher was coaching beginners from half past five to half past six in the morning (the man did for pleasure what professionals would do for hard cash)—that is, before he reported for work at the mill. Marianne had to have a good night's sleep if she wanted to be in form for tennis. Moreover, Conrad disturbed her rest, especially of late, by tossing frequently, sleeping uneasily, and even talking in his sleep. On one occasion Marianne said—for the first time: "You ought to take up sports again. You obviously need the exercise."

Once, in the middle of the night, while they were still sleeping in the same room, Marianne's bedside lamp, abruptly switched on by startled fingers, scooped a dim cave of light out of the darkness of the bedroom. Conrad had screamed in his sleep, screamed horribly. She bent over him and shook him by the shoulders. "Did you have a bad dream?" she asked, angry rather than comforting.

"I don't know," he said, staring sleepily at her, still frightened. But he did know. When the light was put out again, the dream hung above him in the darkness, still dense and coherent; in fact its pressure seemed to return, so that Conrad began groping for the light switch. In the middle of the nocturnal "dressing room," which was illuminated by a strangely high and pale light, something sat on the parquet floor. Black, moist, glistening, with a kind of terrible shamelessness. He recognized it as a yard-long, thick-bodied, giant Japanese salamander. Behind it on the wall towered the big mirror which hung between the windows. The salamander's name was "Young Fellow." It was impossible to get rid of him, if only because Conrad would have had to lay hands on the creature. But he could not prevent several persons from coming through the hall, whose floor was covered with jute matting (since when?). Among them were his father and his Aunt Erika von Spresse. To put this business into proper order, to settle it, would have taken a little time, a little calm and composure. He would have to walk very slowly toward the mirror, squinting his eyes, even though he might come very close to the salamander. Only by looking composedly into the mirror with eyes slightly squinted could he make "Young Fellow" disappear. Desperately, in the impotence of the dream, Conrad struggled for the strength it would take to perform the one act which would allow the affair to turn out well. And then he conquered. Slowly, heavily as stone, he was able to move toward the mirror. Already "Young Fellow" was disappearing. But what Conrad then saw in the mirror opened up like a howling abyss. He screamed.

And then Marianne had turned on the light.

35 ॐ

THE advancing spring passed gradually into the warm, cloying stasis of midsummer. We may say that at this time Conrad Castiletz "ripened." A pressure, which had hitherto held his life captive in a definite, unassailable form and order, gradually diminished, began giving way to a more receptive attitude. That is how he experienced his new condition. And to the extent that the things in his life had surface names (every name expresses an obligation on the part of the object, a witty philosopher once remarked), he began to see, beneath the surface of more or less showy titles, the prolongation of each object or act. These extensions back into the past sometimes made things seem very different from their names. That, for example, was the fate of such labels as "put in order" or "boyhood realm and land of childhood in the water meadows," or even "turning your attention to something of your own free will and decision." He was able to trace a good many things back to their origin, which simply consisted in his having at some time or other begun to parrot his father. Often, he discovered, he had not only taken over certain words and expressions, but he had adopted even his father's manner of moving his mouth and lips. He did not do this only with regard to anecdotes, those honorable family heirlooms. Rather, to give one example: there was the attitude Conrad had always taken toward a man's changing the course of his life and shifting from an existing track. He began to suspect that his closed mind toward this sort of thing was again a kind of contraband smuggled into his personality from his father's territory, without his ever having noticed.

Perhaps he was not so clearly conscious of the more "receptive attitude" he was developing as these excessively plain words suggest, but the attitude was there, and was entirely serious. Conrad was beginning to yield and to let some things slips from his hands. If we may compare his youthful character with a tightly drawn knot, the only metaphor that would suit his present condition would be that of a basin or bowl or some other vessel which freely receives what is poured into it.

And this process was gratifying. He began to conceive of "the serious side of life" as something entirely different from his previous notions of it. (This term is usually thrown at a young person's face at graduation, when grownups resort to the makeshift of such solemn phrases.) The serious side of life, he had come to feel, was this: that something really happened, and that you straightened up out of a stooped position to confront it— rather surprised at your own stature.

All the same, summer is a season which affords people relatively little intellectual freedom. Everything is lush and densely overgrown, with leaves rounding into domes of foliage. A man can do little more than let the honey flow into his bowl, provided he is so fortunate as to have a bowl temporarily empty.

In August Marianne went to Bavaria with several of the crowd, Peter Duracher among them, for some mountain climbing. This was the one sport she had practiced as a girl. A week after her departure, Conrad received greetings—a post card splattered with signatures—from the ice-capped peaks of the Austrian Silvretta. Shortly afterwards she wrote from Northern Styria that she had found climbing the Bischofsmütze and the Buchstein fairly easy.

This made no impression on Conrad, not even a momentary one. He was alone, and enjoying it. When he had had a bit of gin, the serious side of life opened out like a bowl, sometimes in the strange fashion that a heavy truck passing outside could make him vividly aware of the irrevocability of the moment. One moment everything shook from the rumbling on Weissenborn Strasse and then on Hans Hayde Strasse. Then the stillness closed in. Mute objects like the furniture seemed to be far more familiar with stillness than he himself, for which reason they looked down at him haughtily without betraying their thoughts. Never again would this truck pass by at this time as it had just done. The word "past" filled with a summary fragrance, like a bowl with honey. And yet it remained in some curious way ambiguous, even dubious. Such were Conrad's current intellectual experiences— and they were thoroughly untextilian.

Then his vacation came and he met Marianne in Innsbruck. They were to go to an Italian seaside resort together. She walked at his side along one of those streets at whose end a grayish-green mountain invariably looks down with a rough, brisk mien, in spite of the summer's heat. Marianne's hair seemed ash-blonde; the nape of her neck was brown as a nut. Conrad stood about, a bit at a loss, though he felt with extraordinary clarity how well Marianne fitted into these athletic surroundings. He proudly ignored this.

Venice reminded Conrad of the costly, magnificent robes of

state he had seen in museums. An uncomfortable garment, he felt, which seemed not to fit him; rather, he remained half outside it, condemned to a constant, pointless astonishment—which he felt to be curiously obligatory. From the start the prospect of staying here for a week or longer seemed a terrible imposition, and rides out to the Lido made it no easier. The beach edged by hotels, the suspect pomp of the "Stabilimento" (at that time the old one still stood; shortly afterwards the vexed gods let it be burned down)—they all afflicted him, along with the heat, which had seemed far less intense in Rimini, where they had gone around most of the day with a minimum of clothing on. Marianne, more-over, developed a new and curious eagerness for seeing sights and art treasures, which struck Conrad as a transference of her athletic discipline to areas ill-suited to it. On the first day he went along—putting off an intended excursion to Padua—and so he stood beside his wife in the Palace of the Doges and gazed into monstrous quantities of limbs and clouds which Tintoretto had housed there. Now and then he experienced a freer moment, when a breeze touched his brow and he caught a glimpse of a softer, more distant view—on the outermost Riva Schiavoni, for instance, beyond the Spezia Inn. The water lapping against stone, the steps descending into the canal, the marble railings, seemed for a few moments like a bridge that could lead him to a better frame of mind.

But soon the whole knot was untied. This occurred on the Calle S. Felice, outside a building that bore the number 4082A. Marianne wanted to stroll among the narrow streets of Venice, and Conrad had gladly joined her. Somewhat distractedly he was reading a sign on the house in question: it read *Laboratorio Tedesco*, that is, "German Workshop," and belonged to a hat-maker. Suddenly Marianne's voice leaped high; the noise and laughter of greetings filled the narrow street; and a new situation, new circumstances, had come into being. They had run into three of their crowd from the tennis court.

Marianne instantly fell into a gay and comradely relationship with them. She seemed not especially surprised to have run into them ("Peggy" was one of the party). That came out in the ensuing chatter. Conrad became conscious of a kind of paralysis in himself. He lay like a stone in a bubbling brook under all the laughter and talk. Then a way to escape came to him, and he began planning it as they walked together down the Calle S. Felice—although for an instant he perceived that perhaps his plan might not be quite the right course to take, at least not from a certain point of view. . . . At this stage in his reflections he thought fleetingly of Aunt Erika.

That evening he asked Marianne whether she liked Venice. He came out with the question perhaps too suddenly, so that it sounded somewhat crude; but after her surprise had subsided, she replied that she thought the city "absolutely gorgeous" and was sorry that they hadn't come there on their wedding trip. That had been her own fault, her prejudice against "newlyweds in Venice." Conrad, having assured himself that this joint was in order and would move easily, then suggested that Marianne spend another week in Venice. That would be all the easier since she had now found companions and would have the three men at her disposal; they had already said they intended to stay a while. He himself would give up the last days of his vacation for Eisenmann's sake; things were probably too much for the old fellow to handle by himself.

The following night Conrad left. But he did not go home. He traveled by way of Innsbruck and Munich to Stuttgart.

36 ?∾

wwwwwwwwwwwwwwwwwwwwwwwwwwwwwwwwwwwwwwwwwwwwwwwwww

THERE, standing on the top-floor landing of a house on Stift Strasse, the envelopment and constraint of late summer for the first time receded from him. He became really and fully aware that it was autumn, October. The window on the landing looked out over lower-lying parts of the city to the wide and open hills and the neighboring mountains. Innumerable points of light flashed here and there out of the sea of houses, knobs on the ridges of roofs, panes of glass in open casement windows that glittered under the sun.

A sheet of watercolor paper was thumbtacked to the door, and on it was written in brown brush strokes: Maria Rosanka. Conrad rang. But there was no sound of a bell. He knocked, and now footsteps approached—long but light strides.

"My name is Conrad Castiletz and I should like to speak with you, *gnädige Frau*," he said. As he spoke, he realized fully that the assurance he had lately felt and displayed sprang from sources other than the previous competencies of his life. It came, one might say, from an upright, and no longer from a stooped, bearing.

Maria Rosanka had opened the door wide, without mistrust. "Come in," she said, stepping aside. She wore denim overalls, the trousers of which were completely covered with dots and dashes of paint. They looked as if strewn with confetti. Maria Rosanka wore this outfit with dignity. It suited her, and yet would lead no one to doubt that he was in the presence of a lady.

"I should have let you know that I was coming, through Herr von Hohenlocher, whom you may remember," Conrad said as he followed her.

"Hard to forget him," she replied, "since he came to see me only a week ago and bought two pictures. Incidentally, he mentioned your name."

"Why—in what connection?"

They entered the studio. Conrad was stunned by the stroke of fortune which had smoothed his path here—for only half an hour ago he had succeeded in extracting Maria Rosanka's address from the telephone book at the railroad station.

"In connection—actually in connection with your wife's deceased sister. That is, Herr von Hohenlocher gave me a very amusing description of a stag night at his house in the spring. . . ."

It was all perfectly natural. Everything here seemed perfectly natural, including the fact that she looked exactly as Hohenlocher had described her. Conrad looked out through the big, slanting window. The city, the mountains, the remoter distances lay golden under a sky as blue as in spring and yet deep as an organ's bass. The studio smelled of paint and varnish. Things lay about everywhere, scattered with a masterly touch, as it were—tossed here and there with a certain elegance: brushes on the long deal table by the window, or a jacket over a chair, its lemon-yellow silk lining turned outward, or a pair of gloves almost falling from the edge of the table. . . . A large bouquet of asters in front of the slanting pane of glass seemed to gather the autumnal undulations outside into a single distinct point.

As Maria Rosanka cleared a chair for Conrad, he said: "That is why I have come—on account of Louison."

"Ah?" she said. And then she added, pensively and emotionally: "On account of Louison."

"You were a close friend of hers?" Conrad said cautiously.

"Yes, I loved her," the painter replied candidly.

His intentions, the question he had planned to ask struck him just then as totally parched, pitiful, very nearly contemptible. This woman had known Louison face to face.

At last I am living! These words came to his mind with great distinctness, and at the same time he was intensely astonished. Maria Rosanka had risen and gone into an adjoining room. Now she returned with three framed pictures and expertly, as a painter will do, placed them in the proper light.

Ah yes, it was Louison. Holding flowers. Not a prim little nosegay, but a large bunch, and posed not in an eighteenth century manner, as in Derainaux's portrait, but leaning forward, her face animated. In the second picture, she was laughing. In the third she was half naked, wrapped in a Javanese sarong.

"Did you know Derainaux?" Conrad asked abruptly.

"Yes," she said. "In Paris."

"And had you seen the portraits—the ones he painted of Louison?"

"No, to my sorrow. All through that period I heard virtually nothing from Louison. I didn't dare go to Leipzig—although she asked me to come. Because of her, because of Derainaux, because of—of Marianne, I mean—because of your present wife. But especially because of Derainaux. Since I was so in love with him. The most wonderful man I ever met. And at the same time—I know perfectly well that I'm absurd-looking. Oh, Derainaux— good Lord, when I think of Marianne. . ."

She broke off, profoundly alarmed. Her dark, brilliant eyes, candid as those of an animal, in her big, leathery-brown face, nevertheless seemed to assert that she would not regret any of the things she had said. Yes, she had loved Derainaux. And she did look absurd. And she had not dared go to Leipzig while Derainaux was there.

"Please let me have the pictures," Conrad said.

"I'm sorry, but I must say no," Maria Rosanka replied. "I'm not selling these pictures to anyone at any price, even though I am no Derainaux."

Conrad was silent. What would he have done with the paintings anyhow? Could he have taken them with him, hung them anywhere? No. For the first time, sitting in this studio, he felt that his present and his previous life and its circumstances—literally, the things in it and the things standing around it—were in the final analysis only accidental and temporary. Something that—that could be abandoned. But the thought restored his bearings and his erectness, and so he managed to return to the original purpose of his visit.

"You are the last person," he said slowly, with a careful enunciation that somehow tasted novel in his mouth, "among all Louison's friends, relatives, and acquaintances, who saw her alive. That is why I have come to you. From the moment I first heard about it, I was deeply shaken by Louison Viek's tragic end. And beyond that, I have decided to attempt to solve this unsolved mystery."

His last words struck a ridiculous note, he thought.

Maria Rosanka said: "Oh, you mean who did it and what happened to the jewelry and so on. . . . Odd, but none of that ever interested me. Incidentally, the police had me in for questioning, too, but there was very little information I could give."

"Were you by any chance interrogated by a Herr Inkrat?"

"The very man," she said. "*Varanus aridus Inkrat*, later a specimen in Hohenlocher's collection."

Conrad laughed, but only out of politeness. "So you know that, too!" he exclaimed.

"I always know everything," Maria Rosanka said. "Because I'm a witch, you see."

She said this last without the trace of a smile, her dark, shiny animal's eyes gazing steadily into space. For a moment Conrad felt as if the floor were receding beneath his chair, as though the chair were swaying and he himself dreaming. But then he suddenly felt able to classify those eyes. They belonged in the same category as the eyes of the cat in the photograph.

"I sense that about you, too," he replied with utter sobriety. "That is why I should like to ask you, if you will, to tell me first of all what you think of Herr Inkrat as a person."

"A very unhappy person," she said. "He should have been a philosopher or a doctor. He slid, or rather slipped, into the wrong profession. In his misplaced role as a criminologist, he struggled intently and sincerely to fill the position into which he had stumbled, that is, to make up for having been miscast by life. He wanted to remedy his false situation by accepting it, by taking it into himself and stowing it away inside him, if I may so express it. And so he tried to determine what a criminologist really is. That did not make him one, but he did become a theoretician. One can only regret that he didn't shift to literature."

"As a matter of fact, I think he once intended to," Castiletz said. "But you, my dear lady, are really and truly a witch."

They fell silent. It was easy being silent with Maria Rosanka; you could sit still with her in the most relaxed manner, without any tension arising out of the growing silence. For some moments Conrad forgot everything and sat looking at the paintings of Louison. Even the one with the sarong was as close to him as his own heart; and no heated margin within him kindled at the russet tint of the flesh, as it had once done at the sight of Marianne's white skin, when the very air above it had seemed to quiver like a smoldering fire. A tender, infinite yearning gripped him, and this feeling seemed to enter from outside, from the landscape outside, filtering finely and powerfully through the wide sally port of the slanting window.

"You wanted to hear about my last meeting with Louison," Maria Rosanka said after a while, speaking easily and fluently. "There isn't much to say, and you will be just as disappointed as Herr Inkrat was. Of course I instantly volunteered as a witness. Since she was passing through Stuttgart, I'd gone to the railroad station with a few posies." (At this point Conrad felt what Hohenlocher had mentioned, that Maria Rosanka had a tendency to be ironic about herself. But she went about it in the most restrained way—in this case perhaps only by her choice of the word "posies" and the tone in which she spoke it.) "Louison sent me away about a quarter of an hour before the train was to leave, so that I spent no more than five minutes with her. She said she wanted to go to her compartment—it was a ladies' compartment, second class. She'd never wanted to travel in a sleeping car. I wish she had, for I've always felt somehow that you were safer from danger in a sleeping car. Perhaps that's silly. All the same, in a sleeping car there's always some member of the train crew standing around in the aisle. Herr Inkrat also said that this idea of mine was silly and that fate was not in the habit of drawing back from those who take sleeping cars. . . . Anyhow, Louison sent me away. She was obviously in a bad mood—that was the only thing about her that I noticed and was able to report to the police. But all her friends knew about those moods of hers. I mean her depressions. When I was doing those portraits of her, one day she would come to the studio as pliant as a shrub in spring and the next day she would stumble about uncertainly, keep turning around every moment, and start with fright when a sparrow fluttered its wings on the roof guttering. During that last year, after the affair with Derainaux, her nerves were generally in a bad state, or so I thought. Not surprising after such an accumulation of misunderstandings on the part of everyone involved. That whole story always struck me as a perfect example of what might be called a 'fundamental error.' . . . Anyhow, the last time I saw her, Louison was in one of her bad states. I remember we were standing on the platform and she was frightened altogether out of proportion because a baggage cart rolled past close behind her back. She jumped aside and gave a little cry. But in other respects she was anything but timid. Right after this incident, we embraced for the last time and said good-bye."

If Conrad had not been looking at Maria Rosanka, he would not have known that she was crying. She wept without a sound, and her voice as she spoke those last words had not betrayed her. Rapidly and easily, with no trace of a sob, the tears flowed from her big, wide-open eyes, which had the helpless look of a frightened child, frightened by its own weeping. Conrad himself was close to tears. He probably would have broken down but for the fact that at a certain point in his life, back "in the remoteness of time," the possibility of any such flowing release and relief seemed to have vanished like a river going underground in the limestone caverns of the Carso.

And so he checked himself, waited, kept silent, and looked out into the sunlit expanse that leaned gently against the big, slanting window. He knew that he ought to go. And for some moments parting came hard. Once again, as he kissed Maria Rosanka's hand with a feeling of warmth and profound respect, the word "past" filled his consciousness, and, like a full honeycomb at the end of the summer, this replete hour in the bright studio remained in him, with its lingering smell of paint.

He walked, but missed the shortest route to the railroad station. He walked, in fact, as if surrounded by a thin, transparent membrane, past the Botanical Gardens and the Polytechnical School, and came out on a straight street that led to the left-hand corner of the big railroad station. He should have taken the time for a full meal, but he ate standing at the counter, gulping down Russian eggs or something of the sort. Then he checked the trains. His inner turmoil wore a façade of untroubled composure, for he still had four days left of his vacation and therefore did not have to travel straight home. If he wanted seriously to investigate the case of Louison Veik—and he no longer had any doubts about that—it would undoubtedly be useful to become better acquainted with the whole stretch of railroad line, perhaps a segment at a time; and to concentrate especially on the part of the line to which the police, to judge by Inkrat's story, had paid less attention. . . . At the moment this reasoning seemed to Conrad completely convincing. He saw his course as clearly as a small, brightly lit circle. After collecting his baggage from the checkroom, he bought a ticket to Heilbronn.

Conrad was alone in the compartment. Shortly after leaving the station, the train roared through the so-called Prague Tunnel.

Conrad abruptly sat up straight on his seat. Oh well, he could leave that out of consideration for the present. But even in those first minutes of the ride he learned something new, or rather recalled something he had forgotten. He was alert and excited. Then, as the landscape opened out and the Neckar came in sight, the windings of the river and the rises and dips of the rolling hills passed with great freshness and clarity before his illuminated inner eye, which was washed clean like a meadow after rain and stretched in a glassy arch like a clear evening sky. Smoke hovered over tile roofs, and between the gables of houses he saw deep into the narrow streets of the villages. The late afternoon light bathed the distant hills in neutral tints and cloaked the nearer landscape in the golden blur of slanting rays of sunlight. The train stopped twice. Conrad stood at the window, which he had lowered, and leaned out slightly, looking in the direction of the train. The cool country air mingled with the smoke of the train, which flitted along on the tracks, accompanied by vigorous banging and rattling noises, leaving everything behind, from gables and treetops to ducks on ponds. Half an hour had passed since the train had started from Stuttgart.

A broad golden hump blocked the tracks. As the distance shrank, it swelled into a wall. High up against the blue sky the foilage of grapevines climbed jaggedly. The train roared past a station and straight toward the wall. At the foot of it, a small, black, sooty mouth appeared. Then the train slipped with a roar into the tunnel, whose walls seemed made of smoke.

Conrad leaped up from his seat. Outside, the darkness howled and crashed, and within the long-drawn-out thunder innumerable smaller noises exploded like barrels full of shards being dumped all at once. This seemed to last for a long time. Suddenly the roar was swallowed up behind, as if absorbed by the soft palate of a great mouth, and the train once again ran quietly along, swathed in soft, scraping noises. Conrad looked out into a new world, which now, with the lowering evening, extended farther and farther, yet at the same time became more and more enclosed: a wide circle of mountains, perfectly straight at the top, squared off almost alarmingly just on the verge of the twilight sky; the gray foam of leafy woods on the dimming hillsides, which with the regularity of a series of funnels enclosed a succession of valleys in which the train was turning a long, steady curve. And now, looking back, Conrad espied at the bottom of the wall the twin nostrils of the sooty tube out of which the train had roared only a moment before. In his excitement he shifted his weight from one leg to the other. If only the train would stop now!

Next moment he noticed the slowing movement, the screech of the brakes, the clank of switches, and the station. He grabbed his suitcase from the baggage net and came within an inch of smashing it through the windowpane. His manner of leaving the train could justly be called frantic—as if this leisurely local train were going to be stopping for no more than ten seconds. Yet everywhere men and women, weighed down by suitcases and baskets, were climbing slowly and deliberately out of the train, while Conrad Castiletz broke through their sluggish lines in a flash and reached the platform. Once there, his haste obviously no longer had the least sense, but it diminished only slightly. When the conductor at the barrier, observing that Conrad's ticket was to Heilbronn, asked him whether he wished to make a stopover here, Conrad simply left the ticket in the man's hand and rushed out to the square in front of the railroad station, his hand clenched tightly around the handle of his suitcase—so overpowering was the feeling that he had reached the goal of his journey. There, at the terminus and final quietus of his catapulted emergence, he found someone who thought it quite reasonable for a man with baggage to ask for a good hotel. And so he was directed to the inn directly across the station plaza, whose portico was adorned by red grapevine foliage.

37 ॐ

~~~~~~

THE walls were covered chest-high with a dark figured wall-paper. Then came a molding, from which point the walls were painted in a bright, amiable, naïvely complacent pattern. That was the first thing Conrad saw when he awoke in the wide wooden bed. After a while, life once again assumed its usual forms, overcoming the shapes of dream. Details began to appear —for example, surprise at his finding a hotel like this, with central heating, a big washbasin, and running hot and cold water in so tiny a locality. (In this, however, Conrad was mistaken, for he had seen only the outermost edge of the town from the railroad station.) Footsteps sounded outside, and he heard shoes being set down at his door; evidently they had been cleaned, as had his suit, which was hung with a clinking noise on the coat hook beside the door. There was a light knock and the footsteps receded. Amid all these trivia Conrad, still in bed, recalled with regret that he did not have with him that blue notebook in which he had been entering everything of any significance connected with the case. (It would scarcely have been wise to have taken it along on the trip to Italy with Marianne!) As it was, without that particular aid, it was somewhat harder to attack the subject in an orderly fashion, as a freely elected pursuit.

Barely an hour later he was walking through the town: its life moved deliberately in the morning sunlight—a cart laden with straw, and a truck with barrels. As he came out on the highway, which rose at a gradual incline toward the surrounding wall of mountains, he saw the mighty three-quarters circle of the range lying before him in the morning sun, towering several hundred feet at the highest point—a steep enclosing wall topped by the cloudy foliage of the trees like frozen foam.

Inhabitants of this region often explain the unusual landscape as due to the Neckar, which they say flowed here ages ago and gouged out a precise arc. But this is a casual explanation which will not stand examination. Why should the river, which avoids this entire hollow, once have turned in a narrow curve—running backward, in fact—to flow for the second time around a mountain that to this day it has not broken through? But no, these perfectly straight edges, these slopes that look as if they had been drawn with a compass in a slightly elliptical curve whose greatest arc is about one and three quarter miles, do not deny their origin, even though the wine-golden sun at times spins a gossamer of softness and distance over their excessive angularity and lies upon the slopes like the fading glow of a joyful smile on a harsh countenance. If Conrad had ever "studied" such matters ("studied" as the boy Günther had once studied antediluvian monsters), he might have understood the mystery of the region. Very likely it owed its origin to something not of this world. Perhaps its aspect faithfully and rigidly preserves the memory of a super-human catastrophe, when some celestial body struck the area like a projectile, forcing the soft shell limestone out into a bulging ring and itself boring deep into the ground in the center, which is heaped up to form a cone-shaped vault, a tomb for the giant that descended in white heat, amid thunderous howls, to bury itself. That giant, to be sure, was only a grain of dust compared with the planet that drew it with fearful attractive force from its celestial orbit. The place still looks harsh, solitary, and rigid; for all its dress of fine forest, it resembles one of the craters of the moon.

Conrad saw a dirt road branching off to the right of the highway and leading toward the crater. He strode rapidly along it between bare fields, looking distinctly enterprising in his sports outfit, for he wore shorts and heavy shoes. In his pocket he carried a bar of chocolate, a pack of cigarettes, and a good flashlight.

Now, in the morning, it was cool; the sun was thin and kindly. Everywhere there was silence, as though left over from the previous night. The dirt road ended in a dry ditch that ran between willows approximately parallel to the mountain wall, which lunged upward steeper and steeper on Conrad's left. It was, however, not yet forested at this point, but planted with grapes. A path bordered the ditch. Conrad followed it. The grass was green here, but farther off, among the leafy crowns of the steep slopes, bright streaks of red and yellow hues showed. After a few hundred paces, a hill approached from the left, terminating in a kind of dike, which ran straight across the ditch. When Conrad climbed the hill, he found himself standing before a pond whose swampy odor had been with him for some time. Only now, however, did he become aware of it. There was a bench close to the water.

Conrad went up to the edge of the pond, leaned forward, and looked down into the water—for a moment he was tempted to kneel so as to see better. But he could see nothing in the water. The rather muddy pool lay still before him, an oily depth like the cheek of overripe, half-rotten fruit. The circlet of reeds surrounding the pond had been bleached by the autumn; here and there a stalk would be withered like a dried bone or bent forward, submissive and somnolent, preparatory to sinking into the water. The willows—indecent, octopus-like trees, their plump heads exploding into innumerable arms—seemed to express full assent to the watery decay and autumnal weariness. But the other trees behind them, tall and slender, held their beautifully colored leaves against the distant sky.

Beyond the pool there was a water-filled ditch, which led somewhat closer to the mountain; it came within a stone's throw of the wall and then held that distance. On Conrad's left there were now meadows and brush filling the space between the ditch and the almost vertical slope. These meadows and the whole area seemed moist, cool, filled with a hundred little clearings and paths to invite the stroller. A sense of homecoming stirred in Conrad, as if he had been away from the country for years. The dense, domed forest made up of all sorts of trees, which now appeared above the vineyards on the slope, struck him as a precious, luxuriant sight—as though only now were the heat and the barrenness of the Italian summer receding from him. The autumn cascaded down the declivity, poured from the woods in streamers, clouds, and streaks of red and brown, mixed with a bright yellow that rose into the sky like a shout. The sky itself, now that the sun was higher, was swelling into a sonorous blue deep. From the shrubs in the meadow, barberries showed up as bright, madder-red spots. The ground was breathing; the leaves, water, and grass smelled strongly. It was growing warm. Yet Conrad walked faster. Swinging around the central cone in a wide curve, the railroad embankment was approaching. It ran directly in front of Conrad, across the ditch and, on the left, perpendicularly toward the mountain.

Conrad broke through thickets, nettles, and low-growing trees. Then he climbed the embankment at the mouth of the tunnel. Up on top, everything was leveled out, covered with broken rock and gravel. There was an oily or tarry smell from ties baking in the sun. The view was wide and open.

But Conrad turned his back upon the landscape.

Like the forgotten temple of some deity, the entrance of the twin tunnel faced him, with its dark nostrils and its broad brow rammed into the woods, presenting its slanting retaining walls like a pair of huge feet. At a point where the stone had been weathered clean and bright, while elsewhere it was black from accumulations of smoke, nature seemed to shrink away agitatedly to one side and upward, with bushes and trees crooked and tangled. But there also seemed to be a kind of accommodation, something akin to friendship, between the austere, square-cut stones and the mass of plant life growing cheek-by-jowl with the tunnel. Some bushes had even rooted in wind-drifted soil on the cornices.

Conrad stayed to one side, where there was a small, level place fenced off by a grating. Here he could lean forward and peer into the tunnel.

At this moment, the god of the place filled the interior of the temple's maw with swelling thunder. Then he blackly emerged. Conrad, shrinking back, felt as if the grating protected him from some wild beast. It roared past, and behind it came a freight train full of heavy, mute goods, car upon car, rumbling, rattling, and clanging from the tube. Then the whole long russet chain was running in the sun, swerving in the slow curve to the left, around the cone-shaped mountain and out into the flatland. Some wisps of sacrificial smoke puffed out of the temple's maw after it, floated upward a little, and vanished among the bushes which trustfully leaned over the railing up above, their frail bodies touching the heavy portal.

Before long, another, altogether different sound emerged from the tunnel, faint at first, then growing more distinct, a kind of clatter, or perhaps the sound of many small, rapid footsteps. Every so often there was a resounding blow. Conrad, whose instincts of citizenship whispered to him that he had no business being here, skillfully drew back among the bushes.

From his post he could see the trackwalker, who after a while appeared from the tube on Conrad's side—the right-hand tube as you faced out into the country side. Now Conrad realized what the noise had been. The man was walking in the center of the tracks, on the ties, which were too far apart for a walker to omit a single one, and too close together to permit anything but that short, tripping step, which eventually must grow very tiring. The trainman now left the track and stepped over to the wider space between the two tunnel mouths, where a large signaling apparatus stood. Behind it was a telephone, which the trackwalker cranked several times, apparently to make his report. Then he picked up the long-handled hammer that he had laid aside, and vanished, tripping along the ties, in the mouth of the other tunnel.

The calm with which Conrad now lit his cigarette had a certain romanticism. He would have to wait here a while in any case. Very well. Meanwhile, however, Sherlock Holmes experienced a surprise. When that while had passed—almost thirty minutes, by Conrad's watch—the tripping footsteps approached once more and the man in the blue jacket reappeared, carrying a pouch and with a signaling horn slung over his shoulder. This time he walked on, his gaze fixed upon tracks and ties, tripping along with his tiny footsteps like some small machine. Conrad gazed after him for a long time. His assurance was somewhat shaken by the obscure habits of railroad employees.

He reflected, and waited. Out in the open, along the tracks, a rumbling began, and the signal bells nearby began ringing vigorously. A banner of steam came curving around the cone-shaped mountain. Soon the locomotive roared briefly and plunged into the darkness. It was another freight train; rattling and clanking, the russet cars vanished into the tube one after the other. Conrad observed that no smoke emerged from the tunnel behind the train, nor did the entrance on that side show any signs of blackening. The vault was blackened only on his side, the right side.

He decided to wait for one more train to emerge. Then he could venture it.

After another quarter hour, he heard the roaring in the tunnel. Then a locomotive, hot and snorting, charged forth, with only a few passenger cars attached to it. On the rear platform stood a conductor. But he could not see Conrad, who was hidden by the bushes. The distant rumble of the train could still be heard, although the train was already out of sight around the curve, when Conrad sprang up and, with the feelings of a firm believer in authority who is doing something altogether unbelievable, vaulted over the grating. Anxious not to be observed, he ran straight into the still smoke-filled tunnel, using the ties rather clumsily. Now he could see the end of the tunnel on the other side of the mountain. In the smoke it looked strangely red, then yellow, and finally became a white, round disk. It seemed not far away. The thought flashed through his mind that he had come here in haste, without any preparatory reflection—in fact, without actually having made up his mind what he wanted to look for. The jewelry—that is, the fruits of the robbery, which Inkrat imagined might have been thrown out of the train and perhaps scattered? If this tunnel had been the scene of the murder, he would scarcely find the jewelry right here. Like a sink-hole which threatened to swallow up his whole undertaking, the realization dawned on him that no rational reflections had led him to this point. But this writhing knot of crisscrossing ideas was suddenly slashed through like the famous Gordian knot by a single question—behind which Conrad almost triumphantly perceived, for a brief second, a flaw in Inkrat's thinking.

The question: along the right or the left wall?

A kind of purely muscular decision answered this question. It was that, not reasoning. The cone of light from his flashlight was aimed to the right of the track, along the narrow strip of ground, partly covered with broken stone, between the ties and the wall of the tunnel. But almost at once his heart misgave him. To find any small objects among these innumerable sooty stones and the spaces between them, and to do so now, after more than eight years had passed, so that they would be just as covered with sooth as everything else—it was impossible. At least impossible to do hurriedly. What he needed was formal permission to investigate; a second, stronger flashlight; and people to work with him. Conrad stumbled. He was not sure whether to walk on the edges of the ties or in the narrow space alongside them. So far, he had penetrated about a hundred paces into the tunnel. He turned back, still stooping and flashing his light along the ground. A leaf had blown in from outside, a tiny green leaf. He looked down at it. Suddenly, instantaneously, a moment out of the past returned. He had once seen several small stones, in a damned-up brook, which looked exactly like crabs. And then

there had really been a crab. But here it was a beryl earring, set
in gold.

Conrad knelt down slowly. While his heart seemed to stop
entirely deep down inside, so that within his chest there was
nothing but silence, he inserted two fingers into the crack in
which the tiny piece of jewelry lay, pulled it out, and held it
close to the flashlight.

Yes.

Conrad emerged from the tunnel and descended the embankment with his left fist tightly clenched. He swept the bushes
aside with his shoulders, stepped under the trees which climbed
in stages steeply up the slope, and cautiously, slowly, opened his
hand as though he held a captive insect.

Yes.

One must be orderly. With his handkerchief he gently rubbed
the thin coating of soot from the gold and the stone, opened his
wallet, and placed the earring in a compartment which had
hitherto held only a key.

Then orderliness ceased. After he had replaced the wallet in
his trousers pocket and carefully buttoned the pocket, he began
hastily climbing the extremely steep slope, helping himself up
by clinging to an occasional bush or a tree. This steady, strenuous upward movement in some measure calmed him. Farther up,
the steepness diminished slightly; there were little humps and
terraces on the mountain. Conrad sat down in the woods. A
variety of branches crisscrossed against the sky, bright-colored
and brown. There were also some branches of conifers, which
now appeared quite black.

At last he reached the top and climbed over the quarrylike
edge. On that side, perfectly level fields extended for a great
distance. Breathing deeply, Conrad turned and looked back over
the valley from which he had come. The land below seemed
swollen and vaulted, with the rusty brown, sharply delineated
rectangles of the fields, the bright limpid green of the winter

rye, and, farther off, the horizon no longer showing in autumnal clarity, but heavily misted. He stood on the summit as if on the roof of his life, like someone who has occupied a house for many years but for the first time climbs to the top of it and peers out through a hatch, seeing familiar things from that height as entirely new.

38

CROSSING the fields, he found the highway again and followed it. As he tramped along at a steady gait, the tumult within him shook down into one spot. As yet there could be no question of thinking, but it did become possible to eat the chocolate he carried. He broke off piece after piece, without removing the bar from the right-hand pocket of his coat. His gaze remained fastened to the ground; he hardly observed his surroundings, was aware only in the corners of his eyes of the grayish-green edges of the road. For some time the highway sloped downhill. Conrad kept to his even pace. He felt a bit hungry, but, more than that, he had a distinct craving for wine—a condition usually but not altogether justifiably called "thirst." And that fact alone tells us how much our young man had changed. Three years before, any such "thirst" would have been incomprehensible to him. But, you know, family patterns, influence of the parental home—how a young person is inclined to underestimate such things. Though probably Conrad no longer underestimated them, for of late, we may recall, he had engaged in closer investigation of his psychic foundations and had started to trace one thing and another to its source.

At the outermost fringe of the town, close to the spot where he had turned off from the highway that morning, a sign on a building proclaimed a tavern. Still overwrought, he entered the place, to find himself not in a proper tavern but in a private home, one of whose rooms was used as a pub; perhaps the liquor license went with the house. As soon as he was inside, Conrad felt that something was in thorough confusion here: two different ways of living, possibly of speaking, thinking, being. The furniture alone expressed that duality; it was like something out of a dream in its intermingling of kitchen and—music room. There were several stools, a small washtub, a gigantic sideboard of altogether naïve atrociousness (did it not have a certain spiritual relationship with Aunt Berta's pictures?). And in the corner, filling out the scene, stood a large black concert grand. The woman who brought Conrad the wine—refilling his glass almost at once, for he downed the first as if it were that "most sensible drink anyhow"—was like her furniture, a novel and confusing mixture of kitchen smells, gray-haired dignity, and a touch of the artistic. The picture was completed by a few robust words that she called out to the garden from the window of the adjoining room. On her finger she wore a very pretty chalcedony on a gold band. "Ah, I see you're wondering about this instrument, aren't you?" she said as she set the little glass pitcher of wine on the table. "My daughter is married to an engineer in Bamberg, you see, from a very good family. She plays the piano beautifully. The *Moonlight Sonata*, for instance, and all those classical things that a person really has to be pretty good for. So I bought the grand so she wouldn't have to do without her music when she's visiting home. We're very musical too."

Conrad was not exactly a lover of classical music. But we will have observed that he'd developed a keener nose of late; otherwise he would not have noticed in Venice that his wife was applying the principles of athletic discipline to the enjoyment of art. . . . Things of the spirit are like the drinking of spirits: a novel but not entirely safe source of vitality.

The husband looked in at the door. He was as big and fat as a Hungarian ox, but with a strikingly smooth-shaven face. It positively gleamed. Otherwise he seemed mute, and quickly obeyed a glassy look from his wife and removed himself away from the doorway.

"Are you on business here, sir, or on vacation?"

"Half and half," Conrad said, and as had once happened to him at Herr von Hohenlocher's, he quietly observed that he was rather lit. For all that, he was actually frightened, in a strangely clairvoyant manner. For some moments he seriously considered whether this whole affair might not be somehow a belatedly erupting disorder that had its source in his early life. . . . But how?

In the next breath he no longer understood this thought. But he had another, although he rejected it all too simply, feeling that one discovery could not possibly come so rapidly on top of another; that would have made things too clear. ("I'm drunk!") This other thought established an easy connection between lucky finders of scattered jewelry and a daughter for whom people bought a concert grand just so she could play it on visits home. Ah yes, daughters sometimes do play the *Moonlight Sonata*. . . .

Conrad paid and left this weird place behind him. When he reached the hotel, it was long past noon. He ate a substantial meal in the comfortable restaurant—the more he ate, the hungrier he became—went up to his room, removed his shoes and jacket, and instantly fell asleep, since with his meal he had again imbibed two quarter liters of that splendid Lauffener wine.

39 ८⁀

~~~~~~

THE pattern above the molding on the wall represented an invariably gay encounter between two quarter-circles or sickles which seemed to be dancing and teasing each other. Conrad awoke feeling beautifully refreshed, and at once began thinking effortlessly and fluently. The native wine, it seemed, gave all its goodness to the limbs and left no evil effects in the head.

Inkrat must have assumed from the first that the jewelry had been thrown out on the right side—right from the direction in which the train was moving. Thrown out as a "package of loot." (Conrad suddenly laughed aloud in the quiet room at this expression.) The package might have broken open. All that was nonsense. The things had been thrown out as they were, on the open track, where they might have been found right away, perhaps by dawn the same day. The passage through the tunnel had lasted at most a minute (in this Conrad was mistaken; the train rushed through in far less time). Out of the question for any "package" to have been made in that short time.

Well, then, where had the earring come from?

Thoughts flashed through his mind. There had been a struggle; the earring had been torn off. The condition in which Louison's compartment had been found rather argued in favor of that theory. Conrad jumped up from his bed and dressed to go out. He raced down the stairs, which were covered with some kind of jute runner, and across the square to the post office alongside the station. He put through an "urgent" telephone call to Maria Rosanka, after having once more looked her up in the telephone book. He did not have long to wait. First there was a humming, then a chirping.

There she was.

"Hello, this is Conrad Castiletz calling, *gnädige Frau.*"

"Yes, this is Maria Rosanka." The voice sounded near, clear, calm.

"Can you hear me well, *gnädige Frau?*"

"Very well," she said as if she were only two yards away.

"I'm out in the country—looking over the railroad line—in regard to Louison Veik. I have two questions I'd like you to answer, if you can. Have you got that?"

"Perfectly well," the voice came, altered by the telephone but quite clear. "What are your questions?"

As he spoke to her he sensed her—her happiness, her superiority. The golden, sunlit studio on Stift Strasse. The criminals, the jewelry, had never interested Maria Rosanka. She had lost her best friend, perhaps her only intimate friend. That was all that mattered to her. She had wept quietly. He had to force himself to speak.

"My first question is: did Louison ride in a car with compartments on the left and the aisle on the right, reckoning from the direction of the train's motion? So that, for example, if as you stood on the platform and had the train on your right, Louison would have been able to shake hands with you through the window of her compartment, without going out to the aisle, which would be on the other side, to the right, reckoning from the direction of the train. Have I made myself clear?"

"Perfectly clear," she said quietly, deliberately. "It was just as you've described it. Louison stood in the compartment and did shake hands with me once through the window, before I left the platform. Besides, I'd been in the car before and seen the 'ladies' compartment' she was in. It was to the left of the aisle. That is, after you boarded the train you crossed the platform to reach the aisle. I remember that to this day and am absolutely sure of it. You must remember that as a painter I am naturally an eye-centered person. Stuttgart is a terminal station, you know; the

train came in and went out on the same track. For that reason
the aisle would be on the right, in the direction of motion."

"Thank you," Conrad said, doing his best to control his excitement. "Now my second question—I don't know whether you'll
be able to answer this one. When you said good-bye to Louison
Veik, was she wearing earrings?"

"No, definitely not," Maria Rosanka replied firmly. "I would
certainly have been aware of it if she had been. You see, she
never wore earrings and owned only a single pair, exactly the
same as a pair your wife had at the time and perhaps still has.
She did not wear them but almost always had them with the
other jewelry she carried with her, since she was very fond of
beryls."

"A green stone with a gold setting?" Conrad asked.

"Quite right," the near and distant voice replied.

"Then you are certain that Louison was not wearing earrings
that night."

"Certain. I would undoubtedly have noticed. A woman sees
that sort of thing."

Conrad thanked her repeatedly before he hung up. When he
stepped out to the square in front of the post office and railroad
station, the sun had matured to such a golden glow that it was
like a bursting fruit pouring down the sweetness of the autumn
upon every nook and corner of the scene. Its shifting, almost
tangibly dense light enclosed him. This flood of light, after the
long tense telephone call in the dusky booth, plunged him into
confusion. He fled into the station restaurant and had a cup of
coffee. In one respect Maria Rosanka seemed to have reinforced
the structure of deductions which he was trying to consolidate;
in another respect—the earrings—she had dealt the structure
quite a blow. And just as had happened in the course of Conrad's
first hasty rush into the tunnel, a kind of fissure seemed about to
open once more and swallow up his whole undertaking. He
began to feel that what he was doing was too cheap, too "light"

(this was the word that came to him); and back of it all he sensed that there was a far more deliberate, slower, more thorough approach. Strangely, not even the finding of the earring, which after all was a clear triumph, now appeared to justify the way he had chosen. Had he not come upon it virtually by chance? If he were bent on attacking the case in an orderly way, could he tolerate such overhasty, far too "dark" procedures? Everything seemed to dissolve, as had happened the day before in Maria Rosanka's studio. But just as a deep depression was about to descend upon him, a cloud of distress which blew up from all sides out of those great roomy areas of life that contain no definable affairs, details, reasons, or causes—just at that moment there appeared on the edge of the fissure, with its seething depths, a fixed point.

Yes (he said to himself), a struggle took place in the "ladies' compartment" while the train was passing through the tunnel. The murderer was unable to wrest the jewel box from Louison, which she held even in death. The earrings were in that box. One of them fell out, perhaps at the moment Louison reeled against the open window from the force of the blow. But the criminal must have seized the loot at once, reaching out and sweeping up the contents of the box. Perhaps he hurried back to the spot at dawn to find whatever jewelry had fallen out the window. The attack must have taken place shortly before the train emerged from the tunnel. That's it! (Now Conrad saw the clean, graveled space between the two tracks where the signal apparatus stood.) Everything could easily be found there. The major part of the loot would have been packed up and thrown out of the train elsewhere, much later, either to the right or the left, from the aisle or from a compartment. Probably from the toilet. Peitz was sitting calmly (and drunk!) in Erfurt when the train pulled in there! Quite possibly. He had an accomplice. This other man got off soon after the crime, perhaps to ride back—and took the loot with him. They did not have to throw

anything else out the window; there's no need to assume they
had to. But perhaps Peitz had nothing to do with the whole
affair. No, he had to. There was the business of Inkrat's compartment key. He certainly handled that very well; in fact, admira-
bly. Peitz stayed in his seat to avoid suspicion. And then in the
end he slipped up. My next trip must be to Berlin; I want to take
a look at the man. But, according to my deductions, it isn't likely
that anything more can be discovered in the tunnel here. And
even if there were, would it add anything new to my theory?
No. Finding the earring is one of those glorious coincidences that
often bring a murderer to justice. They probably missed the second earring—and at the beginning were probably pretty worried
about it, not so much on account of its value as because it would
identify the exact scene of the crime.

His thoughts ran on lightly, with a playful fluency, like the
lines of a man who is well into a letter and is writing along
smoothly. Now, however, he left the hotel. His intense excitement lengthened his stride, and so he walked in golden sunlight
ripe as a juicy pear on the tree (did not the air here taste of
fruit?) farther and farther through the town. Smoke of evening,
spicy to the nostrils, hung between the slanting rays of the sun.
In the farmyards stood blacksmiths, drovers, and hired hands,
and under the beams of the overhanging roofs hung rows of
yellow Indian corn. Between old walls, narrow passages, stiles,
and stairs, swung the blond braids of children at play; and
Swabian faces, sly and shrewd, sharp of nose like an alchemist's
retort, peered out of arched gateways and windows at the running and jumping children who stood for their own past lives.
They looked on with the same wise equanimity as the steep,
high-shouldered old walls with which one half of the town confronted the river. You looked across at the other half when you
stood among boys, girls, and chickens at the top of the pre-
cipitous Hintere Gasse. So doing, Conrad realized the size of
the town. The ponderous citadel set upon the mountain, the

old crumbling city walls across the river, whitish-gray as they climbed the hill beyond vineyards—all of that and the parts beyond seemed like a blue scaffolding against the broad chest of the distant range. Shadows, cool and delicate, touched the wall of a house here and there on the street where he stood. A number of tall, handsome young men were smearing clay over vintner's vats to seal the chinks. A flock of geese waddled on the river bank, as ancient a feature of the town as this way of sealing vats, or as the walls, which now seemed to be floating freely, their outlines dimmed by twilight. They looked like natural rock. It seemed to Conrad that he had really come to the south in coming here, entering into a mild, spicy air which like the belly of a violin caught up the vibrations of every voice: the cries of the playing children, and the drover's commands to his horse. Actually, it was far more Italian here than it had been over there, across the Alps.

That evening in the hotel's bar Conrad chanced to make the acquaintance of the stationmaster of the railroad. He was a merry, good-looking, sociable man; and in spite of Conrad's present "theory" that no further finds could be expected in the tunnel, it was as if his blue notebook back home in the desk stirred when he learned who was sitting across the table from him. With new assurance and a skill that flowed from hitherto unplumbed sources in his nature—but of late he had been displaying quite an assortment of such gifts—Conrad contrived to turn the conversation to a personal matter: some time ago, while his train was passing through the tunnel just outside town, he had lost a small object out the open window—a cigarette case, or, rather, actually a snuffbox (ah well, we take what comes to mind, when we have to improvise, and no matter how it came to mind!). Had any of the trackwalkers found such a thing and turned it in?

No, the stationmaster replied; as a matter of fact, a trackwalker was the last person who would find anything on the side of the track, because his whole attention was concentrated on the ties and tracks. (Conrad had already learned that earlier in the day.)

Conrad asked whether he might go along through the tunnel some time when the trackwalker was inspecting the stretch. (In the course of this little chat Conrad learned the length of the tunnel; it was only some 1,800 feet.) The stationmaster replied that he could not authorize it, but he would gladly telephone Heilbronn for permission.

"Suppose you come to my office at the station at half past seven tomorrow morning," the stationmaster suggested. "If they say yes, you can take the early morning train to the station on the other side of the mountain, where the trackwalker starts, and you'll be there in time to catch him at the stationmaster's office there. I'll take care that he knows." (The blue notebook positively flapped its wings at this prospect of an orderly survey.) "But," the stationmaster continued, "you say you were traveling toward Heilbronn—do you remember whether your window was on the left or on the right, reckoning from the direction of the train's motion? Everything depends on your remembering that— otherwise you'll have no idea where to look."

"Oh yes, I'm certain," Conrad said. (How certain he was!)

"As far as finding anything, I can't hold out much hope, with all those stones and all the soot," the stationmaster commented.

"It was pretty much toward the end of the tunnel on this side," Conrad said.

The following morning everything worked out well. Conrad rode through the tunnel once more, but he felt only a feeble duplication of his earlier excitement as the train, turning in the long curve, approached the dark maw. Half an hour later, Conrad was tripping along the high railroad embankment at the side of the trackwalker, taking the same small steps as the other man, for the pace was set by the distance of the ties. The golden shield of a slope planted entirely to vineyard towered almost vertically into the blue of the sky. Below, the sooty twin mouths yawned. At the watchman's cabin they waited for a train to pass. Even its looming, thundering, and vanishing did not reawaken the deep agitation of the previous day. As on the day before, the tunnel's other opening first flared red in the smoke, then yellow, and at last appeared as a white disk. Now, incidentally, Conrad learned why—on this side, too—only one of the two mouths appeared sooty: the air current moved in a different direction in each of the two tubes. They entered. Herr Schmidt, the track-walker, a small, serious man, the father of several children, carried a hammer. In spite of the monotonous and exacting nature of his work, he emanated that salty shrewdness and cheerfulness which the common people unquestioningly possess. After all, it is upon them that the heaviest weight of life falls, and they are accustomed, by age-old habit, to hold up under this pressure by virtue of invincible traits. On the whole, it was like a walk through a cellar which smelled of coal smoke instead of wine. Conrad lit their path as well as he could with two flashlights— the evening before he had hurriedly bought another, of the kind used as a headlight for bicycles. He could see well, yet several times he nearly fell on his nose. It did not trouble him that he found nothing whatsoever. This inspection was only a matter of form and orderliness, so to speak—an apology to the blue notebook. Herr Schmidt was concentrating on his work and paid no attention to his companion. He tripped along, the lantern at his chest. Every so often he stopped, swung the hammer, tightened a wedge, tripped on. The blows clanged and echoed in the cool isolation of the tunnel. Conrad was shown the emergency niches, and on the other side, but not directly opposite these, the passages which led to the other tunnel. These were not low passages one would have to crawl through, but were quite high, neatly walled with stone blocks, cleanly sheered off, and had sustaining arches at the top. One should on no account use one of these passages for protection if a train were approaching, the track-walker warned, since the air pressure would hurl anyone stand-

ing in the passage all the way into the other tube and against the
farther wall. If an emergency niche were too far away, the thing
to do was to lie down in the narrow space between the ties and
the walls—and with your head facing the approaching train.
Otherwise the tremendous air pressure could tear your coat off
its buttons and blow it up like a balloon. And if any piece of
your clothing were caught by the train, it was certain death. The
tube was so narrow that a standing man was bound to be overcome by dizziness at the sight of the masses of cars roaring past,
and would fall right into them—unless he were caught by a
running board.

Conrad learned many such details of a different world—
knowledge which he had fortunately not had to draw upon the
previous day—from the gay and serious Herr Schmidt. But to the
very end he found nothing more, no further "clue," although he
walked the tunnel twice, lighting up the space to the left of the
tracks as best he could. Inevitably, he fell far behind Herr
Schmidt, but fortunately the trackwalker had to pause now and
then for a few hammer blows, to test or tighten.

They emerged into the light at last and continued on together
to the railroad station—Herr Schmidt tripping along the ties all
the while and searchingly eying the tracks, while Conrad, whose
legs were not accustomed to this sort of exercise, found a path
alongside. On the way, at the point where the tracks made the
widest arc around the cone in the center of the moon-mountain,
Herr Schmidt and Conrad paused at the barriers by the watchman's cabin and had a chat with the two railroad officials who
were stationed there. One of them, a vigorous elderly man,
walked capably and rapidly on a wooden leg. Yes, of course, he
had been in the war; so had the other man, and so had Herr
Schmidt. Only Conrad had not. He thought of the soldiers who
had once drilled in the water meadows back home; for the first
time he was seeing as a palpable fact that all that could lead to
the loss of a leg. At bottom, that was alien and incomprehensible,

and an empty gulf yawned between this realization and his boy-hood memories. One of the men told an amusing anecdote about something that had recently happened in the vicinity. It included the sentence: *"Ja, was wollt denn ihr da?"* But the man said: *"Ja, was wellet denn ihr do?"* It was Middle High German. Even Conrad noticed it. Had he been just a little less "textilian," his thoughts would have leaped to the fact that the country he was in was the birthplace of his native speech, far back in the remote-ness of time. And here, in the morning sunlight, under the blue sky of a day swelling to sonorous depths, a man who had passed through peace and war turned afresh upon his tongue the same age-old language.

At the station Conrad thanked the obliging stationmaster. No, he admitted, he had not found anything, but he had satisfied his conscience, so to speak. The stationmaster laughed and shook hands with him. Conrad ate his dinner early, with the feeling that he had accomplished a good deal. Now only the blue note-book awaited him.

He slept off his noonday Lauffener wine again, and again his first awakening glance was caught by the patterns on the wall, the two quarter circles or sickles dancing and teasing each other. This time, however, he had slept far longer than the day before. He got up quickly and walked through the village, which once more was awash with golden sunlight and seemed almost to be floating in space. Out on the highway once more, he had a piece of good luck that shortened his walk up to that height which he had reached breathlessly by way of the steep slope the day before. Without considering why, it now seemed to him abso-lutely essential that he conclude his stay with one more visit to the peak. A man in the driver's seat of a heavy truck near the end of town saw him tramping along and took it for granted that he would prefer riding in the empty seat beside him. "Well, now—" Why, certainly. Thumping and rattling, but making good speed, the truck carried him to the top within a few minutes. Conrad casually observed that the tunnel had been built to pierce the mountain at its narrowest point, a pinched-in constriction of the flat slate of fields on top of the circular natural wall. Here, too, the road forked. He thanked the truck driver, who took a cigarette out of courtesy, laughingly refusing to accept anything more. With an enormous clatter and a thumping roar, the truck rumbled downhill.

Slowly, rather hesitantly, Conrad walked over the soft earth of the balk between two fields, toward the edge of the precipice. In the late afternoon sunlight the farthest horizon seemed to be fluid and smoldering. A barberry bush had playfully posted itself to the fore, a red punctuation mark neatly dividing the great arc in the distance. Here and there in the fields were fires of potato vines, the flames looking more alive against the sky because the first hint of twilight was descending. Conrad sat down. He did not stand but sat, on the roof as it were, while below him, far down in the cellar, straight beneath him, the tunnels marched through the mountain. And something filtered up through hundreds of feet of ground to him: the knowledge that he was alive. At last I am alive. Everything that was small and excessively "clear," everything drifting about in the foreground, vanished away for some moments, as if scattered by a high wind. He suddenly clapped his hands over his face, and his face plunged into the darkness as into a deep, deep shaft.

40 ଛଛ

www.www.wwwwwwwwwwwwwwwwwwwwwwwwwwwww

BEFORE Marianne's return from Italy, Conrad visited his aunt Erika von Spresse. Although it was late in the year, he found her outside, by the sunny rear wall of the house, which faced the garden. With most of the leaves gone, the garden had once more resumed its springtime state; except that everything—trellises, espaliers, and benches—had been charged during the summer with the warmth of many sunny hours, and seemed to radiate this heat, so that things did not look so gaunt as in spring, after the long dampness and cold of winter. The autumn hung fulsomely in the air, like the aroma of wine in a glass; the drifting colored leaves which scurried from the gardens in thick flocks over the asphalt of the streets had nothing sad about them. They made up a merry, particolored dance, beyond which, at the street's end, a blue banner of sky whipped in the wind.

Aunt Erika—as much of her as was visible—lay in a deck chair on the low terrace. She had swathed herself in a blanket and was surrounded by piles of books. Conrad sat beside her and talked with her about all these treasures of the spirit. He had come seeking something else entirely, but she was too full of her present studies and endeavors—for she was always engaged in some. Now, for example, there was Latin paleography—here was Steffens's text as well as Thompson's excellent book in English on the manuscripts of Monte Cassino. Conrad did not ask: "What is Latin paleography?" The question would have been too crude in this intellectual atmosphere, posed from too low a standpoint—he could feel that. In any case, he soon learned that reading medieval manuscripts, especially those written in the ancient Roman cursive script, called for a great deal of training, and that you had to study the "Tyronian notes"—the Roman stenography, or shorthand (which Cicero had introduced for Senate debates!). Many remnants of it, he was informed, had passed over into medieval handwriting. . . .

Aunt Erika showed him a leaf of the big book full of plates. Against a yellowish background he saw hooks and curlicues of various sizes, and a number of strokes that looked like diagonal dashes. Conrad shook his head admiringly. "You can read that?" he said.

"Not yet," she replied. "But if I keep at it, I'll eventually master the meaning of the connecting lines, or ligatures, as they're technically called, and recognize them when I see them again."

Conrad rather felt as he had that day the time drew nearer for taking the streetcar to the last stop, where Ida Plangl was waiting for him. When he'd called on Albert Lehnder across the canal, there had still been time to make it, if he had been able to bring himself to ask Albert at once for the money. Then they had gone walking in the water meadows. . . . Yes, of course, how depressing it all was! On account of five and a half or six marks. Conrad forgot that at the time the passing minutes had played on his nerves like an aching tooth, whereas the piece of information he now wanted from Aunt Erika was not tied to any specific time; he could inquire about it later. But he seemed to have a certain mistrust of himself in this respect, so that his visit really amounted to a "now or never." In fact, he had already abandoned his intentions, was almost glad to listen to Frau von Spresse's scholarly explanations because in a way they concealed a weakness on his part. If she did not give him the chance to speak, he could certainly not ask any questions, let alone such odd ones as he had in mind.

A silence ensued. Surrounded but undisturbed by it, the great men stood in the empty garden: Pascal and Giordano Bruno. For several moments the air seemed transformed into glass as Conrad —carried along by an awkward and disorderly impulse of his vocal cords—said: "There's something I've been wanting to ask you about, Aunt Erika—something I'm interested in—about the time I was here with you—when I was a little boy. . . ." He saw her head raised from the pillow; at the moment it looked quite flat, like a small board. ". . . Do you think you could remember the precise day I left?"

Her hand emerged from under the blanket like the neck of a waterfowl probing a pond. With extended forefinger, she pressed a bell which was on the table beside her.

"The yearbook for 1921," she said to the maid.

A small volume bound in red leather was brought in.

"This is the entry." Aunt Erika read: "Conrad left this afternoon for Stuttgart on the way to Mergentheim. He will not reach home until one o'clock in the morning. Would not be dissuaded from the night trip. It seems a pity for my sister to have to receive the boy so late, but he has his heart set on traveling by night, so I have let him have his way. July 24, 1921."

The upright board fell silent. Conrad did not speak.

"You did not reach Stuttgart until evening," she said. "Then you boarded an express train about half past nine and had to change trains in Lauda shortly before midnight."

She seemed still to be reproaching him for his boyhood stubbornness. Perhaps it was as a kind of counterblow to this reproach that he said, speaking with precise enunciation: "If I was traveling in the express train between Stuttgart and Lauda on the night of July 24, it may be that I was in the very train in which Louison Veik was murdered."

"Yes," the board spoke, remaining perfectly immobile. "That has occurred to me. But what of it, after all? Besides, the crime took place much farther along the stretch, so far as I know. A mere coincidence."

Conrad looked down at the ground. He was beside himself with horror at this personality. A chimera, a harpy clinging like a wasp close to a sunny wall, dry and cold, utterly merciless— that was this aunt of his. This purely rational inflexibility far exceeded his capacity for understanding. He could not grasp it at all, and yet there was no possible vent for his indignation. He said nothing, not even: "Well, it still strikes me as remarkably odd, and I've often shuddered at the idea of it," or something of the sort. There was absolutely nothing more that could be said here, no way to create a more breathable atmosphere; here airless space, a pure vacuum began. He avoided looking at Frau von Spresse, and his agitation was so intense and so helpless that it stayed with him long after he was out on the street—in fact, almost the whole of the way home.

Winter paradoxically arrived with Marianne's return from Italy. Or at least the preparations for it began at once. Duracher stood near the chairs and the table, metallic, contemporary artifacts which formed islands on the gray-green floor-covering of the hall. He had a short pipe in his mouth. But he did not act self-important; that was not his way. In fact, he was rather laconic. Perhaps he knew that this is the tone to take with a woman who wants to learn to ski. . . . The floor was a warehouse of winter-sports articles that had been sent up. Marianne was to select her skis, her bindings.

"No," Duracher said, "that pair is out of the question. Once you improve, you can have hickory skis, of course. For the present you can't even walk uphill, and there are a few other things you have to learn, besides. So, ash."

She studied a complicated set of safety bindings.

"No use for a beginner. And by the time you can ski properly, you'll be long past those things, as sure as my name is Peter."

After Christmas she left, Duracher having recommended that she spend a month in the "beginner's course" at St. Anton on the Arlberg. Her tan, when she returned, was indescribable. Her blue eyes seemed to flash from somewhere deep behind it. The following weekend she went off with Duracher for an easy tour in the Allgäu, and he seemed satisfied. A week later there was a trip to Oberstdorf, in Swabia, with a large party; and in March —in the Arlberg—Marianne graduated into the "intermediate class." Duracher remarked to one of the young men that Marianne was in prime condition from her summer, and that the ski gymnastics had also been of enormous benefit.

Along with the young people who often visited—many of them deeply tanned, like Marianne—a new atmosphere entered their home, and a mysterious background of existence. Conrad envisioned that background, on the whole, as blue and white, and occasionally brown, when the ski huts and the life in them were talked about. He was separated from all that by a glass wall. A kind of obstinacy—which, oddly, he regarded in the depths of his soul as wholesome—kept him away from it all, although sometimes he felt a pang of longing. It seemed to him that a short while ago, yesterday, the day before yesterday, he would have been permitted to plunge right in, to go along, to take part. And, after all, it was not exactly that he lacked the physical equipment to do so. But nowadays that was all over, and he remained alone. What most attracted him, what seemed most enviable was the sociability, the adventures, the incidents—all of which he gathered from chance remarks made by one or another of the participants. In other words, he was attracted precisely by what was most natural in this world of athletes. In that world up in the high mountains, from which people returned tanned, with flashing eyes and freshly tautened skin, there obviously existed permanent figures, intrigues, entanglements, surprises, which took place in ways all their own and upon rare and strange planes of life, in huts and on glaciers, on slopes and in ravines at altitudes of six to ten thousand feet.

But he was fond of solitude; he had long since frankly admitted that to himself, with no attempt to contradict this aspect of his nature. Moments such as the one when Marianne had had a fit of temper in the bathroom, and he had found himself powerless to soothe her (and actually happy at this incapacity!)—such moments had assumed a kind of permanent form, an even course from which he deviated only rarely.

At the mill everything went on as usual. Eisenmann was everywhere, sometimes swearing mightily, smoking cigars, dispensing cigars. Now and then he had talks with "my boy"—one of which was noteworthy. It took place in the director's office toward the end of February.

"I'd been wanting to have a word with you, my boy; about Marianne, but don't take it amiss, coming from old Eisenmann—"

(this came out in spurts; he puffed away at the cigar between phrases). "It's all very well and all that. Pity no babies have come along. So something seems to have got started that might lead after a while to, let's say, to an undesirable point. I knew from the start, my boy, that you wouldn't have an easy time of it. An oldish maid like that—come now, that's what she was before you married her!—is like a compressed steel spring, sort of. Now she's springing. You should try to share your wife's interests more than you do. After all, you used to be quite an athlete yourself and now you don't even play tennis any more. What has got into you? You can't blame Marienne for present developments; she's in with a gay group, thank God, and all the tongue-wagging around here is idiotic. People trying to apply standards that belong to our pavements to mountains and ski huts thousands of feet up. Naturally, that sort of thing makes for another style of living. Different codes of behavior, I mean. Well, well. Anyhow, pay a little more attention to your wife. Look at an old donkey like me, still getting in some tennis in the summer. And you were pretty much in the master class. Duracher couldn't beat you, that time. And—don't take it amiss, my boy."

Word for word, sentence for sentence, just as the dear old fellow spoke them. In Conrad they caused a kind of paralysis to well up like ground water, more and more of it. Even before the director had finished, Conrad found himself in the situation of a man who receives good advice, in fact the only correct advice, but whose hands are tied; yet he does not quite see what kind of cord binds them. Yes, the glass stood right on the edge of the table, so to speak, and it would certainly fall. Eisenmann was right. Reason perceived that, but reason alone, and in reason's own fashion, which is to say schematically, like a crystallographic cardboard model of life. That did not suffice to produce action. It was preferable to look the other way. There was something stronger. Conrad felt as if he were being held back by something behind him. Yes, he ought to do something about this situation, do it swiftly and soon, or otherwise the irrevocable would happen. But to arrange this matter satisfactorily, to settle it, to put it in order, required time, calm, composure. He would have to proceed slowly, very slowly, by a much longer route. Conrad strenuously squinted his eyes more and more tightly while Eisenmann spoke, and looked out the window over the new low buildings of the mill, the bare trees behind twining octopod branches against the gray sky. That he imagined he could smell a kind of swampy odor coming from some nearby source, or had some such taste permanently on his tongue, was too close and too muted a sensation to be actually noted, yet too distinct to be overlooked.

"Sir," he said with some effort—and with the feeling that in spite of all the pains he was taking he would be unable to express what he meant—"I am extremely grateful to you for your kindness, for your concern. You are quite right in what you've said. Only, the way—the way I could put all that in order may be more involved, rather longer, a kind of detour—what I really mean is, it can't be done just like that—"

He felt greatly relieved after he had brought this out, and exhaled as if he had performed a strenuous physical feat. Eisenmann looked down at the desk. No doubt he understood Conrad otherwise than Conrad meant. For Conrad's words were half-deliberately misleading. But the old fellow was too wise to raise objections to something he did not grasp; in his own fashion, and with his kindness and intelligence, he tried to understand what he could and, beyond that, simply to respect the other man's view.

"Right you are, my boy," he said. "I see you've understood me perfectly. And of course you can't go about it just like that, as though you were splitting some kindling. What you say about a 'detour' is quite to the point. Don't think old Eisenmann means to butt into your private affairs. He doesn't. But he's your friend, do believe that."

He extended his hand.

"Now to get down to practical matters," he said jovially, "I'd like to give you one more piece of advice, my boy. And it's this: take a trip one of these days. It's against nature for the wife to be gallivanting around all the time and the husband to be hanging around home. If you don't want to go skiing—though that would be the most sensible and natural thing to do—then I can suggest something else for you."

"Sir. . . ?" Conrad said.

"Yes," old Eisenmann replied, "something fine. As you know, the prices for our raw materials have been fluctuating throughout 1929, especially jute. Perhaps we're in for a few surprises. I don't care to talk in riddles, but the fact of the matter is that we may be heading for great changes. So, about jute and also about the other stuff: various parties have suggested that we get in touch. I mean, our pro tem competitors. The present situation offers certain advantages which we should seize. If we don't, we might run into some rough seas in the near future. Yes, things have reached that point. There are a number of persons who expect a larger group to influence new pricings, and where there's smoke, there's fire. Hints have been dropped to me, and to the Councilor, too, twice. So, in the spring there's going to be a kind of rendezvous, on the quiet, sub rosa and no obligations—that was strongly stressed. I haven't made up my mind to go in with them, nor has the Councilor. We only want to send an observer, an ambassador. A good many others will be doing just that. You might be the ambassador. A bit young, of course. But no matter, no matter at all. Besides, you are one of the family. That will strengthen your position in every respect. Which is important for the future. Also, establishing personal relations. And you've never been in Berlin. That isn't right. Have to look around a bit. Let them see you. They'll like you, all right. Yes. Who knows how long I'll be at the helm. So you would go this spring, and of course you'll be perfectly accredited beforehand, by letter.

As far as you're concerned, you're merely an observer. No need to worry. We'll let you know our decision in good time, insofar as we make one. All it will be is sitting in on a few informal meetings and conferences. But stay a while in Berlin—don't be stingy about your time there, understand? Look the city over, amuse yourself, and every so often they'll call you in when they've got something to discuss. I'll take care of things here for the time. Yes, and with regard to what we were talking about before, I think the trip is absolutely indicated. Separation clears the air— that's the story. Better than hanging around home all the time and being put on the shelf."

"I'll be glad to go to Berlin, sir, if this mission is entrusted to me," Conrad said eagerly.

"Come now, mission and entrust—there's no missionary work about it. You're a good-looking fellow, make a nice impression— take your dress suit along—and have a good time!"

After work, Conrad took the streetcar home; Marianne was using the family car and old Eisenmann was planning to work late that evening, so that the mill's car had to wait outside for him. As Conrad, after passing through the bright lights of Wackenroder Strasse, got out by the dark park, he recognized the gentleman strolling slowly and loose-jointedly along in front of him as Herr von Hohenlocher. He was highly pleased at this encounter; it meant a suspension of all the stresses which were holding him clamped tight, resting upon the bottom of his soul with a weight to which he was already habituated.

"How have you been?" he asked.

Herr von Hohenlocher replied: "Fairly well, considering that things have become a bit rough about the house." And then he added, with a touch of that archaic metaphor he was so partial to:

"Frau Schubert has put on her cap and bells."

"Oh—how so?" Conrad asked.

"Once more," Herr von Hohenlocher explained. "She has reached the point of least resistance. Item: she wants to marry."

"Item," Conrad said, "but can she?"

"Of course not. But what she can do is anticipate the outward circumstances of the wished-for condition. She's struck her tents, has moved out of my place, taken an apartment, and bought furniture on installments."

"And what are you doing now, in the face of all this?"

"As I told you, the situation is relatively complicated, but only relatively. For Schubert has chosen her new—as yet—bridal domicile above your former head, Herr Castiletz—that is, she's rented the little apartment directly above the rooms you once had. Two weeks ago the apartment was left vacant. So that she hasn't entirely ceased working for me, although this shift in locale hasn't exactly improved the service. This time I seriously considered giving her her notice, but at the very bottom of these considerations of mine I perceived my own actual desires. And they aim at something altogether different."

"And what may that be?"

"Having her stuffed."

"What's that?"

"Exactly. . . . I shouldn't really like to dismiss Schubert. Nor to tell the truth, to do without any of the people I know. I had to admit that to myself in all honesty. My real desire in regard to all of them is to own some of the more striking specimens, stuffed. For example, Doctor Velten. And, of course, Frau Schubert."

"Mm—I beg your pardon, but exactly how do you imagine that?" Conrad asked. (He felt that his leg was being pulled, but you could never be really angry with Herr von Hohenlocher. And Conrad felt honestly sorry about this trouble with Frau Schubert.)

"Well, I sometimes toy with the thought of giving a party, a 'mute evening,' at which each of my friends, stuffed, would express his personality much more clearly than with a whole slew of words. In the final analysis, words only disguise the physiognomy."

"You're serious—this story about Frau Schubert is really true?" Conrad asked when they had reached the door of his house on Weissenborn Strasse.

"Unfortunately, it is," Herr von Hohenlocher said.

"Perhaps she'll come to her senses again," Conrad suggested.

"Only under the pressure of extreme necessity," Herr von Hohenlocher replied. "That is, when she can't meet the installments for the furniture and falls behind on her rent. Though, when the debts start mounting, I'm afraid she may simply become desperate. The furniture has already been delivered. I have seen it. It is incredibly atrocious. For the present, old Schubert is sitting in her dear little apartment like a spider in its web, hoping to lure the bridegroom that way."

Conrad watched Herr von Hohenlocher until that gentleman turned the corner of Hans Hayde Strasse, and for a moment Conrad felt as if he were gazing at an unalterably fixed point, while he himself was in perpetually shifting motion. A stir, a breath of animation, seemed to be coming from the low railing around the park. The grip of winter was relaxing, letting go of the earth, which was beginning to breathe. Conrad felt a kind of happiness at the realization that he would have the apartment to himself. Marianne was not due back until long after supper.

He ate alone in the dining room. The way the table was neatly set for him affected him strangely. The saltcellars, pepper shakers, and mustard pots—it was as if he were viewing his self-evident needs from outside. And thus, for the briefest moment, he saw a good part of his life.

After eating, he went to the "library," going around by way of the vestibule rather than straight through the door from the dining room. He brought the needful to the divan. The first swallow trickled down hotly. He saw the bridge into his further life no longer suspended, broken off over the first pier. It ran on. He would go to Berlin. After all, he had already achieved an incontestable success. The earring existed; it could not be denied.

This was the way; this way he could settle everything, including matters with Marianne.

At this point there was a distinct relapse within him. He saw himself with Marianne in Italy on their honeymoon. He felt—as if some warm body were rolling like a ball swiftly through his chest—he felt once more the expectation, agitation, tension of those days. It rolled by and passed. But now hope lingered in him like a solid body. Outside, someone closed the door to the bathroom. Once more he had failed to hear his wife's home-coming, so quiet was the front-door lock. Conrad rose quickly, took his key ring, opened a drawer in the desk, and from its far end took a little packet of white tissue paper which contained the earring he had found. He took it from its wrappings and went to the hall, which was now lighted. Just as he passed the island of table and chairs, the bathroom door opened and Marianne emerged. She was wearing pajamas, as she had been doing lately, although they were not becoming to her robust figure. "Good evening, Mariannchen," he said, going up to her. "Look what I've found."

She took the earring from the palm of his hand without a word. What flashed in her eyes and her tanned face might have been difficult for him to see, for the light was fairly dim in the hall. But it changed the whole situation for him, blocking his advance. She left Conrad where he stood, walked swiftly and lightly into her bedroom, and he heard the key turning in the lock. Could he have seen Marianne through the door, he would no longer have been able to ignore that glass of water perched on the edge of the table. From a hiding place between batiste handkerchiefs she took the small key to the drawers in which she kept her jewelry, and violently pulled one open. The green and brown marbleized lid of the case sprang open at the touch of her finger, and there were the two beryl earrings, one of which she had said was lost. In her hand she held the third earring, exactly like the other two. "He's had it copied," she tried for a moment to think. But that frail wall collapsed at once, and behind it was revealed the incomprehensible thing that oppressed her. She stared at it, and in her eyes was militancy, readiness to hate, in fact hatred itself. Glowing, a moment later flaring high, this wall of flames leaped up from Marianne, forever parting her from her husband.

In the next few days—and, in fact, throughout the time that followed—not a word about the earrings was exchanged by the couple.

EVERY MAN

A MURDERER

Part Four

~~~~~~~~~~~~~~~~~~~~~~~~~~~~~~~~~~

৺৻ 41 ৻৺

THE OVERWHELMING MAJORITY of people spend their time in the middle stories of life; only a few dwell permanently in the cellar or on the roof. And even for the latter, the eye eventually becomes accustomed to the altered perspective. Climb around where we will, if we do it constantly, in time our surroundings seem commonplace. Let the average citizen drop in, as a customer or for a friendly cup of coffee, at the painter's bright and lofty studio, where everything smells of varnish and paint and a host of things in process of creation. He can only wonder at having for a neighbor this steeplejack, as it were, who clambers about casually and with breath-taking boldness on the nearest roof—a man who lives above abysses, closer to the sky, where winds blow that never find their way down to the deep canyons of the streets, any more than do the rays of light that flow through the big, slanting windows of the studio.

But under the belly of the city, too, men go about, officiating, handling this and that with the greatest aplomb. There are rushing and splashing sounds in the darkness. The keen glints, examining, checking; the eye (obeying orders) looks over the gears and apparatus of the sluice at the weir of a collecting sewer.

There are rumblings in the bowels of the city. Storms pass

over; there is a thundering and drumming almost like that of the war, back in the remoteness of the years. Such noises come from the nearby tunnels of the subway. Perhaps you think of the war. Once again, for a moment, you see the sky above a springtime battle, see the magically sprouting trees of soil as shells strike, cones standing on their tips, still fattened by the earth they have ripped up, now bursting into fragments, dissipating in smoke. Such is life. And now you have this job. The lantern turns; you follow the path alongside the water, alongside this underground river (this Styx). But you no longer wonder. The protruding edges of such a life, of such an occupation, have long since been sanded down and rounded off. You step around a corner, take the telephone from a niche, and make your report. One more day's round is done.

The subway moves through the cellar of the city, and high up along its roof also, for part of the way it is an elevated line. The tracks glitter far ahead. The hand rests on the brake. The engineer's cab is dark. Below it, two round eyes of light, lifeless eyes, though bright, forewarn the approach of a crawling caterpillar of cars. Now the mouth of the tunnel is behind; the nearby rumble and roar is swallowed up behind, as by the soft palate of a great maw. In the cellar, in the bowels, there had been rumblings; now other material sings and swings behind the ascending trains: bridges, girders, grating upon grating. Everything that man has built, has used for years. All that substance alienated from the womb of earth, iron ore, vaultings of steel, pitiless construction, assumes an almost malignant rigidity compared to soft and suffering life. An unhappy lover, a victim of any other kind of desperation, looks upon such objects as if they were rocky, inflexible mountains. And yet there is a lamenting reverberation in the sounds they give out, the voice of the ore when once more a storm roars out of the dark maw and clangs over the thundering bridges.

Tangential to the curves, the lighted sky of the city, the morbid stars of earth, flash and play. Whole torrents and webs of tracks cut across beneath; chains and shorter caterpillars of cars stand still. Far off, great bales of steam are puffed out. Now, down below, there is animation, familiar sights: the wide square, spacious clearing in the hive of the city. Automobiles, tiny, dart along, ignoring the roof of the city, which the man in the street is not accustomed to see. Now another platform speeds into sight; the waiting passengers on the left loom larger, and just as the movement stops, a few of them come a few steps toward the first car. At certain times of day the engineer recognizes familiar faces—in the morning, say, and in the evening around seven or half past seven. A fat, dark man who looks complacent: brief case, snout like a pig's. A thin, fair-haired man who always stands leaning backward a little, somehow keeping his distance, slightly offended; looks as though he had been nailed into the floor askew. He always stands in one place while waiting for the train, never paces back and forth, as though such action were somehow beneath his dignity, beneath the dignity of his permanently insulted state. Then he immediately heads for the first car. So presumably is a non-smoker.

The signalman on the platform raises his baton. "Ready!" the conductor calls out. Usually he lays his hand briefly against the windowpane as he says this, and then hops upon the platform of the moving train and closes the folding gate.

Grayish-brown, the permanent way stretches on ahead. The tracks glisten, two rails for the wheels and the third rail for the juice, wearing a lesser sheen than the others. The train swallows up moving ties beneath its belly, innumerable ties. Ahead, the black maw of the tunnel now appears, still distant, a tiny mouth, a dark hole, a yawning black rectangle, a black shaft, in which the tracks vanish. (But no worry, they go on and on, right through, as always!) Now the train plunges rumblingly into the tube, whose wall seems to be made of smoke. But there is no smoke here, it only seems so; the swift movement dissolves the nearby wall into a flowing body. Besides, there is a wall only on the right; on the left, nothing but a few iron piers separate the train from the second track.

The next station platform opens out, a long, lighted cave, already in an entirely different quarter of the city which has been reached underground by a short cut difficult to picture, by a kind of short circuit. The areas traversed, roared through underground, vanish away in the darkness, dissolve into the nothingness which they are. It smells clean in the tunnels. Not really cellar-like. No smell of smoke. Rather, like the air in a box.

You studied something once upon a time. (It had been medicine; a smell in the dissecting room, among other things; emerging into the street outside the Anatomical Institute; the spring sunlight—and one more wasted day, without having memorized the bones at the base of the skull.) But since then you've looked into life through entirely different windows. And it's been better so. That abandoned track, from which you shifted over into this one by way of an unfortunate-fortunate switch, that former track had brought with it a constantly rising crescendo of pain, a quivering wait to see whether Uncle would pay the bills to the end of the semester. . . . That uncle was uncoupled by now, done with—besides, he had gone and died. But in the spring sunlight, standing outside the arched gateway of the Institute—a few students stood within the arch, in their white lab coats—for all the banter, you had already felt an inner pressure that cast gloom over everything, numbed all vitality, made it more impossible than ever to catch up with neglected studies, to go home (to that coop of a room with its excess of curtains, plush, furniture) and attack one by one the innumerable things to be learned. The books were killing. As soon as you opened them, the sleep of death rose out of the pages. Certainly this one day more or less didn't matter, and so you went along to the tavern. Besides, the whole business was stupid; what was the sense of living like this, with that eternal uncle and his panicky or threatening letters (which only made you nervous, interfered with your studies—

but who could make the man understand that?). What was the
sense of living like this—there were other ways to live. You
weren't compelled to, not a bit. It was too silly. And grew sillier
all the time. Finally you'd had enough. All that studying was
beginning to hurt the base of your skull. Bah!

Your hand rests on the brake. Now you have this job. Though
it didn't come so fast. There was the entrance examination on
Köthener Strasse, where the head office of the subway was
located—Company for Electric Elevated and Underground Rail-
roads, as it was called at the time, in 1921, to be exact—the
examination in taking dictation and the four branches of arith-
metic. The ex-student had been ashamed because an exam like
that was child's play for him, while the others had to approach it
seriously and alertly. His situation had seemed to him somehow
unclean. All very well, but in learning to be a gateman he'd had
no advantage over anyone; in fact, many of the others proved to
be smarter at it than he. The same was true for platform work.
Finally he'd taken another examination—the third, for before that
one there had been a "ticket examination," after he'd finished his
training as gateman. And then he was trained as a conductor,
and so life began on bridges and in tunnels, day in and day out,
through the cellar and along the roofs. (But still another examination first, of course! Odd that you never escaped exams; only,
here, at least you could actually pass them.) To be precise about
it, an accident, an unfortunate incident that you carried around
with you bottled up—not always well bottled up!—had given the
decisive impulse to shift into the other track. And now it was a
lucky accident on this same other track which propelled you
decisively ahead. In 1923 the need for personnel had increased
due to the opening of the north-south line; and in 1925 that part
of the line which leads to Neukölln was put into operation. And
so one day you were again out on the West Side on the test track
you'd become acquainted with during your training as conductor
—and likewise in the rooms for theoretical education at Stralauer
Tor (lecture halls, real ones!). Those hundred deviltries the

teacher practiced—one time unscrewing a fuse, another time pull-
ing the emergency brake, another time doing something to the
hand brake, creating every imaginable trouble and incident,
whose cause had to be determined quickly and countermeasures
taken, quickly, quickly!—those hundred deviltries became a regular game. You discovered in yourself an entirely new talent, a
technological talent, and a real fondness for things technical. And
the signals! Automatic and semi-automatic. There was a pleasure
here that was somehow, deep underground, connected directly
with boyhood.

The training to be an engineer lasted six weeks.

Now once more the patterns of lights of the city swayed
tangentially in the curves, seen from the darkness of the engine
cab (at that time the instructor stood by): the gridiron of endless lines of streets, leading out to areas where the sprinkling of
lights becomes thinner and thinner, the dim and sharp radiance
of a thousand sick, twinkling earthly stars. A day will come when
you will stand here alone, in this dark box, in this tiny closet, in
this sentry box which electricity drives whiningly onward. This
day is near. And on this day perhaps it will happen to you . . .
perhaps the thing bottled up will break out when you are de-
pendent entirely on yourself, on these hands, on these (medically
tested) eyes; when there is no one standing at your side and only,
behind the partition wall with the small glass window, the conductor outside, in the same car as the passengers.

After six months, the tension of those first two weeks of driving
the train became incomprehensible. That is, virtually nothing of
it could be recaptured. Only the known fact remained that it
had once been like that. And, perhaps as the sole living memory,
the vision of the noiseless alcohol flame over which you had
made coffee the morning of your first solo trip—the darkness still
unbroken, intense, and for moments only a single desire in you:
to have it over with. But then, hand on the brake, train in movement—and, like a good mother, the regulated automatism of

action preserved you from all the dangerous powers of life which
in the morning, before the silent alcohol flame, had still waited,
lurking, in your own dark, unknowing breast. The next station
sped cheerfully up to you; the waiting people on the platform
loomed larger, came toward the train; the lights hewed out the
space. Yes, this was your proper place. And nothing caught up
with you. Soon all that was warmed through and through by the
quiet fires of habit.

Within that habit, as tension slackened off and disappeared,
there appeared again, more distinctly, the anxiety common to all,
a bleak spot, a pressure point, a kind of unexpressed thankful-
ness. . . . Now you had this job; you looked out through these
windows; you rose through the cellar and over the roof. And you
could tell a whole flock of uncles to go to the devil. What a life.
You went way up there, in the north of Berlin, to Kremmener
Strasse, at least once, usually twice a week, to see your girl; you
took with you a package of coffee and sugar or some other
groceries. The walls of her small apartment, consisting of a single
room and a kitchen, could speak of all sorts of things in common,
of mutual obligations, just as the wrinkles on a forehead speak
like runes of the lived past.

For everyone has that; an engine driver is a man like everyone
else. And, in view of this undeniable fact, it is significant that
for hours he reduced himself to a hand, an eye, an ear, to a pure
apparatus, a geometrical pattern or model of the full life of the
senses.

There are rumblings in the bowels of the city. Storms move
past, reverbrating from the tunnel, thundering onto the bridge,
whose iron wails like the statue of Memnon in the rising sun.
Triangle of tracks. Bülow Strasse. Lights red and blue, left and
right, well known, shining far, sharply. Thundering into the
tunnel. Wittenberg Platz. Zoologischer Garten. Knie. This is
Berlin: from the roof and from the cellar.

42 &

CONRAD arrived on a Sunday, early in the morning, and stepped out of the sleeper. The first part of the night had been bad—a twilight sleep accompanied by the humming and motion of the train, never knowing whether he felt too cold or too hot. But it had been better during the second half of the night; his semi-insomnia exhausted itself at last, and turning over on his right side produced a relaxation of all his limbs. Now Conrad walked in a crowd of passengers toward the exit. The city seemed light gray, a dove-gray perhaps, in the light of a cold and overcast spring morning. The wetness from intermittent drizzles lay on the pavement. As he paid the porter and stepped into a cab, he quickly ran down his inner list and noted that of course everything must be in order. Eisenmann had arranged all the details in advance, including the hotel he was to stop at and the kind of room (the best, with bath and telephone). The receptionist came forward to meet him, a mild, pale man with dark hair who looked the very image of "Monsieur Jules," a character in a French picture book for children. Conrad sank into this lively giant hotel as if it were a citadel of silence, surrounded by rugs and with far too much gilt on the banisters, and everywhere. His room—317—was blue; the bed stood at the rear of it, in an alcove graced by a curtain with a tasseled pull cord.

Conrad opened his bags. He wanted to bathe. The telephone was on the table; beside it lay the telephone book. He paused in front of it. Five of the men who were to join in the conference were staying in the same hotel. (Eisenmann had written their names down for him—what had Eisenmann not written down? The oddest things!) Good, then tomorrow he would send a boy around to them with his card. Today it was too early; besides, it was Sunday. (But then, he had deliberately chosen to travel on Saturday night.) Letter L. Lehnder? No. Too many questions! "You're looking well. You used to look better." There it was: Ligharts, Günther.

With that, the burned picture post card was found again, so to speak, replaced. It must be he; the name was not a common one, and besides there was the "Günther." Occupation was listed also. So Günther was in the Foreign Office! Conrad lifted the rceiver, gave the number.

"Günther Ligharts speaking," a pleasant, rather indolent-sounding voice answered.

"This is Conrad Castiletz."

There was a tiny pause. Then, briskly, loudly: "Kokosch?"

"Yes, Kokosch."

"Good Lord, where are you?"

Conrad gave the name of the hotel.

"Then get moving and come over here for breakfast. Listen carefully: Keith Strasse is by the Zoo. The Friedrich Strasse station is right in front of the hotel. You take the Stadtbahn and get out at the fourth stop, Zoologischer Garten. . . ."

"I'll take a cab," Conrad said. "I don't know my way about—this is my first trip to Berlin."

"All right—though that's an expensive way to go about it. You could take the subway, very easily; there'd only be one change. But do as you like, only hurry over here."

"I think I'd better have a bath first."

"All right. Don't drown. You can take in all the liquid you like over here. So be quick about it, Kokosch. See you soon!"

As he was replacing the receiver, Conrad heard a strange cry, as though Günther were calling someone. It sounded like "Quiiiii. . ."

Conrad splashed. He felt good. The post card had been found again; it was as if a kind of lid had been raised.

Half an hour later the cab turned corners, careened down wide avenues in which the few Sunday walkers seemed lost. The city looked far too large, like a cleared, empty stage which had been built spacious enough for tumultuous events. Broad areas of park stood withdrawn within themselves by cold and dampness. Streets fell away, approached, joined; now the cab swung to the left, around another corner, and, rolling more slowly, puffed to a stop by a garden gate.

A maid stood white-aproned at the top of the steps, door held open; but at once Günther came forward. Not changed a bit, except that his clothes were different. The two had undergone parallel growth, as it were. There was no interval. Günther seized Conrad by the wrist and pulled him along behind him into a small, very warm, brightly colored room, through one of whose windows the branches of trees could be seen. The walls were lined with black shelves full of books. In the corner was a wide couch, upholstered in a rosy red; and a number of deep armchairs clustered around a low table covered with a white cloth which looked positively virginal amidst all the vivid colors.

They exchanged a few helter-skelter words which missed their mark, scurried past one another—on what had brought Conrad to Berlin, on where he lived at present. "I'm married too," Günther said, and now that strange sound came again:

"Quiiie . . . k . . ."

"Quiiie . . . k . . ." a high-pitched voice replied from somewhere outside, and then a woman said: "Be with you in a moment, Günther."

A blue book lay on the rose-red upholstery of the couch. Conrad picked it up, in a momentary pause in the conversation—a pause which, however, stood filled to the brim with the waters of life, like a wellspring of many words yet to be exchanged.

"You read Latin?" he said in surprise.

"Yes, Gaius Valerius Catullus," Günther replied. "It's elegant and charming. Look, the way this begins:

> *"Cui dono lepidum novum libellum*
> *arida modo pumice expolitum?*
> *Corneli, tibi; namque tu solebas*
> *meas esse aliquid putare negas. . . ."*

And promptly improvised a translation:

> *"To whom shall I dedicate my pretty little book*
> *Just polished with dry pumice stone?*
> *To you, Cornelius; for you have always thought*
> *There is something to these light little things of mine."*

The door was thrown open. In it stood an exclamation mark lit up by a pale beam of sunlight from the garden. Günther hastened toward her and kissed her hand. "This is Conrad Castiletz, called Kokosch; and this is my wife, called Quiek. You must call each other by your nicknames, of course."

"I've heard so much about you, Kokosch," she said, her hand resting in his. He looked into the face before him, which was charming. She was exceedingly pretty: a lovely sight, with her thick brown hair lying close to her head and her somewhat outsized eyes, so that her head seemed akin to that of an attractive insect. In those seconds in that small, warm, brightly colored room whose window looked out on the garden—where the new, glassy-green leaves seemed ill suited to the cold, clammy air— a space became hollowed out within Conrad. A receptive space, which nevertheless quickly filled itself. He remained separated from these happy people. For a moment the figure of Herr von Hohenlocher passed briefly through his imagination. He, too, was happy. And curiously, his happiness seemed to Conrad closer to his own possibilities.

43 &

HE stayed to dinner with the Ligharts, and after the meal sat alone with Günther, since Quiek always took a nap at this time. Her image lingered within Conrad for quite a while after she had retired. It was like some bump that had sprung into being within him, which he could not smooth out and on the whole felt to be a nuisance. There was no category into which to place this woman; she was a unique case, possessed of a troublesome, uncanny originality. Where the spell of sex between human beings is silenced, where those particular parti-colored veils are looped aside from the start and those particular mists will never rise, there exists an unnatural and abstract ease, a kind of cheapening intimacy between man and woman, a short circuit across empty space. And it was by virtue of this short circuit that Conrad now could grope toward the notion of what it must be like to look out through those eyes, those insect eyes, while riding through the Tiergarten (at breakfast they had mentioned this as one of their pleasures); or in general how it must be to live, to speak, to assume rights and have needs, out of such depths of self-assurance and idiosyncrasy. Briefly, Conrad thought of Maria Rosanka, but he knew at once, with absolute certainty, that the two women, the two worlds, were not to be compared. He was tempted to try to imagine a man like Quiek; but had immediately to recognize that such a person would be a freak, a horror of boundless affectedness, something very close to a monster. And yet she was altogether natural. Her form seemed to have grown in some incomprehensible fashion, like the armor of a strange beetle. Every object she touched in conversation became light. She seemed, as skillfully as a prestidigitator who substitutes one card for another, to empty all things in a flash and then to offer them up as objects of amazing weightlessness, like a true magician.

Conrad had never felt such utter, uncomprehending envy of anyone as he did of Quiek Ligharts. Not even of Herr von Hohenlocher.

"She's an odd one, our Quiek, eh?" Günther said, as if he had guessed Conrad's thoughts.

"Yes, I think she must keep you—holding your breath," Conrad replied, surprised at his own expression; for all its terseness, it struck him as the product of new-found mental powers.

"She's supposed to!" Günther said, laughing. "You might call that her mission. Incidentally, when Quiek said that she's heard a great deal about you, that was more than just a phrase. I actually did speak of you often, Kokosch, though that may surprise you."

"It does surprise me, especially in view of the fact that I never did let you hear from me."

Ah yes, burned post cards could be found again; the mail was put in order and settled; this point no longer had to be listed among the sins of omission. This fault could slumber for good! Over the span of several moments Conrad felt the touch of fresh courage like a fragrant breeze; and, while that zephyr lingered, the hollow vessel of his life displayed itself tranquilly just as it was. It was possible to be content with it. He suddenly imagined that he smelled fresh paint. But that passed. It only looked as though there might be fresh paint, here in this warm, small, brightly colored library where Günther read Gaius Valerius Catullus.

"I had these bookshelves built just recently," Günther said, as though he had noticed Conrad gazing at the walls. Conrad did not reply.

"You say, keep me holding my breath," Ligharts resumed the thread. "But it's really more than that. A woman must be constantly making the world at the same time transparent and mysterious to us. The pictorial drapery of life hangs pretty stodgily, on the whole; what the woman does is gather it up at some point, introduce folds into it, actually distort it—in such a way, I might say, that we sense from the nature of the distortion just how it is suspended up above, and that we're glad to sense that, just as the curtain itself is glad to be distorted. Perhaps because otherwise our lives would be threatened by the danger of continual didacticism, a wearisome unanswerable didacticism as dead as a museum. Death can creep into homes and take up its seat in drapes and pictures and even invade our views with his skeletal presence. We have to hold our breath, the breath of life. By that I don't mean anything especially sensational. But there are small modest aids that perhaps come to no more than the gym teacher's giving a boy a slight push to help make his giant circle on the horizontal bar—or even just holding his arm out in readiness to push if needed. In regard to you, Kokosch, I've made it a matter of holding my breath. That is why I often spoke of you."

"Although I did not answer your friendly card, the one with the white Pierrot." It seemed almost monstrous to Conrad that he should be saying this; it was as if he were carelessly revealing one of the most closely guarded secrets of his life. "Just think," he went on in a somewhat louder voice, drowning out this baring of his heart by the vigor with which he spoke, "I had that card until quite recently, when unfortunately, quite by accident, it got burned. Your address was on it, and even though I never made use of that address, I held on to the card as a possible link. I'm glad we've come together again, Günther. It's a catching up with a piece of my life that had slipped away."

Now he was done, he felt he had spoken stupidly.

"The address would have been no use to you," Ligharts said. "I had written: Uschatius Strasse. There is no such street in Berlin and, so far as I know, never has been. If you had written to that address, it would never have reached me. I simply made it up. In reality, I stayed temporarily with my aunt in Charlottenburg, on Grolman Strasse, near the Knie, and later, when my parents moved, in their house, fairly near here."

Conrad sank deeper into the soft chair.

"But why. . . ?" he said.

"If you like—in order to keep myself holding my breath, as you put it. To create disorder that might some day produce something fruitful, that might put something to the test—instead of a commonplace exchange of letters or cards between two schoolmates, a letter or a post card every three months or so: 'I am well, not learning much because I'm involved in so many things; my parents are well; I've won the fencing prize for our school, a silver medal at the high-school meet.' That bored me a priori. I preferred to see whether we would somewhere and somehow run into each other again without that. That's what I meant by 'putting it to the test.' Well, here we are. The result was that I thought of you often through all these years, kept you fresh in my mind. Otherwise we would have written those letters with our grubby schoolboy fingers; after a while we would have stopped writing and never would have seen each other again. A mystery must remain a mystery."

Conrad did not quite understand these last words, and yet they touched him more than all the rest.

"How are your parents?" Günther interrupted his thoughts.

"They are both dead," Conrad said.

"That's very sad," Ligharts replied gravely, in the tone of stating a fact rather than delivering condolences. "I still have mine, thank God. Your father, though, if I remember rightly, had heart trouble. Was it that?"

"Yes," Conrad said.

"He was much older than your mother?"

"Yes."

"And your mother? She was wonderful and very sweet, I remember."

Conrad did not answer at once. He was hindered by a sudden outbreak of inward confusion.

"Mother died of some sudden, awful circulatory thing. I haven't quite understood it to this day." He hesitated briefly.

Then he said: "Look, Günther, a moment ago you said it would have bored you a priori, keeping up a correspondence and so on. Do you remember that feeling so distinctly? I mean, did you think it at the time? In those very words? Were you—so—so free, if that's the word, that you could think that way, could simply refuse to be bored? Didn't it ever bother you as an—an unsettled matter, an element of disorder you'd left behind?"

"No. That disorder was exactly what I wanted."

"You wanted it. Yes. You say, 'I wanted.' Do you feel with such certainty that you are really the same person. . . ? Because—then in that case—to be exact—you were already grown up?"

"I was," Ligharts said lightly.

"There are many things I cannot exactly pin down—very many. You know, I couldn't say, for example: at that time I—fished for salamanders."

"And it almost ended in a fight," Ligharts said gaily. "Oh, I remember the whole thing. I used to ride by that pond twice a week. With Herr Brokmann. But why couldn't you say you fished for salamanders? That's a fact, after all!"

"Oh yes, I suppose it is. But if I said it, it would become—not genuine. It would stop belonging to me, as it were."

"Odd," Günther said, and sipped cognac. Conrad lost the thread which he had suddenly taken up with such eagerness. Perhaps to make up for this loss and to fill the gap in the conversation—a gap caused by so hazy and rapidly evaporating a subject—he spoke out the things that rose to his lips: "I was sent to Berlin by my general manager, as I've told you, to see about our going into this cartel, or whatever it is they have in mind—we don't know for certain yet. But I also have something else to take care of here—something that is far more important to me personally."

"And what might that be?" Ligharts asked, puffing out cigarette smoke and leaning forward. He looked up at Conrad, and now his clear, open face was that of the boy, a little mischievous, a little peculiar. Pierrot. Of course he would hit it off with such a person as Quiek.

"I'm trying to solve a crime."

He had not meant to bring that out so self-importantly; but there it lay, like a shapeless lump instead of a pretty statuette.

"I see—does that happen to be your sideline?" Ligharts asked, slightly sobered, possibly disappointed.

"No," Conrad said. Then he told the story in approximately the same manner that Inkrat had done, at some points even using Inkrat's very words; but he condensed drastically.

"Your sister-in-law!" Ligharts exclaimed. "No, I never heard of the case."

Conrad told on. Günther repeated the name Henry Peitz. After a few second's silence, he said: "I know him."

"What?" Conrad cried, in a completely unregulated voice.

"Does he have an electric appliance shop here in Berlin?" Günther asked quickly.

Both were seized by momentary excitement, which in Günther's case quickly passed over into jollity and enthusiasm.

"That's right," Conrad said. "That's what his business was."

"Then he's the man!" Ligharts cried loudly, rising to his feet. "Down with Peitz! Just wait, Herr Peitz, we'll fix you. Robber, murderer! He has to be the one. Otherwise the whole thing will be no fun. He simply has to be. And has to be unmasked. Down with Peitz! *Abasso il* Peitz. . ." He broke off in dismay. Perhaps he thought he might be trampling on Conrad's feelings with his attitude. But he was mistaken. Conrad looked at him and at his sallies the way a ski beginner on the Arlberg might watch the winged champion.

"You see, I simply can't bear the fellow," Ligharts said, rather apologetically. "Look here, Kokosch—if he looks like this, there's no doubt it's the same man."

A small hassock stood near the bookshelves, probably to be used to stand on to reach a book from the top shelves. Ligharts sat down on it, opposite Conrad, rather askew and with his trunk tilted stiffly backward and to one side. He brought his hands to the corners of his eyes, drew his eyelids down slightly, and in this posture of someone insulted and shrinking away from a pressing or importunate question, he said: "My name is Henry Peitz. What do you want of me?"

"That's the man!" Conrad exclaimed. This time he sprang to his feet. "That's just the way Herr Inkrat of the police described him!"

"Why, you don't even know me personally?" Günther said, still acting the part of Henry Peitz, and profoundly offended.

"No, Herr Peitz," Conrad replied. "And that is just the difficulty."

"You're going to meet him," Ligharts cried, dropping his pose. "I can arrange that right away. Although you should be able to identify the man by now, without ever having seen him. Wait a moment, I'll show you him standing, too."

He took his stand in front of the bookshelves. "Imagine," he said, "that Peitz is waiting here for some public transportation, the streetcar, the subway train, or a bus. It comes from that direction (he indicated the door) and now our appliance dealer —murderer, robber, *abasso il* Peitz!—sees it approaching. . ."

Ligharts stood as if he had been hammered at an angle into the floor, leaning back stiffly, indignant (was the bus late?) and at the same time keeping his distance from the approaching vehicle. The outer corners of his eyelids were drawn down slightly. "Is the man trying to run me over?" he said.

Günther abandoned his pose. "He stands at the stop as if rooted there," he said. "Never takes a step back or forth. Beneath his dignity. All right, I'll introduce you."

"I don't think that would exactly suit my purposes," Conrad said, speaking slowly and precisely, to make it plain that he had given the matter long and careful thought. (Library room? Most sensible drink anyhow? Blue notebook!) "I want to know him, but he must not know me."

"Right! Splendid!" Ligharts cried out.

"I want to observe him," Conrad continued quietly.

"In other words, to use the technical term, to shadow him," Günther said.

"You must point him out to me," Conrad said.

"It will be done, it will be done!" Ligharts shouted, dancing around the room. Outside, a slight noise was heard.

"Quiiiiek. . ."

"Quiiiiek. . ."

She reappeared. Ligharts drew his wife into the room, holding both her hands. "Peitz is to be destroyed," he told her. "Done for, unmasked, beaten. . . ."

"A punishment long overdue," she said, her big eyes growing more prominent.

During those few seconds a kind of masculine, businessman's sobriety regained possession of Conrad. "What exactly has he done to you?" he asked.

"Done?" Quiek answered. "Nothing at all. Never. We don't associate with him. It's just that we can't bear the man." In her eyes was something resembling the innocence of deep, clear, glittering water.

"That's enough," Günther declared. "This robbing and murdering on trains must end. You'd never believe, Quiek, the sort of thing that has been coming out about Peitz. . . ." He gave a brief summary of Conrad's story. Quiek, however, seemed totally unmindful of the fact that Louison Veik had been a kind of relation of Conrad's. As Günther told the tale, her eyes again protruded slightly, at once greedy and amused; she really looked just like a beautiful insect.

"Now listen closely," Günther said. "My plan is as follows. I'll make an appointment with Peitz. And in his regular café; that's the Tyrolean Wineshop on Koch Strasse. He almost always drops in after business hours. In any case, I want to see him; I bought a radio from him two years ago and want to trade it in for a newer, more expensive model. I'll have to pay considerably more on the exchange. Which will delight Peitz—*abasso!* On the pretext of discussing this, I'll arrange to meet Peitz at his café. You come by, Kokosch, and look the fellow over. Shadowing can start immediately thereafter. And now we call Peitz. In this bad weather he may be home on a Sunday afternoon."

Günther dropped to the couch and reached for the telephone.

"*Abasso!*" he cried into the mouthpiece. "No, I mean: Blücher A 9. . ." and the number followed.

Shortly, Conrad heard a voice whose smothered tone could not have been caused by the wire alone; it must be cramped by nature. Günther leaned back and to one side on the couch, offended and slightly disdainful. And in fact his play-acting went perfectly with the sound that squawked from the receiver: a little curt, a little broken off. The whole conversation did not last long; the arrangements seemed to be easily made. Conrad stood beside Quiek, who was listening eagerly, her nose wrinkled in charming little creases. He felt a wave of that mood which had overcome him in Stuttgart, when he called on Maria Rosanka. Here, too, everything seemed to fall effortlessly onto the proper track. The switches snapped of their own accord.

"Settled," Günther said, after he had replaced the receiver. "I am meeting him tomorrow. At the café. At a quarter to eight. But you and I will meet somewhat earlier. First so that I can show you the place, and second to give you the opportunity to see where Peitz lives—in a detective story, as you know, a good deal can hinge on whether the suspect's apartment is lighted or not. You also should see his shop. If one is going into such a thing, one should go into it thoroughly. An investigation is an investigation. Incidentally, the scene of your novel is set in a neighborhood

I know well from my school days. The Friedrich Wilhelm Gymnasium is near there. Let's meet tomorrow at half past seven in front of the former Palais Albrecht."

Conrad was glad Günther was not treating the matter lightly—he had been afraid he might. Günther explained the best subway route from Conrad's hotel. "Or you might take a cab, if you feel nervous about the subway," he concluded. "There's a firebox in front of the Palais Albrecht. Let's make that our meeting point."

44 ₰

LATE in the afternoon Conrad returned to his blue hotel room. The heat had been turned on, the curtains drawn. Outside, wind-driven raindrops now and then streaked the windowpanes, their impact sounding like the claws of small running birds. Conrad ordered his supper sent up and then made his preparations for the next day. First of all, there was Eisenmann's remarkable list, which went like this:

Tall and stout, black bull's head: Director Klinkart (there followed the name of the firm). Pay close attention to what he says. Always has an end in view; never talks idly. Hard to see through. Make notes on all his points.

Pale earthworm, pince-nez: Stolzenbach (name of firm). Wants to be asked. Goddamned professor. Delivers lectures. Now and then says something worthwhile. Mostly rot.

Pig's head, sagging paunch, black bags under the eyes: Grumbach (name of firm). Women—his sore point. At night clubs don't poach on his preserve when he's making a deal with higher-class chippies. Proud of successes that cost a lot. Otherwise intelligent.

Gentle bookkeeper type, glasses, sparse red pointed beard: Wirchle (name of firm). You can ignore his chatter. Fool. Ask him about coins (as I explained to you, if you recall, my boy). Then let him talk.

Round head, close-cropped, thick neck, stocky, always puffing on cigar: Wedderkopp (name of firm). Mouthpiece like a revolver. Shrewd article. Watch out over champagne, don't try to pick up the tab. He doesn't like that. Let him pay.

In regard to "picking up the tab," Eisenmann had given Conrad thorough instructions. The young man had to find a delicate middle way, a veritable golden mean between the simplicity and modesty of his own person and the magnitude of the firm he was representing, though only as an observer (and son-in-law).

Conrad sat at the desk and went over these lessons. His room was on the fourth floor. (To reach it he used a heavy, slowly rising elevator in which at least six persons could have fitted comfortably.) Yet Conrad had the feeling of being somewhere deep down, in silence, swathed in a kind of upholstery which completely shut him away from the city and the streets outside.

And from everything else. His visit to Ligharts, as he afterwards discovered, had tired him greatly. At the same time it had placed a clear goal before him. He realized he must try to attack this affair of Henry Peitz with a lighter hand, to leave some things to luck, to occupy himself with it as a sport. After all, he stood far above the whole thing. The situation was extraordinarily favorable. Nothing in it that was not in order. He made an entry in the blue notebook:

"G. L. arranges opportunity for observing H. P."

The notebook contained a great deal. Including the matter of the earring. Likewise some "theoretical" notes. A good many lines were crossed out. Conrad had grown quite accustomed to making these entries.

His supper was brought. Expeditiously and silently, the waiter set the table behind Conrad, who remained sitting at the desk, and departed. As Conrad caught sight of the food and the wine he had sent for, he was seized by a kind of fierce hunger. At the same time he became aware, now that tomorrow's schedule was settled, of besetting sleepiness. The half-wakeful night in the train was taking its toll.

But he went on traveling after a fashion, at night, in this hotel: his sleep was filled with motion. At first there were realistic railroad trains. But as the ride went on, these tended to dissolve; the cars became more and more open, and there were fewer and fewer of them; in fact, he was really walking on the tracks, and yet it remained a railroad journey. It was simply called that. The railroad consisted for the most part only of tubes or pipes of an organic nature; he was actually tramping through the innards of a terribly long salamander, to the accompaniment of an incessant rumble.

But in spite of such dreams he slept well, and almost unbrokenly, only awakening pleasantly and briefly once or twice. He felt wonderfully fresh in the morning. For some moments he sat in his pajamas on the edge of the bed, trying to recognize a kind of rhythm that was going on all around him. Sitting thus, he visualized Günther's small, warm, brightly colored library over on Keith Strasse.

Of course, it was that Latin poem. But he couldn't look it up here. Here it was!

. . . *Arida modo pumice expolitum!*

"Pumice expolitum"—tum—tum—tum—yes, that was it, the *pumice expolitum*. He had ridden through the tunnels during the night to the rhythm of those words. Now, with some satisfaction and reassurance, Conrad recaptured a few fragments of his dreams.

Shortly after the bellboy had delivered his cards, the telephone rang. Director Klinkart. The group was going to meet for breakfast, or actually for luncheon, in the hotel restaurant; this was felt to be the simplest, most informal way for those who didn't yet know the others to make their acquaintance ("the case with you, too, isn't it"). They could also get the ball rolling.

The small restaurant was decorated in almost the same colors as Günther's library, which struck Conrad oddly. Everywhere the rough, tweddy cloth of the upholstery showed that rich rose-red. Most of the tables were unoccupied. There was a bar in the room also, with high stools. As he passed these, Conrad saw the group of men assembled in the adjoining room, where several tables had been moved together. He went straight up to Director Klinkart (whom he identified by Eisenmann's data), introduced himself, and said modestly: "I had the pleasure of speaking to you on the telephone this morning, sir." It may be that this little maneuver had the effect of surprising the others and predisposing them favorably toward him. At any rate, Conrad contrived to present himself adroitly, without those awkwardnesses which usually accompany such situations; he was introduced around the tables, and all went smoothly. From that point on, Conrad remained consistently on the right track, and was well aware of it (along with this awareness came the significant insight that, a year or two before, he would scarcely have been able to make such intelligent use of Eisenmann's hints; he could do so now only because of his newly acquired abilities). Of the whole group, Conrad knew only two men, and those very casually; he had seen them at Councilor Veik's home. But he was easily able to chart the others on Eisenmann's graph, which proved to have virtually no gaps.

Klinkart seemed to be presiding, although apparently without especially wanting to. Everyone addressed him, turned to him, and he answered, in each case allowing a moment's interval of silence before speaking. He never omitted this pause. It was highly characteristic—and probably highly useful. Once Klinkart began to speak, he was rather sparing of words, casual of tone, and low-voiced—but each sentence was spoken with extreme grammatical precision. This manner of his seemed to have a compelling, almost hypnotic effect. Once he took the floor of his

own accord, after two new participants had arrived, and he made
the following remarks:

"When we breakfast here, or meet on other occasions, I regard
it as our private affair, which does not concern the association.
Nevertheless, we may find it advisable to pass on to the association any fruitful ideas which may grow out of our private dis-
cussions, provided that these proposals find sufficient support
among us. Nor is there any need for us to restrict ourselves to
vague 'suggestions' and nothing more. I believe I am expressing
the views of most of you."

He fell silent. But no pause ensued; instead, the others came
quickly forth with their assent.

"After all, the private group is a factor like any other in life
in general and therefore in business. We hence declare ourselves
here and now a private group." This was Stolzenbach, speaking
in a soft voice that ran out of the corners of his mouth like thin
sour milk.

There was a general "bravo," laughter, and a rustle of movement. The meeting did indeed seem to be proceeding along
most informal lines. Klinkart, having made his crucial statement,
seemed to veer away from the subject of the conference and its
aims. He began chatting with his neighbor at the table about
other things, of a casual and neutral character. In the course of
this general conversation it turned out that the group was by no
means complete—several other persons were expected during the
following week. However, most of them seemed glad to be in
Berlin, and from the remarks dropped Conrad gathered that some
of the men were anxious to pretend that the conference was a
mere pretext for their coming to the city, and that for others
this was actually the case. One referred to relatives he had in
Berlin, and some family affairs he had to settle (even an inheritance was mentioned). Wirchle chattered enthusiastically about
a numismatic exhibition, and Grumbach seemed to have come all
the way to Berlin solely to attend a première.

Conrad filled in the remaining gaps by going over the Eisen-

mann catalogue (but without having to mutter the items to himself, as he had once done, back in the mists of time, in the
bedroom of Frau Anny Hedeleg). The party included several
young men, a few of whom had not been listed by Eisenmann.
Two of these, Conrad later learned, were "secretaries" who had
accompanied their employers.

Gradually Conrad formed a more distinct impression of the
meeting—the more easily since, with a modesty becoming to his
age and station, he did not do very much talking. Once he was
asked—and with a good deal of sympathy—about his father. On
the whole, however, Conrad was left with a sensation of emptiness. He was forced to realize that he was here merely as a
symbol, that he stood for the mill, for the Veik family, but not
for himself. A good while back, perhaps, before certain changes
or displacements had taken place within him, he might have felt
at sea and been sustained merely by what he represented, rather
than what he was. But at the point Conrad had by now reached,
no such mistaking of roles could take place. Not any longer.

Most of the older men gave the impression that they were being
thrown off by the luxury which surrounded them. It seemed as
though a good many of them would have by far preferred a cup
of coffee and a roll taken at the office to this chic breakfast with
its courses of shellfish and Rhine wine. The waiters swarmed like
flies around the table, of whose "private" importance the manager
of the hotel was well aware. A certain sullen lethargy, with which
some of the men submitted to being served, showed that they
would much prefer to have served themselves, and in simple
fashion. They seemed predominantly—the younger men excepted
—to endure with patience rather than to enjoy these signs of their
upper-class status. And Conrad was to notice this feeling emerging even more forcefully in respect to all the "pleasures" which
the metropolis offered. The men seem to have consented to put
up with all that rot (for the others' sake—and each of them was
in the same boat). The things they really liked to do in Berlin,
they did quietly and by themselves: paying tribute to memories

of their youth by visiting a dingy café they had once frequented, or seeing some girl they had kept in a small room for a year or two, somewhere off in Charlottenburg, in the vicinity of Lietzensee, or elsewhere (*"ipsa olera olla legit,"* says that impudent Gaius Valerius Catullus).

On the whole, it was an aquarium of fat, not very gay fish who for the most part sluggishly nosed the bottom. In the evening, incidentally, they did not choose to go out together, even in small groups. Each probably had his own special cat to brush (*olera legere*). Conrad was more than pleased, since he had something definitely in mind: he was going to officiate, to go a-Peitzing, to brush (unmask, annihilate) Peitz. He had to take it lightly, to go at it playfully. As a sport.

The impression of an aquarium was intensified by a green ridge, or wreath, along the ceiling (from which at night a spotlight was beamed), and by certain ceramic plaques along the walls, of a green color, apparently representing water plants. All that was lacking were caves of tufa rocks and a passage down the middle along which Director Grumbach might have glided, swimming with his belly barely grazing the sand and peering pop-eyed. Yes, no doubt about it, he was sitting at the bottom of an aquarium, along with its inhabitants. Conrad was certainly beginning to feel the Rhine wine.

45 ৯৵

THE double row of columns lining the approach to the one-time Palais Albrecht stretched coldly away in the gathering darkness. The huge building itself (which at that time was completely empty) melted into massive blackness.

Conrad stood by the firebox for a while. Then he walked up and down under the colonnade. It was far too early. He did not notice that the background he was moving against looked like the stage set for a tragic opera—except for the fact that every so often an automobile crossed the front of the stage. The darkness increased, established itself among the gray columns. When Conrad took up his post beside the firebox, he faced the entrance to Koch Strasse. To the right, on the corner, was a closed tobacco shop; to the left, at roof level, a hotel sign glowed intensely; and just in front of him, suspended over the center of the street, a row of street lamps receded into the distance. Now and then a cold breeze swept across the asphalt, and at such moments he could feel that the air was laden with raindrops.

Inwardly, Conrad was looking forward to what was about to happen in much the same way that one regards a spinning top, amazed at how firmly it stands on its point. It was really Günther who was giving the impetus to Kokosch's top. Conrad was merely looking on, more or less pensively. That, at any rate, was how he felt about it for the few minutes that he stood before this dark, tragically self-contained colonnade. Things had to change! Ligharts was simply becoming a model for him, a point to be aimed at. Of course Conrad did not know how this adventure would turn out. But everything had been conscientiously prepared. Back at the hotel, Conrad had once more studied the exact description of the stolen jewelry which he had obtained from Inkrat. (Which list was the more important, that list or Eisenmann's?) The description was tucked into the blue notebook, as a kind of supplement. As to Eisenmann, and his undoubtedly well-intentioned remarks about Marianne: no need to get worked up about that. Solving the case of Louison Veik would of course turn everything onto the right track again. In fact, that was the only way to do it; no other approach was possible. If he could carry through this self-appointed mission, the rest would clear up of its own accord.

This opinion was firmly established in Conrad; it had become a deeply cut stream bed in his mind, a channel into which all the thoughts which bobbed up in reference to Marianne were promptly forced and borne away. In his talk with Eisenmann, too, he had tried to formulate this basic conviction of his. He had chosen to do this by taking the long way around, as it were, rather than pursuing a series of shortcuts; but the upshot would be a total victory. On this question Conrad had no doubts whatsoever.

A cab rolled up, slowed, stopped at the firebox. "I was delayed," Ligharts said quickly. "Let's go." They crossed the street, walking past the tobacco shop on the right. "Here," Günther said, "you see a building strikingly low compared to the others. Only two stories. Peitz lives in the one adjacent to it, on the third floor, where the bow windows are. Note the number. As we see, the lights are on in his apartment. This does not necessarily mean he is at home. He has a wife. She is, I think, completely unimportant. The shop is down below. Already closed, of course. A big place, as you see. There: Electrical Appliances. Now we go on; we'll be at the café in a moment. My old school, over there. I didn't do as well in Greek as I should have, but I've been making up for it. I'll go in now. It's high time. One thing I want to impress on you: if you trail him on the subway, always buy a ticket that will take you to the end of the line and allow for transfers. Otherwise you're sure to lose him when you're held up at the gate to pay additional fare. Quiek reminded me to tell you that. A little slip of that sort can wreck all your plans. I'll go in now. You can't miss seeing him; this café doesn't have any booths or anything. Take a short walk, then come in. He usually sits in the rear room."

Günther vanished. Conrad went over the instructions, engraved them on his mind. What made the strongest impression upon him was the point about the subway ticket. Günther and Quiek were really keen on the case. For a moment he felt himself freshly fired by their excitement. From far back in the mists of time he saw glimmerings of all those neon signs that once emblazoned the façade of life. What a glorious adventure, and what a big city!

He took one turn round the block—it lasted longer than he had imagined and in the end he hurried. The whole thing would not quite settle in on his consciousness. What did settle was a fresh faith in the possibility of lucky accidents, such as the one in Stuttgart and, come to think of it, the even greater one in Lauffen-on-the-Neckar. . . . He entered the café. It smelled of fresh floor wax. On the walls were oil paintings of well-known mountain peaks—the Pasterze glacier, rock cliffs. The Tyrol. A cozy-looking place: old implements were used as decorations. There were shelves of stoneware beer mugs with a design of red eagles, and the tables were covered with pleasant blue-checked tablecloths. He passed through the first room and promptly caught sight of Ligharts. As for Peitz, fantastically enough, the man conformed exactly to the mental image he had formed of him. To make matters worse, Peitz was sitting askew, leaning back slightly away from Günther. Conrad was dangerously tempted to laugh, an act which, occurring in a tragic opera against a background of classicistic colonnades, would have constituted a horrible betrayal of the situation and led straight to disaster. But what Günther was saying, which Conrad of course could not hear, seemed to affect Peitz as so extraordinarily insulting that the man never noticed Conrad's entrance. Conrad walked right by Henry Peitz and took a seat from which he could watch him easily. As he did so, he looked straight into Günther's face, across the whole width of the room.

There followed two episodes which nearly robbed Conrad of his composure again. The first was simply a prank on Günther's part. While Peitz was looking over the wine card and discussing choices with the waitress, Günther threw a glance across at Conrad and then for several seconds played Peitz, regarding his table mate with an offended air, his trunk tilted back. He even went so far as to use his fingertips to draw down the outer corners of his eyes. Peitz did not notice this brazen behavior, but Conrad was seized by such a convulsion that his soup threatened to spurt from his nose. He recovered by the utmost effort, fixing his eyes rigidly on the blue checks of the tablecloth, and forcing his mind to focus on all sorts of serious matters (salamanders, tunnel at Lauffen), and finally skirting this reef by a hair's breadth. For a while, however, he did not dare look across at the pair.

When he did look again, he saw an altogether different scene, which stirred him to the quick. He recognized it as the closing of a link, the beginning of a track into which he was once again being drawn, for this was certainly not the first time! Günther's expression seemed completely changed, transformed; he had grown very serious, tense, clearly on edge. Peitz was speaking. Günther shook his head and apparently said something negative. . . . But then he started, as though he had forgotten something of importance or in some way made a mistake. Conrad turned his eyes away, lest he be caught staring. When he glanced across again, Günther looked straight at him and for a second raised his eyebrows. There was no doubt as to his meaning; he was conveying the message: watch out, things are getting hot.

Conrad called the waitress and paid his check. Shortly afterwards Peitz did the same. Günther remained seated. Two minutes later Conrad unobtrusively followed his man along the sidewalk, in the direction of Friedrich Strasse and at a considerable distance.

What that last fragment of the scene meant, Conrad could not possibly tell; but Günther's signal plainly indicated that it had had something to do with his affair. Hope flowed through him. He felt wonderfully free, with a freedom he had scarcely ever enjoyed of late.

Peitz crossed the street, which was very narrow at this point, and vanished down the steps of the subway. Conrad followed him more closely. At the ticket window he followed Günther's instructions. The underground platform, which Conrad was seeing for the first time, seemed to him enormously wide and long. Peitz stood on the left, at the head of it. He stood exactly as Günther had portrayed him; but now Conrad was not in any laughing mood. From the dark maw at the other end of the long platform there came a low thunder, like a rumble of drums; then the train flew forward and up to him, yellow, low, wide, with lifeless headlamps. Peitz, who had first taken a step backward, moved toward the first car. The rapidly moving train came to a stop after a surprisingly short braking distance. The sliding doors opened for passengers to pour out and in. Now, in sudden excitement, Conrad made a mistake. He ran forward a few steps, was caught in a whirlpool of people; this was now the second car, but he had to get in; he could not make his way back. The sliding doors closed, the movement began. Conrad was astonished at his clumsiness and misfortune. Things had not gone calmly and easily; this had been an unsporting trick of fate. Everything seemed spoiled. He was in the front part of the car, standing in the central aisle between the upholstered benches; he turned (while the pounding of his heart refused to abate) in the direction of the train's movement. As he did so, the saving thought struck him that he need only change to the first car at the next stop. In fact, even that was unnecessary; he could see through to the other car. There was a window at the front and at the rear of each car. Now that he had Peitz under surveillance again, Conrad calmed down and considered. But, on the whole, it wouldn't do to shadow his man from the adjoining car. Let only a few passengers in the other car get in the way and he would lose sight of Peitz. He decided to change to the first car, as he had intended.

Once more the train rumbled out of the tunnel and along another platform. Peitz stood up. Conrad, too, left the train. There were hordes of people; the situation grew difficult, and

Conrad remained close on the heels of our offended Henry, keeping his brown hat just two arm's lengths in front of him. The brightly lighted tunnel through which the people were pouring in a slow stream—toward the exit, so Conrad thought—seemed to go on forever. But now it turned crosswise and up a flight of stairs. To another underground platform! Peitz stayed on the right, walked down the whole length of the platform, and there once more took up his stand. Conrad, who this time had quite skillfully caught up with him unseen, by going around the line of magazines and cigar booths in the center of the platform, stood just two paces behind him.

Once more a train flew toward them. The yellow front of the train came to a stop alongside Peitz. This time they were in the same car. Conrad had a seat near the middle. Peitz stood to one side of the door. No, Peitz could not escape.

With moderate rumbling and thundering, they coursed through the tunnels. They flew into caves where perpetual lights burned; they stopped. Conrad turned his head: he wanted to know where they were. He tried to read a sign. A green-bordered elliptical tablet read: *Märkisches Museum*. But no, this was not the Brandenburg Museum, of course; it was only a subway station named after that institution: but in a dream the station could have been a museum also; in a dream it would bear that name but would look like a station and have such a sign. . . . Conrad wondered at himself and again looked at the sign. The man sitting next to him concluded that he must be a stranger in the city, and with typical Berlin friendliness spoke to him. "We're traveling under the Spree now," he said to Conrad.

"There's water above this tunnel?"

"Yes," the man replied laughing, "but don't let that bother you."

Vacant, insubstantial, the stretches between stations fell away into blackness, into rolling nothingness. This was not riding, but waiting. You sat in this brightly lighted box, which might just as well have been rumbling and shaking without moving from the spot, and along whose windows a uniform wall vibrated past, changed from a solid to a liquid state. It was as if covering a distance manifested itself in the abstract, the only indication of motion being that at every stop a different name appeared on the signs. Conrad was waiting until the posssible murderer of Louison Veik got off. That, too, was abstract; though Conrad did not apply that word to it, he had the feeling of the word. Schönhauser Tor. Senefelder Platz. Suddenly the tunnel was swallowed up at the rear; the train ran high, free, above the street. Now they were really riding again. The color of the treetops, somewhat below the elevated tracks, stood out clearly and sharply, the glassy green here and there illuminated by the street lights. It looked cold. Below, people and automobiles moved in long, wide, undifferentiated lines of streets that ran on and on to the horizon. Danziger Strasse. Schönhauser Allee. Rumbling into the tunnel. This one was short, promptly opened out into the lighted cave of the terminal station. Everyone stood up to get out.

When Conrad, following Peitz, once more stepped out into the upper world, it seemed to him that it had grown colder. But rain and wind had ceased entirely. The wide streets through which Conrad's quarry now hastened, turning several times to the left, were nearly deserted. Conrad had to keep his distance. He looked out for street signs. Odd; a while back he had sat in a Tyrolean café, and now he seemed to have entered a virtually Tyrolean quarter of town. "Zillertal Strasse" was the name of the street. Why not out-and-out Salzburg Strasse? It seemed logical. At an intersection, Peitz headed straight for a brightly lighted restaurant and dived in. The thing was to enter and find some good observation post inside. Conrad hung back a moment. When he finally entered, he found himself in a huge and almost empty room. Peitz was nowhere in sight, and the place did not seem to have a rear room. Along one wall were booths separated by wooden partitions between the tables. Even from the door Conrad could see that two of these were empty. So was the third; therefore Peitz must be in the fourth, from which the waiter was at that moment coming. Conrad took a seat in the adjoining booth.

Here Conrad was pleasantly surprised by what seemed an extraordinarily favorable circumstance. The partition did not extend fully to the wall; there was a fairly wide crevice through which it was possible to see into the next booth if he moved his chair fairly far back and then tipped it slightly on its back legs. Conrad cautiously tried this, and sure enough, he was able to see Peitz plainly; he could have looked into his plate if he had wanted to. However, the abstract murderer was only drinking a glass of beer.

Perhaps this discovery of Peitz's visibility had something to do with the sudden stirring of Conrad's appetite. In the Tyrolean café he had only toyed with his food, ready to jump up at any moment (besides which his soup had nearly spurted out of his nose). Such semiconscious meals apparently did not satisfy. He strongly craved rolls, butter, and a plate of cheese, and promptly ordered these from the waiter—speaking *sotto voce*, for it seemed to him best if Peitz's ears, on the other side of the partition, remained in ignorance of his voice.

Scarcely had he finished his repast when the door opened and a young girl, pretty and respectable-looking, entered. She wore a long, dark coat and a little toque of the kind that was in fashion at the time. Crossing the restaurant, she made promptly for the booth in which Peitz sat. Peitz shifted his chair and greeted her.

Conrad tipped back a little, and was able to see that the new arrival had sat down beside Peitz without removing her hat or coat. She was poised on the edge of the chair, like someone who intends to leave almost at once. Apparently she addressed a question to him, for he nodded, and, as if in reply, took from his pocket an oblong object wrapped in tissue paper and laid it on the table. The girl reached for it, removed the wrappings, and pressed the spring catch of a fairly large, marbleized case. The lid sprang open. Of the jewelry inside, Conrad caught only a flash, like the fire of diamonds, because the girl had her back to him and was leaning forward to examine the precious objects. She closed the case—Conrad could hear the low click of the lid—wrapped it up, and dropped the package into her bag. A minute later she had left the restaurant.

Conrad was left hanging, tormented by the need to do something, to intervene in some way. Meanwhile Peitz, in the adjoining booth, drank another beer and drummed his fingers on the tablecloth. Quite some time passed, perhaps half an hour. What Conrad had just witnessed seemed to him to be directly connected with the signal Günther had given with his eyebrows in the Tyrolean café earlier in the evening. Beyond that, he had nothing to go on. In order to be ready, and because the waiter happened to be standing nearby, Conrad beckoned to him and paid his check. Almost immediately thereafter Peitz called the waiter. The girl reappeared and came toward the table. Peitz rose and reached for his hat and coat. He directed a question to the girl which Conrad could hear distinctly. It consisted of only two syllables: "Met him?"

"Yes," she replied. "You'll hear tomorrow."

The two left the restaurant. And Conrad left after them. As at Stuttgart and Lauffen, he felt caught up in a particular channel which invisibly constituted life. Everything inescapably ran in that channel, confined by so-called coincidences as if by firm, thick walls.

The way was not long this time. Turning into a side street on whose corner stood a terribly decrepit, apparently very old building, the couple walked along the deserted sidewalk, crossed the street, and went into a doorway. Conrad, who had had to keep at a considerable distance from them, hastily noted the number of the building and the name of the street.

The thing to do was to wait: that seemed obvious. Close by, across the street, shone the curtained windows of a café from which it would be possible to keep an eye on the entrance to the building. But it seemed to Conrad that such a trial of patience could be dispensed with at the moment. He had had enough; he was satiated. Carefully noting the route, he found his way back to the subway station without difficulty. And later, proceeding down the long tunnel at the *Stadtmitte Station,* he found the right train, which within a few minutes brought our Sherlock Holmes to the vicinity of his hotel. Conrad was already finding his bearings in Berlin. Where experience comes to us, we are soon at home.

46 ॐ

EARLY next morning (before turning in, Conrad had spent more than an hour recording his data in the blue notebook) the telephone rang. He had set it beside the bed before going to sleep.

"Kokosch," Günther said, "the man asked me yesterday whether I would be interested in some unusually beautiful jewelry he wants to sell, family heirloom and all that. His wife never wears the things, he said; he'd bought some of it years ago as an invest-ment, and now he needed cash. You know, I was so stunned that I did something frightfully stupid."

"What was that?" Conrad asked.

"I said no, I wasn't interested. I said it automatically, the way you say such things. My wife has enough jewelry and doesn't much care for it, besides. Perhaps I said it defensively, too, posi-tively frightened at such a proposal. In any case, it was a bad mistake. I could have had a chance to look at the jewelry, and we might have found out all sorts of things."

"We certainly might have," Conrad agreed; he sat up in bed.

"I can tell you even more. If you had played along, you might have seen the jewelry last night. He had it with him."

"How in the world did you find that out?"

"I trailed him out to Pankow, in the northern part of the city. He has a confederate there, a woman. She took the jewelry from him. Such stuff often passes through many hands. For my part, I have the distinct impression that this man leads a double life."

"Just a moment, Quiek, and I'll tell you all about it. . ." Conrad heard Günther saying.

Then he spoke directly into the telephone: "It certainly looks as though things are coming to a head. We must catch him. After nine years, he's worked up the courage to bring out the jewelry. Well, I'll get in touch with him and see whether I can rectify my error. I'll make up some pretext. I'll say I've thought it over or that I'd like a piece or two for a present."

"He'll become suspicious," Conrad said.

"Well, that would be one more straw in the wind!"

"So it would," Conrad agreed.

"When do I see you? You must give us a blow-by-blow report. Quiek is dying of curiosity."

"That's just the trouble. It's going to be hard to find any time for this. There's to be a conference this morning, and this evening I suppose I'll have to go out with the group. As soon as I'm free, you'll hear from me."

It was remarkable, and somehow quite professional, that the two of them carefully avoided mentioning the name Peitz on the telephone. This little detail afforded Conrad considerable satisfaction.

Half an hour later word came from Klinkart. They had secured a conference room in the hotel, and were to assemble for a formal session. Conrad sat opposite one of the new arrivals, whose name he had hardly caught, the introduction having been very casual. But the man looked like a blond Jupiter of Otricoli in a business suit—without a beard, to be sure, but no less handsome for all that. One of the secretaries who had participated in the

breakfast the day before—as deputies of the god, so to speak—
sat beside him. This dapper assistant bore the name of Nernstel;
Conrad already knew that. The god, incidentally, was chary with
his words; when someone asked him something, he would only
raise his eyebrows, occasionally drop his head in agreement, or
shake it dubiously. Yet Conrad felt that this significant silence
possessed as much force as the keenest of discourses; it exerted a
kind of pressure on all sides. The trick was basically no more
than a version of the Klinkart pause before a reply—only the
dosage was increased a hundredfold, so that the reply could be
omitted entirely. No doubt about it, the technique significantly
simplified procedure, without in the least detracting from the
prestige and gravity of its user. Conrad was curious as to the
place this personage would occupy in the Eisenmann scale—
which he could consult without embarrassment since almost
everyone had a pad in his hand or on the table in front of him
(not Jupiter; his secretary took care of such details). Conrad
glanced briefly at his list. Eisenmann had written:

Blond, handsome, rather spongy: General Manager Kötl (name
of firm). Looks down out of the clouds with vast benevolence.
A great encourager, especially of young people; kind of professional patter-on-the-shoulder. But above all: significant silences.
Complete idiot, but has managed to get the reputation of a sage
by maintaining this pose. An achievement not to be underestimated.

It was odd that both names, that of the master and that of the
servant, ended in a diminutive—Kötl and Nernstel. Eisenmann
was fabulous! Conrad loved him in these moments. He also
understood that the "achievement not to be underestimated" was
meant in all earnestness. (Try sometime to be significantly silent.
It sounds easy, but in practice it soon becomes evident that this
is an art.)

Conrad had barely peeped at the Eisenmann list when something astounding happened.

Jupiter spoke.

At once he commanded everyone's attention. What he said was well-turned. Afterwards, it was impossible to say what the content had been. Perhaps this was the reason his secretary transcribed his every word on a pad.

"What's that you're scribbling, Nernstel?" Jupiter asked casually after Nernstel had finished, and he glanced at the pad.

"I was taking notes on what you said, sir," the secretary murmured modestly. "For my own instruction."

Conrad heard these words. In his short life he had never descended to this (nor would Eisenmann have put up with it). Entirely new attitudes, of a kind he had never suspected, seemed to be the order in this circle. He later observed that this tone was kept up all the time, even outside the conferences. When the men were bantering with some tart, and Grumbach was treated as a formidable rival, or when Wedderkopp's generosity was alluded to as virtually proverbial, much the same attitude prevailed.

On the occasions of group expeditions to the fleshpots of the metropolis, incidentally, Conrad became aware that he was hoeing a tough row, as the phrase is, or at least that he was assigned a very special row which gave him a very special sense of what he was about. He put up with such nights, and put up with his companions, but he stood with one foot in a kind of other world. We might assume that this other world was comprised of the case of Henry Peitz. But that was not really so. In spite of its gay and sportive beginnings, the case was being conducted on the same plane as the conferences, as the amusements, or as the outings to the countryside around Berlin—these last were failures because of the weather. At Potsdam, where the group drove out under a blue sky, it was icy cold; and the city, in which a kind of eternally clean and freshly washed morning seemed to prevail, surrounded with an alien chill the cold and alien little palace on the height. A belt of airlessness separated the aristocratically withdrawn past, in its by now impersonal perfection, from its visitors, contemporary men experiencing all the problems and sufferings of their time. Conrad lingered on the terrace of Sanssouci, where the pink foam of magnolias stood firm and spherical in air that seemed to skim by the blossoms, that did not play about them, so that the fine contours of the trees were not dissolved but stood stark against the sky. Back toward the horizon, the sharp needle of the Church of the Saviour thrust into that sky. But this rare sight was accepted by Conrad, like everything else that he saw, with the same attitude: the dull feeling that he might some day possibly see it all with new eyes, but that time had not yet come. And so he remained in a state of waiting until the given sight was past. (It was the same with the evening pleasures on the town.) On the ride back through the somber landscape with its distant views, through a spring triad consisting of bright bursts of blossoming trees, the glassy green of young leaves, both quietly upheld by the dark, restrained hue of the pine woods—on that ride back, they stopped at the Schlachtensee to take a little stroll along the beautiful shoreline path of the lake. "You know," one of the men said, "in summer you can get a motorboat here and sail as far as the Krumme Lanke."

That sort of thing would have been tempting. The lake wound between the woods, its soft reflections turning left and right, its waters after a while threading between weeping willows. Nothing came of the walk. Above the pines, which soon closed in blackly, a bank of clouds swelled. They rushed back to the cars, and as they reached them the first grains of hail fell, then snow. Everywhere, it lay thinly sprinkled in the woods.

But the fact remained that if Conrad did not feel quite at ease in this company it was not because of the "H.P. case" or because of his age—though the fact of his youth might seem to have been the basic reason for his maladjustment. For all the inner modesty which, we concede, was characteristic of him, he had the distinct feeling that in certain respects he was far ahead of these people.

And this was something Conrad had never felt before! The only trouble was that he did not know in what respect he could be ahead of them. These men, it seemed to him, all had a completely established and therefore easily determinable way of working, living, and amusing themselves. Everything about them was wrapped up, encapsulated, closed in. Whereas Conrad had newly discovered all sorts of potentialities in himself. Merely that put him in a different world from theirs. Moreover, it enabled him to be forbearing, patient, even understanding. As a stranger, as one who was basically independent of everything that seriously concerned this circle (though in reality he was not independent at all!). And so it was that when Grumbach, in the red-upholstered booth of an expensive night club, launched into morose and cautious negotiations with a tart, Conrad was not put out. In fact, he was able to look on quite benevolently as the man gradually warmed to his task. He even helped build up the general manager by addressing him with marked respect—immediately afterwards turning from him and his prospective lady friend to talk with someone else.

On the stage there was a whirl of legs, powdered legs, powdered right up to the panties. The music went something like *pumice expolitum—pumice expolitum.* Conrad felt hungry. His hunger took the form of a craving for bread or pastry, a request the extremely high-minded waiter found hard to understand. At last, two tiny rolls on a plate were produced.

When Conrad regarded these with some disappointment, Wedderkopp remarked: "No, there aren't any Kimmicher here, Castiletz." The old grads of Reutlingen laughed. But the fact that Wedderkopp had said this seemed to change everything for Conrad, and the effect lasted all night. When at the next stage in their fancy "pub crawl" they came to a dance hall that looked like a huge hollow in whipped cream, he made no fuss about obliging Grumbach by dancing with one of the nymphs, who had caught the fancy of the general manager. Grumbach wanted to see how the girl danced (one of the group used the phrase "trying her paces"), and since he himself was too lazy, he deputized Conrad for the task. Conrad drank champagne and danced with the red-haired female, who lay in his arms like perfumed straw. The band with its glittering instruments sat in tiers in a kind of gold-colored equilateral triangle which had been scooped out of the whipped cream. During the dance the girl asked him what his role was with regard to the older men. "Secretary," Conrad told her. A huge green wreath festooned with satin ribbons was suspended from the ceiling over the dance floor. Conrad's state of mind was surprising to himself. It was receptive, open as a funnel, ready, courageous. But ready for what, courageous about what? For a moment it seemed to him that the wreath was getting smaller and smaller and was descending from the ceiling to land on his head. That was the effect of the champagne—a weak beverage, no doubt, compared to "the most sensible drink anyhow," but he'd been having a great deal of it. The dancing seemed to earn Conrad some popularity; he had broken the ice and the others started dancing. "*Prosit*, young fellow!" they cried.

So it went for several nights. In between two illuminated hollows of whipped cream or red velvet you sat in the purring, rolling darkness of automobiles, blindly traversing short distances, stopping and popping anew into differently colored light. They also sought out less fashionable places. At Alexanderplatz the décor consisted of sultry red glows and small fountains whose spray was dyed the colors of the rainbow by eternally changing spotlights—for someone already reeling, not exactly a sight to restore stability.

Not until the third day was Conrad able to see Günther, thanks to a lull in the negotiations. After a somewhat brittle agreement in the conference room, the group felt sufficiently strong to meet with the men of the other party ("jute and the other stuff," to use Eisenmann's phrase). But the delegates could

scarcely be expected to arrive before the beginning of the following week. Conrad telephoned Marianne to explain that things
would take at least another ten days. He wanted to make sure
there would be time enough for Peitz. Marianne's voice on the
telephone sounded friendly and gay, which considerably encouraged and reassured Conrad.

Günther and Quiek were beside themselves. They shouted and
jumped about the room. Günther swore and called himself an
idiot. For Henry Peitz, when Günther telephoned him, had not
taken the bait; he had been peculiarly evasive about the jewelry
and had pleaded lack of time. That same evening Conrad stood
on Koch Strasse, on the sidewalk opposite Peitz's shop, and had
luck. Peitz came stalking out before closing time. Once more,
Conrad stood at the head of the platform behind that brown,
stiff hat, and once more the subway ride out to Pankow ended
in front of the particular house in that "Tyrolean" quarter of
town. Peitz dived into the building without first dropping into a
café.

Thus everything seemed to be standing still, or revolving in
the same spot. Somehow he had apparently slipped out of the
channel of lucky accidents. Conrad once more recalled the days
at Lauffen where his first impulsive thrust had yielded him his
great success, the find in the tunnel, whereas the deliberate and
reasoned survey of the place had brought to light nothing
whatsoever.

Almost every morning, while he dressed, Conrad's thoughts
would veer toward two matters which had no connection, but
which followed on the heels of one another. The first was that
he ought to call Albert Lehnder. That was still to be done; he
kept pushing it in front of him like a ball being kicked along.
But he could not pick up this ball, could not activate the telephone—even though he had the number of Lehnder's office in
his notebook. Aunt Berta had sent it to him when she learned
that Conrad would be going to Berlin. He realized, in a moment

of remarkable calm, when he listened with a keener ear to the depths of his own being, that an almost insuperable sluggishness held sway over him in this matter. There was an invisible wall present.

The second thing that crossed his mind in the morning was connected, in a sense, with Herr von Hohenlocher. Its site was the bathroom.

Conrad saw that he was developing a paunch. That, to be sure, was scrutinizing himself by strictly athletic standards. Still, the flat shield was beginning to push out just a shade more than in the past, and those grooves along the loins which in a male body normally delimit the belly, and which are so great a feature in classic sculpture, seemed to be filling in. In the long run then, Conrad might yet develop into the sort of fellow blessed with wealthy aunts and influential connections, who ends up as a general manager . . . the very type, that is, which he suspected Herr von Hohenlocher wanted to bring out in him that time they talked about Frau Erika von Spresse and her sizable fortune.

Conrad tended to exaggerate this unpleasant discovery, so that he did not see what the mirror actually showed; he saw an already full-blown director's paunch parading before him. It was therefore in a spirit of reaction that he fell back on the adventurousness of his boyhood, on that spirit of meeting life head-on and beholding upon its starred face huge cloudy symbols of high romance. Certainly this big city offered abundant scope for adventure. Solitary walks and explorations—quite aside from the Peitz trail—were called for. And they were undertaken. (Though nothing like a real collar-and-tie period developed here; that was a thing of the past.)

The days were growing warmer, which also furthered such sorties; everything assumed a hazy margin these days. Late one sunny afternoon, Conrad again went to Pankow, not precisely in pursuit of Peitz, but in order to look at the milieu of the romance by daylight. The extraordinary roominess of this suburb, the tremendous width of its main thoroughfare, made it seem that here at its margin the city was fanning out, as though sucking into its open, funneling maw the wind of the Brandenburg countryside. As Conrad came up the stairs of the subway station and reached the upper world, the sun broke through from his left, coming out of a long street as if through a gateway filled with molten gold. The glassy spring green of the trees had reached its highest, most translucent pitch.

Here, too, he sought to recall something. Many memories returned to him nowadays, as clear as those that come to the very old when they summon back their youth: while the middle of life remains in shadow, the beginning and the end glow. Conrad's wanderings brought him to the vicinity of the Lehrter Bahnhof. The station's gigantic, semi-cylindrical body lay outstretched in a sunny waste in this quiet section of town. Conrad tramped through Moabit, past the brick structure of the famous courthouse, opposite which the pale arches of the Walderseesche Villa slept in its garden. He asked his way, turned right, found himself on the high bridge, with its wind and distant prospect. Beneath the bridge flowed the broad stream of tracks. From this elevation he could see the green foam of the trees near Virchow Hospital. He stood on the open platform of the brightly colored elevated car and toured outlying sections of the city, between high embankments, along rows of sidings, factories, and rows of houses turning slowly as the train curved.

Conrad did not confine himself to the suburbs. He also tramped about the quarter where Günther lived, for example. From the nocturnal jaunts in search of entertainment, he had a slight acquaintance with this district. And here he encountered himself, as it were, and a self of the fairly recent past. The choir of a large Romanesque church seemed to have influenced the building opposite by radiation in much the same manner as the church back home on Wackenroder Strasse had affected Inkrat's house behind it. Here was the same ponderosity, the same arches and capitals.

Conrad walked all around the Gedächtniskirche, made his way safely through the swarm of vehicles which at twilight shot from all sides into the broad plaza, left the upper world, and walked back and forth on the underground platform. In contrast to the streets, it was quite peaceful, with a smell like a box of shut-in air.

He had quickly grown accustomed to Berlin, for one can adapt to a metropolis much more quickly than to a small town. The big city has the tracks of life smoothed to a much higher polish; it provides those convenient short circuits in the cellar and on the roof. At Stadtmitte, Conrad got out knowledgeably. He was making his way through the passenger tunnel when he saw a stiff brown hat hurrying past him in the opposite direction.

47 &

CONRAD himself was hurrying—why, it is hard to say, but probably because everyone was doing so. He decided to follow Peitz—from a simple sense of duty! At the same time a kind of certainty leaped up in him that this accidental meeting would lead to some decisive point. With dismay he noticed the red railing which separated the streams of passengers moving in opposite directions. But a moment later he observed openings in the railing and promptly shifted to the other stream.

Breathing somewhat rapidly, he stood behind Peitz at the head of the platform, saw the low yellow train come flying up, stepped aboard the first car along with Peitz. And later, in Pankow, entered the same café as before. Once more they sat in adjacent booths, drinking beer, separated only by a partition.

And here it happened—Conrad could see by tipping back his chair. Peitz, obviously quite calm about it, took a large case from his pocket—a different case, this time!—and laid it on the table before him. Conrad had not yet recovered from this shock when the red drape at the front door was drawn back, and there entered none other than Herr Albert Lehnder, Ph.D. Swiftly making his way among the tables, in a dark coat and homburg, not noticing Conrad, he entered Peitz's booth, said casually: "Evening," took off his coat, sat down, and commented: "Aha, so that's it. Let me see."

Albert's appearance had a vastly sobering and disillusioning effect upon Conrad. He felt instantly that it marked the end of all his efforts. So dashed was he that he almost gave up the chance to look by tilting his chair. Lehnder sat in the same position as had the girl that first time, bent over the opened case, so that Conrad could not possibly see it.

"I'll give you a receipt," Lehnder said—he spoke fairly loudly, in a sonorous voice—"and then we'll see. Naturally I cannot promise you anything."

"I would in any case be greatly obliged to you, Herr Doktor," Peitz answered. His voice sounded much as it had on the telephone, at Günther's, extremely compressed, with a kind of yellow tone to the vowel sound in *greatly*. "I must ask you to excuse me now—I've an appointment in town. I came out here just to hand them over to you."

A minute later the stiff hat departed through the red drape.

Conrad stood up and walked around the partition. "Good evening, Albert," he said.

"My word, what are you doing here?" Lehnder asked with perfect *sang-froid*.

"Just what I wanted to ask you," Conrad replied, trying to consolidate what remnants of equilibrium he had left. A while back in the passenger tunnel at the Stadtmitte Station it had seemed as if Life were going to make a tremendous, momentous entrance. Now Life seemed far more inclined to prove how very seldom it condescended to put in an appearance.

"There's nothing very strange about my being here," Lehnder said. "The Pankow courthouse is only a few blocks away. I was on two cases there today. I also have a dinner invitation out this way. One of our clients wanted to have a talk with me, so I arranged to meet him here."

"It was about some jewelry," Conrad said. He laughed, to his own surprise and suddenly and successfully dissimulating. "I already know."

"I suppose you were eavesdropping from the next booth," Lehnder said quietly. It struck Conrad that his old tutor had aged considerably. His color was poor and his face was tending toward puffiness. A few gray hairs could be seen on his temples. "Eight or nine years ago the man had the smart idea of putting part of his money into jewelry, to beat inflation and all that. Only it happened that he picked on pearls. Idiot. The Japanese are raising them artificially, you know, and pearls have dropped. He'll be taking a big loss."

Albert's manner was casual and careless, slightly morose, but in no way hostile. He seemed to have changed greatly. The very fact that he spoke so bluntly of such matters, without bothering to ask Conrad about himself, seemed to suggest that in recent years his whole personality must have undergone a metamorphosis. Oddly, at this moment he reminded Conrad of the Grumbachs, Stolzenbachs, and Wirchles. Albert Lehnder's present existence (which he knew nothing about, after all) must be as static and as easily comprehensible as that of those other men. Conrad was now well on to their relationships, their motivations, and their amusements—the effects of the latter could be plainly seen in Lehnder.

"The dealer from whom he originally bought the pearls—a man on Friedrich Strasse with whom I recently discussed the deal—won't pay him anything like the original purchase price. So the fellow's making a stab at selling them on his own, and I offered to help. I thought I'd show the things around at a party this evening—perhaps someone there will want them. Would you care to take a look at them? If you should need them—for your wife or something of the sort—they're a good value."

He lazily took the case from his coat pocket and snapped the lid open. Inside, gleaming and still very much alive, lay a four-fold string of pearls.

"An old client of ours who pays well and on the dot—otherwise I'd hardly bother," Albert said. "In other respects he's disgusting. Yet, though it's hard to believe, he has a very pretty mistress—out here in Pankow, incidentally. She's been running around to all the rich butcher-shop owners of the neighborhood, trying to interest them in another necklace. But that one isn't nearly as good as this."

Conrad snapped the case shut.

"You don't like them?" Lehnder said.

"They're very fine," Conrad replied. "But my wife doesn't care for pearls. Anyhow, she's all for the outdoor life these days, which rather rules out jewelry."

"So I'd heard, from your Aunt Berta. She told me all about your wife's new interest in sports. A good thing when a wife has her whims. Simplifies life in lots of ways." And then, with belated surprise, Lehnder added: "But now tell me, what are you doing in Pankow!"

"The Veiks wanted me to visit an old cook of theirs. She was with them for years and years. Now she's married and lives in this neighborhood." He tossed that off easily, casually, without faltering or stumbling.

"Family obligations," Lehnder said, and actually yawned. "Incidentally, your aunt wrote me that you were in Berlin and what hotel you were at. Meant to ring you up one of these days, except that I had so much to do. By the way, you're looking awful, my boy."

"I probably am," Conrad said effortlessly. "You have no idea, the kind of life I've been leading in Berlin. Conferences by day and so-called amusements at night."

"Oh yes, I have an idea," Lehnder replied. "I can imagine. Besides, I know why you were sent to Berlin and what your meetings are all about. The little birds are shouting it from the housetops. But not a thing will come of the whole business— I can assure you. At any rate, no effective association; and your jute, or whatever the stuff is, will go on doing just as it pleases."

"It looks that way to me, too," Conrad said.

"Oh well, it's no skin off your back. At least it brought you to Berlin. Your name's been down on my memo pad for days. There are things that take care of themselves. That's sometimes true of letters that are overdue and should have been written long ago."

"Then we shouldn't feel too badly about such things," Conrad said with considerable verve.

"Quite right," Lehnder replied. "Have you any special plans for this evening?"

"I have to get back to town right away," Conrad said. Like most people, necessity had not taught him to pray, but to lie glibly, even when there was no cause.

"And I have this party I must go to. Oh well, I may be able to unload the pearls. Peitz—that's the man's name—promised me a fat percentage."

They arranged for Conrad to telephone Albert at his office the following afternoon. "So we can get together for an evening before you leave."

Conrad left. His legs felt strangely hollow and loose, as though he were tramping through thick sand. A feeling of nakedness, of defenselessness accompanied him on his walk to the subway station; he strode toward it mechanically, as if he were at home in this sector of the city. So vast was the emptiness within him that he became far more keenly conscious of his surroundings than would have been the case in a more filled state of mind. The dark streets, the solitary lampposts with their street signs on the corners, the trees whose greenery emerged sharp and

bright in the lamplight, stiff as colored paper—he absorbed all
this with a cold clarity, while a feeling of danger grew within
him, as though the vacuum in which he was moving were attracting it, were sucking everything indefinite from that further, less
definable circle of life which lay like a ring around the moon
about this inner ring and was the realm of all intangibles and
unknowns. Everything from that space seemed to have moved
concentrically one step closer, enclosing him in a tighter circle.
It enclosed Conrad on all sides in the cold evening air, drew
close to him like some hard substance—but one to which there
was no communicating, reassuring bridge. In this state of mind,
he descended the subway stairs, took up his stand on the platform, and since the last car of the train happened to draw up in
front of him, entered it. Shortly before the train started, the
sliding door was opened once more. A man in the dark-gray loden
uniform of the subway employees, with green lapels, entered the
almost empty car. He approached Conrad, who automatically
reached for his ticket, thinking there might be some reason for
checking it again.

"I beg your pardon, sir," the man said. "It's not about the
ticket."

Conrad looked up, with that bias of embarrassment one feels
toward officials, and looked into a face that appealed to him. It
was a face, not a mere official physiognomy. It was a highly animated face: long and high, somehow soft and weak, the emaciated
cheekbones and temples a little pale and damp, apparently from
sweat.

But he looks firmer now, tougher. . . . Conrad thought this
distinctly, in those very words. The man had sat down beside
him on the bench. "I suppose you don't remember me?" he said.

"But I do," Conrad replied. A space inside him had suddenly
been cleared, a receptive, absorptive space which could no longer
be sealed off. "From a railroad journey," he added, or rather
blurted out.

"That's right," the subway official said. And Conrad became

aware of the man's strange excitement and the tremendous effort he was making to master it. Moreover, Conrad realized—with a clarity that bordered on actual fright—that for some time he had been seeing things with greater sharpness than in the past—in fact, simply seeing more. This clearer vision had been born of the complete emptiness of the past few minutes—an emptiness that was determined to be filled and consequently refused nothing, let everything invade it.

"You've been out to Pankow several times lately," the man said, every word an effort. But he spoke precisely. "I am an engine driver. I saw you from the cab. Three times. You always stood at the very front of the platform at Stadtmitte. I must talk to you. I couldn't the other times, because I was on duty. It was horrible, because I had to talk to you. I saw you just at the last moment, just as I was about to enter another car. Please, let me have a talk with you. Would you mind getting out at the station after next with me. That's Danziger Strasse. I'll explain later why it must be there. I—I cannot talk here."

His enunciation did not suit his occupation. It was too precise, even in his state of excitement. Conrad was no longer surprised by that.

"I'll get out with you," he said.

"Thank you, sir," the man replied. The sweat was plainly visible on his cheekbones now. The train had meanwhile stopped. It started again.

"Do you know . . ." the man said, "do you know—but of course there's no reason that you should—only I know, oh God—I know—who Louison Veik was?"

"I do know," Conrad said, emphasizing his words.

They said no more. They got out at Danziger Strasse, beneath the short roof that vaulted the elevated tracks; the cold night sky hung a dirty blue in the arches of the vault. The streets stretched before them, almost deserted. Ahead, on the right, ran a garden wall over which greenery showed in bright light.

"Wouldn't you care to know where we are going?" Conrad's

companion said humbly; it must have seemed odd that Conrad failed to ask any questions. But Conrad, walking beside him on the broad sidewalk, was at the moment preoccupied with something else entirely. He was trying to grasp how he had come to undertake those—those romantic, adventure-seeking walks which he had formerly indulged in, back in the mists of time, and had resumed only a few hours ago. He saw the bridge before him, like a comb above the veering tracks: old Moabit, the prison, then again the stop—ah yes, Putlitz Strasse!—over there by the bridge, with the open platform and the bright, rapidly moving cars of the Ringbahn. All that was not just hours, days, or even years in the past (not back in the real collar-and-tie period!), but had simply been cut off sharply. It was all incomprehensible, no longer even ludicrous. What he was going through here and now, his present walk, belonged to another person, to a different, a second life. And the discovery of this seemed to wipe out everything else that had ever been.

"If you've no objection, sir, I'd like to take you to my—my fiancée's apartment. Because, you see, I wouldn't be able—anywhere else, in a café, say—I wouldn't be able to speak. Besides, I'd like her to be a witness of what I'm going to say. I'm perfectly calm now, thank God. I felt very bad before. You know the girl, of course, because she was with me that night nine years ago in the night express from Stuttgart. At first she even sat next to you."

"Blonde, thin?"

"Yes. Very thin, unfortunately, and that won't change. There are reasons why she lives in this district and not somewhere else. One of them is that over there"—he raised his arm and pointed across the street at the garden wall, in which Conrad saw a wide gate, now closed—"is the Municipal Hospital for Bone and Joint Diseases. She has to have almost constant treatment. We'll be there in a moment. She won't be at home; she's with a neighbor right now. But I have the key."

They crossed the street, turned left, and almost immediately turned right, into a very narrow street. At the door of the corner house the man said: "Here we are. Let me lead the way."

The building was old, of a greenish color, and had several balconies. That much Conrad saw before they entered. He followed the man through the entrance hall and stairwell. A bunch of keys jingled, a light switch clicked, and Conrad entered a small apartment that smelled of some slightly oily hair dressing or some other unfamiliar and penetrating perfume.

That was the first thing he noticed. Then a machine for making stockings, such as home workers have; a sewing machine; and in the corner a dressmaker's model and an ironing board. The second room looked presentable, or attempted to. In the center was a table covered with a green, long-fringed runner, and toward the back of the room a sideboard with metal objects on the top, and an ash tray ornamented with a pottery dwarf.

"Please sit down," the man said. "For my part, I must have a shot of rye. Would you care for one?"

"Gladly," Conrad said.

The man returned from the back of the room with a bottle and two glasses. The whisky had a certain kinship with the "most sensible drink anyhow." It had a stimulating effect upon Conrad, sharpening his firm, palpable sense that everything was altered. Half an hour before, he had been sitting with Lehnder. Lehnder had been the tutor of a person who was beginning to fall into place and become fully comprehensible.

"My name is Botulitzky," the man said, extending his hand.

"Castiletz," Conrad said with clear articulation. He smiled lightly. "Though I think names matter little between us." He reached into his coat pocket and found a pack of cigarettes. Botulitzky brought over the ash tray with the drawf.

"May I talk now?" he said inhaling deeply.

"Please tell me everything, but really everything," Conrad replied calmly and clearly.

48 ᣰ

"THE death of Louison Veik," Botulitzky said, looking down at the tablecloth, "did not take place, as the police assumed at the time, on the stretch through the Thuringian Forest between Grimmenthal and Erfurt, but some thirty minutes after the train left Stuttgart, in the tunnel between Kirchheim and Lauffen on the Neckar. And you and I, Herr Castiletz, were responsible for it. What happened was this: In a moment of weakness, when my point of least resistance—*punctum minimae resistentiae*—had been touched, I had to boast to my traveling companions, and especially to those two goddamned snot-nosed boys who happened to be in our compartment—I had to boast that I was at the university and a medical student. And so I brought out that skull, which you—on the brilliant suggestion of one of those two bums! —were to hold in front of the window of the next compartment, in which there was only one passenger. That passenger was Louison Veik. While the rest of you prepared to carry out the joke, I began to feel uncomfortable about it, and so I went out to the aisle, with my girl friend. Do you remember that?"

"Very well," Conrad said.

"Now I'll tell you what I saw from the aisle. The breeze coming in through the open window had swirled aside one of the curtains which otherwise would have kept anyone from seeing into the compartment. Margit—that's my girl's name—and I peeped in through the glass pane of the door. The woman was standing, half turned away from us, against the back seat, close to the window. She was holding an open casket and turned it this way and that with evident pleasure. It flashed brilliantly in the light, and we could see quite well what was inside. It was filled right to the brim with jewelry; no individual cases at all. That was what we saw for perhaps five seconds. Then—and just at this point Louison Veik turned somewhat toward the window—there appeared, brilliantly lighted, the turbaned skull you were holding on the cane. It bobbed away again immediately. But Fräulein Veik either lost consciousness or momentarily became giddy. Anyhow, she cried out and reeled toward the window, in the direction of the train's motion. For a second the upper part of her body pitched through the window and hung out; immediately afterwards she was hurled back with a fearful impact. We saw a huge red splash of blood fall over her face, while an open suitcase which had been standing on the seat was knocked down by her falling body and overturned, so that the contents rolled all over the floor. What I saw at once was that the girl's hand still clutched the casket. But now the casket was empty. At that moment the train left the tunnel. What we had seen had taken place within at most twelve to fifteen seconds. I reasoned that all the jewelry had been scattered along the tracks, either at the very end of the tunnel or just outside it."

Conrad saw Derainaux's portrait of Louison in the small room with the topaz-colored lamp shades. The pain was brief and intense. It passed at once. This sphere of emotion, too (of late the focus of so many activities and hence scarcely felt), sank down forever, and thus became comprehensible.

"She screamed?" he asked.

"Yes, a short, sharp scream. It sounded like the smashing of a plate."

"Then I wasn't mistaken at the time," Conrad said.

Botulitzky continued his story: "I knew that after this idiocy I was going to have to fight for my life, and the way I acted was almost clairvoyant. I opened the sliding door of the compartment —it wasn't bolted—snapped the curtains together, closed the door again, and locked it with a compartment key I always carried. Then I arranged with Margit—she was wonderfully brave about it all—to get out at the next station. That was Heilbronn, no more than fifteen minutes away. We quietly went back to our seats. I had to keep on yawning without being in the least sleepy. I remember that. I wished I could have thrown the skull out the window, instead of packing it up. While we sat there through those painful minutes, it occurred to me that I would have been wise to switch out the light in the next compartment. But it was too late for that now. For some reason the train was moving very slowly—probably the track wasn't free—and it took somewhat longer than normal for us to reach Heilbronn. We got out there. And didn't go out through the gate. We had tickets to Würzburg. I thought it was absolutely essential not to attract attention by having a stopover noted, or anything of the sort. I didn't want to have anything to do with any trainman. And so we sneaked out at another part of the station, and were lucky enough not to be seen. That turned out to be our salvation. The newspapers reported that no one had left the train along the whole route with a ticket that entitled him to travel farther."

"You mean you read about it all in the newspaper afterwards?" Conrad asked.

"Of course! The following night. So as to find out who the victim was, Herr Castiletz. But, before that, several things happened which perhaps you'll understand better if I tell you what a fix I was in at the time."

"You went back for the jewelry and were greatly upset to find one earring missing," Conrad said lightly.

He had not been particularly concerned about saying this, about giving the man proof of his knowledge. The words had not been spoken out of any inner pressure. He had only said them playfully, yet now he listened to their reverberations and realized quite calmly that to have said them was a blunder. Up to this time he had only listened, letting the other man talk; probably embarrassment over the grotesque adventure had kept him silent. But that capacity for listening had been part of the slumbering of faults, as he had once called it. Some of his faults had not only gone to sleep; they were beginning to wither. For example—he was so far developed that it would have cost him a vast effort to come forth with the anecdote about his father's uncle, the old colonel, and the two singing and wine-drinking servants. . . .

Botulitzky's face, up to this moment, had been composed from the effort he was making to tell his story with exact fidelity to the truth. It had, in a way, been ennobled by the burden on his conscience. Now it fell apart as Conrad's remark about the earring rolled across the table to him like a marble. In his face appeared all sorts of switches that could lead to very different tracks; unsavory crow's-feet formed around his eyes and at the base of his nose.

"What does that mean, sir!" he said, his eyes darkening with a sense of persecution. He would undoubtedly retaliate. "Haven't I spoken to you of my own free will! I'm being absolutely frank with you. Are you trying to trap me? Who do you think you are, anyhow? I suppose you're what they call upper class. . . . But better not fool with me. I have a lot less to lose than you. I fancy such a scandal wouldn't be exactly pleasant to you—I mean, if it came out that you were the key figure in a murder case. That sort of thing doesn't go over well in your circles—I'm well aware. . . . Even if you were only a teenager at the time and didn't realize what you were doing. Your hidden threats don't bother me, my friend—I've got something on you as well. . . ."

He had worked himself into a rage. Conrad watched him thoughtfully, as if he were sitting at a great remove. The various changes the man had undergone in the hour since their meeting were only too apparent to Conrad. He himself, holding to one fixed point, had observed them carefully, as if he were watching a play.

Botulitzky's face came closer. "Under certain conditions," he said, "I would of course be prepared to keep my mouth shut. . . ." Conrad saw his fear; it rattled through all the switches, coursed through all the tracks of his face, impelled by the desperate effort to repair what he must suddenly have seen as inexcusable stupidity—to repair it by the most threadbare insolence, if there were no other way.

But Conrad, cut off as he now was from that too easily comprehensible person whose former tutor had sat at a café table with him so short a time before (a messenger from the beginning arriving barely half an hour before the close)—Conrad was now dominated by feelings of forbearance, understanding, even kindliness.

"Herr Botulitzky," he said, "whatever those conditions are, they do not matter to me because it does not matter in the least to me what you do or do not do in this affair. You cannot imagine how little it interests me. Do exactly what seems best to you and without the slightest consideration for me, because I have no need at all of consideration. If it would really relieve you to clarify to the world at large the mystery of Louison Veik's death, I urge you to do so in spite of the harm you might be doing to yourself. In any case, don't be held back by any consideration for me, because there would really not be the slightest sense in that."

His newly acquired faculties, it seemed, were completely at his command. He had reached a point at which he could display that paradoxical—because altogether cold-blooded—courage which is truly the bravery of the lion because it comes from utter resolution. Out of the deepest and coldest need of his heart, he reached out for nothing less than the laurel wreath.

Botulitzky, for his part, collapsed over the ruins of his feeble position, over his terror-stricken audacity, which had advanced against Conrad not so much on feet of clay as on broken toothpicks.

"But what will you do. . . ?" he asked, bending low over the top of the table.

"What will I do? In the first place, that is my affair. In the second place, I can tell you because I have nothing to hide: I'll do nothing at all, because I have already done everything that could possibly be done. For well over a year I have pursued the murderer of Louison Veik. That is, I have tried to solve the mystery. Last autumn I went to Lauffen on the Neckar for that purpose and there, close to the end of the Kirchheim Tunnel, as it's called, on the side toward Lauffen, I found an earring, a beryl set in gold. On the basis of that, I deduce that you likewise found only one piece of the pair. A correct deduction, isn't it? Finally, I came to Berlin on the track of the murderer. Sherlock Holmes went to Pankow, the pitcher went to the well—and I found the murderer, in other words, myself."

"You . . . actually thought that . . . that there had been an actual murderer, like. . . ?"

"Let's drop that," Conrad said. "When I was a fifteen- or sixteen-year-old brat, I didn't read the newspapers. It was years later that I learned the whole story, when I happened to meet the family of the dead girl. That was when I started to take an interest in the case. With success, as you see. I don't feel like telling you any more than that. But what I do want to tell you, Herr Botulitzky, is this: the jewelry and whatever may have happened to it matters no more to me than your silly threats of a moment ago. You don't have to account to me, and I'll forget your whole story because I don't want you spending sleepless nights over having been so indiscreet. That would be foolish and unnecessary. As I said before: do whatever suits you."

"Sir," Botulitzky said, his forehead by now touching the green tablecloth, "you must forgive me for saying what I did. I just went off the rails for a moment."

"You seem to have a tendency to do that," Conrad replied ruthlessly. "Not as an engine driver, I hope."

"Well, you rode in my train more than once," Botulitzky said, and there was a heartbroken note in his voice, a deep crack that reached through to the very depth of its tone.

"Yes, to Pankow," Conrad said slowly.

They remained silent for a minute or longer. "But I had to—I had to talk to you," Botulitzky said softly at last, still bowed over the table. "Could I—could I possibly—let you pass? After nine years! Oh my God, you were fifteen or sixteen at the time. The most upsetting part of it was, when I saw you—you've hardly changed at all. . . ."

"I've made up for that," Conrad replied calmly. "There are people who hardly change. Then at some point the change seems to take place all at once—when they've carried through their investigations. After that. . ." He broke off this line of thought. "You, too, haven't aged at all," he said.

"I waited for you, Herr Castiletz, to—to be able to begin aging."

He let his forehead drop to the tabletop. A heavy sob, which sounded somehow as though he had been shot through the chest, shook his shoulders in the loden uniform jacket. Kokosch looked calmly down upon this battlefield. He was a veteran of life.

"I'd like to make some comment on the story you told," he said after a short while, disregarding the other man's state. "The train was going from Stuttgart toward Heilbronn and naturally passed through the right-hand tube of the Kirchheim twin tunnel. In our car the aisle was on the right, and the windows of the compartments were on the left, going by the train's motion. As I reconstruct it, this must have been what happened: in her momentary faint, Louison Veik leaned out the window and must have struck her forehead against the edge of one of the protruding cornices of the cross-passages to the other tube. I noticed them when I was in the tunnel."

"You're right," Botulitzky said, straightening up. He was very pale now, but composed. "Otherwise—if she had just grazed the side—there would have been another sort of wound, and she wouldn't have been thrown back on her seat the way she was. I went into the tunnel too, though not very far. As you will hear. For—naturally I want to tell you the whole story. Otherwise, what point would this meeting have for me. There isn't much to say; I'll be finished soon."

He tried to explain to Conrad his situation, the position of the clock of his life at the critical time, insofar as such things can be explained to any other person. Botulitzky was not a bad story-teller; after his fashion, he had a command of his mother tongue such as is possessed only by those who have measured its protean nature against the sparser and firmer linguistic forms of the ancients. "In the end, my uncle in Würzburg became simply a drag on my conscience," he said. "I absolutely could not study under such circumstances." When the time came for his first set of examinations for the degree, he did not pass one. And there was his uncle in Würzburg, waiting for tangible results. Some-how, he had to explain why the results were not forthcoming—that had been the purpose of his unfortunate summer trip in 1921. Referring to Vienna, where he had idled away two semesters, Botulitzky said: "To this day, when the train emerges from the underground and I see the myriad lights of the city, this twinkling sky on earth, I remember how we sat in a tavern somewhere up in the hills, on the slopes above the sea of houses, singing student songs—and it was just the same: a gridiron formed of endless glowing streets crisscrossing one another. It gives you a sense of the unity of life everywhere and under all conditions. Oh, well."

Then he had tried his luck at Munich University, and then somewhere else—anywhere but Würzburg, where he would have had to live with his fund-supplying uncle. In any case, the whole situation had become unendurable. "The plain fact, Herr Cas-tiletz," he said, "was that studying itself had become a kind of torture. I could no longer look at a book, not even at its cover."

He was silent a moment. "I sensed that—something was going to happen."

And it had happened. The means of independence and freedom lay in the Lauffen tunnel, glowing like the treasure in the moun-tain on Midsummer Eve. He and the girl walked across the

Heilbronn athletic field and went through Böckingen, choosing the longer route by way of Klingenberg and Nordheim. Thus they avoided tramping through the city of Heilbronn itself with suit-cases in hand. "I was super-cautious," he said, "determined not to attract any attention or be remembered by anyone." By and by, the girl could no longer toil along with the suitcase. Luckily, they had a big rucksack with them, and were able to transfer the contents of one of the suitcases to it. That helped a good deal. "At Klingenberg, where the Neckar touches the railroad and the highway again, I threw the skull into deep water, giving it a big follow-through, like a discus. I had to get rid of it, even at the risk of attracting attention. It hit with a thump, and with a kind of gulping sound vanished forever into the night."

The worst of the ten-mile tramp had been the last stage, about a third of the whole. Keeping Lauffen on the left, they followed the Zaber River, which curves along the mountain. "It was an enormous detour, for the sake of safety. If I hadn't known the vicinity very well from having hiked there, I think we would probably have gone astray somewhere and lost a lot of precious time. Besides, Margit's nerves began to give out, during that night march, from the aftereffects of our experience."

They had turned off the road. They crossed the narrow-gauge track to Brackenheim and Leonbronn, leaving the river behind, and then, still at the foot of the mountain, followed the same ditch that had guided Conrad eight years later, except that they approached the right-of-way and the tunnel mouth from the other side.

"Well then, you found all the jewelry," Conrad said, a bit im-patient. "And I can even tell you where: just outside the tunnel, between the tracks, on the space where the signal apparatus stands. A few pieces might have been within the last fifty yards of the tunnel."

He spoke almost irritably, but he was swept with admiration for this other type of human being, for the qualities which enabled such a type to switch tracks in life. Never—he saw that

clearly, as he surveyed himself and the life he called his own—
would he have had the capacity to endure that night on the road
between Klingenberg and Lauffen, to live through such a night
cherishing such aims, or with such disorder prevailing in his own
existence. Now that he had, as it were, caught up with himself,
comprehended, seen through himself down to his weakest point,
and was therefore freed of himself and deliciously enjoying this
freedom—now for the first time he saw another human being with
unprecedented clarity. He gazed across that abyss which sep-
arates character from character. He was a creature of consistency
(at what cost!), and for all his admiration of the other man, that
left him with a feeling of distinct superiority. He had his fixed
point, clung to it, while the other man was possessed by restless
alternations; his face changed, his spirit flickered like a candle
flame in a draft.

"You're wrong about that," Botulitzky said with an effort.
"Though you may not believe me. We found some pieces, yes."
And as though he saw a vision before him, as though he were
staring into it, he went on, with wide, blank eyes: "The dusk was
still thick in the woods where we waited. Not a leaf stirred. Then,
when it was light enough to see, we made a dash for the tracks.
We didn't dare waste another minute. As I scrambled up over the
embankment, I spied the first piece. There it lay, a tiny thing, but
real. We snatched it up. I can still see Margit before me, a
crouching, scurrying shadow, as though she were gray from the
night out of which we had sprung. In the end, I went through the
tunnel, shining my flashlight, to the right of the track. I stumbled,
but my eyes pulled the ground up to me as though I meant to
sift every inch of it. A bracelet lay fairly close to the entrance,
then the earring, then nothing more."

He fell silent, subsided into heavy gloom. It was as if he were
actually staring into the dark double mouth of the tunnel, and
deep into those moments of his life; and as if he felt as he had
then, not knowing whether there were any way out.

Conrad thought that he had never really lived—not in the sense

Botulitzky had. He had been passed on from place to place like a parcel-post package. This insight came to him calmly, coolly. There was nothing offensive about it. It was like a biological observation. Momentarily, he thought of Maria Rosanka. And then, with a further, rapid flight of thought, his mind lighted upon that urchin whom Ligharts had once punched, down by the salamander pool. And the other urchins had mentioned the police! Botulitzky, with his silly threats a while back, had basically the same temperament.

"At any rate, what loot you did find had considerable value," Conrad said. (Even to himself, the word "loot" sounded rather ruthless.) "Perhaps some of the things rolled between the stones and into cracks. After all, the jewelry was mostly emeralds, whose value has risen enormously in the interval."

"Yes," Botulitzky said, his cheekbones damp from the strain. "But, all the same, it wasn't so overwhelming. . . . The major part was lost. . . . Possibly more was found afterwards and nothing said about it."

For a moment Conrad thought of the strange tavern with the grand piano and the married daughter who could play the *Moonlight Sonata*. He smiled and waved away the thought.

"Please go on with your story about the jewelry, Herr Botulitzky," he said. "What happened to the rest is unimportant. I only hope that the incident brought about an improvement in your circumstances."

"It didn't turn out that way," Botulitzky said. His humiliation had reached such a low point—it was as low as it could possibly get—that it seemed to have a liberating effect upon him. "I see you're losing interest, so I'll make it short. We walked to Bietigheim—as you may know, that is a railroad junction. On the way we scarcely dared buy food. From Bietigheim we rode by detours, changing trains several times, through Mannheim or Ludwighafen or some other place, and finally reached Berlin. Very little of that trip has remained in my memory. I only recall it was hot. Thank God we had some cash on us—that is, Margit—where can she be?—had some. I didn't. She took me along to Berlin with her. She had a job there, quite a good one. We'd met in Stuttgart, where Margit was visiting relatives. She'd decided to come with me to Würzburg to give me moral support. But now I'd given up all thought of seeing that uncle of mine. And, in fact, given up everything. I sat in Berlin at Margit's place like Fafnir over his hoard, read the newspapers, and was in constant terror of the police, who hadn't wasted a moment's thought on us."

He seemed to hesitate about going further, and was silent for a moment.

"It really was a turning point," he went on softly. "After six weeks, Margit lost her job. Probably because of my living with her. That must have been the reason. We didn't dare do anything about the jewelry. For my part, I was good for nothing. And I found nothing. No job, I mean. That was a horrible summer. Out in the country occasionally, at the Nikolassee, among the pine woods I'd known in the past, I would be conscious of the blue sky, the boat rides, all my old pleasures. . . . But for me they were over. I was cut off, isolated, from the life of the big city in which I huddled like a shipwrecked man on a deserted beach."

Botulitzky's voice dropped lower and lower, from sentence to sentence. His head found a resting place on his arms, which lay folded on the table.

"She pulled me through. Don't ask how, Herr Castiletz. Imagine it for yourself, to yourself. That's the reason, too, why I can't marry Margit, today. I would be out on my ear; they are very strict about such matters at the Transit Authority. I looked on, powerless to do anything; that is, I saw it coming and I looked away. One day she told me, confessed it, here in this room. I knew she loved me—could I help knowing, after everything? Now I was clearly carrying on both shoulders a load that I had previously felt or guessed at only as an increasing, dull pressure

from the side. Once she'd arrived at—at that point"—Botulitzky
had suppressed some word—"Margit also disposed of our 'loot,'
as you called it, Herr Castiletz. She had made various contacts.
I myself went out to Neukölln with her several times—I recall
that—but only as if it were a hole in life—sitting on some bench
in some unknown park with children playing all around. Then
Margit came; we walked with our small, frightful things tied up
in handkerchiefs—it was an agony to carry them, they felt so
hard. . . . My hands were constantly sweaty and dirty in those
days—why, I couldn't imagine. . . . You know, it really seems too
ironic—you would think that among all those painfully broken up
and dissected pieces of jewelry we might have had a few of
those sad little green stones that were the most valuable of all?
We didn't have one. Our terror lowered the price; we made the
deals faster and faster, just to get rid of the stuff. But you know—
I want to tell you this here and now, Herr Castiletz—" he raised
his head, which had been pillowed on his arms—"there's something awesome about the fact that after the last sale, and really,
after we'd hastily, greedily, consumed the last money from that
source—everything changed overnight. Within a week or a
month, anyhow. For Margit and for me."

His eyes floated in tears as he again lifted his head.

"Well," he went on, "I'm sure you want to be spared the
details. Here"—Botulitzky plucked at the tunic of his uniform
by way of referring to the subway—"I made remarkably rapid
progress. They had built new lines in 1925 and 1926, which meant
that more men were needed for the trains. . . ."

He said this last almost in a murmur. Now he seemed to have
come to an end. Conrad remained silent. After a while, Botulitzky
produced one more sentence, spoken from between the arms
folded on the table: "It has broken me, the way you break a stick
over your knee. Ruined my whole life. . . ."

"Mine too," Conrad wanted to say. The words almost reached
his teeth, his lips. But then he saw the irrationality of what he

intended to say, and the folly of the way he had spoken all his
life, the way everyone spoke, taking from mouth to mouth smooth
and borrowed phrases. It was like a flash of grace, illuminating
everything with a surpassing clarity. No, that stupid practical
joke, that turn of a switch in the boy's soul, that "folly," had not
"ruined his life" (what else had his life consisted of?). It was
his life, his real life, then and today—no, not today, but up to two
hours ago. Everything else during the long subsequent years,
which he had considered his life, had in fact been piled-up rubble
concealing his true life. And he had been well on the way to aging
along with that rubble.

Now for the first time he would really speak out. Not to just
anyone, not in order to be heard; but as if speaking in solitude,
to himself in an empty room. Not a thinker by trade, and therefore with no skill at expression, he thought of this as a monstrously heavy task.

He was preparing himself, with remarkable boldness, to strive
for this impossible laurel wreath, when a key found its way into
the lock at the door, the light was switched on and sprang into
all the cramped corners (over dressmaker's dummy, ironing
board, stocking machine). A light footstep outside the door of
the room. It was opened swiftly, as by a person who is late.

"Oh heavens!" she said, and her gaze, capitulating in the face
of the monumentality of life, rested on Conrad, quivering, transparent as egg white. Her body, a frail clinging plant, seemed no
longer able to stand upright by itself, but to be supported only
by the doorjamb against which she leaned. Both men had risen
to their feet.

"It's him," Botulitsky said.

"Does he know . . . ?" she asked.

"Yes," Botulitsky replied.

"Everything?"

"Yes," Botulitsky whispered, slowly dropping his head, full of
shame in the face of this woman because of his imprudence, his

lack of caution. It was the bowing of the neck before Hera, the oldest gesture of man—and what made man what he is.

Conrad leaped forward toward her. "Margit!" he cried out. "There's nothing to be afraid of! Don't be afraid!" He shouted, crying out to her as if for help. The sea of suffering rose, overflowed from her eyes.

"Is that true?" she said, nodding behind a veil of tears.

Botulitsky collapsed at the table, his face plunging into the darkness of his folded arms. "It's all right, everything is all right now," he murmured.

49 ‽

CONRAD did not travel that night. No trains rushed through his dreams; there were none that had to be caught and then dissolved during the journey, so that, still traveling on the railroad, he would be walking the ties with tripping steps. His sleep was stationary. In the morning, the train stood in the same terminal into which it had pulled that evening.

Broad daylight filled the blue hotel room. Conrad flexed his right arm, felt a hard object in his hand, opened his fingers, and saw on the heavily perspiring palm a tiny cigarette case, or, rather, a snuff case of old silver, with the initials M and V on the lid. That was the one thing that was left. Margit had given it to him.

He wanted to leave Berlin at once and, disturbed but also pleasantly surprised, found that his watch read only six o'clock. That meant he could easily catch the morning train. Conrad

sprang out of bed and rang. Between breakfast, bath, and dressing—which he went about without haste, though he let everything lie in disarray around the room—he wrote a note to Herr
Klinkart, a few lines in which he said that his wife's sudden illness
made it imperative for him to go home at once, but that he hoped
to be back in time for the impending conferences. Conrad then
forgot this letter; he did not give it to a bellboy or a waiter or
the chambermaid, but simply left it lying on the desk. He also
forgot his baggage, and while he paid his check was reminded
of it with mild, cosmopolitan courtesy. He was only taking one
suitcase, he said, the small yellow one. Would they mind storing
his things somewhere—the wardrobes were full, the suit he'd
worn yesterday lay half on the chair, half on the floor—since he
expected to be back in a few days. In the yellow suitcase, incidentally, he had the blue notebook. During his journey, Conrad
read through it with amusement, while he was alone in the compartment; then he left it on the upholstered seat, together with
the unlocked suitcase, and went to the dining car. There he spent
a large part of the ride; he breakfasted and had his noon meal,
but he did not drink a drop of beer, wine, or even brandy. It did
not occur to him; he felt no need for anything of the sort, and
merely had a carbonated beverage.

At the low, oblong station, he took Line 3, rode to the end
down long, narrow Wackenroder Strasse, and got out at the park,
carrying his foolish little suitcase. The gold of late afternoon
flooded slantwise through the warm air. Things were spacious
and still, scarcely a vehicle in sight. The treetops stood motionless
in stiff, young greenery. In the stairwell, too, the sunlight silently
cast nets upon the walls. But then, from the Castiletz apartment,
a fine phonograph began to boom the *paso doble* to which
Conrad had danced with the red-haired tart inside the whipped-
cream hollow in Berlin. He inserted the key into the noiseless
lock. Through the silently widening crack of the door, Conrad
could see across the hall and straight into the "dressing room,"

whose door stood open. He beheld Marianne stooping over the
phonograph and, incidentally, clad only in step-ins. Her strong,
nut-brown neck looked decidedly like the period after a declara-
tory sentence, whose subject she was, and whose object—a completely undressed man—stood beside her. There could be no
doubt whatsoever as to the nature of the verb. Both were fussing
with the phonograph, which was giving forth an extraordinary
blare of trumpets. Conrad, who now very softly drew the door
closed from without, had, at the first glimpse of this apocalyptic
scene, expected to see Peter Duracher. But it was someone else.
He had to run through a whole roster of possibilities before his
mental eye lighted upon another figure, that of the young man
who for inscrutable reasons was called by a woman's name:
"Peggy." But this was not the man either. Breaking through at
last to optical reality *(demonstratio ad oculos)*, Conrad was
forced to realize that he did not even know the name of the
young man. It was one of those nineteen-year-old, whited sepulchers from the tennis court. Standing on the landing outside his
door, he could hear the phonograph; it was playing more softly,
but, on the other hand, there was some loud laughter. He picked
up his small suitcase and slowly descended the stairs. This matter
was completely in order. The only excess, from his point of view,
was the fact that Marianne had not thought it necessary to insert
the chain bolt. But then, the maid had been sent away and probably given no key, and who else might be expected to come?

In general, everything was in order. It had been ludicrous of
him to have spent a thought now and then, during the railroad
journey, on how he was going to "confront" Marianne with his
present knowledge. As he turned the corner of Weissenborn
Strasse, opposite that birch behind the low park fence (the tree
stood bright green now, its foliage like colored paper), and
started to cross Hans Hayde Strasse, an old acquaintance unexpectedly met him and equally unexpectedly came within a hair
of running him down: a big, yellow tank truck. Conrad's ear had

ignored the horn; this time it was really a matter of a hair's breadth and a leap. He jumped back out of the way. A young man sitting beside the driver turned and favored Conrad with a number of not unjustified insults. Hans Hayde Strasse was bathed in sunlight, too, the rays slanting so sharply that they seemed stretched out along the whole length of the street. Frau Schubert came down the stairs. She greeted Conrad, swishing rapidly by, with a curious little squeaking noise. She raised her handkerchief. Her face looked like a small, clenched, wet fist.

"Herr von Hohenlocher," Conrad said as the door opened, "can you put me up for the night?"

"Of course," the gentleman replied without emotion, throwing a glance at Conrad's small suitcase. "Even in your former quarters. *Castrum Conradi* is at present ungarrisoned. No one home at your house?"

"I'll explain that in a moment," Conrad said quietly as he entered. "But before I do so, may I ask you for a glass of gin."

"*Fiat libatio!*" Hohenlocher exclaimed. Bottles, soda, Angostura bitters were produced. Once more Conrad sat in his old place—but this time Hohenlocher did not sprawl on the divan. His posture was, on the contrary, extremely composed and attentive, full of suspense. It soon became more so.

Conrad told him everything. While he spoke, the daylight subsided; the gilt of sunlight in the windows was extinguished; his host lit the parti-colored lamp. It was as though time were running backward and meeting once more in a closed circle, just as the story Conrad told closed a circle; as though he had arrived the day before, fallen asleep in the hotel by the railroad station (whispering: "Yes, this is it, of course—life!"); and as if he now sat here, having come about the apartment, and were being given instructions. In regard to the last, however, there was now a profound difference. Throughout his narrative, Conrad felt it. He was speaking now on the same plane, from equal to equal. Herr von Hohenlocher's mission as an authority had come to an end.

Henceforth, the sole possible future for them would be to become friends.

When Conrad finished, Hohenlocher rose, strode to the center of the big room, and stood there in silence. His face looked very grave and handsome; but probably this was due only to the favorable lighting. At last he produced a statement.

"Herr Castiletz," he said sharply, "my attitude in this matter depends first of all upon what you will answer if, instead of expressing my concern and my profound sympathy, I flatly and with utmost conviction congratulate you most heartily."

"My reply," Conrad said, "is first that this seems only natural to me, and second that I thank you from the bottom of my heart."

"Then you have won the laurel wreath," Herr von Hohenlocher said. (At these words Conrad gave a slight start.) "You have traveled with unusual success upon that longest road which heals all evils. That the road had to end with yourself is the eternal law—which we spend a considerable portion of our life's efforts trying to evade. Those who follow this road to the end and win the wreath obtain possession of something granted only to an infinitesimally small number of persons: the knowledge of who they really are. Through the dead rock of life's mountain you drove a tunnel, pursuing another man's supposed guilt. But the proof that you directed your tunnel accurately is provided by the fact that, when you broke through to the other side and stepped out of the darkness, you saw yourself standing in the floodlit expanse of your boring."

Conrad had risen. He went up to Hohenlocher. They shook hands—the erstwhile ironic teacher and the textilian pupil, who had reached the point of being friends. In a low voice, Hohenlocher added one more comment: "The measure of freedom you have won is very great," he said. "Almost too great, I would say; I can scarcely see how you are going to live with it. . . ."

He broke off, as if disturbed. It seems remarkable, and therefore must be remarked on, that both men now turned with a casual air to totally different subjects of conversation. They discussed, for example, the two paintings by Maria Rosanka which Hohenlocher had bought the year before, but which had only recently been framed according to the artist's specifications. They were two still-lifes executed with almost scientific strictness. One of them showed a top hat, gloves, a plate of grapes, and back of it, curiously intersected by the slanting studio window and brought almost resoundingly into the rectangle of the picture, the edge of a distant building with a narrow vertical row of windows.

They also talked about Frau Schubert; that was inevitable, since there was no servant in evidence, and the apartment was beginning to wear a look of neglect. "You know," Herr von Hohenlocher said, "I am confronted with these alternatives: to throw her out or to have her stuffed. As you know, I would prefer the second. This time the woman really seems to be frozen at a low, turned to ice at her weakest point. She sits up there in her apartment above your rooms, Herr Castiletz, and savagely glooms all day long. Scarcely ever in sight. The last time I saw her, days ago, she looked like one of those gnomes people carve out of roots, with bright button-eyes."

Shortly after an evening snack that Herr von Hohenlocher improvised, Conrad grew sleepy. It was a weightless sleepiness with nothing heavy about it, merely a gentle evaporation of his strength, which seemed to be pleasantly dissipating. It was a state in which he was equally far and near to all things, like the center of a small world. After he had gone across the hall and lain down in his own room—it smelled very delicately of paint— and after he had switched off the light, it seemed to him it had become a different room, despite its familiar ochre-colored furniture trimmed in red. It was as if he would live in an entirely different way here. He decided to remain for the present. Hohenlocher had said "your rooms." He'd buy paintings from Maria Rosanka in Stuttgart and hang them here. That was the last clear thought he had, while his hand groped on the night table and found the little snuffbox. Then he was walking toward the mirror, effortlessly now, in the drawing room of his parental home. He felt just a little frightened of the figure approaching him out of the mirror. The fear lasted for the space of a heartbeat, and concerned especially the head, the face. But although he squinted his eyes in the proper way, the vision was not at all what he expected: modestly, in a white dress, the figure came over the small bridge by Frau Rumpler's laundry. "Are you in Salzburg?" he asked. "Yes, Kokosch, and how lovely it is in Salzburg!" she said, smiling. "Yes, but aren't you angry with me?" he asked. She gave him her small, very warm hand. "Why not at all, Kokosch, how could you think that? I only cried because I love you." Now, climbing on a chair, she began taking down the curtains, which Frau Rumpler was to wash. He held out his arms to receive a batch of washing. "No, my child," she said, "you should go to sleep now. We don't need the little pencil any more, never again. Sleep now, sleep, my darling." She placed her hand over his eyes. As under the patriarch's rod the water had once sprung from the sheer rock, so now, accompanied by a feeling of boundless joy, the spring welled from the Carso, the hot stream of tears rose to the surface again—the stream that from a definite point in boyhood had flowed underground throughout a whole life, like a hidden hemorrhage.

50 ߷

HERR von Hohenlocher's analysis of Frau Schubert had been correct. She came scurrying back from her errand with six bottles of beer in her apron and ascended to her dreadful little apartment. Those bottles, or rather their contents, were in a sense the last thread on which her life hung at the moment. (Is the figure lame? It is. A little patience; it will soon stand firmly on both feet.) Having landed in her little kitchen, and, thus alone, Frau Schubert was seized with fear. But she could no longer go running perpetually about the streets, for her feet were too tired. The door from the kitchen into the only other room in this tiny apartment, where the "furniture" was enthroned, stood open. The furniture was yellow and flashed like false teeth—false because life refused to thrust anything to bite between them. The mighty twin beds, set plumb in the middle of the room, were the outstanding pieces, a highly varnished trumpet blast, a broadside of a hint.

At this sight, Frau Schubert's fear was once more converted into rage, an emotion more in character. She slammed the door upon the mocking sight, switched on the kitchen light, and began gulping beer from a pint glass. With this, she hoped to keep her fear at bay. The little iron cot, on which she had thought to sleep only a short while longer, stood in the kitchen beside the stove. She sat on it, with her beer glass, and looked out into the hall, the door to which remained open so that she would not miss the door bell. But the bell never rang. Except in the mornings, when the bills came for the installment payments.

Intoxication gave her strength, though false. Frau Schubert's eyes changed. She felt grandeur. Her rage took courage and launched itself into the world, which could do nothing to stop it but had to submit to being shouted at, locked up as the world was with the infuriated woman. By the time the third bottle was reached, it was given a name and was shattered, along with the invention of the name, against the white plaster of the wall, having been hurled straight at the face of one and all. The name was: "Lousy dog!" The sound "ou" gaped like a maw black as ebony. The shards, however, did not stick to the wall or bore into it like an arrow. They clinked pedantically and soberly to the floor, except for a few which, with due regard to the laws of physics, had to bounce sidewise and land in a corner. Frau Schubert drank the fourth bottle. Hurled the fifth. Opened the sixth, vigorously and resolutely poured it into the pint glass; and then suddenly grabbed the rubber pipe from the stove as though about to strangle a snake, like Heracles in his cradle. It was a wild triumph and a deep, deep swallow; but at that moment she was simply knocked down by the beer as if hit on the head with a bludgeon. She could not manage to down the last of it. Her mouth still full, she sank back on her cot, hanging over slightly on the right side, so that from the corner of her mouth a thin thread of beer flowed (accounting for the aforementioned figure of speech). The thread soon broke up into single drops. Things looked pretty bad. But life was still so strong in her that her body rearranged itself for proper sleep.

Like a steadily blowing wind, the gas poured out of the pipe, mingled with the air, gathered near the ceiling of kitchen and hall. The mute furniture and household articles that cohabit at night, under the cover of indulgent darkness—these objects could pursue their intimacies only in the adjoining room. In the kitchen they were disturbed by the fixed glow of the bulb, were held off from one another hour upon hour, and stood weary for lack of sleep in the gradually growing dawn which dimmed and quarantined the electric light.

51 ߷

THE letter carrier climbed the stairs of Number 5 Hans Hayde Strasse: a decent, dependable man, like all letter carriers. He was forty, knew life and knew what he was placing in Frau Schubert's box: a court order, probably having to do with overdue payments. A letter carrier handles such communications by the thousands. Still, a good heart does not weary so easily, cannot easily be reduced to indifference. He thought: "Poor woman." Then he dropped the letter into the box, pressed the bell, and—the author very nearly wrote here: "and turned to start down the stairs again." But this time his publisher really would have given him the devil. Because that pressure upon the bell produced an overwhelming change in the situation, for the letter carrier himself, for Frau Schubert, for everyone concerned.

The letter carrier did not turn at all. He flew, just as he was, with his pouch on his back—flew across the landing and into the wall. Fortunately the good man came out of the affair pretty well, aside from some minor injuries. His statement and the subsequent official investigation explained the cause of the explosion. The action of the bell over the door had produced a fairly large spark. Perhaps the setscrew of the interrupter had been shaken loose in the course of years by the passage of so many heavy vehicles, tank trucks and the like, so that the size of the spark was greater than normal. This spark, then, had acted like a fuse. The gas which had accumulated mainly on the ceiling in Frau Schubert's apartment, mingled with air penetrating through cracks, produced a terrifying detonation. The letter carrier, who was only grazed by a few falling bricks, was left unconscious on the landing, which had become a balcony suspended in mid-air. But before he lost consciousness, he declared, he experienced a very odd moment: when everything around him was thrown into movement, a shaking, thumping, and low rumbling began and grew fantastically, while firm, smooth, rectangular things dissolved into rubble-filled clouds which seemed to fall rather slowly. Their thudding impact at the bottom sent back more ethereal, floating clouds of thin dust, more and more and more. Beams and joists were revealed, window and door frames cracked and vanished, tearing loose from their surroundings with an earth-shaking noise. As for Frau Schubert, she escaped with comparatively few injuries. In fact the disaster, which smashed the windowpanes, ripped everything open, and admitted air into her apartment, saved her from suffocation.

The low drum roll of the blast shook windowpanes throughout the neighborhood. But its greatest effect, of course, was felt in the immediate vicinity. Marianne Castiletz ran out to see what was happening. Since she had taken up athletics, she feared nothing at all. She was courageous as a hussar lieutenant. Behind her ran the maid, and behind her the chauffeur, to keep an eye on the two women. On Hans Hayde Strasse the police cordon had not yet been drawn as tight as it would be ten minutes later, and the crowd that had gathered was still small. Number 5 looked at first glance like a broken corset extruding its whalebone. On its left side were beams and rafters. Rooms exposed their wallpaper to the open sky. On the second story a chair was wedged in the rubble with its four legs turned upward, as though it had desperately stood on its head and bored into the debris in order not to see so much destruction. The middle of the house, with the entryway, seemed almost undamaged; on the right only a few missing windowpanes could be seen. The rescue crew was at work; they cried for room; stretchers, long and stiff, swayed toward the ambulances.

Marianne pressed forward as far as the front garden. On one stretcher an arm was raised, waved, beckoned to her. The stretcher was set down; one of the rescue crew bent over the man on it and had some words with him. Marianne was allowed through at once. Now she stood in the inside of the circle of excitement and spectators, in a relatively empty space, and recognized Herr von Hohenlocher peering at her out of the depths of a huge bandage around his head—how odd it was to see him entirely without a forehead! His mouth smiled, or tried to; he greeted Marianne, pressed her hand, and answered her question: "No, I'm not too badly hurt. A pistol box was shaken loose along with the shelf and had the kindness to land on my head, that's all. Frau Castiletz, you must be very brave. This man will lead you." He indicated the ambulance assistant. The stretcher was lifted. Herr von Hohenlocher attempted to sit up to bid Frau Castiletz good-bye; but his face twisted painfully and somewhat irritably, and he sank back. Marianne followed the man through the entryway, which seemed to her endless, like a long tunnel. They emerged into the cobbled courtyard. Off to one side, on the right, stood two covered stretchers; there was another at the left, against the whitewashed wall. The ambulance man pointed to this one. "I must ask you to be very brave," he said, unwittingly repeating Hohenlocher's words; he assumed a solemn expression, in spite of all the heavy work he had been doing. "It is your husband." Then he drew the sheet back, whipped off his cap, and stepped aside.

Kokosch looked as if he were seventeen. There was no sign of any external injury. His head lay tilted back somewhat; his chest under the open pajama jacket seemed arched, though not inflated any longer by the breath of life. Marianne understood nothing; it was altogether impossible. But as she fell to her knees beside him, feeling under her hands the classical shape of those shoulders—as she did so, she capitulated to what was here and was real. In these minutes no riddles could be propounded to her—not even by the snuffbox which protruded from his right, half-closed hand so that she was able to turn it a little and recognize it. His right arm was drawn lightly against his chest. Though not too long ago hatred had billowed in a wall of flame against what was uncanny and incomprehensible in her marriage, this too collapsed in ashes. She raised her head. Her eyes wildly sought the lower-lying parts of the city, which could be seen from this height. The sky of this April morning had that distracted and faded expression which matches the earth's alternations when spring is only half come, a hovering between death and life. At its margin a number of strange shapes melted and vanished, tousled white cirrus clouds, like sails dipping below the horizon.

A NOTE ON THE TYPE

THE text of this book is set in *Caledonia*, a Linotype face designed by W. A. DWIGGINS, the man responsible for so much that is good in contemporary book design and typography. Caledonia belongs to the family of printing types called "modern face" by printers—a term used to mark the change in style of type-letters that occurred about 1800. Caledonia borders on the general design of Scotch Modern but is more freely drawn than that letter.

Composed, printed, and bound by
The Haddon Craftsmen, Inc., Scranton, Pa.
Typography and binding design by
GEORGE SALTER